OUTSTANDING ACCLAIM FOR THE EPIC NOVELS OF

WILBUR SMITH

THE EYE OF THE TIGER

"A bonanza of excitement." —*The New York Times*

"Wilbur Smith rarely misses a trick." —*Sunday Times*

"Action follows action . . . mystery is piled on mystery . . . tales to delight the millions of addicts of the gutsy adventure story." —*Sunday Express*

"Raw experience, grim realism, history, and romance welded with mystery and the bewilderment of life itself." —*Library Journal*

"The world's leading adventure writer." —*Daily Express*

"The pace would do credit to a Porsche, and the invention is as bright and explosive as a fireworks display." —*Sunday Telegraph*

MORE . . .

BIRDS OF PREY

RIVER GOD

THE SEVENTH SCROLL

CRY WOLF

WILBUR SMITH

St. Martin's Paperbacks

Previously published in Great Britain by William Heinemann Ltd and Pan Books/Macmillan Publishers Ltd

CRY WOLF

ISBN: 0-312-98258-5

Printed in the United States of America

St. Martin's Paperbacks edition / December 2001

St. Martin's Paperbacks are published by St. Martin's Press, 175 Fifth Avenue, New York, NY 10010.

10 9 8 7 6 5 4 3 2 1

This book is for my wife Danielle

To Jake Barton, machinery was always feminine — with all the female's fascination, wiles and bitchery. So when he first saw them standing in a row beneath the spreading dark green foliage of the mango trees, they became for him the iron ladies.

There were five of them, standing aloof from the other heaps of worn-out and redundant equipment that His Majesty's Government was offering for sale. Although it was June and the cooler season between the monsoons, yet the heat on this cloudless morning in Dar es Salaam was mounting like a force-fed furnace and Jake went thankfully into the shade of the mangoes to stand closer to the ladies and begin his examination.

He glanced around the enclosed yard, and noticed that he seemed to be the only one interested in the five vehicles. The motley crowd of potential buyers was picking over the heaps of broken shovels and picks, the rows of battered wheelbarrows and the other mounds of unidentifiable rubbish.

He turned his attention back to the ladies, as he slipped off the light tropical moleskin jacket he wore and hung it on the branch of a mango tree.

The ladies were aristocrats fallen on hard times, their hard but rakish lines were dulled by the faded and scratched paintwork and the cancerous blotches of rust that showed through. The foxy-faced fruit bats that hung inverted in the mango branches above them had splattered them with their dung, and oil and grease had oozed from their elderly joints and caked with dust in unsightly black streaks and blobs.

Jake knew their lineage and their history and as he laid aside the small carpet bag that held his tools, he reviewed it swiftly. Five fine pieces of craftsmanship lying rotting away on the fever coast of Tanganyika. The bodies and chassis had been built by Schreiner – the stately high cupola in which the open mounting for the Maxim machine gun now glared like an empty eye-socket, the square sloping platform of the engine housing, with its heavy armour plate and the neat rows of rivets and the steel shutters that could be closed to protect the radiator against incoming enemy fire. They stood tall on the metal-bossed wheels with their solid rubber tyres, and Jake felt a sneaking regret that he would be the one to tear their engines out of them and toss aside the worn-out but gallant old bodies.

They did not deserve such cavalier treatment, these fighting iron ladies who in their youth had chased the wily German commander von Lettow-Vorbeck across the wide plains and over the fierce hills of East Africa. The thorns of the wilderness had deeply scarred the paintwork of the five armoured cars and there were places where rifle fire had glanced off their armour, leaving the distinctive dimple in the steel.

Those were their grandest days, streaming into battle with their cavalry pennants flying, dust billowing behind them, bounding and crashing through the dongas and ant-bear holes, their machine guns blazing and the terrified German askaris scattering before them.

After that, the original engines had been replaced by the beautiful new 6½-litre Bentleys, and they had begun the long decline of police patrol work on the border, chasing the occasional cattle raider and slowly being pounded by a succession of brutal drivers into the condition which had at last brought them here to the Government sale yards in this fiery May of the year of our Lord 1935. But Jake knew that even the savage abuse to which they had been subjected could not have destroyed the engines completely and that was what interested him.

He rolled up his sleeves like a surgeon about to begin his examination.

'Ready or not, girls,' he muttered, 'here comes old Jake.'

He was a tall man with a big bony frame that was cramped in the confined area of the armoured car's body, but he worked with a quiet concentration so close to rapture that the discomfort went unnoticed. Jake's wide friendly mouth was pursed in a whistle that went on endlessly, the opening bars of 'Tiger Rag' repeated over and over again, and his eyes were screwed up against the gloom of the interior.

He worked swiftly, checking the throttle and ignition settings of the controls, tracing out the fuel lines from the rear-mounted fuel tank, finding the cocks under the driver's seat and grunting with satisfaction. He scrambled out of the turret and dropped down the high side of the vehicle, pausing to wipe away with his forearm the thin trickle of sweat that broke from his thick curly black hair and ran down his cheek, then he hurried forward and knocked the clamps open on the side flaps of the armoured engine-cover.

'Oh sweet, sweet!' he whispered, as he saw the fine outlines of the old Bentley engine block beneath the layer of thick dust and greasy filth.

His hands with the big square palms and thick spatulate fingers went out to touch it with what was almost a caress.

'The bastards have beaten you up, darling,' he whispered. 'But we will have you singing again as lovely as ever, that's a promise.'

He pulled the dipstick from the engine sump and took a drop of oil between his fingers.

'Shit!' he grunted with disgust, as he felt the grittiness, and he thrust the stick back into its slot. He pulled the plugs and, with the promise of a shilling, had a loitering

African swing the crank for him while he felt the compression against the palm of his hand.

Swiftly he moved along the line of armoured cars, checking, probing and testing, and when he reached the last of them he knew he could have three of them running again for certain and four maybe.

One was shot beyond hope. There was a crack in the engine block through which he could have ridden a horse, and the pistons had seized so solid in their pots that not even the combined muscle upon the crank handle of Jake and his helper could move them.

Two of them had the entire carburettor assemblies missing, but he could cannibalize from the wreck. That left him short of one carburettor – and he felt only gloom at his chances of finding another in Dar es Salaam.

Three, then, he could reckon on with certainty. At one hundred and ten pounds apiece, that was £330. Less an estimated outlay of one hundred, it gave him a clear profit of two hundred and thirty pounds – for surely he would not have to bid more than twenty pounds each for these wrecks. Jake felt a warm spreading glow of satisfaction as he tossed his African helper the promised shilling. Two hundred and thirty pounds was a great deal of money in these lean and hungry times.

A quick glance at the fob-watch he hauled from his back pocket showed him there was still over two hours before the advertised time of the commencement of the sale. He was impatient to begin work on those Bentleys – not only for the money. For Jake it would be a labour of love.

The one in the centre of the line seemed the best bet for quick results. He placed his carpet bag on the armoured wing of the mudguard and selected a ³⁄₈th-inch spanner. Immediately he was totally absorbed.

After half an hour he pulled his head out of the engine,

wiped his hands on a handful of cotton waste and hurried around to the front of the car.

The big muscles in his right arm bunched and rippled as he swung the crank handle, spinning the heavy engine easily with a steady whirring rhythm. After a minute of this, he released the handle and wiped off his sweat with the cotton waste that left grease marks down his cheeks. He was breathing quickly but lightly.

'I knew you for a temperamental bitch the moment I laid eyes on you,' he muttered. 'But you are going to do it my way, darling. You really are.'

Once more his head and shoulders disappeared under the engine cowling and there was the clink of the spanner against metal and the monotonous repetition of 'Tiger Rag' in a low off-key whistle for another ten minutes, then again Jake went to the crank handle.

'You are going to do it my way, baby – and what's more you're going to like it.'

He spun the handle and the engine kicked viciously, back-fired like a rifle shot, and the crank handle snapped out of Jake's hand with enough force to have taken his thumb off if he had been holding it with an opposed grip.

'Jesus,' whispered Jake, 'a real little hell cat!' He scrambled up into the turret and reached down to the controls and reset the ignition.

At the next swing of the crank handle she bucked and fired, caught and surged, then fell back into a steady beat, quivering slightly on her rigid suspension, but come alive.

Jake stepped back, sweating, flushed, but with his dark green eyes shining with delight.

'Oh you beauty,' he said. 'You bloody little beauty.'

'Bravo,' said a voice behind him, and Jake started and turned quickly. He had forgotten that he was not the only person left on earth, in his complete absorption with the machine, and now he felt embarrassed, as though he had been observed in some intimate and private bodily function. He glowered at the figure that was leaning elegantly against the bole of the mango tree.

'Jolly good show,' said the stranger, and the voice was sufficient to stir the hair upon the nape of Jake's neck. It was one of those pricey Limey accents.

The man was dressed in a cream suit of expensive tropical linen and two-tone shoes of white and brown. On his head he wore a white straw hat with a wide brim that cast a shadow over his face. But Jake could see the man had a friendly smile and an easy engaging manner. He was handsome in a conventional manner, with noble and regular features, a face that had flustered many a female's emotions and that fitted well with the voice. He would be a ranking government official probably, or an officer in one of the regular regiments stationed in Dar es Salaam. Upper class establishment, even to the necktie with its narrow diagonal stripes by which the British advertised at which seat of learning they had obtained their education and their place in the social order.

'It didn't take you long to get her going.' The man lolled gracefully against the mango, his ankles crossed and one hand thrust into his coat pocket. He smiled again, and this time Jake saw the mockery and challenge in the eyes more clearly. He had judged him wrongly. This was not one of those cardboard men. They were pirate eyes, mocking and wolfish, dangerous as the glint of a knife in the shadows.

'I have no doubt the others are in as good a state of repair.' It was an enquiry, not a statement.

'Well, you're wrong, friend.' Jake felt a pang of dismay. It was absurd that this fancy lad could have a real interest in the five vehicles – but if he did, then Jake had just given him a generous demonstration of their value. 'This is the only one that will run, and even her guts are blown. Listen to her knock. Sounds like a mad carpenter.'

He reached under the cowling and earthed the magneto. In the sudden silence as the engine died, he said loudly, 'Junk!' and spat on the ground near the front wheel – but not on it. He couldn't bring himself to do that. Then he gathered his tools, flung his jacket over his shoulder, hefted the carpet bag and, without another glance at the Englishman, ambled off towards the gates of the works yard.

'You not bidding then, old chap?' The stranger had left his post at the mango and fallen into step beside him.

'God, no.' Jake tried to fill his voice with disdain. 'Are you?'

'Now what would I do with five broken-down armoured cars?' The man laughed silently, and then went on, 'Yankee, are you? Texas, what?'

'You've been reading my mail.'

'Engineer?'

'I try, I try.'

'Buy you a drink?'

'Give me the money instead. I've got a train to catch.'

The elegant stranger laughed again, a light friendly laugh.

'God speed, then, old chap,' he said, and Jake hurried out through the gates into the dusty heat-dazed streets of noonday Dar es Salaam and walked away without a backward glance, trying to convey with his determined stride and the set of his shoulders that his departure was final.

J ake found a canteen around the first corner and within five minutes' walk of the works yard, where he went into hiding. The Tusker beer he ordered was blood warm, but he drank it while he worried. The Englishman gave him a very queasy feeling, his interest was too bright to be mere curiosity. On the other hand, however, Jake might have to go over the twenty pounds bid that he had calculated – and he took from the inside pocket of his jacket the worn pigskin wallet that contained his entire worldly wealth and, prudently using the table top as a screen, he counted the wad of notes.

Five hundred and seventeen pounds in Bank of England notes, three hundred and twenty-seven dollars in United States currency, and four hundred and ninety East African shillings was not a great fortune with which to take on the likes of the elegant Limey. However, Jake drained his warm beer, set his jaw and inspected his watch once more. It gave him five minutes to noon.

Major Gareth Swales was mildly dismayed, but not at all surprised to see the big American entering the works yard gates once more in a manner which was obviously intended to be unobtrusive but reminded him of Jack Dempsey sidling furtively into an old ladies' tea party.

Gareth Swales sat in the shade of the mangoes upon an upturned wheelbarrow, over which he had spread a silk handkerchief to protect the pristine linen of his suit. He had set aside his straw hat, and his hair was meticulously trimmed and combed, shining softly in that rare colour between golden blond and red, and there was just a sparkle of silver in the wings at his temples. His moustache was the same colour and carefully moulded to the curve of his upper lip. His face was deeply tanned by the tropical sun to a dark chestnut brown, so that the contrasting blue of his eyes was startlingly pale and penetrating, as he watched Jake Barton cross the yard to join the gathering of buyers under the mango trees. He sighed with resignation and returned his attention to the folded envelope on which he was making his financial calculations.

He really was finely drawn out, the previous eighteen months had been very unkind to him. The cargo that had been seized in the Liao River by the Japanese gunboat when he was only hours away from delivering it to the Chinese commander at Mukden – and receiving payment for it – had wiped away the accumulated capital of ten years. It had taken all his ingenuity and a deal of financial agility to assemble the package that was stored at this moment in No. 4 warehouse down at the main docks of Dar es Salaam port. His buyers would be arriving to take delivery in twelve days – and the five armoured cars would have rounded out the package beautifully.

Armour, by God, he could fix his own price. Only aircraft would have been more desirable from his client's point of view.

When Gareth had first seen them that morning in their neglected and decrepit state of repair, he had discounted them completely, and was on the point of turning away when he had noticed the long muscular pair of legs protruding from the engine of one of the vehicles and heard the barely recognizable strains of 'Tiger Rag'.

Now he knew that one of them at least was a runner. A few gallons of paint, and a new Vickers machine gun set in the mountings, and the five machines would look magnificent. Gareth would give one of his justly famous sales routines. He would start the one good engine and fire the machine gun – by God, the jolly old prince would pull out his purse and start spilling sovereigns all over the scenery.

There was only the damned Yankee to worry about, it might cost him a few bob more than he had reckoned to edge him out, but Gareth was not too worried. The man looked as though he would have difficulty raising the price of a beer.

Gareth flicked at his sleeve where a speck of dust might have settled; he placed the panama back on his golden head, adjusted the wide brim carefully and removed the long slim cheroot from his lips to inspect the ash, before he rose and sauntered across to the group.

The auctioneer was an elfin Sikh in a black silk suit with his beard twisted up under his chin, and a large dazzling white turban wrapped about his head.

He was perched like a little black bird on the turret of the nearest armoured car, and his voice was plaintive as he pleaded with the audience that stared up at him stolidly with expressionless faces and glazed eyes.

'Come, gentlemens, let me be hearing some mellifluous voice cry out "ten pounds". Do I hear "ten pounds each" for these magnificent conveyances?'

He cocked his head and listened to the hot noon breeze in the top branches of the mango. Nobody moved, nobody spoke.

'Five pounds, please? Will some wise gentlemens tell me five pounds? Two pounds ten – gentlemens – for a mere fifty shillings these royal machines, these fine, these beautiful—' He broke off, and lowered his gaze, placed a delicate chocolate brown hand over his troubled brow. 'A price, gentlemens. Please, start me with a price.'

'One pound!' a voice called in the lilting accents of the Texan ranges. For a moment the Sikh did not move, then raised his head with dramatic slowness and stared at Jake who towered above the crowd around him.

'A pound?' the Sikh whispered huskily. 'Twenty shillings each for these fine, these beautiful—' he broke off and shook his head sorrowfully. Then abruptly his manner changed and became brisk and businesslike. 'One pound, I am bid.

Do I hear two, two pounds? No advance on one pound? Going for the first time at one pound!'

Gareth Swales drifted forward, and the crowd opened miraculously, drawing aside respectfully.

'Two pounds.' He spoke softly, but his voice carried clearly in the hush. Jake's long angular frame stiffened, and a dark wine-coloured flush spread slowly up the back of his neck. Slowly, his head swivelled and he stared across at the Englishman who had now reached the front row.

Gareth smiled brilliantly and tipped the brim of his panama to acknowledge Jake's glare. The Sikh's commercial instinct instantly sensed the rivalry between them and his mood brightened.

'I have two—' he chirruped.

'Five,' snapped Jake.

'Ten,' murmured Gareth, and Jake felt a hot uncontrollable anger come seething up from his guts. He knew the feeling so well, and he tried to control it, but it was no use. It came up in a savage red tide to swamp his reason.

The crowd stirred with delight, and all their heads swung in unison towards the tall American.

'Fifteen,' said Jake, and every head swung back towards the slim Englishman.

Gareth inclined his head gracefully.

'Twenty,' piped the Sikh delightedly. 'I have twenty.'

'And five.' Dimly through the mists of his anger, Jake knew that there was no way that he would let the Limey have these ladies. If he couldn't buy them, he would burn them.

The Sikh sparkled at Gareth with gazelle eyes.

'Thirty, sir?' he asked, and Gareth grinned easily and waved his cheroot. He was experiencing a rising sense of alarm — already they were far past what he had calculated was the Yank's limit.

'And five more.' Jake's voice was gravelly with the

11

strength of his outrage. They were his, even if he had to pay out every shilling in his wallet, they had to be his.

'Forty.' Gareth Swales's smile was slightly strained now. He was fast approaching his own limit. The terms of the sale were cash or bank-guaranteed cheque. He had long ago milked every source of cash that was available to him, and any bank manager who guaranteed a Gareth Swales cheque was destined for a swift change of employment.

'Forty-five.' Jake's voice was hard and uncompromising; he was fast approaching the figure where he would be working for nothing but the satisfaction of blocking out the Limey.

'Fifty.'

'And five.'

'Sixty.'

'And another five.'

That was break-even price for Jake – after this he was tossing away bright shining shillings.

'Seventy,' drawled Gareth Swales, and that was his limit. With regret he discarded all hopes of an easy acquisition of the cars. Three hundred and fifty pounds represented his entire liquid reserves – he could bid no further. All right, the easy way had not worked out. There were a dozen other ways, and by one of them Gareth Swales was going to have them. By God, the prince might go as high as a thousand each and he was not going to pass by that sort of profit for lack of a few lousy hundred quid.

'Seventy-five,' said Jake, and the crowd murmured and every eye flew to Major Gareth Swales.

'Ah, kind gentlemens, do you speak of eighty?' enquired the Sikh eagerly. His commission was five per cent.

Graciously, but regretfully, Gareth shook his head.

'No, my dear chap. It was a mere whim of mine.' He smiled across at Jake. 'May they give you much joy,' he said, and drifted away towards the gates. There was clearly nothing to be gained in approaching the American now. The man was in a towering rage – and Gareth had judged him as the type who habitually gave expression to this emotion by swinging with his fists. Long ago, Gareth Swales had reached the conclusion that only fools fight, and wise men supply them with the means to do so – at a profit, naturally.

I t was three days before Jake Barton saw the Englishman again – and during that time he had towed the five iron ladies to the outskirts of the town where he had set up his camp on the banks of a small stream among a stand of African mahogany trees.

With a block and tackle slung from the branch of a mahogany, he had lifted out the engines and worked on them far into each night by the smoky light of a hurricane lamp.

Coaxing and sweet-talking the machines, changing and juggling faulty and worn parts, hand-forging others on the charcoal brazier, whistling to himself endlessly, swearing and sweating and scheming, he had three of the Bentleys running by the afternoon of the third day. Set up on improvised timber blocks, they had regained something of their former gleam and glory beneath his loving hands.

Gareth Swales arrived at Jake's camp in the somnolent heat of the third afternoon. He arrived in a ricksha pulled by a half-naked and sweating black man – and he lolled with the grace of a resting leopard on the padded seat, looking cool in beautifully cut and snowy crisp linen.

Jake straightened up from the engine which he was tuning. He was naked to the waist and his arms were greased black to the elbows. Sweat gleamed on his shoulders and chest, as though he had been oiled.

'Don't even bother to stop,' Jake said softly. 'Just keep straight on down the road, friend.'

Gareth grinned at him engagingly and from the seat beside him he lifted a large silver champagne bucket, frosted with dew, and tinkling with ice. Over the edge of the bucket showed the necks of a dozen bottles of Tusker beer.

'Peace offering, old chap,' said Gareth, and Jake's throat contracted so violently with thirst that he couldn't speak for a moment.

'A free gift – with no strings attached, what?'

Even in this cloying humid heat, Jake Barton had been so completely absorbed by his task that he had taken little liquid in three days, and none of it was pale golden, bubbling and iced. His eyes began to water with the strength of his desire.

Gareth dismounted from the ricksha and came forward with the champagne bucket under one arm.

'Swales,' he said. 'Major Gareth Swales,' and held out his hand.

'Barton. Jake.' Jake took the hand, but his eyes were still fixed on the bucket.

Twenty minutes later, Jake sat waist-deep in a steaming galvanized iron bath, set out alfresco under the mahogany trees. The bottle of Tusker stood close at hand and he whistled happily as he worked up a foaming lather in his armpits and across the dark hairy plain of his chest.

'Trouble was, we got off on the wrong foot,' explained Gareth, and sipped at the neck of a Tusker bottle. He made it seem he was taking Dom Pérignon from a crystal flute. He was lying back in Jake's single canvas camp chair under the shade flap of the old sun-faded tent.

'Friend, you nearly got a wrong foot right up your backside.' But Jake's threat was without fire, marinated in Tusker.

14

'I surely understand how you felt,' said Gareth. 'But then you did tell me you weren't bidding. If only you had told me the truth, we could have worked out an arrangement.'

Jake reached out with a soap-frothed hand and lifted the Tusker bottle to his lips. He swallowed twice, sighed and belched softly.

'Bless you,' said Gareth, and then went on. 'As soon as I realized that you were bidding seriously, I backed out. I knew that you and I could make a mutually beneficial deal later. And so here I am now, drinking beer with you and talking a deal.'

'You are talking – I'm just listening,' Jake pointed out.

'Quite so.' Gareth took out his cheroot case, carefully selected one and leaned forward to place it tenderly between Jake's willing lips. He struck a match off the sole of his boot and cupped the match for Jake.

'It seems clear to me that you have a buyer for the cars, right?'

'I'm still listening.' Jake exhaled a long feather of cheroot smoke with evident pleasure.

'You must have a price already set, and I am prepared to better that price.'

Jake took the cheroot out of his mouth and for the first time regarded Gareth levelly.

'You want all five cars at that price in their present condition?'

'Right,' said Gareth.

'What if I tell you that only three are runners – two are shot all to hell.'

'That wouldn't affect my offer.'

Jake reached out and drained the Tusker bottle. Gareth opened another for him and placed it in his hand.

Swiftly Jake ran over the offer. He had an open contract with Anglo-Tanganyika Sugar Company to supply gasoline-powered sugar-cane crushers at a fixed price of £110 each. From the three cars he could make up three units – maximum of £330.

The Limey's offer was for all five units, at a price to be determined.

'I've done one hell of a lot of work on them,' Jake softened him a little.

'I can see that.'

'One hundred and fifty pounds each – for all five. That's seven hundred and fifty.'

'You would replace the engines and make them look all ship-shape.'

'Sure.'

'Done,' said Gareth. 'I knew we could work something out,' and they beamed at each other. 'I'll make out a deed of sale right away,' Gareth produced a cheque book, 'and then I'll give you my cheque for the full amount.'

'Your what?' The beam on Jake's face faded.

'My personal cheque on Coutts of Piccadilly.'

It was true that Gareth Swales did have a chequing account with Coutts. According to his last statement, the account was in debit to the sum of eighteen pounds seventeen and sixpence. The manager had written him a spicy little letter in red ink.

'Safe as the Bank of England.' Gareth flourished his cheque book. It would take three weeks for the cheque to be presented in London – and bounce through the roof. By that time, he hoped to be on his way to Madrid. There looked to be a very profitable little piece of business brewing up satisfactorily in that area, and by then Gareth Swales would have the capital to exploit it.

'Funny thing about cheques.' Jake removed the cheroot from his mouth. 'They bring me out in a rash. If it's all the same to you, I'll just take the seven fifty in cash money.'

16

Gareth pursed his lips. Very well, so it wasn't going to be that easy either.

'Dear me,' he said. 'It will take a little while to clear.'

'No hurry,' Jake grinned at him. 'Any time before noon tomorrow. That's the delivery date I have for my original buyer. You be here with the money before that, and they are all yours.' He rose abruptly from the bath, cascading soapy water, and his black servant handed him a towel.

'What plans have you for dinner?' Gareth asked.

'I think Abou here has cooked up a pot of his lion-killing stew.'

'Won't you be my guest at the Royal?'

'I drank your beer for free — why shouldn't I eat your food?' asked Jake reasonably.

The dining room of the Royal Hotel had high ceilings and tall insect-screened sash windows. The mechanical fans set in the roof stirred the warm humid air sluggishly into a substitute for coolness, and Gareth Swales was a splendid host.

His engaging charm was irresistible, and his choice of food and wine induced in Jake a sense of such well-being that they laughed together like old friends, and were delighted to find that they had mutual acquaintances — mostly barmen and brothel-keepers in various parts of the world — and that they had parallel experience.

Gareth had been doing business with a revolutionary leader in Venezuela while Jake was helping build the railroad in that same country. Jake had been chief engineer on a Blake Line coaster on the China run when Gareth had been making contact with the Chinese Communists on Yellow River.

They had been in France at the same time, and on that terrible day at Amiens, when the German machine guns had accelerated Gareth Swales's promotion from subaltern to major in the space of six hours, Jake had been four miles down the line, a sergeant driver in the Royal Tank Corps – seconded from the American Third Army.

They discovered that they were almost of an age, neither of them yet forty, but that both of them had packed a world of experience and wandering into that short span.

They recognized in each other that same restlessness that was always driving them on to new adventure, never staying long enough in one place or at one job to grow roots, unfettered by offspring or possessions, by spouse or responsibilities, taking up each new adventure eagerly and discarding it again without qualms or regrets. Always moving onwards – never looking backwards.

Understanding each other a little, they began to respect one another. Halfway through the meal, they were no longer scornful of the other's differences. Neither of them thought of the other as Limey or Yank any longer – but this didn't mean that Jake was about to accept any cheques or that Gareth had given up his plans to acquire the five armoured cars. At last Gareth swilled the last few drops around his brandy balloon and glanced at his pocket watch.

'Nine o'clock. It's too early for bed. What shall we do now?'

Jake suggested, 'There are two new girls down at Madame Cecile's. They came in on the mail boat.'

Gareth quickly turned the suggestion aside.

'Later perhaps – but too soon after dinner, it gives me heartburn. You don't, by any chance, feel like a few hands at cards? There is usually a decent game down at the club.'

'We can't go in there. We aren't members.'

'I have reciprocity with my London club, old boy. Sign you in, what?'

They had played for an hour and a half. Jake was enjoying the game. He liked the style of the establishment, for he usually played in less salubrious surroundings – the back room behind the bar, an upturned fruit-crate behind the main boiler in an engine room, or a scratch game in a dockside warehouse.

This was a hushed room with draped velvet curtains, expanses of dark wood panelling, dark-toned oil paintings and hunting trophies – shaggy-maned lions, buffalo with huge bossed horns drooping mournfully, all of them staring down with glassy eyes from the walls.

From the three billiard tables came the discreet click of the ivory balls, as half a dozen players in dress shirts and braces, black ties and black trousers, evening jackets discarded for the game, leaned across the heavy green-topped tables to play their shots.

There were three tables of contract bridge from which came the murmur of bid and counterbid in the cultivated tones of the British upper class, all the players in the dress that Jake thought of as penguin suits – black and white, with black bows.

Between the tables, the waiters moved on silent bare feet, in ankle-length white robes and pillbox fez, like priests of some ancient religion – bearing trays of sparkling crystal glass.

There was only one table of draw poker, a huge teak structure with brass ashtrays set into the woodwork, and niches and trays to hold the whisky glasses and the coloured ivory chips. At the table sat five players, and only Jake was not in evening dress – the other three were the type of poker players that Jake would dearly love to have kept locked up for his exclusive pleasure.

There was a minor British peer, out in Africa to decimate the wildlife. He had recently returned from the interior, where a white hunter had stood respectfully at his elbow with a heavy-calibre rifle, while the peer mowed down vast numbers of buffalo, lion and rhinoceros. This gentleman had a nervous tic under his right eye which jumped whenever he held three of a kind or better in his hand. Despite this affliction, a phenomenal run of good cards had allowed him to be the only winner, other than Jake, at the table.

There was a coffee planter with a deeply tanned and wrinkled face who made an involuntary little hissing sound whenever he improvised on the draw or squeezed out a pleasing combination.

On Jake's right hand was an elderly civil servant with thinning hair and a fever-yellow complexion who broke out in a muck sweat whenever he judged himself on the point of winning a pot – an expectation which was seldom realized.

In an hour's careful play, Jake had built up his winnings to a little over a hundred pounds and he felt very warm and contented down there where his dinner was digesting. The only element in his life that afforded him any disquiet was his new friend and sponsor.

Gareth Swales sat at his ease, conversing with the peer as an equal, condescending graciously to the planter and commiserating with the civil servant on his run of luck. He had neither won nor lost any significant amount, yet he handled the cards with a dexterity that was impressive. In those long tapering fingers with the carefully manicured nails, the pasteboards rustled and rippled, blurred and snapped, with a speed that defied the eye.

Jake watched carefully, without appearing to do so, whenever the deal passed to Major Gareth Swales. There is no way that a dealer, even with the most magical touch, can stack a deck of cards without facing them during the shuffle – and Gareth never faced the deck as he manipulated it. His eyes never even dropped to the cards, but played lightly over the faces of the others as he chatted. Jake began to relax a little.

The planter dealt him four to an open-ended flush, and he filled it with the six of hearts. The civil servant, who had an insatiable curiosity, called his raise to twenty pounds and sighed and muttered mournfully as he paid the ivory chips into the pot and Jake swept them away and stacked them neatly in front of him.

'Let's have a new pack—' smiled Gareth, lifting a finger for a servant, 'and hope that it breaks your run of luck.'

Gareth offered the seal on the new pack for inspection, then split it with his thumbnail and unwrapped the pristine cards with their bicycle-wheel designs, fanned them, lifted the jokers and began to shuffle, at the same time starting a very funny and obscene story about a bishop who entered the women's rest room at Charing Cross Station in error. The joke took a minute or two in the telling and in the roar of masculine laughter that followed, Gareth began to deal, skimming the cards across the green baize, so that they piled up neatly before each player. Only Jake had noticed that during the bishop's harrowing experiences in the ladies' room, Gareth had blocked the cards between shuffles, and that each time as he lifted the two blocks he had rolled his wrists so that for a fleeting instant they had fanned slightly and faced.

Guffawing loudly, the baron gathered up his hand and looked at it. He choked in the middle of his next guffaw, and his eyelid started to jump and twitch, as though it was making love to his nose. From across the table came a loud hiss of indrawn breath as the planter closed his cards quickly and covered them with both hands. At Jake's right hand, the civil servant's face shone like polished yellow ivory and a little trickle of sweat broke from his thinning hairline, ran down his nose, and dripped unheeded on to the front of his dress shirt, as he stared at his cards.

Jake opened his own cards, and glanced at the three queens it contained. He sighed and began his own story.

'When I was first engineer on the old *Harvest Maid* tied up in Kowloon, the skipper brought a fancy little dude on board and we all got into a game. The stakes kept jumping up and up, and just after midnight this dude dealt one hell of a hand.'

Nobody appeared to be listening to Jake's story, they were all too absorbed with their own cards.

'The skipper ended up with four kings, I got four jacks and the ship's doctor pulled a mere four tens.'

Jake rearranged the queens in his hand and broke off his story while Gareth Swales fulfilled the civil servant's request for two cards.

'The dude himself took one card from the draw and the betting went mad. We were throwing everything we owned into the pot. Thanks, friend, I'll take two cards also.'

Gareth flicked two cards across the table, and Jake discarded from his hand before picking them up.

'As I was saying, we were almost stripping off our underpants to throw it all in the middle. I was in for a little over a thousand bucks—'

Jake squeezed open the new cards – and could hardly suppress a grin. All the ladies were there. Four pretty little queens peered out at him.

'We signed I.O.U.s, we pledged our wages, and the dude came right along on the ride, not pushing the betting but staying right there.'

Gareth gave the baron one card and drew one himself. They were listening now, eyes darting from Jake's lips to their own cards.

'Well, when it came to the showdown, we were looking at each other across a pile of cash that came to the ceiling – and the dude hit us with a straight flush. I remember it so clearly, in clubs – three to the eight. It took the skipper and

22

me twelve hours to recover from the shock and then we worked out the odds on that deal just happening naturally – it was something like sixteen million to one. The odds were against the dude and we went looking for him. Found him down at the old Peninsula Hotel, spending our hard-won gold. We were preparing for sea at the time. Our boilers were cold. We sat the dude on top of them, and fired them. Had to tie him down, of course, and after a few hours his knackers were roasting like chestnuts.'

'By God,' exclaimed the peer. 'How awful.'

'Quite right,' Jake agreed. 'Hell of a stink in my engine room.'

A heavy charged silence settled over the table – all of them aware that something explosive was about to happen, that an accusation had been made, but most of them not certain what the accusation was, and at whom it had been levelled. They held up their cards like protective shields, and their eyes darted suspiciously from face to face. The atmosphere was so tense that it pervaded the gracious room, and the players at the other tables paused and looked up.

'I think,' Gareth Swales drawled in crisp tones that carried to every corner of the listening room, 'that what Mr Barton is trying to say is that somebody is cheating.'

That word, spoken in these surroundings, was so shocking, so charged with dire consequence, that strong men gasped and blanched. Cheating – in the club, by God, better a man be accused of adultery or ordinary murder.

'I must say that I have to agree with Mr Barton.' The icy blue eyes snapped with angry lights, and he turned deliberately to the bewildered member of the House of Lords beside him.

'I wonder if you would be good enough, sir, to inform us as to the exact amount of our money that you have won.' The voice cracked like a whiplash, and the peer stared at him with complete incomprehension for a moment and then his face mottled purple and crimson, and he gobbled angrily.

'Sir! How dare you. Good God, sir!—' and he rose in his seat, breathless, choking with outrage.

'Have at him!' cried Gareth, and overturned the heavy teak table with a single upward thrust of both hands. It crashed over, pinning the planter and the civil servant under it, and scattering ivory chips and playing cards in such profusion that nobody would ever know what cards Gareth Swales had dealt to himself in that last remarkable deal.

Gareth leaned across the struggling mass of downed players and clipped the peer smartly under the left ear.

'Cheating! Ha! Caught you cheating!'

The peer roared like a bull and swung a full-armed punch under which Gareth ducked lightly, but which went on to catch the club secretary between the eyes, as he hurried up to intervene.

The room erupted into violence, as the other members rushed in to assist the secretary.

Jake tried to reach Gareth, through the sudden seething storm of bodies.

'Not him – you!' he shouted angrily, flexing his arms and knotting his fists.

There were forty club members in the room. Only one person was not dressed in the uniform that showed they belonged – Jake in his baggy moleskins – and the pack turned on him.

'Watch out behind you, old boy,' Gareth warned Jake in a friendly fashion, as he reached out to take the lapels of Gareth's suit in his hands.

Jake whirled to meet the rush of angry members, and the fists that were bunched for Major Swales thudded into the charging group. Two of them dropped but the rest swarmed on.

'Lay on!' Gareth encouraged him merrily. 'And damned be he who cries "Enough".' Miraculously he had armed himself with a billiard cue.

By now, Jake was almost totally submerged under a heaving mound of black evening dress. There were three of them riding on his back, two hanging around his legs, and one tucked under each of his arms.

'Not me, you fools. Not me – him!' He tried to point to Gareth, but both his arms were occupied.

'Quite right,' Gareth agreed. 'Dirty cheating dog!' and he wielded the billiard cue with uncanny skill, holding it inverted and tapping the thick end smartly against the skulls of the well-dressed gentlemen riding on Jake's back. They dropped away, and freed of their weight Jake turned to Gareth once more.

'Listen—' he bellowed, advancing despite the bodies that clung to his legs.

'Listen, indeed.' Gareth cocked his head, and the sound of a police whistle shrilled, and there was the glimpse of uniforms beyond double doors. 'Peelers, by Jove,' Gareth announced. 'Perhaps we should move on. Follow me, old son.' With a few expert swings of the billiard cue, he knocked the glass from the window beside him, and stepped lightly and unruffled into the darkened garden.

Jake strode along the unlit footpath under the dark jacaranda trees. He followed the main road out towards his camp beside the stream. The outraged cries and the sound of police whistles had long since died away in the night behind.

Jake's anger had also died away, and he chuckled once as he thought of the peer's purple face and his bulging affronted eyes. Then behind him, following along the dark street, he heard the rhythmic squeak of the springs of a ricksha, and the pad of bare feet.

Even before he looked back, he knew who was following.

'Thought I'd lost you,' Gareth Swales remarked lightly, his handsome noble features lit by the glow of the cheroot between his teeth as he lolled against the cushions of the ricksha. 'You took off like a long dog after a bitch – fantastic turn of speed. I was very impressed.'

Jake said nothing, but strode on towards his camp.

'You can't possibly be bound for bed.' The ricksha kept station beside Jake. 'The night is still a pup – and who can say what beautiful thoughts and stirring deeds are still to be thought and performed.'

Jake tried not to grin, and kept going.

'Madame Cecile's?' Gareth wheedled.

'You really do want those cars – don't you?'

'I am hurt,' announced Gareth, 'that you should imply gross materialism to my friendly overtures.'

'Who is paying?' demanded Jake.

'You are my guest.'

'Well, I've drunk your beer, eaten your food – why should I stop now?' He stopped and walked to the ricksha. 'Move over, then,' he said.

The ricksha driver wheeled in a tight turn and trotted back into the town, while Gareth pressed a cheroot between Jake's lips.

'What did you deal yourself?' Jake asked, between puffs of the fragrant smoke. 'Four aces? Straight flush?'

'I am appalled at the implied slur on my character, sir. I shall ignore the question.'

They jogged a little farther in silence until it was Gareth's turn to ask the next question.

'You didn't really roast that poor fellow's chestnuts, did you?'

'No,' Jake admitted. 'But it made a better story.'

They reached the door of Madame Cecile's, discreetly set back in a walled garden, with a lamp burning over the lintel. Gareth paused with his hand on the brass knocker.

'You know – damned if I don't owe you an apology. I've misjudged you all along the line.'

'It's been a lot of laughs.'

'I think I'm going to have to be honest with you.'

'I don't know if I can stand the shock.' They grinned at each other and Gareth punched his shoulder lightly.

'It's still my treat, what?'

Madame Cecile was so tall and thin and bosomless that she seemed in danger of snapping off like a brittle stick. She wore a severely cut dress of dark and indeterminate colour which swept the ground and buttoned up under her chin and at the wrists. Her hair was drawn back tightly into a large bun at the back of her neck and her expression was prim and disapproving, but it softened a little when she let them into the front room.

'Major Swales, it is always a pleasure. Mr Barton, we haven't seen you in a long while. I was afraid you'd left town.'

'Let us have a bottle of Charlie Champers, my dear.' Gareth handed his silk scarf to the maid. 'Have you run out of the Pol Roger 1923?'

'Indeed not, Major.'

'And we'd like to talk alone for a while before meeting any of the young ladies. Is your private lounge vacant?'

Gareth was settled comfortably in one of the big leather armchairs with a glass of champagne in one hand and a cheroot in the other.

'Il Duce is about to put himself in to bat. Though God alone knows what he hopes to gain by it. From all accounts, it's the most desolate stretch of desert and mountain one could imagine. However, Mussolini wants it – perhaps he has visions of empire and glory. The old Napoleonic itch, you know.'

'How do you know this?' Jake was sprawled on the buttoned couch across the room. He wasn't drinking the champagne. He didn't like the taste.

'It's my business to know, old chap. I can smell out a barney before the fellows themselves know they are going to fight. This one is a racing certainty. Il Duce is going through all. the classic stages of protestations of peaceful intentions, combined with wholesale military preparations. The other big powers – France, our chaps and yours – have given him the wink. Of course, they'll all squeal like blazes, and make all sorts of protests at the League of Nations – but nobody is about to stop old Benito making a big grab for Ethiopia. Haile Selassie, the king of kings, knows it and so do all his princes and rases and chieftains and merry men. And they are desperately trying to prepare some kind of defence. That's where I come in, old boy.'

'Why must they buy from you – at the prices you say they are offering? Surely they could get this sort of stuff direct from the manufacturers?'

'Embargo, old chap. The League of Nations have slapped an arms embargo on the whole of Eritrea, Somaliland and Ethiopia. No imports of war material into the area. It's intended to reduce tension – but of course it works out completely one-sided. Mussolini doesn't have to go shopping for his armaments – he has all the guns, aircraft and armour that he needs already landed at Eritrea. Just ready to go – and the jolly old Ethiop has a few ancient rifles and a lot of those long two-handed swords. It should be a close match. You aren't drinking your Charlie Champers?'

'I think I'll go get myself a Tusker. Back in a minute.' Jake rose and moved to the door and Gareth shook his head sadly.

'You've got taste buds like a crocodile's back. Tusker, forsooth, when I'm offering you a vintage Charlie.'

It was more for a chance to think out his position and plan his moves than desire for beer that made Jake seek the bar in the front room. He leaned against the counter in the crowded room, and his mind went swiftly over what Gareth Swales had told him. He tried to decide how much was fact and how much was fantasy. How the facts affected him – and where, if there were any, the profits to himself might lie.

He had almost decided not to involve himself in the deal – there were too many thorns along that path – and to go ahead with his original intentions, selling the engines as cane-crushing units – when he was made the victim of one of those coincidences which were too neat not to be one of the sardonic jokes of fate.

Beside him at the bar were two young men in the sober dress of clerks or accountants. Each of them had a girl tucked under his arm and they fondled them absentmindedly as they talked in loud assertive voices. Jake had been too busy making his decision to follow this conversation until a name caught his attention.

'By the way, did you hear that Anglo Sugar has gone bang?'

'No, I don't believe it.'

'It's true. Heard it from the Master of the Court himself. They say they've gone bust for half a million.'

'Good God – that's the third big company this month.'

'It's hard times we live in. This will bring down a lot of little men with it.'

Jake agreed silently. He poured the beer into his glass, tossed a coin on the counter and headed back for the private lounge.

They were hard times indeed, Jake thought. This was the

second time in as many months that he had been caught up in them.

The freighter on which he had arrived in Dar es Salaam as chief engineer had been seized by the sheriff of the court as surety in a bankruptcy action. The owners had gone bust in London, and the ship had been unable to pay off.

Jake had walked down the gang-plank with all his worldly possessions in the kit-bag over his shoulder – abandoning his claim to almost six months' back wages, together with all his savings in the bankrupt company's pension fund.

He had just started to shape up with the cane-crusher contract, when once again the tidal waves of depression sweeping across the world had swamped him. They were all going bang – the big ones and the small, and Jake Barton now found himself the owner of five armoured cars for which there remained but a single buyer in the market.

Gareth was standing by the window, looking down to the harbour where the lights of the anchored ships flickered across the dark waters. He turned to face Jake and went on as though there had been no break in the conversation.

'While we are still being disgustingly honest with each other, let me estimate that the Ethiopians would pay as much as a thousand pounds each for those vehicles. Of course, they would have to be spruced up. A coat of paint, and a machine gun in the turret.'

'I'm still listening.' Jake sank back on the couch.

'I have the buyer lined up – and the Vickers machine guns, without which the cars have no value. You have the vehicles themselves and the technical know-how to get them working.'

Jake was seeing a different man in Gareth Swales now. The lazy drawling voice and foppish manner were gone. He spoke crisply and once again there was the piratical blue sparkle in his eyes.

'I have never worked with a partner before. I always

knew I could do it better on my own – but I've had a chance to get a good look at you. This could be the first time. What do you think?'

'If you cross me, Gareth – I will truly roast your chestnuts for you.'

Gareth threw back his head and laughed delightedly. 'I believe you really would, Jake!' He crossed the room and offered his hand.

'Equal partners. You put in the cars, and I'll throw in my pile of goodies – everything down the middle?' he asked, and Jake took the hand.

'Right down the middle,' he agreed.

'That's enough business for tonight – let's meet the ladies.'

Jake suggested that Gareth as a full partner might like to assist in refitting the engines and painting the bodywork of the cars, and Gareth blanched and lit a cheroot.

'Look here, old chap. Don't let's take this equal partners lark too far. Manual labour isn't really my style at all.'

'I'll have to hire a gang, then.'

'Please don't stint yourself. Hire what and who you need.' Gareth waved the cheroot magnanimously. 'I've got to get down to the docks – grease a few palms and that sort of thing. Then I'm dining at Government House this evening, making the contacts that may be useful to us, you understand?'

In a ricksha, bearing the silver champagne bucket full of Tusker, Gareth appeared at the camp under the mahogany trees the following morning to find half a dozen blacks labouring under Jake's supervision. The colour Jake had chosen was a businesslike battleship grey, and one of the

31

cars had received its first coat. The effect was miraculous. The vehicle had been transformed from a slovenly wreck into a formidable-looking war machine.

'By Jove,' Gareth enthused. 'Even I am impressed. The old Ethiops will go wild.' He walked along the line of cars, and stopped at the end. 'Only three being painted. What about these two?'

'I explained to you. There are only three runners.'

'Look, old chap. Don't let's be too fussy. Slap paint on all of them – and I'll put them into the package. We aren't selling with a guarantee, what?'

Gareth smiled brilliantly and winked at Jake. 'By the time the complaints come in, you and I will have moved on – and no forwarding address.'

He did not realize that the suggestion was trampling rudely on Jake's craftsman's pride, until he saw the now familiar stiffening of the wide shoulders and the colour coming up Jake's neck.

Half an hour later they were still arguing.

'I've got a reputation on three oceans and across seven seas that I'm not likely to pass up for a couple of pox-ridden old bangers like these,' shouted Jake, and he kicked the wheel of one of the condemned vehicles. 'Nobody's ever going to say that Jake Barton sold a bum.'

Gareth had swiftly gained a working knowledge of his man's temper. He knew instinctively that they were on the very brink of physical violence – and quite suddenly he changed his attitude.

'Listen, old chap. There's no point in shouting at each other—'

'I am not shouting—' roared Jake.

'No, of course not,' Gareth soothed him. 'I see your point entirely. Quite right too. I'd feel exactly the same way.'

Only slightly mollified, Jake opened his mouth to protest

further, but before sound passed his lips, Gareth had pressed a long black cheroot between them and lit it.

'Now let's use what brains God gave us, shall we? Tell me why these two won't run – and what we need to make them do so.'

Fifteen minutes later they were sitting under the sun-flap of Jake's old tent, drinking iced Tusker, and under Gareth's skilful soothing the atmosphere was once more one of friendly co-operation.

'A Smith-Bentley carburettor?' Gareth repeated thoughtfully.

'I've tried every possible supplier. The local agent even cabled Cape Town and Nairobi. We'd have to order one from England – eight weeks delivery, if we are lucky.'

'Look here, old son. I don't mind telling you that this means facing a fate worse than death – but for the good of our mutual venture, I'll do it.'

The Governor of Tanganyika had a daughter who was a spinster of thirty-two years, this despite her father's large fortune and respected title.

Gareth glanced sideways at her and saw all too clearly why this should be. The first adjective which sprang to mind was 'horsey', but it was not the correct one, Gareth decided. 'Camely' or 'camel-like' would convey a much more accurate description. A besotted camel, he thought, as he intercepted the adoring gaze which she fixed upon him as she sat sideways upon the luxurious leather seats.

'Jolly good of you to let me take your Pater's bus for a spin, old girl.'

And she simpered at the endearment, exposing the huge yellowish teeth under the large nose.

33

'Definitely thinking of buying one myself, when I get home. Can't beat the old Benters, what?'

Gareth swung the long black limousine off the metalled road and it plunged forward smoothly over the dusty rutted track that led northwards along the coast through the palm trees.

An askari policeman recognized the fluttering pennant on the front wing, red and blue and gold with rampant lion and unicorn, and he pulled himself to foot-stamping attention and flung a flamboyant salute. Gareth touched the brim of his hat to the manner born, then turned to his companion who had not taken her eyes from his tanned and noble face since they had left the grounds of Government House.

'There is a good view place up ahead, looks out across the channel, very beautiful – actually. Thought we'd park there for a while.'

She nodded vehemently, unable to trust herself to speak. Gareth was glad of that – she had a squeaky little treble – and he smiled his gratitude. That brilliant, completely irresistible smile, and the girl blushed a mottled purple.

She had good eyes, Gareth tried to convince himself, that is if you like camels' eyes. Huge sorrowful pools with long matted lashes. He would concentrate on the eyes – and try and avoid the teeth. He felt a sudden small twinge of concern. 'I hope she doesn't bite in the critical moments. With those choppers, she could inflict a mortal wound.' For a moment he considered abandoning the project. Then he made himself imagine a pile of one thousand sovereigns, and his courage returned.

Gareth braked the Bentley and searched for the turn-off. It was well concealed by underbrush and he missed it and had to back up.

Gently he eased the gleaming limousine down into a small clearing, walled in by fern and scrub and roofed over by the cathedral arches of the palms.

'Well, here we are, what?' Gareth pulled on the hand-brake, and turned to his companion. 'Actually you can see the channel if you twist your neck a bit.'

He leaned forward to demonstrate, and with a convulsive leap the Governor's daughter sprang upon him. Gareth's last controlled thought was that he must avoid the teeth.

Jake Barton waited until the huge glistening Bentley began to heave and toss on its suspension like a lifeboat in a gale, before he rose from the cover of the ferns and, carpet-bag in hand, crept around to the bonnet with its gleaming winged initial 'B' and the stiffly embroidered household pennant.

The noise he made in opening and lifting the engine cowling was effectively smothered by the whinnying cries of passion that issued from the car, and Jake glanced through the windscreen and caught one horrifying glimpse of the Governor's daughter's white limbs, long and shape-less and knobbly kneed as a camel's kicking ecstatically at the roof of the cab before he ducked his head into the engine.

He worked swiftly, his lips pursed but the tune stealthily muted, and his brow creased with concentration as the carburettor jumped and heaved unpredictably under his hands and the whinnies of passion and the high-pitched exhortations to greater effort and speed rang louder.

The resentment he had felt at Gareth Swales's refusal to assist in painting the iron ladies faded swiftly. He was pushing and pulling his full weight now, and his efforts made even the most gruelling manual labour seem insignificant.

As Jake lifted the entire carburettor assembly off the engine block and stowed it into the carpet-bag, there was one last piercing shriek and the Bentley came to an abrupt rest while a ringing silence fell over the palm grove.

Jake Barton crept silently away through the undergrowth

leaving his partner stunned and entangled in a mesh of lanky limbs and expensive French underwear.

'I want you to believe that in my weakened condition it was a long walk home. At the same time, I had to try and convince the lady that we were not betrothed.'

'We'll get you a citation,' Jake promised him, and emerged from the engine housing of the armoured car. 'With disregard for his own personal safety Major Gareth Swales held the pass, stormed the breach, battered down the gates—'

'Terribly amusing,' growled Gareth. 'But, just like you, I have a reputation to maintain. It would embarrass me in certain circles if this got out, old son. Mum's the word, what?'

'You have my word of honour,' Jake told him seriously, and stooped over the crank handle. She fired at the first turn and settled to a steady rhythm to which Jake listened for a few moments before he grinned.

'Listen to her, the bloody little beauty,' and he turned to Gareth. 'Wasn't it worth it just to hear that sweet burbling song?'

Gareth rolled his eyes in agonized memory and Jake went on. 'Four of them. Four lovely, well-behaved ladies. What more could you ask out of life?'

'Five,' said Gareth promptly, and Jake scowled.

'We'd put my name on the fifth one,' he wheedled. 'I'd sign a statement to protect your reputation.' But the expression on Jake's face was sufficient answer.

'No?' Gareth sighed. 'I predict that your sentimental, old-fashioned outlook is going to get us both into a lot of trouble.'

'We can split up now.'

'Wouldn't dream of it, old son. Actually, it would have been dicey peddling a dead 'un to those Ethiops. They've got these dirty great swords, and it's not only your head that they lop off – or so I hear. No, we'll settle for just the four, then.'

On May 22nd the *Dunnottar Castle* anchored in the Dar es Salaam roads and was immediately surrounded by a swarm of barges and lighters. She was the flagship of the Union Castle Line, outward bound from Southampton to Cape Town, Durban, Lourenço Marques, Dar es Salaam and Jibuti.

Two suites and ten double cabins of the first class accommodation were taken up by Lij Mikhael Wasan Sagud and his entourage. The Lij was a scion of the royal house of Ethiopia that traced its line back to King Solomon and the Queen of Sheba. He was a trusted member of the Emperor's inner circle and, under his father, the deputy governor of a piece of mountain and desert country in the northern provinces the size of Scotland and Wales combined.

The Ras was returning to his homeland after six months of petitioning the foreign ministers of Great Britain and France, and lobbying in the halls of the League of Nations in Geneva, trying to gather pledges of support for his country in the face of the gathering storm clouds of Fascist Italian aspirations towards an African Empire.

The Lij was a disillusioned man when he disembarked with four of his senior advisers and made the short journey by lighter to where two hired open tourers awaited his arrival on the wharf. Hire of the motor vehicles had been arranged by Major Gareth Swales and the drivers had been given their instructions.

'Now, you leave the talking to me, old chap,' Gareth

advised Jake, as they waited anxiously in the cavernous and gloomy depths of No. 4 Warehouse. 'This really is my part of the show, you know. You just look stern and do the demonstrating. That will impress the old Ethiop no end.'

Gareth was resplendent in a pale blue tropical suit with a fresh white carnation in the buttonhole, and silk shirt. He wore the diagonally striped old school tie, his hair was brilliantined and carefully brushed, and the sleek lines of the moustache had been trimmed that morning. He ran a judicious eye over his partner and was mildly satisfied. Jake's suit had not been cut in Savile Row, of course, but it was adequate for the occasion; clean and freshly pressed. His shoes had been newly polished and the usually unruly profusion of curls had been wetted and slicked down neatly. He had scrubbed all traces of grease from his large bony hands and from under his fingernails.

'They probably don't even speak English,' Gareth gave his opinion. 'Have to use the old sign language, you know. Wish you'd let me have that dead 'un. We could have palmed it off on them. They are bound to be a gullible lot, throw in a handful of beads and a bag of salt—' He was interrupted by the sound of approaching engines.

'This will be them, now. Don't forget what I told you.'

The two open tourers pulled up in the bright sunlight beyond the doors and disgorged their passengers. Four of them wore the long flowing white shammas, full-length robes like Roman togas draped across the shoulder. Under the robes they wore black gaberdine riding breeches and open sandals. They were all of them elderly men, the dense bushes of their hair shot through with strands of grey and the dark faces wrinkled and lined. In dignified silence they gathered about the taller, younger figure clad in a dark western-style suit and they moved forward into the cool gloom of the warehouse.

Lij Mikhael was well over six feet in height, with a slight

38

scholarly stoop to his shoulders. His skin was the colour of dark honey and his hair and beard were a thick curly halo about the finely boned face, with dark thoughtful eyes and the narrow nose with its Semitic beak. Despite the stoop, he walked with the grace of a swordsman and his teeth when he smiled were glisteningly white against the dark skin.

'By Jove,' said the Lij, in the drawling accent that echoed Gareth's with surprising accuracy. 'It is Farty Swales – isn't it?'

Major Gareth Swales's composure seemed to fall away, leaving him tottering mentally at the use of a nickname he had last heard twenty years before. He had been so branded when his unexpected attack of flatus had clapped and echoed from the vaulted ceiling and stone walls of College Chapel. He had hoped never to hear it spoken again, and now its use took him back to that moment when he had stood in the cold stone chapel and the waves of suppressed laughter had broken over his head like physical blows.

The Prince laughed now, and touched the knot of his necktie. For the first time Jake realized that the diagonal stripes were identical to those that Gareth Swales wore at his own throat.

'Eton 1915 Waynflete's. I was Captain of the House. I gave you six for smoking in the bogs – don't you remember?'

'My God,' gasped Gareth. 'Toffee Sagud. My God. I just don't know what to say.'

'Try him with the old sign language, then,' murmured Jake helpfully.

'Shut up, damn you,' hissed Gareth, and then with a conscious effort he resurrected the smile that lit the gloomy warehouse like the rising of the sun.

'Your Excellency – Toffee – my dear fellow.' He hurried forward with hand outstretched. 'What a great and unexpected pleasure.'

They shook hands laughing, and the solemn dark faces of the elderly advisers lightened with sympathetic merriment.

'Let me introduce my partner, Mr Jake Barton of Texas. Mr Barton is a brilliant engineer and financier – Jake, this is His Excellency Lij Mikhael Wasan Sagud, Deputy Governor of Shoa and an old and dear friend of mine.'

The Prince's hand was narrow-boned, cool and firm. His gaze was quick and penetrating before he turned back to Gareth.

'When were you expelled? Summer of 1915 – wasn't it? Caught boffing one of the maids, as I recall.'

'Good Lord, no!' Gareth was horrified. 'Never the hired help. Actually, it was the house master's daughter.'

'That's right. I remember now. You were famous – went out in a blaze of glory. Talk about your feat lasted for months. They said you went to France with the Duke's, and did jolly well for yourself.'

Gareth made a deprecating gesture, and Lij Mikhael asked,

'Since then what have you been doing, old chap?'

Which was a thoroughly embarrassing question for Gareth. He made a few airy gestures with his cheroot.

'This and that, you know. One thing and another. Business, you understand. Importing, exporting, buying and selling.'

'Which brings us to the present business, does it not?' the Prince asked gently.

'Indeed, it does,' agreed Gareth and took the Prince's arm. 'Now that I realize who is buying, it only increases my pleasure in managing to assemble a package of such high quality.'

The wooden crates were stacked neatly along one wall of the warehouse.

'Fourteen Vickers machine guns, most of them straight from the factory – hardly a shot through the barrels—'

They passed slowly down the array of merchandise to where one of the machine guns had been uncrated and set up on its tripod.

'As you can see, all first-class stuff.'

The five Ethiopians were all warriors, from a long warlike line, and they had the true warrior's love of and delight in the weapons of war. They crowded eagerly around the gun.

Gareth winked at Jake, and went on, 'One hundred and forty-four Lee-Enfield service rifles, still in the grease—' Half a dozen of the rifles had been cleaned and laid out on display.

No. 4 Warehouse was an Aladdin's Cave for them. The elderly courtiers forgot their dignity, and fell upon the weapons like a flock of crows, cackling in Amharic as they fondled the cold oiled steel. They hoisted up the skirts of their shammas to crouch behind the demonstration machine gun and traversed it happily, making the staccato schoolboy imitations of automatic fire as they mowed down imaginary hordes of their enemies.

Even Lij Mikhael forsook his Etonian manners and joined in the delighted examination of the hoard, pushing aside an old greybeard of seventy to take his place at the Vickers gun and triggering off a noisy squabble amongst the others in which Gareth diplomatically intervened.

'I say, Toffee, old chap. This isn't all I have for you. Not by a long chalk. I've kept the plums for the last.' And Jake helped him to gather up the robed and bearded group of excited old men and herd them gently away from the display of weapons and down the warehouse to the open tourers.

The motorcade, headed by Gareth, Jake and the Prince in the leading tourer, came bumping down the dusty track through the mahogany forest and parked in the clearing in front of the candy-striped marquee that had taken the place of Jake's weather-beaten bell tent.

The Royal Hotel had undertaken to cater for the occasion, despite Jake's protests at the cost.

'Give them a bottle of Tusker each – and open a tin of beans,' he insisted, but Gareth had shaken his head sadly. 'Just because they are savages doesn't mean that we have to behave like barbarians, old chap. Style. One has to have style – that's what life is all about. Style and timing. Fill them up with Charlie and then take them for a stroll down the garden path, what?'

Now there were white-robed waiters with red sashes and little red pillbox fezes upon their heads. Under the marquee, long trestle-tables were laden with displays of choice food – decorated sucking pig, heaped salvers of boiled scarlet reef lobster, a smoked salmon, imported apples and peaches from the Cape of Good Hope – and case upon case, bucket upon bucket of champagne. Although Gareth had been swayed by Jake's pleas for economy sufficiently to order a Veuve Clicquot not of a selected vintage.

The Prince and his entourage disembarked to a salvo of champagne corks and the elderly courtiers crowed with delight. Quite by chance, Gareth had struck upon the Ethiopians' love of feasting and strong sense of hospitality. Little that he could have done would have endeared him more to his guests.

'I say, this is very decent of you, my dear Swales,' said the Prince. With his innate sense of courtesy, he had not used Gareth's nickname since the first greeting. Gareth was grateful and when the glasses were filled he called for the first toast.

'His Majesty, Negusa Nagast, King of Kings, Emperor Haile Selassie, Lion of Judah.'

And they drained their glasses, which seemed to be the

correct form, so Gareth and Jake imitated them, and then they fell upon the food, giving Gareth a chance to whisper to Jake,

'Think up some more toasts – we've got to get them filled up.' But he needn't have worried for the Prince came in with:

'His Britannic Majesty, George V, King of England and Emperor of India.' And no sooner were the glasses filled again than he bowed to Jake and lifted his glass.

'The President of the United States of America, Mr Franklin D. Roosevelt.'

Not to be outdone, each of the courtiers shouted an unintelligible toast in Amharic, presumably to the Prince and his father and mother and aunts, uncles and nieces, and the glasses were upended. The waiters rushed back and forth to the steady report of champagne corks.

'The Governor of the British Colony of Tanganyika.' Gareth lifted his glass, slurring slightly.

'And the Governor's daughter,' Jake murmured sardonically.

This provoked another round of toasts from the robed guests, and then it dawned on Jake and Gareth simultaneously that it was folly to try drinking level with men who had been bred and reared on the fiery *tej* of Ethiopia.

'How are you feeling?' muttered Gareth anxiously, squinting slightly to focus.

'Beautiful,' Jake grinned at him beatifically.

'By God, these fellows know how to pack it away.'

'Keep pounding them, Farty. You've got them on the run.' With his empty glass he indicated the smiling but sober group of courtiers.

'I'd be grateful if you could refrain from using that name, old chap. Distasteful, what? Not in the best of style.' Gareth slapped his shoulder with bonhomie and almost missed. A look of concern crossed his face. 'How do I sound?'

'You sound like I feel. We'd better get out of here before they drink us flat on our backs.'

'Oh God, there he goes again,' Gareth muttered with alarm as the Prince raised his brimming glass and looked about him expectantly. 'Wine with you, my dear Swales,' he called as he caught Gareth's eyes.

'Enchanted, I'm sure.' Gareth had no choice but to acknowledge and toss off the contents of his glass before hurrying forward to intercept the waiter who darted in to recharge the Prince's empty glass.

'Toffee, old sport, I do want you to see this little surprise I have for you.' He grabbed the Prince's drinking arm and prised the glass from his grip. 'Come along, everybody. This way, chaps.'

Among the grey-bearded courtiers there was a decided reluctance to leave the marquee, and Jake had to assist Gareth. Both of them spreading their arms and making shooing noises, they finally got them moving down the track through the forest which emerged a hundred yards farther on into an open glade the size of a polo field.

A stunned silence fell upon the party as they saw the row of four iron ladies, gleaming in their new coats of grey, with the heavily jacketed water-cooled barrels of the Vickers machine guns protruding from the ports and the rakish turrets emblazoned with the tricolour horizontal bars of the Ethiopian national colours – green, yellow and red.

Like sleep-walkers, they allowed themselves to be led to the row of chairs under the umbrellas, and without removing their gaze from the war machines they sank into their seats. Gareth stood in front of them like a schoolmaster, but swaying slightly.

'Gentlemen, we have here one of the most versatile armoured vehicles ever brought into service by any major military power—' And while he paused for the Prince to translate, he grinned triumphantly at Jake.

44

'Start them up, old son.'

As the first engine burst into life, the elderly courtiers came to their feet and applauded like the crowd at a prize fight.

'Fifteen hundred quid each,' whispered Gareth, his eyes sparkling, 'they'll go fifteen hundred!'

L ij Mikhael had invited them to dine in his suite aboard the *Dunnottar Castle*, and over Jake's protests a short-order tailor had run up a passable dinner jacket to fit Jake's tall rangy frame.

'I look like I'm in fancy dress,' he objected.

'You look like a duke,' Gareth contradicted. 'It gives you a bit of style. Style, Jake me lad, always remember. Style! If you look like a tramp, people will treat you as one.'

Lij Mikhael Sagud wore a magnificently embroidered cloak in gold and scarlet and black, clasped at the throat with a dark red ruby the size of a ripe acorn, tight-fitting velvet breeches and slippers embroidered with twenty-four carat gold wire. The dinner had been excellent – and the Prince seemed in a mellow mood.

'Now, my dear Swales. The prices for the machine guns and the other armaments were decided months ago – but the armoured cars were never mentioned. Would you like to suggest a reasonable figure?'

'Your Excellency, I had in mind a fair figure before I realized it was you I was dealing with—' Gareth drew deeply on one of the Prince's Havana cigars, steeling himself for the wild flying chance he was going to take. 'Now, of course, I am prepared merely to cover my costs and leave only a modest profit for my partner and myself to share.'

The Prince showed his appreciation with a gracious gesture.

'Two thousand pounds each,' said Gareth quickly, running the words together to make it sound less shocking, but still Jake almost choked on a mouthful of whisky soda.

The Prince nodded thoughtfully. 'I see,' he said. 'That is probably five times the actual value.'

Gareth looked shocked. 'Your Excellency—'

But the Prince silenced him with a raised hand.

'During the last six months, I have spent a great deal of time inspecting and pricing various items of military equipment. My dear Swales, please don't insult us both by protesting.'

There was a long silence and the atmosphere in the cabin was taut as guitar strings – then the Prince sighed.

'I could price those weapons – but I could not buy. The great powers of the world have denied me that right – the right to defend my country against the predator.' There was an age of weariness in the dark eyes and smooth brow furrowed with thought. 'My country is land-locked, as you know, gentlemen. We do not have access to the sea. All imports must come through the territories of French and British Somaliland – or Italian Eritrea. Italy the predator – or the French and the British who have placed us under embargo.' Lij Mikhaël sipped at the drink in his hand, and then frowned into the depths of the glass, as though it were a crystal ball and he could read the future there.

'The great powers are prepared to deliver us to the Fascist tyrant, with our swordhand empty and trussed behind our back.' He sighed again heavily and then looked up at Gareth. His expression changed.

'Major Swales, you have offered me a collection of worn and obsolete vehicles and weapons at many times their actual value. I am a desperate man. I must accept your offer and the price you demand.'

Gareth relaxed slightly and glanced at Jake.

'I must even accept your condition that payment be made in British sterling.'

Gareth smiled now. 'My dear fellow—' he began, but again the Prince silenced him with a raised hand.

'In turn I impose only one condition. It is vital to my acceptance of your offer. You and your partner, Mr Barton, will be responsible for the delivery of all these weapons into the territory of Ethiopia. Payment will be made only when you hand over the shipment to me or my agent within the borders of his Imperial Majesty, Haile Selassie.'

'Good God, man,' exploded Gareth. 'That involves smuggling them through hundreds of miles of hostile territory. That's ridiculous!'

'Ridiculous, Major Swales? I think not. Your merchandise is of no value to me or to you in Dar es Salaam. I am your only customer – nobody else in the entire world would be foolish enough to buy it from you. On the other hand, any attempt that I should make to import it into my homeland would certainly be frustrated. I am being watched carefully by agents of all the major powers. I know I shall be searched the moment that I land at Jibuti. Lying here, the merchandise has no value.' He paused and glanced from Gareth to Jake. Jake rubbed his jaw thoughtfully.

'I see your point, Your Excellency.'

'You are a reasonable man, Mr Barton,' said the Prince, and then returned his attention to Gareth, and repeated his last statement. 'Lying here it has no value. In Ethiopia, it is worth fifteen thousand British sovereigns to you. The choice is yours. Abandon it – or get it into Ethiopia.'

'I am appalled,' said Gareth solemnly, as he paced back and forth. 'I mean, after all the fellow is an old Etonian. God, I can hardly believe that he would welsh on our agreement. It's absolutely frightful. I mean, I trusted him.'

Jake was sprawled on the couch in Madame Cecile's private room. He had shed his dinner-jacket, and perched on his knee there was a plump young lady with a cap of brassy blonde hair. She was dressed in a flimsy daffodil-coloured dress, the skirts of which had pulled up to show bright blue garters around her ripe thighs. Jake was weighing one of her ample breasts in his hand with all the concentration of a housewife choosing tomatoes from a green-grocer's tray. The girl giggled and wriggled provocatively into his lap.

'Damn it, Jake, listen to me.'

'I am listening,' said Jake.

'The man was positively insulting,' protested Gareth, and then seemed for a moment to lose his concentration as Jake's companion unbuttoned the bodice of her wispy dress.

'By Jove, Jake, they are rather delicious, what?' and they both regarded the display with interest.

'You've got your own,' Jake muttered.

'You're right,' agreed Gareth, and turned to the junoesque female who waited patiently for him on the other couch. Her glossy black hair was piled upon her head in an elaborate nest of curls and plaits, and she had large, intense, toffee-coloured eyes in a face whose paleness was emphasized by the vividly painted crimson lips. She pouted at Gareth, and draped one arm languidly around his shoulders.

'Are you sure neither of them understands English?' Gareth called, as he entered into the practised embrace of the white arms.

'Portuguese, both of them,' Jake assured him. 'But you'd better test them.'

'Very well.' Gareth thought a moment. 'Girls, I must warn you that we aren't paying for your company – not a penny. This is for love alone.'

Neither of their expressions changed, and the enfolding movements of sinuous limbs continued without pause.

'That settles it,' Gareth opined. 'We can talk.'

'At a time like this?'

'We've only got until morning to decide what we are going to do.'

Jake made a muffled remark and Gareth admonished him, 'I can't hear a word.'

'That gullible old Ethiop of yours has us over a barrel,' repeated Jake with sardonic relish. Before he could reply, vivid lips, pouting and red as ripened fruit, closed over Gareth's. There was silence for a while until Gareth wrested himself loose and his head popped up – moustache in disarray and stained with lipstick.

'Jake, what the hell are we going to do?'

And Jake told him in nautical language which left no room for misunderstanding precisely what he was about to do.

'I don't mean that, I mean what are we going to tell old Toffee tomorrow? Are we going to deliver the goods?'

Gareth's companion reached up, took him in a head lock and drew his mouth down again.

'Jake, for God's sake, concentrate on the problem,' he pleaded as he was engulfed.

'I am, I am!' Jake assured him, rolling his eyes sideways to meet Gareth's, but without interrupting his efforts with the plump blonde.

'How the hell do we get four armoured cars ashore on a hostile coast, just for a start – then how do we run them two hundred miles to the Ethiopian border?' Gareth lamented, speaking out of the unemployed corner of his mouth, and then something caught his attention. He pulled free and raised himself on one elbow. 'I say, your companion isn't a blonde after all. Extraordinary.'

Jake glanced sideways and grinned. 'And yours seems to be Scottish – she's wearing a sporran, by God.'

'Jake, we've got to make a decision. Do we go or don't we?'

'Action first, decisions later. Let's engage the targets.'

'Right,' Gareth agreed, realizing the futility of discussion at this moment. 'Driver advance.'

'Gunner. Traverse right. Steady. On. Independent rapid fire.'

'Shoot!' cried Gareth, and the conversation languished. It was half an hour before it was resumed, with the two of them in shirt sleeves, braces dangling and black ties discarded, poring over a large-scale map of the East African coast that Madame Cecile had produced.

'There's a thousand miles of unguarded coast line.' Gareth traced the great horn of Africa in the light of the Petromax lamp and then ran his finger inland. 'And this is marked as semi-desert all the way to the border. We aren't likely to run into a crowd.'

'It's a hell of a way to make a living,' said Jake.

'Are we going then?' Gareth looked up.

'You know we are.'

'Yes,' Gareth laughed. 'I know we are. Fifteen thousand sovereigns say we have to.'

L ij Mikhael received their decision with a curt nod and then asked,
'Have you planned yet how you will accomplish this task? Perhaps I can be of assistance, I know the coast well and most of the routes to the interior.' He gestured for one of his advisers to spread a map upon the stateroom table. Jake ran his finger across it, as he spoke.

'We thought to hire a shallow-draughted vessel here in Dar es Salaam, and make a landing somewhere in this area. Then to load the cases on the cars, and, carrying our own fuel, run directly inland to some prearranged rendezvous with your people.'

'Yes,' agreed the Prince. 'The basic idea is right. But I should avoid British territory. They maintain a very intensive patrol system to discourage the export of slaves from their territory to the East. No, keep clear of British Somaliland. The French territory is more suitable.'

They plunged into the planning of the expedition, both Jake and Gareth realizing swiftly how lightly they had discounted the difficulties that faced them, and how valuable was the Prince's advice.

'Your landing will be one of the critical stages. There is a tidal fall of almost twenty feet on this coast and an unfavourable shelving of the bottom. However, at this point – about forty miles north of Jibuti – there is an ancient harbour called Mondi. It's not marked on the chart. It was one of the centres of the slave trade before its abolition, like Zanzibar and Mozambique Island. It was stormed and sacked by a British force in 1842. The port is without fresh water and since then it has been deserted. Yet it has a deep-water channel and a good approach to the shore. This would be a suitable place to land the vehicles – an awkward task without good wharfage and overhead cranes.'

Gareth was scribbling notes on a sheet of Union Castle notepaper, while Jake leaned attentively over the chart.

'What about patrols in this area?' he asked, and the Prince shrugged.

'There is a battalion of the Légion Étrangère at Jibuti – and they send an occasional camel patrol through this area. The odds are much against an encounter.'

'Those are the kind of odds I like,' muttered Gareth.

'Once we are ashore – what then?'

The Prince touched the map. 'You should then move parallel with the border of Italian Eritrea – a south-westerly heading – until you encounter the swamp area where the Awash River sinks into the desert. Then turn directly westwards and you will cross the French Somali border and enter the Danakil country of Ethiopia. I will arrange to meet your column here—' He turned to his group of elderly advisers and asked a question. Immediately an animated and high-volume discussion broke out, at the end of which the Prince turned back to them with a smile.

'We seem to be in general agreement that the rendezvous should be at the Wells of Chaldi – here.' He showed them the map again. 'As you can see, it is well within Ethiopian territory. This will suit my Government as well – for the cars will be used in the defence of the Sardi Gorge and the road to Dessie – in the event of an Italian offensive in that direction—' The Prince was interrupted by one of his advisers and he listened for a few minutes before nodding in agreement and turning back to the two white men. 'It has been suggested that as your journey from Mondi to the Wells of Chaldi will be through trackless desert country – some areas of which would be impassable to wheeled vehicles – we should provide you with a guide who knows the area—'

'That's more like it,' Jake growled with relief.

'That's absolutely splendid, Toffee,' agreed Gareth.

'Very well. The young man I have chosen is a relative of mine, a nephew. He speaks English well, having also spent three years at school in England, and he knows the area through which you will be travelling, as he has often hunted the lion there as a guest of a chief in French territory.' He spoke to one of the advisers in Amharic, and the man nodded and left the cabin. 'I have sent for him now. His name is Gregorius Maryam.'

When he came, Gregorius was a young man probably in his early twenties. However, he was almost as tall as his uncle with the warrior's fierce dark eyes and eagle features – but his skin was smooth and hairless as a girl's, the colour of pale honey. He also was dressed in Western European fashion, and his expression was intense and intelligent.

His uncle spoke to him quietly in Amharic and he nodded, then turned to meet Jake and Gareth.

'My uncle has explained what is required of me – and I am honoured to be of service.' Gregorius's voice was clear and eager.

'Can you drive a motor car?' Jake asked unexpectedly, and Gregorius smiled and nodded.

'Indeed, sir. I have my own Morgan sports car in Addis Ababa.'

'That's great.' Jake returned the smile. 'But you'll find an armoured car a rougher ride.'

'Gregorius will pack what he needs for the journey, and join you immediately. As you know, this ship sails at noon,' observed the Prince, and the young Ethiopian nobleman bowed to his uncle and left the cabin.

'You now owe me a favour, Major Swales, and I request repayment immediately.' Lij Mikhael turned back to Gareth, whose complacency evaporated immediately, to be replaced by an expression of mild alarm. Gareth had developed a healthy respect for the Prince's ability to drive a bargain.

'Now listen here, old chap—' he began to protest, but the Prince went on as though there had been no interruption.

'One of the few weapons that my country has to exploit is the conscience of the civilized world—'

'I wouldn't give you much change for that,' observed Jake.

'No,' agreed the Prince sadly. 'Not a very effective weapon as yet. But if we can only inform the world of the injustices and unprovoked aggression which we suffer – then we can force the democratic nations to come to our support. We need popular support – we must reach the people. If the common peoples are informed of our lot, they will force their own governments to take action.'

'It's a pretty thought,' Gareth agreed.

'Travelling with me now is one of the most highly thought of and influential journalists in America. Someone who has the ear of hundreds of thousands of readers across the United States of America, and the rest of the English-speaking world as well. A person of liberal conscience, a champion of the oppressed.' The Prince paused. 'However, this person's reputation has preceded us. The Italians realize that their case might be damaged if the truth is written by a journalist of this calibre – and they have taken measures to prevent this happening. We have today heard by radio that transit of English, French and Italian territories will be refused, and that this ally of ours will be denied access to Ethiopia. They do not only embargo weapons – but they prevent our friends from giving us succour.'

'No,' said Gareth. 'I've got enough trouble – that I must act as a taxi service for the entire press corps of the world. I'll be damned if I will—'

'Can he drive a motor car?' Jake interrupted 'We are still short of a driver for the last car.'

'If I know journalists, all he can drive is a whisky bottle,' grunted Gareth gloomily.

'If he can drive – we'd save the wages of hiring another

driver,' Jake pointed out, and Gareth's gloom lightened a little.

'That's true – if he can drive.'

'Let us find out,' suggested the Prince, and spoke quietly to one of his men who slipped out of the cabin. Gareth took advantage of the pause to take the Prince's arm and draw him aside from the main group.

'I have drawn up an estimate of the additional expenses we will encounter – the hire of a ship and that sort of thing – it stretches the old finances. I wonder if you could see your way clear to making a gesture of good faith – just a small advance. A few hundred guineas.'

'Major Swales, I have made the gesture already by giving my nephew into your care.'

'Not that I don't appreciate that—' Gareth was about to enlarge his argument, but he was prevented from doing so by the opening of the cabin door and the entry of the journalist. Gareth Swales straightened up and touched the knot of his tie. His smile broke across the cabin like the early morning sun.

Jake Barton had slumped down into one of the chairs beside the chart table and was about to light a cheroot, the match flaring in the cup of his hands, but he did not complete the movement. The match burned on forgotten, as he stared at the newcomer.

'Gentlemen,' said the Prince. 'I have the honour to introduce Miss Victoria Camberwell, a distinguished member of the American press and a good friend of my country.'

Vicky Camberwell was not yet thirty years of age, and she was also an unusually attractive and nubile young woman. She had learned long ago that youth and feminine beauty were not assets in her chosen career and she tried, with little success, to disguise both.

She adopted a severe, almost mannish, dress. A military-style shirt with cloth epaulets and button-down breast pockets that were pushed out by the large but shapely breasts. Her skirt was tailored in the same cream linen with more button-down pockets on the thighs, and clasped at the slim waist with a leather belt and heavy snake's buckle. Her shoes were of the lace-up type that women call 'sensible'. On her long lovely legs they looked almost frivolous.

Her hair was drawn severely back to expose a long swan neck. The hair was fine and silken, sun-bleached, in places, almost white and shaded over her high broad forehead to the colour of wheat and autumn leaves.

Gareth recovered first. 'Miss Camberwell, of course. I know your work. Your column is syndicated in the *Observer*.' She looked at him without expression, remarkably immune to the celebrated Swales smile. Her eyes, he noticed, were serious and level, sage green in colour, but shot with speckles of tawny gold.

Jake's match burned his fingers and he swore. She turned to him and he stood up quickly.

'I didn't expect a woman.'

'You don't like women?' Her voice was pitched low and had a husky tone that raised goose bumps on Jake's forearms.

'Some of my favourite people are women.'

He saw that she was tall, reaching almost to his shoulder, and that her body had a poised athletic carriage. She held her head at a haughty angle which emphasized the strong independent line of mouth and jaw.

'In fact, I can't think of anyone I like more.' And she smiled for the first time. It had surprising warmth, and Jake saw that her front teeth were slightly uneven – one pushed out of line with the other. He stared at it fascinated for a moment, then he looked up into the appraising green eyes.

'Do you drive a car?' he asked seriously, and her smile turned to surprised laughter.

'I do,' said Vicky, laughing. 'I also ride a horse and a bicycle, I can ski, pilot an aeroplane, play snooker and bridge, sing, dance and play the piano.'

'That will do,' Jake laughed with her. 'That will do just fine.'

Vicky turned back to the Prince. 'What is all this about, Lij Mikhael?' she asked. 'Just what do these two gentlemen have to do with our plans?'

The towering purple hull of the *Dunnottar Castle* swung slowly across the back-drop of palm trees and the high sun-gilded ranges of cumulus cloud, as she pulled her anchors and came around for the harbour entrance.

At the rail of the upper deck, the tall figure of the Prince was flanked by the white-robed figures of his staff, and as the ship increased speed and kicked up a white sparkling bow wave, he lifted an arm in a gesture of farewell.

Swiftly, the shape of the liner dwindled away into the limitless eastern ocean as she made her offing before turning northwards once more.

The four figures on the wharf lingered after it had disappeared, staring out at the horizon whose long sweep was uninterrupted except by the tiny white triangular sails of the fishing fleet coming in off the banks.

Jake spoke first. 'We'll have to find digs for Miss Camberwell.' And at the thought, both he and Gareth made a grab for her single battered portmanteau and the typewriter in its leather case.

'Spin you for it,' suggested Gareth, and an East African shilling appeared in his hand.

'Tails,' decided Jake.

'Rough luck, old son,' Gareth commiserated, and

returned the coin to his pocket. 'I'll take care of Miss Camberwell—' he went on, '— then I'll start looking for a ship to take us up coast. In the meantime, I suggest you have another look at those cars.' As he spoke, he hailed a ricksha from the row which waited at the head of the wharf. 'Remember, Jake, it was one thing driving them down to the harbour – but an altogether different matter driving them through two hundred miles of desert. You'd best make sure we don't have to walk home,' he advised, and handed Vicky Camberwell into the ricksha. 'Driver, advance!' he called, and with a cheery wave they jogged away up town.

'It looks as though we are on our own, sir,' said Gregorius, and Jake grunted, still staring after the departing ricksha. 'I think I should also find accommodation,' and Jake roused himself.

'Come along, lad. You can doss down in my tent for the few days before we leave.' And then he grinned. 'I hope you won't be offended if I wish it was Miss Camberwell rather than you, Greg.'

The boy laughed delightedly. 'I understand your feelings – but perhaps she snores, sir.'

'No girl who looks like that could possibly snore,' Jake told him. 'And another thing – don't call me "sir", it makes me nervous. My name's Jake.' He picked up one of Greg's bags. 'We'll walk,' he said. 'I have a horrible hollow feeling that it's going to be a long weary wait until next the eagle screams.'

They set off along the dusty unpaved verge of the road.

'You said you own a Morgan?' Jake asked.

'That's right, Jake.'

'Do you know what makes it move?'

'The internal combustion engine.'

'Oh brother,' applauded Jake. 'That is a flying start. You have just been appointed second engineer – get your sleeves rolled up.'

G areth Swales had a theory about seduction which in twenty years he had never had reason to revise. Ladies liked the company of aristocrats, they were all of them basically snobs and a coat of arms usually made the coldest of them swoon. No sooner had they settled into the padded seats of the ricksha, than he turned upon Vicky Camberwell the full dazzling beam of his wit and charm.

No one who had built up an international reputation in the hard field of journalism by the age of twenty-nine could be expected to lack perception, or be naïve in the wicked ways of the world. Vicky Camberwell had made a preliminary judgement of Gareth within minutes of meeting him. She had known others with the same urbane good looks and meticulous grooming, the light bantering tone and the steely glint in the eye. Rogue, she had decided – and every second in his company confirmed the initial judgement – but damned good-looking rogue, and very funny rogue with the exaggerated accent and turn of speech which she had recognized immediately as a huge put-on. She listened with amusement as he set out to impress with his lineage.

'As the colonel used to say – we always referred to my old man as the colonel.' Gareth's father had indeed died a colonel, but not in an illustrious regiment, as the rank suggested. He had worked his way up from the lowly rank of constable in the Indian police.

'Of course, the family estates were from my mother's side—' His mother had been the only daughter of an unsuccessful baker, and the family estate had comprised the mortgaged premises in Swansea.

'The colonel was always a bit of a rogue, and moved with a wild crowd, you know. Fast ladies and slow horses. The estates went to the block, I'm afraid.' Victims themselves of the grinding injustices of the British class system, mother and father had devoted themselves to lifting their only son

59

beyond that invisible barrier that divides the middle from the upper classes.

'Of course, I was at Eton and he was mostly on foreign service. Wish I'd got to know the old devil better. He must have been a wonderful character—' Entrance to the school had been assisted by the Commissioner of Police, himself an old Etonian. The mother's small inheritance and the greater part of the father's salary went into the costly business of turning the son into a gentleman.

'Killed in a duel, would you believe it. Pistols at dawn. He was a romantic, too much fire in his veins.' When the cholera took the mother, the father's salary was insufficient to meet the bills that a young man casually ran up when he mixed sociably with the sons of dukes. In India, bribery was a convention, a way of living – but the colonel was found out. It was indeed pistols at dawn. The colonel rode out into the dark Indian forest with his Webley service pistol, and his bay mare trotted back to the stables an hour later with an empty saddle and the reins trailing.

'Had to leave Eton, naturally.' Under considerable duress. It was coincidence that Gareth's friendship with the house master's daughter took place at the same time as the colonel's last ride, but at least it allowed Gareth to leave in a blaze of glory, as Lij Mikhael remarked, rather than as a nobody whose fees had not been met.

He went out into the world with the speech, the manners and the tastes of a gentleman – but without the means to support them.

'Luckily they were having this war at the time—' and even a regiment like the Duke's were not enquiring too deeply into the private means of their new officers. Eton was sufficient recommendation, and, with the help of the German machine guns, promotion was swift. However, after the armistice, things were back to normal and it required three thousand a year for an officer to support himself in the style the regiment expected. Gareth moved on, and had kept moving ever since.

Vicky Camberwell listened to him, fascinated despite herself. She knew that this was the cobra dance before the chicken, she knew herself well enough to realize that part of the attraction he held for her was the very devilry and roguishness she had so readily recognized.

There had been others like this one. Her job took her to the trouble spots of the world, and men of this breed were attracted to the same hot spots. With these men there was always the excitement and danger, the thrill and the fun — but inevitably there was also the sting and the pain in the end.

She tried not to respond, wishing the ride would end, but Gareth's sallies were too much for her and as the ricksha drew up in front of the Royal Hotel entrance, she could not resist the almost suffocating urge to laugh. She threw back her head, shaking her shining pale hair in the wind as she let it ring out.

Gareth had learned also to use the calibre of a woman's laughter as a yardstick. Vicky laughed with an unaffected gaiety, a straightforward physical response that he found reassuring, and he took her arm possessively as he helped her out of the ricksha.

He showed her through the royal suite with a proprietorial air. 'Only one suite in the place. Balcony looks out over the gardens, and you get the sea breeze in the evening.' And, 'Only private loo in the building, even one of those French jobs for sluicing the old privates, you know.' And, 'The bed is quite extraordinary, like sleeping on a cloud and all that rot. Never experienced anything like it.'

'Is this where I am to stay?' Vicky asked, with a small-girl innocence.

'Well, I thought we could make some sort of arrangement, old girl.' And she was left with no doubts as to the type of arrangement Gareth Swales had in mind.

'You are very kind, major,' she murmured, and crossed to the handset of the telephone.

'This is Miss Camberwell. Major Swales is vacating the royal suite for me. Please have a servant move his clothes to alternative accommodation.'

'I say—' gasped Gareth, and she covered the mouthpiece and smiled at him. 'It's so sweet of you.' Then she listened to the manager's voice. 'Oh dear,' she said. 'Well, if that's the only room you have vacant, it will just have to do then, I am sure the major has experienced more uncomfortable billets.'

When Gareth saw the room that was now his, he tried honestly to remember humbler and less comfortable billets. The Chinese prison in Mukden had been cooler and not placed directly over the boisterous uproar of the public bar, and the frontline dugout during the winter of 1917 at Arras had been more spacious and better furnished.

The next three days Gareth Swales spent at the harbour, drinking tea and whisky in the office of the harbour master, riding out with the pilot to meet every new vessel as it crossed the bar, jogging in a ricksha along the wharf to speak with the skippers of dhows and luggers, rusty old coal-burners and neater, newer oil-burners, or rowing about the harbour in a hired ferry to hail the vessels that lay at anchor in the roads.

His evenings he spent plying Victoria Camberwell with charm, flattery and vintage champagne – for all of which she seemed to have an insatiable appetite and complete immunity. She listened to him, laughed with him and drank his champagne, and at midnight excused herself prettily, and nimbly side-stepped his efforts to press her to his snowy shirt-front or get a foot in the door of the royal suite.

By the morning of the fourth day, Gareth was understandably becoming a little discouraged. He thought of taking a bucket of Tusker out to Jake's camp and cheering himself up with a little of the American's genial company. However, he did not relish having to admit failure to Jake, so he fought off the temptation and took his usual ricksha ride down to the harbour.

During the night a new vessel had anchored in the outer roads and Gareth examined her through his binoculars. She was salt-rimed and dirty, old and scarred with a dark nondescript hull and a ragged crew, but Gareth saw that her rigging was sound and that although she was schooner-rigged with masts which could spread a mass of canvas, yet she had propeller drive at the stern – probably she had been converted to take a diesel engine under the high poop. She looked the most likely prospect he had yet seen in the harbour and Gareth ran down the steps to the ferry and exuberantly tipped the oarsman a shilling over his usual fare.

At closer range the vessel seemed even more disreputable than she had at a distance. The paintwork proved to be a mottled patchwork of layer peeling from layer, and it was clear what the sanitary arrangements were aboard. The sides were zebra-striped with human excrement.

Yet closer still, Gareth noticed that the planking was tight and sound beneath the execrable paint cover, and her bottom, seen through the clear water, was clean copper and free of the usual fuzzy green beard of weed. Also her rigging was well set up and all sheets had the bright yellow colour and resilient look of new hemp. The name on her stern was in Arabic and French, *Hirondelle*, and she was Seychelles registered.

Gareth wondered at her purpose, for she was certainly a ringer, a thoroughbred masquerading as a cart horse. That big bronze propeller would drive her handily, and the hull itself looked fast and sea-kindly.

Then as he came alongside he smelled her, and knew precisely what she was. He had smelled that peculiar odour of polluted bilges and suffering humanity before in the China Sea. He had heard it said that it was an odour that could never be scoured from a hull, not even sheep dip and boiling salt water would cleanse it. They said that on a dark night, the patrol boats could smell a slaver from over the horizon.

A man who made his daily bread buying and selling slaves would be unlikely to baulk at a mere trifle like gun-running, decided Gareth, and hailed her.

'Ahoy, *Hirondelle!*'

The response was hostile, the closed dark faces of the ragged crew stared down at the ferry. They were a mixed batch, Arab, Indian, Chinese, Negro – and there was no answer to his hail.

Standing in the ferry, Gareth cupped his hands to his mouth and, with the Englishman's unconscious arrogance that assumes all the world speaks English, called again.

'I want to speak to your captain.'

Now there was a stir under the poop and a white man came to the rail. He was swarthy, darkly sunburned and so short that his head barely showed above the gunwale.

'What you want? You police, hey?'

Gareth guessed he was Greek or Armenian. He wore a dark patch over one eye, and the effect was theatrical. The good eye was bright and stony as water-washed agate.

'No police!' Gareth assured him. 'No trouble,' and produced the whisky bottle from his coat pocket and waved it airily.

The Captain leaned out over the rail and peered closely at Gareth. Perhaps he recognized the twinkle in the eye and the jaunty piratical smile that Gareth flashed up at him. It often takes one to know one. Anyway, he seemed to reach a decision and he snapped an order in Arabic. A rope ladder tumbled down the side.

'Come,' invited the Captain. He had nothing to hide. On this leg of his voyage he carried only a cargo of baled cotton goods from Bombay. He would discharge this here at Dar es Salaam before continuing northwards to make a nocturnal landfall on the great horn of Africa, there to take on his more lucrative cargo of human wares.

As long as the merchants of Arabia, India and the East still offered huge sums for the slender black girls of the Danakil and Galla, men like this would brave the British warships and patrol boats to supply them.

'I thought we might drink a little whisky together and talk about money,' Gareth greeted the Captain. 'My name is Swales. Major Swales.'

The Captain had trained his oiled black hair into a queue that hung down his back. He seemed to cultivate the buccaneer image.

'My name is Papadopoulos.' He grinned for the first time. 'And the talk of money is sweet like music.' He held out his hand.

Gareth and Vicky Camberwell came to Jake's camp in the mahogany forest, bearing gifts.

'This is a surprise,' Jake greeted them sardonically as he straightened up from the welding set with the torch still flaring in his hand. 'I thought you two had eloped.'

'Business first, pleasure later.' Gareth handed Vicky down from the ricksha. 'No, my dear Jake, we have been working hard.'

'I can see that. You look really worn out with your labours.' Jake doused the welding torch and accepted the bucket of Tusker beer. He broached two bottles immediately, handing one to Greg and lifting the other to his own lips. He wore only a pair of greasy khaki shorts.

When he lowered it, he grinned. 'But, what the hell, I was dying of thirst and so I forgive you.'

'You have saved our lives, Major Swales and Miss Camberwell,' agreed Greg, and saluted them with the dewed bottle.

'What on earth is this?' Gareth turned to inspect the massive construction on which Jake and Greg had been working, and Jake patted it proudly.

'It's a raft.' He circled the complicated platform of empty oil drums with its decking of timber slats, indicating its finer features with the half-empty beer bottle.

'Armoured cars don't swim, and we have to land them on a shelving beach. It's unlikely we will be able to get within a hundred yards of the shore. We'll float them off.'

Vicky was looking at the fine muscling of Jake's shoulders and arms, at the flat belly and the dark pelt of hair that covered his chest, but Gareth was fascinated by the crudely constructed raft.

'I was going to talk to you about landing the cars, and suggest something like this,' Gareth said, and Jake lifted an eyebrow at him in disbelief.

'All we must make sure of is that the vessel that lands us has a derrick strong enough to swing the cars outboard.'

'What do they weigh?'

'Five tons each.'

'Fine, the Hirondelle can handle that.'

'The Hirondelle?'

'The vessel that's transporting us.'

'So you *have* been working.' Jake laughed. 'I would never have believed it of you. When do we sail?'

'Dawn, the day after tomorrow. We will load during the night – not wanting to advertise our cargo – and we will sail at first light.'

'That doesn't give me much time to teach Miss Camberwell to drive one of the cars.' Jake turned to her now, and once again felt the thrill of looking into those speckled eyes of green and gold. 'I'm going to need a deal of your time.'

'That's one thing I've got plenty of at the moment.' For Vicky the interlude in Dar es Salaam had served to rest tired and strained nerves – her previous assignment at Geneva had been irksome and wearying. She had spent the last few days exploring the ancient port and writing a two-thousand-word filler on its origins and history. She had enjoyed Gareth Swales's attentions and the by-play of avoiding his more serious advances. Now she was becoming aware of Jake Barton's smouldering admiration. Nothing like being pursued by two tough, dangerous and forceful males to relax a girl, she thought, and smiled at Jake, enjoying his reaction, and watching Gareth Swales bridle and move in to intervene.

'I can give Vicky a bit of instruction on the jolly old machines – don't want to take you off important work.'

Vicky did not turn her head, but went on smiling at Jake.

'I think that's rather Mr Barton's department,' she said.

'Jake,' said Jake.

'Vicky,' said Vicky.

This whole business was turning out very well indeed. A good story to chase, a worthy cause to support, another daring escapade to add to the blooming lustre of her reputation. She knew none of her colleagues had dared the League's sanctions and violated international frontiers with a gang of gun-runners to file a story.

As a bonus, there were two attractive males for company. It all looked very good indeed, just as long as she kept it all on a manageable basis, and did not let her emotions get into an uproar once more.

They followed the path down through the mahogany forest, and she smiled secretly to herself as she watched Gareth and Jake jockeying for position beside her. However, when they reached the clearing, Gareth stopped abruptly.

'What now?' he demanded.

'The paint job is Greg's idea,' explained Jake. 'Make people think twice before they start shooting at us.'

The four vehicles were now painted a glistening snowy white, and the turrets were emblazoned with a flaming scarlet cross.

'If the French or the Italians try to stop us, we are a unit of armoured ambulances of the International Red Cross. You, Greg and I are doctors, and Vicky is a nursing sister.'

'My God, you have been busy.' Vicky was impressed.

'Also the white paint will be cooler in the desert,' Greg explained seriously. 'They call it the "Great Burn" with good reason.'

'The carrying racks I designed,' said Jake. 'Each vehicle will be able to carry two forty-gallon drums of gasoline and one of water at the rear of the turret. The crates of arms and ammunition we will distribute between the four of them and rope them down here across the sponsons – I have welded cleats here to take the ropes.'

'The crates will be a dead give-away,' objected Gareth. 'They are all marked—'

'We'll plane off the marking and re-label them as medical supplies,' Jake told him, then took Vicky's arm. 'I've chosen this one for you. She's the most docile and friendly of the four.'

'Do they have characters of their own?' Vicky teased him, and laughed at the seriousness of his reply.

'They are just like women. My iron ladies,' he slapped the nearest machine. 'This one is an absolute darling – except that her rear suspension is slightly out of alignment, so she waggles her bottom a bit at speed. It's nothing serious, however, but it's why her name is Miss Wobbly. She's yours. You'll grow to love her.' Jake walked on and kicked the tyre of the next car. 'This one is the bitch of the party. She tried to break my wrist the very first time I ever cranked her. She is known as Priscilla the Pig. I'm the only one who can handle her. She doesn't love me, but she respects me.' He moved on. 'Greg has chosen this one and called her Tenastelin – which means "God is with us" – I hope he is right, but I doubt it. Greg is a bit funny about that sort of thing. He tells me he was going to be a priest once.' He winked at the youngster. 'Gareth, this one is yours – she has a brand new carburettor. I think it is only fair you should enjoy her, since you are the one who risked all to obtain it.'

'Oh?' Vicky's eyes lit with interest, the news-hound in her aroused. 'What happened?'

'It's a long story,' Jake grinned, 'but it involved a long and dangerous ride on a camel.' Gareth choked on a lungful of cheroot smoke and coughed, but Jake went on remorselessly, 'She shall therefore be known in future as Henrietta the Hump – the Hump for short.'

'How very cute,' said Vicky.

After midnight the four vehicles moved in column through the dark and sleeping streets of the old town. The steel shutters were closed down over the headlights so that only a narrow strip of light was thrown forwards and downwards. The engines were idling as they moved at walking speed under the trees whose spread branches hung over the road and hid the stars.

The silhouette of the cars was drastically altered by the burden that each of them carried – drums and crates, coils of rope and netting, trenching tools and camping equipment.

Gareth Swales led the column, freshly shaven and dressed in grey flannel Oxford bags and a white jersey with the I Zingari cricket colours adorning the neck and cuffs. He was mildly concerned that the proprietor of the Royal Hotel might become aware of his imminent departure, for there was a bill for three weeks' board outstanding and a formidable pile of unpaid chitties signed with the Swales flourish for champagne supplied. Gareth would definitely feel happier out at sea.

Gregorius Maryam followed him closely. His hereditary title was Gerazmach, 'Commander of the Left Wing', and his warrior blood coursed through his veins mingling with the deeply religious Old Testament teachings of the Coptic Christian Church, so that his eyes shone with an almost mystic fanaticism and his heart soared with a young man's fierce patriotism, for he was still young enough and inexperienced enough to look on the dirty bloody business of war as something glamorous and manly.

Behind him came Vicky Camberwell, driving Miss Wobbly with competence and precision. Jake was delighted with her ability to judge the engine beat, and to mesh the ancient gears with a light touch on clutch and stick. She too was excited by the prospect of adventure, and new experience. That afternoon she had filed her preliminary report, despatching five thousand words by the new airmail service that would deposit them on her editor's desk in New York within ten days. She had explained the background, the clear intent of Benito Mussolini to annex the sovereign territories of Ethiopia, the world's indifference, the arms embargo. 'Do not delude yourselves,' she had written, 'into the belief that I am crying wolf. The wolf of Rome is already hunting. What is about to happen in the mountains of northern Africa will shame the civilized world.' And then she had gone on to expose the intention of the great nations to prevent her reaching the embattled empire and reporting its plight. She had ended the despatch, 'Your correspondent has rejected this restriction placed upon her movements and her integrity. Tonight I have joined a group of intrepid men who are risking their lives to defy the embargo, and to carry through the closed territories a quantity of arms and supplies desperately needed by the beleaguered nation. By the time you read this, we shall have failed and have died upon the desert coast of Africa, which the natives fearfully call the "Great Burn" – or we shall have succeeded. We shall have landed by night from a small coasting vessel and trekked through hundreds of miles of savage and hostile territory to a meeting with an Ethiopian prince. I hope that in my next despatch, I shall be able to describe our journey to you, but if the gods of chance decree otherwise – at least we shall have tried.' Vicky was very pleased with the first article. In her usual flamboyant style, she particularly liked the 'trek-king' bit which gave a touch of local colour. It had everything: drama, mystery, the little guy taking on the big. She knew that the completed series would be a giant and she was excited and aglow with anticipation.

Behind her Jake Barton followed. He listened with half his attention to the engine beat of the Pig. For no apparent reason, except perhaps a premonition of what awaited her, the car had that night refused to start. Jake had cranked her until his arm was cramped and aching. He had blown through the fuel system, checked the plugs, magneto and every other moving part that could possibly be at fault. Then, after another hour of tinkering, she had started and run sweetly, without giving the slightest hint of what had prevented her doing so earlier.

With the other half of his attention, he was mentally

checking out his preparations – knowing that this was his last chance to fill any gaps in his list. It was one hell of a long trail from Mondi to the Wells of Chaldi and not many service stations on the road. The pontoon raft of drums had been stowed aboard the *Hirondelle* that afternoon, and each car carried its own means of sustenance and survival – a load which taxed their ancient suspensions and bodywork.

Thus Jake's conscious mind was fully occupied, but below that level was a gut memory that tightened his nerves and charged his blood with adrenalin. There had been another night like this, moving in column in the darkness, with the throttled-back engine beat drumming softly in his ears – but then there had been the glow of star shell in the sky ahead, the distant juddering of a Maxim firing at a gap in the wire and the smell of death and mud in his nostrils. Unlike Gregorius Maryam in the car ahead, Jake Barton knew about war and all its glories.

P apadopoulos was waiting for them on the wharf, carrying a hurricane lamp and dressed in an ankle-length greatcoat that gave him the air of a down-at-heel gnome. He signalled the column forward, waving the lamp, and his ragged crew swarmed off the deck of the *Hirondelle* on to the stone wharf.

It was clear that they were accustomed to loading unusual cargo in the middle of the night. As each car was driven forward, it was stripped of its burden of drums and crates. These were stowed separately in cargo nets. Then they thrust sturdy wooden pallets under the chassis of the car and fixed the heavy hemp lines. At a signal from Papadopoulos, the men at the winches started the donkey engines and the lines ran through the blocks on the booms of the derricks. The bulky cars rose slowly and then swung inboard.

The whole operation was carried out swiftly, with no raised voices or unnecessary noise. Only a muttered command, the grunt of straining men, the muted clatter of the donkey engines and then the thump of the cars settling on the deck.

'These fellows know their business.' Gareth watched approvingly, then turned to Jake. 'I'll go down to the harbour master and clear the bills of lading. We'll be ready to sail in an hour or so.' He sauntered away and disappeared into the shadows.

'Let's inspect the accommodation,' Jake suggested, and took Vicky's arm. 'It looks like a regular Cunarder.' They climbed the gangplank to the deck and only then did they get the first whiff of the slave stench. By the time Gareth returned from his nefarious negotiations with bills of lading showing a consignment of four ambulances and medical supplies to the International Red Cross Association at Alexandria, the others had made a brief examination of the single tiny odoriferous cabin which Papadopoulos had put at their disposal and decided to leave it to the cockroaches and bed bugs which were already in residence.

'It's only a few days' sailing. I think I prefer the open deck. If it rains, we can take shelter in the cars.' Jake spoke for all of them as they stood in a group at the rail, watching the lights of Dar es Salaam glide away into the night, while the diesel engine of the schooner thumped under their feet and the sweet cool sea breeze washed over the deck, cleansing their nostrils and mouths of the slave stench.

Vicky was awakened by the brilliance of the starlight shining into her face and she opened her eyes and stared up at a sky that blazed with the splendours of the universe, as fields and seas of pearly light swirled across the heavens.

Quietly she slipped out of her blankets and went to the ship's rail. The sea was lustrous glittering sable; each wave seemed to be carved from some solid and precious metal, bejewelled by the reflections of the starlight and through it the ship's wake glowed with phosphorescence like a trail of green fire.

The sea wind was the touch of lovers' hands against her skin and in her hair, the great mainsail whispered above her head, and there was an almost physical ache in her chest at the beauty of this night.

When Gareth came up silently behind her and slipped his arms about her waist, she did not even turn her head, but lay back against him. She did not want to argue and tease. As she herself had written, she might soon be dead and the night was too beautiful to let it pass.

Neither of them spoke, but Vicky sighed and shuddered voluptuously as she felt his hands, smooth and skilful, slide up under the light cotton blouse. His touch, like the wind, was softly caressing.

Through their thin clothing she could feel the warmth and resilience of his flesh pressed against her, feel his chest surge and subside to the urgency of his breathing.

She turned slowly within the circle of his arms and lifted her face to his as he stooped, meeting his body with a forward thrust of her hips. The taste of his mouth and the musky male smell of his body hastened her own arousal.

It took all her determination to tear her lips loose from his, and to draw away from his embrace. She crossed quickly to where her blankets lay and picked them up with hands that shook.

She spread them again between the dark supine forms of Jake and Gregorius, and only when she rolled herself into their coarse folds and lay upon her back trying to control her ragged breathing was she aware that Jake Barton was awake.

His eyes were closed and his breathing was deep and even, but she knew with complete certainty that he was awake.

General Emilio De Bono stood at the window of his office and looked across the squalid roofs of the town of Asmara towards the great brooding massif of the Ethiopian highlands. It looked like the backbone of a dragon, he thought, and suppressed a shudder.

The General was seventy years of age, so he recalled vividly the last Italian army that had ventured into that mountain fastness. The name Adowa was a dark blot on the history of Italian arms, and after forty years, that terrible bloody defeat of a modern European army was still unavenged.

Now destiny had chosen him as the avenger and Emilio De Bono was not certain that the role suited him. It would be much more to his liking if wars could be fought without anybody getting hurt. The General would go to great lengths to avoid inflicting pain or even discomfort. Orders that might be distasteful to the recipient were avoided. Operations that might place anybody in jeopardy were frowned upon severely by the commanding General and his officers had learned not to suggest such extravagances.

The General was at heart a diplomat and a politician — not a warrior. He liked to see smiling faces, so he smiled a great deal himself. He resembled a sprightly, wizened little goat, with the pointed white beard that gave him the nickname of 'Little Beard'. And he addressed his officers as 'Caro', and his men as 'Bambino'. He just wanted to be loved. So he smiled and smiled.

However, the General was not smiling now. This morning he had received from Rome another one of those importunate coded telegrams signed Benito Mussolini. The wording had been even more peremptory than usual. 'The King of Italy wishes, and I, Benito Mussolini, Minister of the armed forces, order that—'

Suddenly he struck himself a blow on his medal-bedecked chest which startled Captain Crespi, his aide-de-camp.

'They do not understand,' cried De Bono bitterly. 'It is all very beautiful to sit in Rome and urge haste. To cry "Strike!" But they do not see the picture as we do, who stand here looking across the Mareb River at the swarming multitudes of the enemy.'

The Captain came to the General's side and he also stared out of the window. The building that housed the expeditionary army headquarters in Asmara was double-storied, and the General's office on the top floor commanded a sweeping view to the foot of the mountains. The Captain observed wryly that the swarming multitudes were not readily apparent. The land was a vast emptiness slumbering in the brilliant sunlight. Air reconnaissance in depth had descried no concentrations of Ethiopian troops, and reliable intelligence reported that the Emperor Haile Selassie had ordered that none of his rudimentary military units approach the border as close as fifty kilometres, to avoid giving the Italians an excuse to march.

'They do not understand that I must consolidate my position here in Eritrea. That I must have a firm base and supply train,' cried De Bono pitifully. For over a year he had been consolidating his position and assembling his supplies. The crude little harbour of Massawa, which once had lazily served the needs of an occasional tramp steamer or one of the little Japanese salt-traders, had been reconstructed completely. Magnificent stone piers ran out into the sea, great wharves bustled with steam cranes, and busy locomotives shuttled the incredible array of warlike stores that poured ashore by the thousands of tons a day for month after month. The Suez Canal remained open to the transports of the Italian adventure, and a constant stream of them poured southwards, unaffected by the embargo that the League of Nations had declared on the importation of military materials into Eastern Africa.

Up to the present time, over three million tons of stores had been landed, and this did not include the five thousand vehicles of war – troop transports, armoured cars, tanks and aircraft – that had come ashore. To distribute this vast assembly of vehicles and stores, a road system had been constructed fanning into the interior, a system so magnificent as to recall that of the Caesars of ancient Rome.

General De Bono smote his chest again, startling his aide. 'They urge me to untimely endeavour. They do not seem to realize that my force is insufficient.'

The force which the General lamented was the greatest and most powerful army ever assembled on the African continent. He commanded three hundred and sixty thousand men, armed with the most sophisticated tools of destruction the world had yet devised – from the Caproni CA.133 three-engined monoplane which could carry two tons of high explosive and poison gas a range of nine hundred miles, to the most modern armoured cars and heavily armoured CV.3 tanks with their 50 mm guns, and supporting units of heavy artillery.

This great assembly was encamped about Asmara and upon the cliffs overlooking the Mareb River. It was made up of distinct elements, the green-clad regular army formations with their wide-brimmed tropical helmets, the blackshirt

Fascist militia with their high boots and cross-straps, their deathshead and thunderbolt badges and their glittering daggers, the regular colonial units of black Somalis and Eritreans in their tall tasselled red fezes and baggy shirts, their gaily coloured regimental sashes and putteed legs above bare feet. Lastly, the irregular volunteers or 'banda' who were a group of desert bandits and cut-throat cattle thieves attracted by the possibility of war in the way that the taint of blood gathers sharks.

De Bono knew but did not ponder the fact that nearly seventy years previously, the British General Napier had marched on Magdala with less than fifty thousand men, meeting and defeating the entire Ethiopian army on the way, storming the mountain fortress and releasing the British prisoners held there, before retiring in good order. Such heroics were outside the realms of the General's imagination.

'Caro.' The General placed an arm about the gold-braided shoulders of his aide. 'We must compose a reply to the Duce. He must be made to realize my difficulties.' He patted the shoulder affectionately and his face lightened once more into its habitual expression as he began composing.

'My dear and respected leader, please be assured of my loyalty to you and to the glorious fatherland of Italy.' The Captain hastened to take up a message pad and scribble industriously. 'Be assured also that I never cease to toil by night and by day towards—'

It took almost two hours of creative effort before the General was satisfied with his flowery and rambling refusal to carry out his orders.

'Now,' he ceased his pacing and smiled tenderly at the Captain, 'although we are not yet ready for an advance in force, it will serve to placate Il Duce if we initiate the opening phases of the southern offensive.'

The General's plans for the invasion, when it was finally put in hand, had been laid with as ponderous regard to detail as his earlier preparations. Historical necessity dictated that the main attack should be centred on Adowa. Already a marble monument, brought from Italy and engraved with the words 'The dead of Adowa avenged . . .' with the date left open, lay amongst the huge mountains of his stores.

However, the plan called for a secondary flanking attack farther south through one of the very few gateways to the central highlands. This was the Sardi Gorge. A narrow opening that was riven up from the desert floor, splitting like an axe-stroke the precipitous mountain ranges, and forming a pass through which an army might reach the plateau that reared seven thousand feet above the desert. The first phase of this plan entailed the seizure of the approaches to the Sardi Gorge – and particularly important in this dry and scalded desert would be the water supplies of the attacking army.

The General crossed the floor to the large-scale map of Eastern Africa which covered one wall, and he picked up the ivory pointer to touch an isolated spot in the emptiness below the mountains.

'The Wells of Chaldi,' he read the name aloud. 'Whom shall we send?'

The Captain looked up from his pad, and observed how the spot was surrounded by the forbidding yellow of the desert.

He had been in Africa long enough to know what that meant, and there was only one person who he would wish were there.

'Belli,' he said.

'Ah,' said the General. 'Count Aldo Belli – the fire-eater.'

'The clown,' said the Captain.

79

'Come, caro,' the General admonished his aide mildly. 'You are too harsh. The Count is a distinguished diplomat, he was for three years ambassador to the court of St James in London. His family is old and noble – and very very rich.'

'He is a blow-hard,' said the Captain stubbornly, and the General sighed.

'He is a personal friend of Benito Mussolini. Il Duce is a constant guest at his castle. He has great political power—'

'He would be well out of harm's way at this desolate spot,' said the Captain, and the General sighed again.

'Perhaps you are correct, caro. Send for the good Count if you please.'

Captain Crespi stood on the steps of the headquarters building, beneath the portico with its imitation marble columns and the clumsily painted fresco depicting a heroic band of heavily muscled Italians defeating heathens, ploughing the earth, harvesting the corn, and generally building an empire.

The Captain watched sourly as the huge Rolls-Royce open tourer bumped down the dusty, pot-holed main street. Its headlights glared like monstrously startled eyes, and its burnished sky-blue paintwork was dulled by a light flouring of pale dust. The purchase price of this vehicle would have consumed five years of his service pay, which accounted for much of the Captain's sourness.

Count Aldo Belli, as one of the nation's great landowners and amongst the five most wealthy men in Italy, did not rely on the army for his transportation. The Rolls had been adapted and designed to his personal specifications by the makers.

As it slid to a graceful halt beneath the portico, the Captain noticed the Count's personal arms blazoned on the front door – a rampant golden wolf supporting a shield with a quartered device of scarlet and silver. The legend unfurled beneath it read, 'Courage arms me.'

As the car stopped, a small wiry sun-blackened little man in the uniform of a blackshirt sergeant leaped from the seat beside the driver and dropped on one knee in the roadway with a bulky camera at the ready to capture the moment when the figure in the wide rear seat of the Rolls should descend.

Count Aldo Belli adjusted his black beret carefully, sucked in his belly and rose to his feet as the driver scurried around to hold open the door. The Count smiled. It was a smile of flashing white teeth and powerful charisma. His eyes were dark and romantic with the sweeping lashes of a lady of fashion, his skin was lightly tanned to a golden olive and the lustrous curls of his hair that escaped from under the black beret shone in the sunlight. Although he was almost thirty-five years of age, not a single grey strand adulterated that splendid mane.

From his commanding position his height was exaggerated, so he seemed to tower god-like above the men who scampered about him. The highly polished cross-straps glittered across his chest as did the silver deathshead cap badges. The short regimental dagger on his hip set with small diamonds and seed pearls was to the Count's own design, and the ivory-handled revolver had been hand-made for him by Beretta; the holster was belted in tightly to subdue a waistline that was showing signs of rebellion.

The Count paused and glanced down at the little sergeant.

'Yes, Gino?' he asked.

'Good, my Count. Just a little up with the chin.'

The Count's chin caused them both much concern. At certain angles, it showed an alarming tendency to duplicate itself like the ripples on a pond. The Count threw up his chin sternly, rather like Il Duce, and the gesture ironed out the jowls below.

'Bellissimo,' cried Gino, and tripped the shutter. The Count stepped down from the Rolls, enjoying the way the soft sparkling leather of his high boots gave like the bellows of a concertina above his instep as he moved, and he hooked the thumb of his gloved left hand into the belt above his dagger as he flung his right arm up and outwards in the Fascist salute.

'The General awaits you, Colonel,' Crespi greeted him.

'I came the moment I received the summons.'

The Captain made a moue. He knew the summons had been delivered at ten o'clock that morning and it was now almost three in the afternoon. The Count's primping had taken most of the day, and now he glowed from bathing and shaving and massaging and smelled like a rose garden in full bloom.

'Clown,' thought the Captain again. It had taken Crespi ten years of unswerving service and dedication to reach his rank, while this man had opened his purse, invited Mussolini for a week of hunting and carousal to his estates at the foot of the Apennines, and had in return been given the colonelcy of a full battalion. The man had never fired a shot at anything larger than a boar, and until six months ago had commanded nothing more formidable than a squad of accountants, a troop of gardeners or a platoon of strumpets to his bed.

'Clown,' thought the Captain bitterly, bowing over the hand and grinning ingratiatingly. 'Have your photograph taken swatting flies in the Danakil desert, or sniffing camel dung beside the Wells of Chaldi,' he thought, and backed away through the wide doors into the relative cool of the administrative building. 'This way, Colonel, if you would be so kind.'

General De Bono lowered the binoculars through which with brooding disquiet he had been studying the Ethiopian massif, and almost with relief turned to greet the Colonel.

'Caro,' smiled the General, extending both hands as he crossed the uncarpeted hand-painted tiles. 'My dear Count, it is so good of you to come.'

The Count drew himself up at the threshold and flung the Fascist salute at the advancing General, stopping him in confusion.

'In the services of my country and my king, I would count no sacrifice too dear.' Aldo Belli was stirred by his own words. He must remember them. They could be used again.

'Yes, of course,' De Bono agreed hurriedly. 'I'm sure we all feel that way.'

'General De Bono, you have only to command me.'

'Thank you, caro mio. But a glass of Madeira and a biscuit first?' suggested the General. A little sweetmeat to take away the taste of the medicine. The General felt very bad about sending anyone down into the Danakil country – it was hot here in Asmara, God alone knew what it would be like down there, and the General felt a pang of dismay that he had allowed Crespi to select anyone with such political influence as the Count. He would not further insult the good Count by too hurriedly coming to the business in hand.

'I hoped that you might have had an opportunity to hear the new production of *La Traviata* before leaving Rome?'

'Indeed, General. I was fortunate enough to be included in the Duce's party for the opening night.' The Count relaxed a little, smiling that flashing smile.

The General sighed as he poured the wine. 'Ha! The civilized life, so far a cry from this land of thorns and savages . . .'

It was late afternoon before the General had steeled himself to approach the painful subject of the interview and, smiling apologetically, he gave his orders.

'The Wells of Chaldi,' repeated the Count, and immediately a change came over him. He leapt to his feet, knocking over the Madeira glass, and strode majestically back and forth, his heels cracking on the tiles, belly sucked in and noble chin on high.

'Death before dishonour,' cried Aldo Belli, the Madeira warming his ardour.

'I hope not, caro,' murmured the General. 'All I want you to do is take up a guard position on an untenanted water-hole.' But the Count seemed not to hear him. His eyes were dark and glowing.

'I am greatly indebted to you for this opportunity to distinguish my command. You can count on me to the death.' The Count stopped short as a fresh thought occurred to him. 'You will support my advance with armour and aircraft?' he asked anxiously.

'I don't really think that will be necessary, caro.' The General spoke mildly. All this talk of death and honour troubled him, but he did not want to give offence. 'I don't think you will meet any resistance.'

'But if I do?' the Count demanded with mounting agitation, so that the General went to stroke his arm placatingly.

'You have a radio, caro. Call on me for any assistance you need.'

The Count thought about that for a moment and clearly found it acceptable. Once more the patriotic fervour returned to the glowing eyes.

'Ours is the victory,' he cried, and the General echoed him vigorously.

'I hope so, caro. Indeed I hope so.' Suddenly the Count swirled and strode to the door. He flung it open and called.

'Gino!'

The little black-shirted sergeant hurried into the room, frantically adjusting the huge camera that hung about his neck.

'The General does not mind?' asked Aldo Belli leading him to the window. 'The light is better here.' The slanting rays of the dying sun poured in to light the two men theatrically as the Count seized De Bono's hand.

'Closer together, please. Back a trifle, General, you are covering the Count. That's excellent. Chin up a little, my Count. Ha! Bello!' cried Gino, and recorded faithfully the startled expression above the General's little white goatee.

The senior major of the Blackshirt 'Africa' Battalion was a hard professional soldier of thirty years' experience, a veteran of Vittorio Veneto and Caporetto, where he had been commissioned in the field.

He was a fighting man and he reacted with disgust to his posting from his prestigious regiment in the regular army to this rabble of political militia. He had protested at length and with all the power at his command, but the order came from on high, from divisional headquarters itself. The divisional General was a friend of Count Aldo Belli, and owed favours. He also knew the Count intimately and decided that he needed a real soldier to guide and counsel him. Major Castelani was probably one of the most real soldiers in the entire army of Italy. Once he realized that his posting was inevitable, he had resigned himself and settled to his new duties – whipping and bullying his new command into order.

He was a big man with a close-cropped skull of grey bristle, and a hound-dog, heavily lined face burned and eroded by the weathering of a dozen campaigns. He walked with the rolling gait of a sailor or a horseman, though he was neither, and his voice could carry a mile into a moderate wind.

Almost entirely due to his single-handed efforts, the battalion was drawn up in marching order an hour before dawn. Six hundred and ninety men with their motorized transports strung out down the main street of Asmara. The lorries were crammed with silent men huddling in their greatcoats against the mild morning chill. The motorcycle outriders were sitting astride their machines flanking the newly polished but passenger-less Rolls-Royce command car, with its gay pennants and its driver sitting lugubriously at the wheel. A charged sense of apprehension and uncertainty gripped the entire assembly of warriors.

There had been wild rumours flying about the battalion for the last twelve hours – they had been selected for some desperate and dangerous mission. The previous evening the mess sergeant had actually witnessed the Colonel Count Aldo Belli weeping with emotion as he toasted his junior officers with the fighting slogan of the regiment, 'Death before dishonour,' which might sound fine on a bellyful of chianti, but left a hollow feeling at five in the morning on top of a breakfast of black bread and weak coffee.

The Third Battalion was in a collectively sombre mood as the sun came up in a blaze of hot scarlet, forcing them almost immediately to discard the greatcoats. The sun climbed into a sky of burning blue and the men waited as patiently as oxen in the traces. Someone once observed that war is ninety-nine per cent boredom and one per cent unmitigated terror. The Third Battalion was learning the ninety-nine per cent.

Major Luigi Castelani sent yet another messenger to the Colonel's quarters a little before noon, and this time received a reply that the Count was now actually out of bed and had almost completed his toilet. He would join the battalion shortly. The Major swore with the practice of an old campaigner and set off with his rolling swagger down the column to quell the mutinous mutterings from the half-mile-long column of canvas-covered lorries sweltering in the midday sun.

The Count came like the rising sun itself, glowing and glorious, flanked by two captains and preceded by a trooper carrying the battle standard which the Count had personally designed. It was based on the eagles of a Roman legion, complete with shrieking birds of prey and dangling silken tassels.

The Count floated on a cloud of bonhomie and expensive eau de cologne. Gino got a few good shots of him embracing his junior officers, and slapping the backs of the senior N.C.O.s. At the common soldiers he smiled like a father and spurred their spleens with a few apt homilies on duty and sacrifice as he strode down the column.

'What a fine body of warriors,' he told the Major. 'I am moved to song.'

Luigi Castelani winced. The Colonel was frequently moved to song. He had taken lessons with the most famous teachers in Italy and as a younger man he had seriously considered a career in opera.

Now he halted and spread his arms, threw back his head and let the song flow in a deep ringing baritone. Dutifully, his officers joined in the stirring chorus of 'La Giovinezza', the Fascist marching song.

The Colonel moved slowly back along the patient column in the sunlight, pausing to strike a pose as he went for a high note, lifting his right hand with the tip of the second finger lightly touching the thumb, while the other hand grasped the bejewelled dagger at his waist.

The song ended and the Colonel cried, 'Enough! It is time to march – where are the maps?' and one of his subalterns hurried forward with the map case.

'Colonel, sir,' Luigi Castelani intervened tactfully. 'The road is well sign-posted, and I have two native guides—'

The Count ignored him and watched while the maps were spread on the glistening bonnet of the Rolls.

'Ah!' He studied the maps learnedly, then looked up at his two captains. 'One of you on each side of me,' he instructed. 'Major Vito – you here! A stern expression, if you please, and do not look at the camera.' He pointed with a lordly gesture at Johannesburg – four thousand miles to the south – and held the pose long enough for Gino to record it. Next, he climbed into the rear seat of the Rolls and, standing, he pointed imperatively ahead along the road to the Danakil desert.

Mistakenly, Luigi Castelani took this as a command to advance. He let out a series of bull-like bellows and the battalion was galvanized into frantic action. Like one man, they scrambled into the covered lorries and took their seats on the long benches, each in full marching order with a hundred rounds of ammunition in his bandolier and a rifle between his knees.

However, by the time 690 men were embarked, the Colonel had once more descended from the Rolls. It was an unfortunate chance that dictated that the Rolls should be parked directly in front of the casino.

The casino was a government-licensed institution under whose auspices young ladies were brought out from Italy on six-month contracts to cater to the carnal needs of tens of thousands of lusty young men in a womanless environment. Very few of these ladies had the stamina to sign a renewal of the contract and none of them found it necessary. Possessed of a substantial dowry, they returned home to find a husband.

The casino had a silver roof of galvanized corrugated iron and its eaves and balconies were decorated with intricate cast-iron work. The windows of the girls' rooms opened on to the street.

The young hostesses, who usually rose in the mid afternoon, had been prematurely awakened by the bellowing of orders and the clash of weapons. They had traipsed out on to the long second-floor veranda, clad in brightly coloured but flimsy nightwear, and now entered into the spirit of the occasion, giggling and blowing kisses to the officers. One of them had a bottle of iced Lacrima Cristi, which she knew from experience was the Colonel's favourite beverage, and she beckoned with the cold dewed bottle.

The Colonel realized suddenly that the singing and excitement had made him thirsty and peckish.

'A cup for the stirrup, as the English say,' he suggested jocularly, and slapped one of the captains on the shoulder. Most of his staff followed him with alacrity into the casino. A little after five o'clock, one of the junior subalterns emerged, slightly inebriated, from the casino with a message from the Colonel to the Major.

'At dawn tomorrow, we advance without fail.'

The battalion rumbled out of Asmara the following morning at ten o'clock. The Colonel was feeling liverish and disgruntled. The previous night's excitement had got out of hand, he had sung until his throat was hoarse and had drunk great quantities of Lacrima Cristi, before going upstairs with two of the young hostesses.

Gino knelt on the seat of the Rolls beside him, holding an umbrella over his head, and the driver tried to avoid potholes and irregularities in the road. But the Count was pale and his brow sparkled with the sweat of nausea.

Sergeant Gino wished to cheer him. He hated to see his

Count in misery and so he attempted to rekindle the warlike spirit of yesterday.

'Think on it, my Count. We of the entire army of Italy will be the very first to confront the enemy. The first to meet the blood-thirsty barbarian with his cruel heart and red hands.'

The Count thought on it as he was bidden. He thought on it with great concentration and increasing nausea. Suddenly he became aware that of all the 360,000 men that comprised the expeditionary forces of Italy, he, Aldo Belli, was the very first, the veritable point of the spear aimed at Ethiopia. He remembered suddenly the horror stories he had heard from the disaster of Adowa. One of the atrocity stories outweighed all others – the Ethiopians castrated their prisoners. He felt the contents of that noble sac between his thighs retracting forcibly and a fresh sweat broke out upon his brow.

'Stop!' he shrieked at the driver. 'Stop, this instant.'

A bare two miles from the centre of the town, the column was plunged into confusion by the abrupt halt of the lead vehicle, and, answering the loud and urgent shouts of the commanding officer, the Major hurried forward to learn that the order of march had been altered. The command car would take up station in the exact centre of the column with six motorcycle outriders brought back to ride as flank guards.

It was another hour before the new arrangement could be put into effect and once more the column headed south and west into the great empty land with its distant smoky horizons and its vast vaulted blue dome of the burning heavens.

Count Aldo Belli rode easier on the luxurious leather of the Rolls, cheered by the knowledge that preceding him were three hundred and forty-five fine rubbery sets of peasant testicles upon which the barbarian could blunt his blade.

The column went into bivouac that evening fifty-three kilometres from Asmara. Not even the Count could pretend that this was a forced march for motorized infantry – but the advantage was that a pair of motorcyclists could send back with a despatch for General De Bono reassuring him of the patriotism, the loyalty and the fighting ardour of the Third Battalion – and, of course, on their return the cyclists could carry blocks of ice from the casino packed in salt and straw and stowed in the sidecars.

The following morning, the Count had recovered much of his good cheer. He rose early – at nine o'clock – and took a hearty alfresco breakfast with his officers under the shade of a spread tarpaulin and then, from the rear seat of the Rolls, he gave a clenched fist cavalry order to advance.

Still in the centre of the column, pennants fluttering and battle standard glittering, the Rolls glided forward and it looked, even to the disillusioned Major, as if they might make good going of the day's march.

The undulating grassland fell away almost imperceptibly beneath the speeding wheels, and the blue loom of the mountains on their right hand merged gradually with the lighter fiercer blue of the sky. The transition to desert country was so gradual as to lull the unobservant traveller. The intervals between the flat-topped acacia trees became greater and the trees themselves were more stunted, more twisted and spiky, as they progressed, until at last they ceased and the bushes of spina Cristi replaced them – grey and low and viciously thorned. The earth was parched and crumbled, dotted with clumps of camel grass – and the horizon was unbroken, enclosing them entirely. The land itself was so flat and featureless that it gave the illusion of being saucer-shaped, as though the rim of the land rose slightly to meet the sky.

Through this wilderness, the road was slashed like the claw mark of a predator into the fleshy red soil. The tracks were so deeply rutted that the middle hump constantly brushed the chassis of the Rolls, and a mist of fine red dust stood in the heated air long after the column had passed.

The Colonel was bored and uncomfortable. It was becoming increasingly clear, even to the Count, that the wilderness harboured no hostile horde, and his courage and impatience returned.

'Drive to the head of the column,' he instructed Giuseppe, and the Rolls pulled out and sped past the leading trucks, the Count bestowing a cheery salute on Castelani as he left him glowering and muttering behind him.

When Castelani caught up with him again, two hours later, the Count was standing on the burnished bonnet of the Rolls staring through his binoculars at the horizon and doing an excited little dance while he urged Gino to make haste in unpacking the special Mannlicher 9.3 mm sporting rifle from its leather case. The weapon was of seasoned walnut, butt and stock, and the blued steel was inlaid with twenty-four-carat gold hunting scenes of the chase – boar and stag, huntsmen on horseback and hounds in full cry. It was a masterpiece of the gunsmith's art.

Without lowering the binoculars, he gave orders to Castelani to erect the radio aerial and send a message of good cheer and enthusiasm to General De Bono, to report the magnificent progress made by the battalion to date and assure him that they would soon command all the approaches to the Sardi Gorge. The Major should also put the column into laager and set up the ice machine while the Colonel undertook a reconnaissance patrol in the direction in which he was now staring so intently.

The group of big dun-coloured animals he was watching

were a mile off and moving steadily away into the mirage-fevered distance, but their gracefully straight horns showed dark and long against the distant sky.

Gino had the loaded Mannlicher in the rear seat and the Count jumped down into the passenger seat beside the driver. Standing holding the windshield with one hand, he gave his officers the Fascist salute, and the Rolls roared forward, left the road and careered away, weaving amongst the thorn scrub and bounding over the rough ground in pursuit of the distant herd.

The beisa oryx is a large and beautiful desert antelope. There were eight of them in the herd and with their sharp eyesight they were in flight before the Rolls had approached within three-quarters of a mile.

They ran lightly over the rough ground, their pale beige hides blending cunningly with the soft colours of the desert, but the long wicked black horns rode proudly as any battle standard.

The Rolls gained steadily on the running herd, with the Count hysterically urging his driver to greater speed, ignoring the thorn branches that scored the flawless sides of the big blue machine as it passed. Hunting was one of the Count's many pleasures. Boar and stag were specially bred on his estates, but this was the first large game he had encountered since his arrival in Africa. The herd was strung out, two old bulls leading, plunging ahead with a light rocking-horse gait, while the cows and two younger males trailed them.

The bouncing, roaring machine drew level with the last animal and ran alongside at a range of twenty yards. The galloping oryx did not turn its head but ran on doggedly after its stronger companions.

'Halt,' shrieked the Count, and the driver stood on his brakes, the car broadsiding to rest in a billowing cloud of dust. The Count tumbled out of the open door and threw up the Mannlicher. The barrel kicked up and the shots crashed out. The first was a touch high and it threw a puff of dust off the earth far beyond the running animal – the second slapped into the pale fur in front of the shoulder and the young oryx somersaulted over its broken neck and went down in a clumsy tangle of limbs.

'Onwards!' shouted the Count, leaping aboard the Rolls as it roared away once again. The herd was already far ahead but inexorably the Rolls closed the gap and at last drew level. Again the ringing crack of rifle-fire and the sliding, tumbling fall of a heavy pale body.

Like a paper chase, they left the wasteland littered with the pale bodies until only one old bull ran on alone. And he was cunning, swinging away westward into the broken ground for which he had clearly headed at the outset of the chase.

It was hours and many miles later when the Count lost all patience. On the lip of another wadi he stopped the Rolls and ordered Gino, protesting volubly, to stand at attention and offer his shoulder as a dead-rest for the Mannlicher.

The beisa had slowed now to an exhausted trot, but the range was six hundred yards as the Count sighted across the intervening scrub and through heat-dancing air that swirled like gelatinous liquid.

The rifle-fire cracked the desert silences and the antelope kept trotting steadily away, while the Count shrieked abuse at it and crammed a fresh load of brass cartridges into the magazine.

The animal was almost beyond effective range now, but the next bullet fired with the rear sight at maximum elevation fell in a long arcing trajectory and they heard the thump of the strike, long after the beisa had collapsed abruptly and disappeared below the line of grey scrub.

When they had found another crossing and forced the

Rolls through the deep ravine, scraping the rear fender and denting one of the big silver wheel-hubs, they came up to the spot where the antelope lay on its side. Leaving the rifle on the back seat in his eagerness, the Count leapt out before the Rolls had stopped completely.

'Get one of me completing the *coup de grâce*,' he shouted at Gino, as he unholstered the ivory-handled Beretta and ran to the downed animal.

The soft bullet had shattered the spinal column a few inches forward of the pelvis, paralysing the hindquarters, and the blood pumped gently from the wound in a bright rivulet down the pale beige flank.

The Count posed dramatically, pointing the pistol at the magnificently horned head with its elaborate face-mask of dark chocolate stripes. Near by, Gino knelt in the soft earth focusing the camera.

At the critical moment, the antelope heaved itself up into a sitting position and stared with swimming agonized eyes into the Count's face. The beisa is one of the most aggressive antelopes in Africa, capable of killing even a fully grown lion with its long rapier horns. This old bull weighed 450 lb. and stood four feet high at the shoulder while the horns rose another three feet above that.

The beisa snorted, and the Count forgot all about the levelled pistol in his hand in his sudden desperate desire to reach the safety of the Rolls.

Leading the beisa by six inches, he vaulted lightly into the back seat and crouched on the floorboards, covering his head with both arms while the beisa battered the sides of the Rolls, driving in one door and ripping the paintwork with the deadly horns.

Gino was trying to disappear into the earth by sheer pressure, and he was making a pitiful wailing sound. The driver had stalled the engine, and he sat frozen in his seat and every time the beisa crashed into the Rolls, he was thrown so violently forward that his forehead struck the windshield, and he pleaded, 'Shoot it, my Count. Please, my Count, shoot the monster.'

The Count's posterior was pointed to the sky. It was the only part of his anatomy that was visible above the rear seat of the Rolls and he was shrieking for somebody to hand him the rifle, but not raising his head to search for it.

The bullet that had severed the beisa's spine had angled forward and pierced the lung as well. The violent exertions of the stricken animal tore open a large artery and, with a pitiful bellow and a sudden double spurt of blood through the nostrils, it collapsed.

In the long silence that followed, the Count's pale face rose slowly above the level of the back door and he stared fearfully at the carcass. Its stillness reassured him. Cautiously, he groped for the Mannlicher, lifted it slowly and poured a stream of bullets into the inert beisa. His hands were shaking so violently that some of the shots missed the body and came perilously close to where Gino still lay, producing a fresh outburst of wails and more mole-like efforts to become subterranean.

Satisfied that the beisa was at last dead, the Count descended and walked slowly towards a nearby clump of thorn scrub, but his gait was bow-legged and stiff, for he had lightly soiled his magnificently monogrammed silk underwear.

In the cool of the evening, the slightly crumpled Rolls returned to the battalion bivouac. Draped over the bonnet and across the wide mudguards lay the bleeding carcasses of the antelopes. The Count stood to acknowledge the cheers of his troops, a veritable triumphant Nimrod.

A radio message from General De Bono awaited him. It

was not a reprimand, the General would not go that far, but it pointed out that although the General was grateful for the Count's efforts up to the present time, and for his fine sentiments and loyal messages, nevertheless the General would be very grateful if the Count could find some way in which to speed up his advance.

The Count sent him a five-hundred-word reply ending, 'Ours is the Victory,' and then went to feast on barbecued antelope livers and iced chianti with his officers.

L eaving the sailing and handling of the *Hirondelle* to his Mohammedan mate and his raggedy crew, Captain Papadopoulos had spent the preceding five days sitting at the table in his low-roofed poop cabin playing two-handed gin rummy with Major Gareth Swales. Gareth had suggested the diversion and it had occurred to the Captain by this time that there was something unnatural in the consistent run of winning cards which had distinguished Gareth's play.

The agreed fare for transporting the cars and the four passengers had totalled two hundred and fifty of sterling. The Captain's losses had just exceeded that figure, and Gareth smiled winningly at Papadopoulos and smoothed the golden moustaches.

'What do you say we give it a break now, Papa old sport, go up on deck and stretch the legs, what?'

Having recovered the passage money, Gareth had accomplished the task he had set himself, and he was now anxious to return to the open deck where Vicky Camberwell and Jake were becoming much too friendly for his peace of mind. Every time Gareth had been forced by nature to make a brief journey to the poop rail, he had seen the two of them together and they seemed to be laughing a great deal, which

97

was always a bad sign. Vicky was in the forefront of any action, passing tools to Jake and offering general encouragement, as he worked at fine-tuning the cars and making last-minute preparations for the desert crossing – or the two of them sat with Gregorius while amidst great hilarity he gave them basic lessons in the Amharic language. He wondered distractedly what else they were up to.

However, Gareth was a man sure of his priorities and his first concern was to recover his money from Papadopoulos. Having done so, he could now return to sheep-dogging Vicky Camberwell.

'It's been a lot of fun, Papa.' He half rose from the table, folding the grimy wad of banknotes into his back pocket and gathering the pile of coins with his free hand.

Captain Papadopoulos reached into the depths of the Arabic gown he wore and produced a knife with an ornately carved handle and a viciously curved blade. He balanced it lightly in the palm of his hand and his single eye glittered coldly at Gareth.

'Deal!' he said, and Gareth smiled blandly and sank back into his seat. He picked up the cards and cut them with a ripping sound and the knife disappeared into Papadopoulos's gown once more as he watched the shuffle intently.

'Actually, I do feel like a few more hands,' Gareth murmured. 'Just getting warmed up, hey?'

The slaver altered course as she cleared the tip of the great horn of Africa and rounded Cape Guardafui. Before her lay the long gut of the Gulf of Aden and a run of five hundred miles westwards to French Somaliland.

The Hindu mate came down and whispered fearfully to his Captain.

'What troubles the fellow?' Gareth asked.

'He worries about the English blockade.'

'So do I,' Gareth answered. 'Shouldn't we go up on deck?'

'Deal,' said Papadopoulos.

Below them they heard the steady thumping beat of the big diesel engine begin, and the vibration of the propeller shaft spinning in its bed. The mate had her under sail and power now, and the motion of the ship changed immediately, the thrust of the propeller combining with the push of the full spread of her canvas, and she flew towards the vivid purple and pink flush of sky and piled cumulus cloud behind which the sun was beginning to set.

The mate had set a course which would take him swiftly down the middle of the Gulf, out of sight of Africa on his port side and Arabia on the starboard. The *Hirondelle* was making twenty-five knots, for the sea breeze was on her best point of sailing and a day and two nights would see them in and out again. He sent one of his best men to the masthead with a telescope and he wondered which the English viewed more sternly – young black girls in chains or Vickers machine guns in wooden cases. Mournfully he concluded that either of them would be lethal and he shrilled at his masthead to keep a strict watch.

The sun was sinking with agonizing slowness, almost dead ahead and the wind rose steadily, driving the *Hirondelle* on deeper into the gut.

Jake Barton wriggled out of the engine hatch of Miss Wobbly and grinned at Vicky Camberwell who sat on the sponson above him swinging her long legs idly, with the wind in her hair and the tan she had picked up in the last few days gilding her arms and flushing at her cheeks. She had lost the dark rings of worry and the paleness of fatigue, and looked now like a schoolgirl, young and carefree and gay.

'That's the best I can do,' said Jake, beginning to scour the black grease from his arms with Scrubbs Ammonia. 'She's running so sweetly, I could take her out at Le Mans.' Her knees were at the level of Jake's eyes and her skirts had rucked up high. He felt his heart stop as he glanced down the smooth length of her thigh. Her skin had a lustre and sheen, as though made of some precious and rare substance. Vicky saw the direction of his gaze and brought her knees together sharply, although a smile touched her lips. She jumped down lightly on to the deck, steadying herself against the *Hirondelle*'s rolling action with a touch on the muscled hardness of his arm. Vicky thoroughly enjoyed the admiration of an attractive male and Gareth had been closeted in the Captain's cabin these last five days. She smiled up at Jake. He was tall but the bush of dark hair that curled around his ears gave him the look of a small boy which was again quickly dispelled by the strong jaw line and the fine networks of creases that radiated from the outer corners of his eyes.

She realized suddenly that he was on the point of stooping to kiss her, and she felt a delicious indecision – the slightest encouragement would set Jake on a violent collision course with Gareth and might seriously endanger the whole expedition and the story she wanted so badly. At that moment she noticed, as if for the first time, that Jake's mouth was wide and full and his lips were delicately shaped for the bigness and hairiness of him. His chin and cheeks were blued with a day's growth of beard and she knew it would feel rough and electric against her own peach-smooth cheeks. Suddenly she wanted to feel that, and she lifted her chin slightly and knew that he would read that want in the sparkle of her eyes.

The masthead shrieked like a startled gull and instantly the *Hirondelle* was plunged into frantic activity. The Mohammedan mate echoed his shrieks, but at a higher volume, and his grubby robes flapped around him in the wind. His eyes rolled in his dark brown skull and his toothless maw opened so wide that Jake could see the little pink glottis dangling in the back of his throat.

'What is it?' Vicky demanded, her hand still on Jake's arm.

'Trouble,' he answered grimly, and they turned as the

door of the poop cabin flew open and Papadopoulos rushed out with his queue twitching like the tail of a lioness and his single eye blinking rapidly. He still clutched a fan of cards in his right hand.

'One more card and I make gin!' he howled bitterly, and threw the cards into the wind and grabbed the mate by the front of his gown, shouting into his open but now silent mouth.

The mate pointed aloft and Papadopoulos dropped him and hailed the masthead in Arabic, and Jake listened to the swift exchange.

'A British destroyer – sounds like "*Dauntless*",' he muttered.

'You speak Arabic?' Vicky asked, and Jake stilled the question irritably and listened again.

'The destroyer has seen us. She's altering course to intercept.' Jake looked quickly at the smouldering globe of the sun, the crinkles around his eyes puckering up thoughtfully as he listened to the heated argument in Arabic taking place on the poop deck.

'Are you two having fun?' Gareth Swales asked, smiling but with a glitter in his eyes as he glanced significantly at Vicky's hand still on Jake's arm. He had come out of the cabin as silently as a panther.

Vicky dropped her hand guiltily and immediately wished she had not. She owed Gareth Swales no debts and she answered his stare defiantly, before turning back to Jake and finding him gone.

'What is it, Papa?' Gareth called up at the poop-deck, and the Captain snarled,

'Your Royal mucking Navy – that's what it is.' And he shook his fist at the northern horizon. 'The *Dauntless* – she based at Aden, blockade for slavers.'

'Where is she?' Gareth's expression changed swiftly and he strode to the rail.

'She's coming fast – masthead watching her. She'll be over the horizon pretty damn quick.' Papadopoulos turned from Gareth and roared a series of orders at his crew. Immediately they swarmed down on to the main deck and gathered about the first car – it was Priscilla the Pig – swaying gently on her suspension as the schooner plunged ahead.

'I say,' Gareth exclaimed. 'What are you up to?'

'They catch me with arms aboard, big trouble,' Papadopoulos explained. 'No arms, no trouble,' and he watched his men fall on the lines that secured the big white-painted vehicle. 'We do same trick with slaves, they go down pretty damn fast with the chains.'

'Now, just hold on a shake. I paid you a fortune to transport this cargo.'

'Where that fortune now, Major?' Papadopoulos shouted down at him derisively. 'I got nothing in my pants – how about you?' and the Captain turned away to urge his men on.

The turret of Priscilla the Pig opened suddenly and from it emerged the head and shoulders of Jake Barton with his hair blowing in the wind and a Vickers machine gun in his arms. He braced himself in the turret with the thick water-jacketed barrel of the Vickers across the crook of his left arm, and the pistol grip firmly enclosed in his other hand. Across his shoulder was draped a heavy necklace of belted ammunition.

He fired a roaring clattering burst, the tracer streaking in fiery white balls of flame a mere twelve inches over the Captain's head. The Greek threw himself flat on his deck, howling with terror, and his crew scattered like a flock of startled hens, while Jake looked down on them benignly from his post in the turret.

'I think we should understand each other, Captain.

Nobody is going to touch these machines. The only way you are going to save your ship is by outsailing the Englishman,' Jake called mildly.

'She can make thirty knots,' protested the Captain, still face down on the deck.

'The longer you talk the less time you have,' Jake told him. 'It'll be dark in twenty minutes. Turn away, and make a stern chase of it until it is dark.'

Papadopoulos rose uncertainly to his feet, and stood blinking his one eye rapidly and miserably wringing his hands.

'Kindly move your arse,' said Jake affably, and fired another burst of machine-gun bullets over his head.

The Captain dropped once again to the deck, howling the orders to bring the *Hirondelle* around on a course directly away from the closing British warship.

As the schooner came around on to her new course, Jake called Gareth across to him, and handed him the machine gun. 'I want this bunch of bastards covered while I work with the Greek. You, Vicky and Greg can batten down the hatches on the cars in the meantime.'

'Where did you get that gun?' Gareth asked. 'I thought they were all cased.'

'I like to keep a little insurance at all times,' Jake grinned, and Gareth selected two cheroots from his case, lit them both, and passed one up to Jake.

'Compliments of the management,' he said. 'I'm beginning to know why I picked you as a partner.' Jake stuck the cheroot in the side of his mouth, exhaled a long blue feather of smoke and grinned jauntily.

'If you've got any pull with your Royal Navy, lad, then get ready to use it.'

Jake stood in the deep canvas crows-nest at the crosstrees of the main mast, and swayed with a gut-swooping rhythm through the arc of the swinging mast as he tried to keep the grey silhouette that closed them rapidly in the field of the telescope.

Although the warship was only ten miles off, already her shape was fading into the deepening dusk, for the sea breeze had chopped the surface to a wave-flecked immensity and the sun behind Jake was touching the watery horizon and throwing the east into mysterious blue shade.

Suddenly a bright prick of light began winking rapidly from the hazy shape of the warship, and Jake read the urgent query.

'What ship?' and Jake grinned and tried to judge how conspicuous the schooner, with her mass of canvas, was to the destroyer, and to decide the moment when he would trade speed for invisibility.

The destroyer was signalling again.

'Heave to or I will fire upon you.'

'Bloody pirates,' Jake growled indignantly, and cupped his hand to bellow down at the bridge.

'Get the canvas off her.' On the deck far below, he saw the Greek's face, pale in the dusk looking up at him, then heard his orders repeated and watched the motley crew climb swiftly aloft.

Jake glanced back towards the tiny dark shape of the destroyer on the limitless dark sea and saw the angry red flash of her forward gun bloom in the dark. He remembered that flash so well and his skin crawled with the insects of fear as he waited out the long seconds while the shell climbed high into the sombre sky and then fell towards the schooner.

He heard it come, passing overhead in a rising shriek, before it pitched into the sea half a mile ahead of *Hirondelle*. A swift, blooming pillar of spray gleamed in the last rays of the sun like pink Carrara marble and then was blown swiftly away on the wind.

The crewmen froze in the rigging, petrified by the howling passage of the shot, and then suddenly they were galvanized into frantic babbling activity and the gleaming white canvas disappeared as swiftly as a wild goose furls its wings when it settles on the lake surface.

Jake looked back at the destroyer and searched for seconds before he found her. He wondered what they would make of the disappearance of the sails. They might believe the Hirondelle had obeyed the order to heave to, not guessing that she was under propeller power as well. Certainly she would have disappeared from their view, her low dark hull no longer beaconed by the towering white pyramid of canvas. He waited impatiently for the last few minutes until the warship itself was no longer visible from the masthead before bellowing down to the Greek the orders that sent Hirondelle swinging away into the wind and pounding back into the head sea along her original track, side-stepping the headlong charge of the destroyer.

Jake held that course while the tropical night fell over the Gulf like a warm thick blanket, pricked only by the cold white stars. He strained his eyes into the impenetrable blackness, chilled by the fear that the destroyer Captain might have double-guessed him and anticipated his turn. At any moment, he expected to see the towering steel hull emerge at close range from the night and flood the schooner with the brilliant white beams of her battle lights and hear the squawking peremptory challenge of her bull horn.

Then suddenly, with a violent lift of relief, he saw the cold white fingers of the lights far behind – at least six miles away – at the spot where the destroyer had seen him taking in sail. The Captain had bought the dummy, believing that Hirondelle had heaved to and waited for him to come up.

Jake threw back his head and laughed with relief before he caught himself and began shouting new orders down to the deck, swinging the schooner once again across the wind

105

on the reciprocal of the warship's course, and beginning the long delicate contest of skill in which the *Hirondelle* ducked and weaved on to her old course, while the warship plunged blindly back and forth across the darkened Gulf, searching desperately with the mile-long beams of the battle lights for the dark and stinking hull of the slaver – or switching them off and running under full power with all her ports darkened in the hope of taking *Hirondelle* unawares.

Once the destroyer Captain almost succeeded, but Jake caught the flashing phosphorescence of her bow-wave a mile off. Desperately he yelled at the Greek to heave to and they lay silent and unseen while the low greyhound-waisted warship slid swiftly across their bows, her engines beating like a gigantic pulse, and was swallowed once again by the night. The nervous sweat that bathed Jake's shirt dried icy cold in the night wind as he put *Hirondelle* cautiously on course again.

Two hours later he saw the lights of the destroyer again, a glow of white light far astern, that pulsed like summer sheet lightning as the arc lamps traversed back and forth. Then there was only the stars and many hours later the first steely light of dawn growing steadily and expanding the circle of the dark sea around the schooner.

Chilled to the bone by the night wind and the long hours of inactivity, Jake swept the horizon back and forth as the light strengthened, and only when he knew that it was empty of any trace of the warship did he close the telescope, climb stiffly from the crows-nest and begin the long slow journey down the rigging to the deck below.

Papadopoulos greeted him like a brother, reaching up to hug him and breathe garlic in his face, and Vicky had the chop-box open and the primus stove hissing. She brought him an enamel mug of steaming black coffee and looked at him with a new respect tinged with admiration. Gareth opened the hatch of the turret from which during the whole night he had commanded the crew with a loaded Vickers machine gun and came to fetch the other mug of coffee from Vicky and gave Jake a cheroot as they moved to the rail together.

'I keep underestimating you,' he grinned, as he cupped his hands around the flaring match he offered Jake. 'Just because you are big – I keep thinking you are stupid.'

'You'll get over it,' Jake promised him. Instinctively they both glanced across the deck at where Vicky was breaking eggs into the pan – and they understood each other very clearly.

She shook them both awake a little before noon. They were sprawled on their blankets in the shade under one of the cars trying to catch up on the sleep they had missed that night. However, they followed Vicky without protest to the bows and the three of them peered ahead at the low lion-coloured coast line, upon which the surf creamed softly and over which the hard aching blue shield of the sky blazed with an intensity that hurt the eyes.

There was no clear dividing line between earth and sky. It was blurred by the low mist of dust and heat that wavered and rippled like the yellow mane of the lion. Vicky wondered whether she had ever seen such an uninviting scene, and decided she had not. She began to compose the words with which she would describe it to her tens of thousands of readers.

Gregorius came up to join the group. He had discarded the western dress and donned instead the traditional shamma and tight breeches. He had become the man of Africa once again, and the smooth chocolate-brown face, with its halo of dark thick curls, was lit by the passion of the returning exile.

'You cannot see the mountains – the haze is too thick,' he explained. 'But sometimes in the dawn when the air is cooler—' and he stared into the west, with his longing expressed clearly in the liquid flashing eyes and upon the full sculptured lips.

The schooner crept inshore, gliding over the shallows where the water was like that of a mountain stream, so clear that they could make out every detail of the reef thirty feet down and watch the shoals of coral fish below like bejewelled clouds through the crystal waters.

Papadopoulos turned the *Hirondelle* to approach the shore at an oblique angle so that the details of the coast resolved themselves gradually and they saw the golden red beaches broken by headlands and points of jagged rock, and beyond it the land rose gradually, barren and awful, speckled only with the low scrubby spina Cristi and camel grass.

For an hour they ran parallel with the shore, a thousand yards off, and the group by the rail stood and stared at it with fascination. Only Jake had left the group and was making the preparations to begin unloading, but he also came back to the rail when abruptly a deep bay opened ahead of them.

'The Bay of Chains,' said Gregorius, and it was clear how it had got its name, for, huddled under the cliffs of one headland and protected from the prevailing winds and the run of the surf by the horn of land, were the ruins of the ancient slave city of Mondi.

Gregorius pointed it out to them, for it did not look like a city. It was merely an area of broken rock and stone blocks running down to the water's edge. They were close enough now to make out the roughly geometrical layout of smothered streets and roofless buildings.

Hirondelle dropped anchor and snubbed up gently. Jake finished his final preparations for unloading and crossed to where Gareth stood by the rail.

'One of us will have to swim a line ashore.'

'Spin you for it,' suggested Gareth, and before Jake could protest he had the coin in his hand.

'Heads!' Jake looked resigned.

'Bad luck, old son. Give the sharks my love.' Gareth smiled and stroked his moustache.

Jake balanced on the clumsy pontoon raft as it was lifted by the donkey engine and lowered over the side, dangling on the heavy lines.

It settled on to the surface and floated alongside as ungracefully as a pregnant hippo. Jake grinned up at Vicky who was leaning over the rail, watching with interest.

'Unless you want to be blinded with splendour, you'd better close your eyes.' For a moment she did not understand, but then as he started to strip off his shirt and unbutton his pants, she turned modestly away.

With the end of a coil of light line tied about his waist Jake plunged naked into the sea and struck out for the shore. Vicky's curiosity got the better of her at this stage, and she glanced slyly overboard. There was something so childlike and defenceless about a man with his trousers off, she thought, as she considered Jake's bobbing white buttocks. She might develop that as a theme in one of her columns, she thought, and then realized that Gareth Swales was watching her with one mockingly raised eyebrow, as he paid out the coil of line that snaked after Jake. She blushed pinkly under her tan and hurried away to make sure her typewriter and personal duffel bag were packed away into Miss Wobbly.

Jake touched bottom and waded ashore to secure the line onto one of the stone blocks, and already the first car was on its wooden blocks, and, with the winch clattering, was being lifted over the side.

With each man performing his own task skilfully, one at a time the cars were lowered on to the bobbing raft. There its wheels were hastily lashed and it was hauled carefully towards the beach by the land line.

As soon as the raft ran aground on the sloping yellow

sand, Jake started the engine while Gregorius clamped the footboards into place. Then with the engine revving noisily and the raft swaying dangerously, it rolled over the footboards and up the slope to park well above the high-water mark. Then the raft was hauled back alongside the schooner for its next load.

Although they worked as swiftly as safety would allow, the hours sped away just as swiftly, and it was late afternoon when the last load of fuel drums and wooden cases, with Vicky Camberwell sitting on top of the precarious load, made the short crossing to the beach.

Almost the instant it left the ship's side, the diesel thumped into life, the anchor chain rattled in over the bows and Papadopoulos gave the order to cast off the line of the raft.

By the time Vicky jumped down on the crunchy sand, the *Hirondelle* was moving steadily out between the horns of the bay, and spreading her wings of white canvas to the evening breeze. The four of them stood upon the beach in the lowering dusk and watched her go. None of them waved, and yet they all felt a loss at her going. Stinking slaver, with a crew of pirates, yet she had been their link with the outer world. *Hirondelle* cleared the cliffs and caught the full drive of the wind, heeled eagerly and went away, with her wake leaving a long oily slick across the surface long after she had disappeared into the Gulf.

Jake broke the spell of silence and loneliness that held them.

'All right, my children. Let's make camp.'

They had landed on the open beach between the ruined city and the headland, and now the evening wind was sweeping dust and grit across their exposed position.

Jake selected a sheltered hollow under the lee of the ruins, and they moved the cars up and parked them in the protective hollow square of the laager.

110

The ancient buildings were choked with piled sand and thick with the spiny camel-thorn growth that blocked the narrow streets. While Jake and Gregorius checked the fuelling and lubrication of the vehicles, and Gareth scraped a fireplace against a shielding stone wall, Vicky wandered off to explore the ruins in the dusk.

She did not go far. A tangible sense of menace and human suffering seemed to emanate from the rubble of buildings that had been burned over a century before. It made her skin crawl, but she picked her way cautiously along a narrow alleyway that opened at last into an open square.

She knew instinctively that this had been the trading square of the slave city and she imagined the long chained lines of human beings. The pervading aura of their misery still persisted. She wondered if she could capture it on paper, and make her readers see that it had not changed. Once again, a consuming greed was to place a nation in chains, once again hundreds of thousands of human beings would be forced to learn the same misery that this city had engendered. She must write that, she decided, she must capture the sense of outrage and despair she felt now and convey it to the civilized peoples of the world.

A small scuffling sound distracted her and she looked down, then drew back with a shudder from the finger-length purple scorpion, with its lobster claws and the high curved tail bearing a single-hooked fang that scuttled towards the toe of her boot. She turned and hurried back along the alleyway.

The chill of horror stayed with her, so that she crossed gratefully to the bright fire of thorn twigs that blazed under the ruined wall. Gareth looked up as she knelt beside him and held out her hands to the blaze.

'I was just coming to look for you. Better not wander off on your own.'

'I can look after myself,' she told him quickly, with an edge to her voice which was becoming familiar.

'I agree.' He smiled placatingly at her. 'A bit too damned well, I sometimes think,' and he dug in his pocket.

'I found something in the sand as I was digging the fireplace.' He held out a broken circle of metal which gleamed yellow in the firelight. It was fashioned as a snake bangle, with a serpent's forged head and coiled body.

Vicky felt her irritation evaporate magically. 'Oh, Gary,' she lifted it in both hands, 'it's beautiful. Is it gold?'

'I suspect it is.'

She slipped the heavy bangle over her wrist and admired it with a glowing expression, twisting it to catch the light.

'Not one of them can resist a gift,' Gareth thought comfortably, watching her face in the dancing firelight.

'It belonged to a princess, who was famous for her beauty and her compassion to besotted suitors,' said Gareth lightly. 'So I thought how fitting that you should have it.'

'Oh!' she gasped. 'For me.' And impulsively she leaned forward to kiss his cheek, and was startled when he turned his head quickly and her lips pressed full against his. For a moment she tried to pull away – and then it did not seem worth the effort. After all, it was a truly magnificent bracelet.

In the light of the single hurricane lamp, Jake and Gregorius were studying the large-scale map spread on the engine bonnet of Priscilla the Pig. Gregorius was tracing the route they must take to the shed of the Awash River and lamenting the map's many inaccuracies and omissions.

'If you had tried to follow this, you'd have got into serious trouble, Jake.'

Jake looked up suddenly from the map, and thirty paces away he saw the two figures in the firelight come together and stay that way. He felt his pulse begin to pound and the blood come up his neck, scalding hot.

'Let's get some coffee,' he grunted.

'In a minute,' Gregorius protested. 'First I want to show you where we have to cross the sand desert—' He pointed at the map, tracing a route and not realizing that he was talking to himself alone. Jake had left him to interrupt the action at the fireside.

Vicky awoke in the first uncertain light of dawn to the realization that the wind had dropped. It had whistled dismally all night, so that now when she pulled back her blanket, it was thickly powdered with golden grit and she could feel it stiff in her hair and crunchy between her teeth. One of the men was snoring loudly, but they were three long blanket-wrapped bundles close together, so she was not sure which of them it was. She fetched her toilet bag, towel and a change of underwear, then slipped out of the laager, climbed the slope of the dune and ran down to the beach.

The dawn was absolutely still, the surface of the bay as smooth as a sheet of pink satin as the glow of the hidden sun touched it. The silence was the complete silence of the desert, unbroken by bird or beast, wind or surf – and the dismay she had felt the previous day evaporated.

She stripped off her clothing and walked down the wet sand that the tide had smoothed during the night and waded out into the pink waters, sucking in her belly against the sudden chill of it, and gasping with pleasure as she squatted suddenly neck deep and began to scrub her body of the night's grit and dirt.

When she waded ashore, the sun was cresting the sweeping watery horizon of the Gulf. The tone of light had altered drastically. Already the soft hues of dawn were giving way to the harsher brilliance of Africa to which she had become accustomed.

She dressed quickly, bundling her used underwear in the towel and combing her wet hair as she climbed the dune. At the crest, she halted abruptly with the comb still caught in the tangle of her hair and she gasped again as she stared out into the west.

As Gregorius had told them, the still cool air and the peculiar light of the rising sun created a stage effect, foreshortening the hundred miles of flat featureless desert and throwing up into the sky the sheer massif of the highlands, so that it seemed she might stretch out her hand and touch it.

It was dark purplish blue in the early light, but as Vicky watched in awe, it changed colour like some gargantuan chameleon, becoming gilded with bright sun colours and beginning at the same time to recede swiftly, until it was a pale wraith that dissolved into the first dancing heat mirages of the desert day, and she felt the sultry puff of the rising wind.

She roused herself and hurried down the dune into the laager. Jake looked up from the pan of beans and bacon that was spluttering over the fire and grinned at her.

'Five minutes for breakfast.' He spooned a mess of food into her pannikin and offered it to her. 'I thought about night travel to avoid the heat – but the chances of smashing up the cars on rough going was too great.'

Vicky took the food and ate with high relish, pausing only to stare at Gareth Swales as he came to the fire freshly shaven and perfectly groomed, wearing a spotless open-neck shirt and a baggy pair of plus-four trousers in an expensive thorn-proof tweed. His brogues gleamed with polish, and he smoothed his golden moustaches and raised an eyebrow when Jake exploded with delighted laughter.

114

'Jesus,' he laughed. 'Anyone for golf?'

'I say, old son,' Gareth admonished him, amiably running an eye over Jake's faded moleskins, scuffed Chukka boots and plaid shirt with a tear in the sleeve. 'Your breeding is showing. Just because we are in Africa, there is no need to go native, what?' Then he glanced at Gregorius and flashed that brilliant smile. 'No offence, of course. I must say you look jolly dashing in that get-up.'

Gregorius swathed in his shamma looked up from his breakfast and returned the smile. 'East is east, and west is west,' he said.

'Old Wordsworth certainly knew his stuff,' Gareth agreed, and dipped a spoon into the pan.

The four vehicles, grotesquely burdened and strung out at intervals of two hundred yards to avoid each other's dust, crawled out of the coastal dunes into the vast littoral where the wind rustled endlessly but brought no relief from the steadily rising heat.

Jake was pointing the column on a compass-bearing slightly southerly of that which he would have chosen without Gregorius's advice. They aimed to pass below the sprawling salt pans which Gregorius warned were treacherous going.

For the first two hours, the fluffy yellow earth offered no serious obstacle to their passage, except that the narrow solid tyres cut in deeply and created a wearying drag that kept the speed down below ten·miles an hour and the old engines grinding in the lower gears.

Then the earth firmed, but was strewn with black stone that had been rounded and polished by the grit-laden wind and varied in size from acorns to ostrich eggs. Their speed dropped away a little more as the cars bounced and jolted over this murderous surface, and the black rock threw the fheat back at them, so they rode with all hatches and engine-louvres wide open. Though all of them, including Vicky, had stripped to their underwear, still they ran with sweat that dried almost immediately it oozed from their pores. The exposed metal of the cars, although it was painted white, would blister the hand that touched it, and the engine heat and stench of hot oil and fuel in the driver's compartments was swiftly becoming unbearable as the sun climbed to its zenith.

An hour before noon, Priscilla the Pig blew the safety valve on her radiator and sent a shrieking plume of steam high into the air. Jake earthed the magneto and stopped her immediately. He climbed, half-naked and shiny with sweat, from the turret and shaded his eyes to peer out across the wavering heat-distorted plain. There was no horizon in this haze and visibility was uncertain after a few hundred yards. Even the other vehicles lumbering far behind him seemed monstrous and unreal.

He waited for the others to come up before calling,

'Switch off. We can't go on in this – the engine oil will be thin as water, and we'll ruin all the bearings if we try. We'll wait for it to cool a little.'

Thankfully, they climbed from the cars and crawled into the shade of the chassis where they lay panting like dogs while Jake went down the line with a five-gallon tin of blood-warm water and gave them each as much as they could drink before collapsing on the blanket beside Vicky.

'It's too hot to walk back to my own car,' he explained, and she took it with good grace, merely nodding and closing one more button of her half-open blouse.

Jake wet his handkerchief from the water can and offered it to her. Gratefully, she wiped her neck and face and sighed with pleasure.

'It's too hot to sleep,' she murmured. 'Entertain me, Jake.'

116

'Well now!' he grinned, and she laughed.

'I said it's too hot. Let's talk.'

'About – ?'

'About you. Tell me about you – what part of Texas are you from?'

'All of it. Wherever my pa could find work.'

'What did he do?'

'Wrangled cattle, and rode rodeo.'

'Sounds fun.'

Jake shrugged. 'I preferred machines to horses.'

'Then?'

'There was this war, and they needed mechanics to drive tanks.'

'Afterwards? Why didn't you go home?'

'Pa was dead – a steer fell on him, and it wasn't worth the journey to go collect his old saddle and blanket.'

They were silent for a while, just lying and riding the solid waves of heat that came off the earth.

'Tell me about your dream, Jake,' she said at last.

'My dream?'

'Everybody has a dream.'

He smiled ruefully. 'I've got a dream—' he hesitated, 'there is this idea of mine. It's an engine, the Barton engine. It's all there.' He tapped his forehead. 'All I need is the money to build it. For ten years, I've tried to get it together. Nearly had it a couple of times.'

'After this trip, you will have it,' she suggested.

'Perhaps.' He shook his head. 'I've been too sure too many times to make any bets, though.'

'Tell me about the engine,' she said and he talked quietly but eagerly for ten minutes.

It was a new design, a lightweight, economical design. 'It would drive anything, water pump, saw mill, motorcycle, that sort of thing.' He was intent, happy, she saw. 'I'd only need a small workshop to begin with, some place back west

– I've thought about Fort Worth—' he stopped himself, and glanced at her. 'Sorry, I was running on a bit.'

'No,' she said quickly. 'I enjoyed listening. I hope it works out for you, Jake.'

He nodded. 'Thanks.' And they rode the heat for a few more minutes in companionable silence.

'What's your dream?' he asked at last, and she laughed lightly.

'No, tell me,' he insisted.

'There is this book. It's a novel – I have thought about it for years. I have written it in my head a hundred times – all I have to do is find the time and the place to write it on paper—' she broke off, and then laughed again. 'And then, of course, it sounds corny – but I think about kids and a home. I have been travelling too long.'

'I know what you mean.' Jake nodded. 'That's a good dream you've got,' he said thoughtfully. 'Better than mine.'

Gareth Swales heard the murmur of their voices and raised himself on one elbow. For a while he thought seriously about crossing the dozen yards of sunbaked black stones to where they lay – but the effort required was just too much and he fell back. A fist-sized rock jarred his kidneys and he cursed quietly.

It was five o'clock before Jake judged they could start the engines again. They refuelled from the cans strapped on the sponsons, and once more they set off in column at an agonized walking pace over the rough surface, each jolt shaking driver and vehicle cruelly.

Two hours later, the plain of black boulders ended abruptly, and beyond it stretched an area of low red sand hills. Thankfully Jake increased speed and the column sped towards a sunset that was inflamed by the dust-laden sky until it filled half the heavens with great swirls of purple and pink and flaming scarlets. The desert wind dropped and the air was still and heavy with memory of the day's heat. Each vehicle drew a long dark shadow behind it and threw up a fat rolling sausage of red dust into the air above it.

The night fell with the tropical suddenness that is alarming to those who have known only the gentle dusks of the northern continents. Jake calculated that they had covered less than twenty miles in a day of travel and he was reluctant to call a halt, now that they had hit this level going and were bowling along with engine temperatures dropping in the cool of night and the drivers' tempers cooling in sympathy. Jake took a bearing off Orion's belt as the easiest constellation, then he switched on the headlights and looked back to see that the others had followed his example. The lights threw a brilliant path a hundred yards ahead of Jake's car, giving him plenty of time to avoid the odd thick clump of thorn scrub, and occasionally trapping a large grey desert hare, dazzling it so that its eyes blazed diamond bright before it turned and loped, longlegged, ahead of the car, seemingly unable to break out of the path of light, dodging and doubling with its long floppy ears laid along its back, until at the last instant it ducked out from under the wheels and dived into the darkness.

He was just deciding to call a halt for food and drink, with a possible further march later that night, when the sand hills dropped away gradually and in the headlights he saw ahead of him a glistening white expanse of perfectly level sand, as smooth and as inviting as the Brooklands motor-racing circuit.

Jake changed up into high gear for the first time that day, and the car plunged forward eagerly – for a hundred yards before the thick hard crust of the salt pan collapsed and the heavy chassis fell through, belly deep, floundering instantly so that Jake was thrown violently forward at the abrupt halt, striking his shoulder and forehead painfully on the steel visor.

The engine shrieked in the frenzy of high revolutions and lifting valves before Jake recovered himself, then slammed the throttle closed. He dragged himself from the turret to signal a halt to the following vehicles, and then mournfully clambered down to inspect the heavily bogged vehicle. Gareth walked out across the snowy surface of the pan, and stood beside him surveying the damage silently.

'Let him make one crack,' Jake thought through the mists of his anger and frustration. He felt his hands curling into big bony hammers.

'Cheroot?' Gareth offered him the case, and Jake felt his anger deflate slightly.

'Good place to camp tonight,' Gareth went on. 'We'll see about hauling her out in the morning.' He clapped Jake's shoulder. 'Come on, I'll buy you a warm beer.'

'I was waiting for you to say something, anything but that – and I would have swung on you.' Jake shook his head, grinning with surprise at Gareth's perception.

'You think I didn't know that, old son?' Gareth grinned back at him.

Vicky woke in the hours immediately after midnight when human vitality is at its lowest, and the night was utterly silent – except for the gentle sound of one of the men snoring. She recognized the sound from the previous evening, and wondered which of them it was. Something like that could influence a girl's decision, she thought, imagine sleeping every night of your life in a saw mill.

It was not that which had woken her, however. Perhaps it was the cold. The temperature had plunged in that phenomenal temperature range of the desert, and she drew her blankets tighter over her shoulder and settled to sleep again – when the sound came again and she shot upright into a rigid sitting position.

It was a long-drawn rolling, rattling sound, quite unlike anything she had ever heard before. The sound rose to a pitch which clawed her nerves, and then ended in a series of deep gut-shaking grunts. It was so fierce and menacing a sound that she felt the slow ice of terror spreading through her body. She wanted to shout to the others, to wake them, but she was afraid to draw attention to herself and she sat frozen and wide-eyed in the next silence – waiting for it to happen again.

'It's all right, Miss Camberwell.' Vicky started at the quiet voice. 'It's miles away. Nothing to worry about.' And she looked round to see the young Ethiopian, still wrapped in his blankets watching her.

'My God, Greg – what on earth is it?'

'A lion, Miss Camberwell,' Gregorius explained, obviously surprised that she did not recognize such a commonplace sound.

'A lion? That is a lion roaring?' She had not expected it to sound anything like that.

'My people say that even a brave man is frightened three times by a lion – and the first time is when he hears it roar.'

'I believe it,' she whispered. 'I truly do.' And she picked up her blankets and went to where Jake and Gareth slept on, undisturbed. She lay down carefully between them, and felt a little easier that the lion had now a wider choice, but still she did not sleep.

Count Aldo Belli had retired to his tent with the sincerest and firmest resolve that in the morning he would press forward to the Wells of Chaldi. The General's pleas had touched him. Nothing would check him now, he decided, as he composed himself to sleep.

He woke in the utter dark of the dog hours to find that the Chianti he had drunk at dinner was now exerting internal pressure. Where a lesser man might have slipped without ceremony from his bed to deal with this problem, the Count did things in greater style.

He lay back on his pillows and let out a single loud bellow, and immediately there was the frantic activity in the night, and within minutes Gino had arrived with a bull's-eye lantern, hastily dressed in a camel-hair gown, and tousle-haired and owl-eyed with sleep. He was followed by the Count's personal valet and his galloper, all in the same state of freshly awoken bewilderment.

The Count stated his physical needs, and the dedicated group gathered around his bed solicitously. Gino helped him up as though he were an invalid, the valet held a dressing-gown of quilted blue Chinese silk, embroidered with ferocious scarlet dragons, and then knelt to place a calf-skin slipper on each of the Count's feet, while his aide hastened to kick the Count's personal guard awake and fall them in outside the tent.

The Count emerged from the tent and a small procession, well armed and lighted, filed down to the latrine which had been dug exclusively for the Count's personal use. Gino entered first and checked the small thatched edifice for snakes, scorpions and brigands. Only when he emerged and declared it safe did the Count enter. His escort stood to attention and listened respectfully to the copious outpouring taking place within – until they were interrupted by the sky-shaking, earth-rattling, heart-stopping roar of a male lion.

The Count shot from the latrine, his face a startled glistening white in the lantern light.

'Sweet and merciful Mother of God!' he cried. 'What in the name of Peter and all the saints is that?'

Nobody could answer him, in fact nobody showed any interest in the question whatever, and the Count had to move swiftly to catch up with his armed escort which had already started back towards the bivouac in a sprightly fashion.

Once within the security of his own brightly lit tent, and surrounded by his hastily assembled staff, the Count's pulse rate returned to normal, and one of his officers suggested that the native Eritrean guides be sent for and questioned on the terrible night sounds that had plunged the entire battalion into consternation.

'Lion?' said the Count, and then again, 'Lion!' Instantly the formless terrors of the night evaporated, for by this time the first light of dawn was gleaming in the east, and the Count's breast swelled with the fierce instincts of the huntsman.

'It appears, my Colonel, that the beasts will be feeding on the antelope carcasses that you left lying out on the desert,' the interpreter explained. 'The smell of blood has attracted them.'

'Gino,' snapped the Count. 'Fetch the Mannlicher and have the driver bring the Rolls-Royce to my tent immediately.'

'My Colonel,' protested Major Luigi Castelani. 'The battalion, by your own orders, is to march at dawn.'

'Countermanded!' snapped the Colonel. Already he imagined the magnificent trophy skin spread before his Louis XIV desk in the library of his castle. He would have it prepared with wide open jaws, flashing white fangs and fierce yellow glass eyes. The picture of open jaws and fangs suddenly reminded him with considerable force of his nerve-racking brush with the beisa oryx.

'Major,' he ordered, 'I want twenty men to accompany me, a truck to transport them, full battle order, and one hundred rounds of ammunition each.' The Count was not about to take any more silly chances.

The lion was a fully mature male, six years of age, and, like most of the desert strain of *leo panthera*, he was much larger than the forest lions. He stood well over three feet high at the shoulder, and he weighed in excess of four hundred pounds. The late sun enhanced the sleek reddish ochre of his skin and transformed his mane into a glowing halo of gold. The mane was dense and long, framing the broad flattened head, reaching far back beyond the shoulder, and hanging so low under his chest and belly as almost to sweep the earth.

He walked stiffly, head held very low and swinging heavily from side to side with each laborious step. His breathing came with a low explosive grunt at each exhalation, and occasionally he stopped and swung his head to snap irritably at the buzzing blue cloud of flies that swarmed about the wound in his flank. Then he would lick at the small dark hole from which pale watery blood oozed steadily. The long pink tongue curled out and, rough as shagreen, rasped against the supple hide. The constant licking had worn away the hair around the wound, giving it a pale shaven appearance.

The 9.3 Mannlicher bullet had caught him at the instant he had begun to turn away to run. It had angled in from two inches behind the last rib, striking with a force of nine tons that had bowled the lion down, rolling him in a cloud of pale dust. The copper-jacketed bullet was tipped with soft expanding lead, and it mushroomed as it raked the belly cavity, lacerating the bowels and tearing four large abdominal veins. The slug had passed close enough to the kidneys to bruise both of them severely, so now, when the lion stopped, arched his back and crouched to pass a spattering of blood-stained urine, he groaned like the roll of drums at an execution. Then, finally, the bullet had struck the arch of the pelvic girdle and lodged there against the bone.

After the first massive shock of impact, the lion had rolled to his feet and flattened into a dead streaking run, jinking away below the level of the coarse scrub. Although a dozen more bullets had thrown up soft jumping spurts of dust around him, one so close as to throw grit into his eyes, not another touched him.

There had been seven lions in the pride. Another older, heavier, darker-maned male, two younger daintier breeding females, one with her lithe-waisted body thickened with the heavy bearing of young in her womb, and three immature animals still dappled with their cub spots and boisterous as kittens.

The younger male was the only one to survive that long shattering roll of rifle fire, and now as he moved on he felt the thick jelly-like weight of congealing blood sloshing back and forth across his belly cavity at each step. There was a heavy lethargy slowing his movements, but thirst drove him onwards. Thirst was a scalding agony that consumed his whole body, and the lower pools of the Awash River were a dozen miles ahead.

In the dawn Priscilla the Pig was heavily bogged down on her belly with all four wheels helpless in the porridge of pale salt mire below the crust of the pan.

Jake stripped to the waist and swung the long two-handed axe relentlessly, while the others gathered the piles of thorny scrub he mowed down, and, cursing at the pricks and scratches, carried them out across the snowy surface of the pan.

Jake worked with a self-punishing fury, angry with his lack of attention which had bogged the car and was going to cost them a day at the least. It was no valid excuse that exhaustion and heat had clouded his judgement – that he had not recognized the treacherous smooth white surface of the pan – for Gregorius had warned him specifically of this hazard. He worked with the axe from an hour before sunrise until the heat had climbed with the sun and a small mountain of cut branches stood beside the car.

Then Gareth helped him build a firm foundation of flat stones and thicker branches under the engine compartment of the car. They had to lie on their sides and grovel in the dust to get the big screw jack set up on the base and they slowly lifted the front of the car, turning the handle between them.

As the front wheels rose an inch at a time, Vicky and Gregorius packed the wiry scrub branches under them. It was slow and laborious work which had to be repeated at the rear of the car.

It was past noon before Priscilla the Pig stood forlornly balanced on four piles of compacted branches – but her belly was clear of the surface.

'What do we do now?' Gareth asked. 'Drive her back?'

'One spin of the wheels will kick that trash out and she'll bog down again,' Jake grunted, and wiped his sweat-glistening chest on the bundled shirt in his hand. He looked at Gareth and felt a flare of irritation that after five hours' work in the sun, after grovelling on his belly in the dust, and heaving on the jack handle, the man had barely raised a sweat, his clothes were unmarked and – final provocation – his hair was still neatly combed.

Working under Jake's direction, they cut and laid a corduroy of branches back to the hard ground at the edge of the pan. This would distribute the weight of the vehicle and prevent it breaking through the crust again.

Then Vicky manoeuvred and reversed Miss Wobbly down to the edge of the pan and lined her up with the causeway of branches. The men joined three coils of the thick manila line and carried it out to the stranded vehicle, unrolling it behind them as they went, until at last the two cars were joined by that fragile thread.

Gareth climbed in and took the wheel of Priscilla while Jake and Gregorius, armed with two of the thickest branches, stood ready to lever the wheels.

'You any good at praying, Gary?' Jake shouted.

'Not my strong suit, old son.'

'Well, stiffen the old upper lip then.' Jake mimicked him, and then let out a bellow at Vicky who acknowledged with a wave before her golden head disappeared into the driver's hatch of Miss Wobbly. The engine beat accelerated and the line came up taut as Miss Wobbly rolled forward up the incline above the pan.

'Keep the wheels straight,' shouted Jake, and he and Gregorius threw their weight on the branches, giving just that ounce of leverage sufficient to transfer part of the vehicle's weight on to the corduroyed pathway.

Slowly, ponderously, the cumbersome vehicle rolled back across the pan, until she reached the hard ground and the four of them shouted with relief and triumph.

Jake retrieved two celebratory bottles of Tusker beer from his secret hoard, but the liquid was so warm that half of it exploded in a fizzing gush from the mouth of each bottle as it was opened, and there was only a mouthful for each of them.

'Can we reach the lower Awash by nightfall?' Jake demanded, and Gregorius looked up and judged the angle of the sun before replying.

'If we don't waste any more time,' he said.

Still on a compass heading, and giving the salt-white pans a wide berth, the column ground on steadily into the west.

In the mid afternoon they reached the sand desert, with its towering whale-backed dunes throwing lovely lyrical shadows in the hollows between. The colour of the sand varied from dark purple to the softest pinks and talcum white, and was so fine and soft that the wind blew long smoke-like plumes from the crest of each dune.

Under Gregorius's direction they turned northwards, and within half an hour they had found the long narrow ridge of ironstone that bisected the sand desert and formed a narrow causeway through the shifting dunes. They crept slowly across this rocky bridge, following its winding course for twelve miles, while the dunes rose on each side of them.

Vicky thought that this was much like the passage of the Red Sea by the fleeing Israelites. Even the dunes seemed like frozen waves that might at each moment come crashing down to swamp them – and she despaired that she could ever adequately describe the wild and disordered beauty of this multicoloured sea of sand.

They emerged at last and with startling suddenness into the dry flat grasslands of the Ethiopian lowlands. The desert proper was at last behind them – and although this was a harsh and arid savannah, there was, at least, the occasional thorn tree and an almost unbroken carpet of sered grass amongst the low thorny scrub. Although the grass was so fine and dry that all colour had been bleached from it by the sun, it shone silver and stiff as though coated with hoar frost.

Most cheering of all was the distant but discernible blue outline of the far mountains. Now they hovered at the edge of their awareness, a far beacon calling them onward.

Over the short crisp grass, the four vehicles roared forward joyously, bumping through an occasional ant-bear hole and flattening the clumps of low thorn that stood in their way as they plunged ahead.

In the last glimmering of the day, just when Jake had decided to halt the day's march, the flat land ahead of them opened miraculously and they looked down into the steep boulder-strewn gorge of the Awash River fifty feet below them. They climbed out of the parked vehicles and gathered stiffly in a small group on the lip of the ravine.

'There is Ethiopia, two hundred yards away. It's two years since last I stood upon the soil of my own country,' said Gregorius, his big dark eyes catching the last of the light. He stopped himself and explained. 'The river rises in the high country near Addis Ababa and comes down one of the gorges into the lowland. A short distance downstream from here it ends in a shallow swamp. There its waters sink away into the desert sand and disappear. Here we are standing on French territory still, ahead of us is Ethiopia, there far to the north is Italian Eritrea.'

'How far is it to the Wells of Chaldi?' Gareth interrupted. That for him was the end of the rainbow and the pot of gold.

Gregorius shrugged. 'Another forty miles, perhaps.'

'How do we get across this lot?' Jake muttered, staring down into the dim depths of the ravine where the shallow pools still glowed dull silver.

'Upstream there is an old camel route to Jibuti,' Gregorius told him. 'We might have to dig out the banks a little, but I think we'll be able to cross.'

'I hope you are right,' Gareth told him. 'It's a long way home, if we have to go back.'

The view of water that she had glimpsed in the depths of the ravine haunted Vicky Camberwell during the night. She dreamed of foaming mountain streams and spilling waterfalls, of moss-covered boulders, swaying green ferns about a deep cold pool, and she awoke, restless and tired, with sweat plastering her hair to her neck and forehead. There was just the first promise of dawn in the sky.

She thought that she was the only one awake and she crept into the vehicle and fetched her towel and toilet bag, but as she jumped down to the ground she heard the clink of spanner on steel and she saw Jake stooped over the engine compartment of his car.

She tried to sneak away before he saw her, but he straightened suddenly.

'Where are you going?' he demanded. 'As if I didn't know. Listen, Vicky, I don't like you wandering around out of camp on your own.'

'Jake Barton, I feel so filthy I can smell myself. Nothing and nobody is going to stop me getting down to the river.'

Jake hesitated. 'I'd better come down with you.'

'This isn't the Folies Bergère, my dear,' she laughed, and he had learned enough not to argue with this lady. He watched her hurry to the lip of the ravine and disappear down the steep slope with vague misgivings, for which he could find no real substance.

The earth and loose stone rolled easily underfoot, and Vicky restrained her impatience and picked her way carefully towards the water, until she reached a narrow game trail that tipped down at a more comfortable angle, and she followed it with relief. Her footsteps, falling silently on to the soft earth, followed faithfully the string of round five-toed pad marks, larger than a saucer, which had been plugged deeply by the heavy weight of the animal that had made them. Vicky did not look down, however, and if she had, it was doubtful if she would have recognized what she was seeing. The faintly reflected light of the pools drew her like a beacon.

When she reached the bottom of the ravine, she found that the river was so shrunken that it was no longer flowing. The pools were shallow, stagnant and still warm from the previous day's sun. The storm waters of the Awash had cut down through the softer upper layers of earth until they exposed the sheet of hard black ironstone that formed the floor of the ravine.

Vicky stripped off her sweat-damp clothing and stepped down into one of the shallow pools, sighing with the pleasurable feel of water on her skin. She sat waist-deep and scooped handfuls of water over her face and breasts, washing away the dust and salt-sticky sweat of the desert.

Then she waded to the edge of the pool and selected a bottle of shampoo from her bag. The water was so soft that she swiftly worked up a thick coating of white suds that covered her head and ran down her neck on to her bare shoulders.

She rinsed the soap off and bound the towel around her wet head like a turban, before kneeling in the shallow pool and soaping her entire body, delighting at the slipperiness of the suds and their fragrance. By the time she was finished, the light had strengthened and she knew that the others would be up and chafing to resume the march.

She stepped out on to the flat black rock that surrounded the pool and stood for a moment to feel the first gentle movement of the morning breeze against her naked skin, and suddenly she had a strong sensation that she was being watched. She turned swiftly, half crouching, her hands flying instinctively to cover her bosom and her groin.

The eyes that watched her were of a savage golden colour, and the pupils were glistening black slits. The stare was steady and unblinking.

The huge reddish-gold beast crouched on a level ledge of rock, halfway up the far bank of the ravine. It lay with its forepaws drawn up under its chin, and there was a sense of deadly stillness about it that was chilling, although Vicky did not readily recognize what she was seeing.

Then very slowly the dark ruff of the mane came erect, swelling out around the head and exaggerating its already impressive bulk. Then the tail twitched and began to slash back and forth with the steady beat of a metronome.

Suddenly Vicky knew what it was. She heard again in her imagination the echoes of that terrible sound in the night – and she screamed.

Jake had just completed the adjustments he was making to the ignition of his car and closed the engine cowling. He picked up the fluted bottle of Scrubbs Cloudy Ammonia to dissolve the grease from his hands. At that instant he heard the scream and he began to run without a conscious thought.

The scream was so high and shrill, an expression of mortal terror, that Jake's heart raced in sympathy and when the scream came again, if anything shriller still, he leaped the bank and went sliding and running down the steep slope of the ravine.

It was only seconds from when he heard the first scream until he came skidding and sliding down on to the rocky floor of the ravine beside the pool.

He saw the naked girl crouching at the edge of the pool, both hands pressed to her mouth. Her body was pale and slim, with the small tight round buttocks of a lad and long graceful legs.

'Vicky,' he shouted. 'What is it?'

And she turned quickly to him, her breasts swinging heavily at the movement, round and white with large pink nipples standing out tightly with cold and shock. Even in the extremity of the moment, he could not help but glance down at the smooth velvety plain of her belly and the fluffy dusky triangle at its base. Then she was running towards him on those long coltish legs, and her face was deadly white, and the speckled green eyes huge and swimming with rampant terror.

'Jake,' she cried. 'Oh God, Jake,' and then he saw movement beyond her, halfway up the bank of the water course.

The wound had stiffened during the night, almost paralysing the lion's hindquarters, and the torn entrails were leaking poison and infection into the belly cavity. It had slowed the animal so drastically that the natural reflexive anger which the sight of a human form had roused was not strong enough to precipitate the charge.

However, the sound of the human voice immediately invoked memories of the hunters who had inflicted this terrible aching agony and the anger flared higher.

Then suddenly there was another of the hated two-legged figures, more noise and movement, all of this enough to counter the stiffness and paralysing lethargy. The lion rose slightly out of his crouch and he growled.

Jake ran four paces to meet Vicky and she tried to throw her arms about his neck for protection, but he avoided the embrace and grasped her upper arm with his left hand, his fingers digging so deeply into her flesh that the pain steadied her. Using the impetus of her run, he swung her on towards the path that climbed the slope.

'Run,' he shouted. 'Keep running.' And he turned back to face the crippled animal as it launched itself from the ledge into the bed of the river.

It was only then that Jake realized that he still carried a full bottle of Scrubbs Ammonia in his hand. The lion came bounding swiftly through the shallow stagnant pool towards him. Despite the wounds, it flowed with a lithe and sinuous menace. It was so close that he could see each stiff white whisker in the curled upper lip and hear the rattle of air in its throat. He let it come on, for to turn and run was suicide. At the last moment he reared back like a baseball pitcher and hurled the bottle. It was an instinctive action, using the only weapon – however puny – that was at hand.

The bottle flew straight at the lion's head, catching it in the direct centre of its broad forehead as it lunged smoothly upwards towards the ledge where Jake stood.

The bottle exploded in a burst of sparkling glass splinters and a creamy gush of the pungent liquid. It filled both the lion's eyes, blinding it instantly, and the stench of concentrated ammonia in its open mouth and flaring nostrils killed its sense of smell and shocked its whole system so violently that it missed its footing and fell, roaring with the agony of scalded eyeballs and burning throat, into the shallow water where it rolled helplessly on its back.

Jake ran forward, seizing the few seconds of advantage he had gained. He stooped to pick up a water-worn ironstone boulder the shape and size of a football, and swung it up above his head with both hands.

As he poised himself on the ledge above the pool, the lion recovered its balance and came up at him blindly. Jake swung the boulder down from on high and, like a cannon ball, it smashed into the back of the animal's neck, where the sodden mane covered the juncture of skull and vertebrae, crushing both so that the dreadfully mutilated beast collapsed and rolled on to its side, half in the water and half on the black rock ledge.

For long seconds Jake stood over it, panting with exertion and reaction, then he leaned forward and touched with his fingertip the long pale lashes that fringed the lion's open staring golden eye. Already the sheen of the eyeball was clouded by the corrosive liquid. At Jake's touch there was no blinking reflex, and he knew that the animal was dead. He turned to find that Vicky had not obeyed his instruction to run. She stood frozen where he had left her, naked and vulnerable, so that he felt his heart shift within him and he went to her quickly. With a sob she flew into his arms and clung to him with startling strength. Jake knew that the embrace was the consequence of terror not affection, but as his own heart-beat slowed and the tingle of the adrenalin in his blood receded, he thought that he had achieved a solid advantage. If you save a girl's life, she just has to take you seriously, he reasoned, and grinned to himself still a little unsteadily. All his senses were enhanced by the high point of recent danger. He could smell the perfumed soap and the stink of ammonia. He could feel with excruciating clarity the slim hard length of the girl's body pressed to his and the smooth warmth of her skin under his hands.

'Oh Jake!' she whispered brokenly, and with sudden aching certainty he knew that in this moment she was his to take, to possess right here on the black rock bank of the Awash, beside the warm carcass of the lion.

The knowledge was certain and his hands moved on her body, receiving instant confirmation – her body was quick and responsive, and her face turned up to his. Her lips trembled and he could feel her breath upon his mouth.

'What the hell is going on down there?' Gareth's voice rang across the murky depths of the gorge. He stood at the top of the bank high above them. He had one of the Lee Enfield bolt-action rifles under his arm and seemed on the point of coming down to them.

Jake turned Vicky, shielding her with his own big body and slipping off his moleskin jacket to cover her nakedness. The jacket reached halfway down her thighs and folded voluminously around under her armpits. She was still shivering like a kitten in a snowstorm, and her breathing was broken and thick.

'Don't worry about it,' Jake called up at Gareth. 'You weren't in time to help, and you aren't needed now.' He groped in his hip pocket and produced a large, slightly grubby handkerchief, which Vicky accepted with a tearful, quivering smile.

'Blow your nose,' said Jake. 'Then get your pants on, before the whole gang arrives to give you a hand.'

Gregorius was so impressed that he was speechless for several minutes. In Ethiopia there is no act of valour so highly esteemed as the single-handed hunting and killing of a full-grown adult lion. The warrior who accomplishes this feat wears the mane thereafter as a badge of his courage and earns the respect of all. The man who shoots his lion is respected, the man who kills with the spear is venerated – Gregorius had never heard of one killed with a single rock and a bottle of ammonia.

Gregorius skinned out the carcass with his own hands. Before he had finished, the black pinioned vultures were sailing in wide circles overhead. He left the naked pink carcass lying in the river bed, and carried the wet skin up to the bivouac where Jake was fretting to continue the trek towards the Wells. He was irreverent in his disdain of the trophy, and Greg tried to explain it to him.

'You will gain great prestige amongst my people, Jake. Wherever you go, people will point you out to each other.'

'Fine, Greg. That's just fine. Now will you kindly haul arse.'

'I will have a war bonnet made for you out of the mane,' Greg insisted, as he strapped the bundle of wet skin to the sponson of Jake's car. 'With the hair combed out, it will look very grand.'

'It could only be an improvement on his present hair style,' Gareth observed drily. 'I agree it's been a beautiful honeymoon, and Jake is a splendid lad – but like he said, let's move on, before I am violently ill.'

As they moved towards their respective cars, Gregorius fell in beside Jake and quietly showed him the mushroomed copper-jacketed bullet he had removed from its niche in the pelvic bone of the carcass.

Jake paused to examine it closely, turning it in the palm of his hand.

'Nine millimeter, or nine point three,' he said. 'It's a sporting calibre – not military.'

'I doubt if there is a single rifle in Ethiopia that would fire this bullet,' said Greg seriously. 'It's a foreigner's rifle.'

'No need to blow the bugle yet,' said Jake, and flicked the bullet back to him. 'But we'll bear it in mind.'

Gregorius almost turned away, then said shyly, 'Jake, even if the lion was already wounded – it's still the bravest thing I ever heard of. I have often hunted for them, but never killed one yet.' Jake was touched by the boy's admiration. He laughed roughly and slapped his shoulder.

'I'll leave the next one for you,' he promised.

They followed the windings of the River Awash through the savannah grassland, running in towards the mountains so that with each hour travelled the peaks stood higher and clearer into the sky. The ridges of rock and the deep-forested gorges came into hazy focus, like a wall across the sky.

Suddenly they intersected the old caravan road, hitting it at a point where the steep banks of the Awash flattened a little. The ford of the river had been deeply worn over the ages by the passage of laden beasts of burden and the men who drove them, so that the many footpaths down each bank were deep trenches in the red earth, that jinked to avoid any large boulder or ridge of rock.

The three men worked in the brilliant sunlight and swung shovel and mattock in a fine mist of red dust that powdered their hair and bodies. They filled in the uneven ground and deeply worn trenches, levering the boulders free and letting them roll and bounce down into the river bed, and slept that night the deathlike sleep of utter exhaustion that ignored the ache of abused muscle and burst blisters.

Jake had them at work before it was fully light the next morning, clearing and levelling, shovelling and packing the dry hard-baked earth, until at last each bank had been shaped into a rough but passable ramp.

Gareth was to take the first car through and he stood in the turret, somehow managing to look debonair and sartorially elegant, under the fine layer of red dust. He grinned at Jake and shouted dramatically,

'Noli illegitimi carborundum,' and disappeared into the steel interior. The engine roared and he went bounding and sliding down the steep ramp of newly turned earth, bounced and jolted across the black rock bottom and flew at the far bank.

When the wheels spun viciously in the loose red earth, blowing out a storm of grit and pebbles, Jake and Gregorius were ready to throw their weight against it and this was just sufficient to keep the vehicle moving. Slowly it ground its way up the almost vertical climb, the rear end kicking and yawing under the thrust of the spinning wheels, until at last it burst out over the top, and Gareth shut down the power and jumped out laughing.

'Right, now we can tow the other cars up the bank,' and he produced a celebratory cheroot.

'What was that piece of dog Latin you recited just then?' Jake asked, as he accepted the cheroot.

'Old family war cry,' Gareth explained. 'Shouted by the fighting Swales at Hastings, Agincourt and in the knocking shops of the world.'

'What does it mean?'

'*Noli illegitimi carborundum?*' Gareth grinned again as he lit the cheroots. 'It means, "Don't let the bastards grind you down".'

One at a time, they brought the other three cars down into the ravine, and hitched them up to the vehicle on the far bank. Then with Vicky driving, Gareth towing, and Jake and Gregorius shoving, they hauled them up on to the level, sunbaked soil of Ethiopia. It was late afternoon when at last they fell panting in the long shadow thrown by Miss Wobbly's chassis, to rest and smoke and drink steaming mugs of hastily brewed tea. Gregorius told them:

'No more obstacles ahead of us now. It's open ground all the way to the Wells,' and then he smiled at the three of them with white teeth in a smooth honey-coloured face. 'Welcome to Ethiopia!'

'Quite frankly, old chap, I'd much prefer to be sitting at Harry's Bar in the rue Daunou,' said Gareth soberly, 'which is exactly what I will be doing not long after Toffee Sagud presses a purse of gold into my milk-white hand.'

Jake stood up suddenly and peered out into the dancing heat waves that still poured from the hot earth like swirling liquid. Then he ran quickly across to his own car and leapt up into the turret, emerging seconds later with his binoculars.

The others stood up uneasily and watched him focus the glasses.

'Rider,' said Jake.

'How many?' Gareth demanded.

'Just the one. Coming this way fast.' Gareth moved across

to fetch the Lee-Enfield and work a cartridge into the breech.

They saw him now, galloping through the dizzy heat mirage, so that at one moment horse and rider seemed to float free of the earth, and then sink back and swell miraculously, growing to elephantine proportions in the heat-tortured air. Dust drifted behind the running horse and it was only at close range that the rider came into crisp focus.

Gregorius let out a bellow like a rutting stag and raced out into the sunshine to meet the newcomer. In a brilliant display of horsemanship the rider reined in the big white stallion so abruptly that he plunged and reared, cutting at the air with his forehooves. With white robes billowing, he flung himself from the horse, and into Gregorius's wide-spread arms.

The two figures joined together rapturously, the stranger suddenly seeming small and delicate in Gregorius's arms, and the cries of laughter and greeting high and birdlike.

Then hand in hand, looking into each other's faces, they came back to the group that waited by the cars.

'My God, it's another girl,' said Gareth with amazement, setting the loaded rifle aside, and they all stared at the slim, dark-eyed child in her late teens with a skin like dusky silk and immense dark eyes fringed with long curling lashes.

'May I introduce Sara Sagud?' asked Gregorius. 'She is my cousin, my uncle's youngest daughter, and she is also without doubt the prettiest lady in Ethiopia.'

'I see what you mean,' said Gareth. 'Very decorative indeed.' As Gregorius introduced each of them to her by name, the girl smiled at them, and the long aristocratic face with the serenity of an Egyptian princess, the delicate features and chiselled nose of a Nefertiti, changed instantly to a sparkling childlike mischievousness.

'I knew you must cross the Awash here, it is the only place – and I came to meet you.'

'She speaks English also,' Gregorius pointed out proudly. 'My grandfather insists that all his children and his grandchildren learn to speak English. He is a great lover of the English.'

'You speak it well,' Vicky congratulated Sara, although in fact her English was heavily accented, and the girl turned to her, smiling anew.

'The sisters at the convent of the Sacred Heart in Berbera taught me,' she explained, and she examined Vicky with frank and unabashed admiration. 'You are very beautiful, Miss Camberwell, your hair is the colour of the winter grass in the highlands,' and Vicky's usual composure was rocked. She blushed faintly and laughed, but Sara's attention had flicked away to the armoured cars.

'Ah, they also are beautiful – nobody has spoken of anything else, since they heard these were coming.' She hoisted the skirts of her robe up over her tight-fitting embroidered breeches, and hopped agilely up on to the steel body of Miss Wobbly. 'With these we shall throw the Italians back into the sea. Nothing can stand before the courage of our warriors and these fine war machines.' She flung her arms wide in a dramatic gesture and then turned to Jake and Gareth. 'I am honoured to be the first of all my people to thank you.'

'Don't mention it, my dear girl,' Gareth murmured, 'our pleasure, I assure you.' He refrained from asking if her father had remembered to bring the cash with him, but asked instead, 'Are your people waiting for us at the Wells?'

'My grandfather has come with my father and all my uncles. His personal guard is with him, and many hundreds of others of the Harari, together with their women and animals.'

'My God,' growled Jake. 'It sounds like a helluva reception committee.'

They camped that last night of the journey on the bank of the Awash under the spreading umbrella branches of a camelthorn tree, sitting late and talking in the ruddy flickering glow of the fire, secure within the square fort formed by the four hulking steel vehicles. At last the talk died away into a weary but friendly silence, and Vicky stood up.

'A short walk for me, and then bed.'

Sara stood with her. 'I'll come with you.'

Her fascination with and admiration for Vicky was increasingly apparent, and she followed her out of the laager like a faithful puppy.

Away from the camp, they squatted side by side in companionable fashion under a night sky splendid with star shot, and Sara told Vicky seriously,

'They both desire you greatly – Jake and Gareth.' Vicky laughed awkwardly again, once more discomposed by the girl's direct manner.

'Oh, come now.'

'Oh yes, when you come near them, they are like two dogs, all stiff and walking around each other as though they will sniff each other up the tail.' Sara giggled, and Vicky had to smile with her.

'Which one will you choose, Miss Camberwell?' Sara demanded.

'Lordy, do I have to?' Vicky was still smiling.

'Oh no,' Sara reassured her. 'You can make love with both of them. I would do so.'

'You would?' Vicky asked.

'Yes, I would. What other way can you tell which one you like best?'

'That's true.' Vicky was becoming breathless with suppressed laughter, but fascinated by this bit of logic. The idea had a certain appeal, she admitted to herself.

'I will make love with twenty men before I marry Gregorius. That way I will be sure I have missed nothing, and I will not regret it when I am old,' declared the girl.

'Why twenty, Sara?' Vicky tried to keep her voice as serious as the girl's. 'Why not twenty-three or twenty-six?'

'Oh no,' said Sara primly. 'I would not want people to think me a loose woman,' and Vicky could hold her laughter no longer.

'But you—' Sara returned to the immediate problem. 'Which of them will you try first?'

'You pick for me,' Vicky invited.

'It is difficult,' Sara admitted. 'One is very strong and has much warmth in his heart, the other is very beautiful and will have much skill.' She shook her head and sighed. 'It is very difficult. No, I cannot choose for you. I can only wish you much joy.'

The conversation had disturbed Vicky more than she realized, and although she was exhausted by the long hard-driven day, she could not sleep, but lay restlessly under a single blanket on the hard sun-warmed earth, considering the wicked and barely thinkable thoughts that the girl had sown in her mind. So it was that she was still awake when Sara rose from beside her and, silently as a wraith, crossed the laager to where Gregorius lay. The girl had discarded the robe and wore only the skin-tight velvet breeches, encrusted with silver embroidery. Her body was slim and polished as ebony in the light of the stars and the new moon. She had small high breasts and a narrow moulded waist. She stooped over Gregorius and instantly he rose, and hand in hand, carrying their blankets, the pair slipped out of the laager, leaving Vicky more disturbed than ever. She lay and listened to the night sounds of the desert. Once she thought she heard the soft cry of a human voice in the darkness, but it may have been only the plaintive yelp of a jackal. The two young Ethiopians had not returned by the time Vicky at last fell asleep.

T he radio message that Count Aldo Belli received from General De Bono on the seventh day after leaving Asmara caused him much pain and outrage.

'The man addresses me as an inferior,' he protested to his officers. He shook the yellow sheet from the message pad angrily before reading in a choked voice, '"I hereby directly order you".' He shook his head in mock disbelief. 'No "request", no "if you please", you notice.' He crumpled the message sheet and hurled it against the canvas wall of the headquarters tent and began pacing in a magisterial manner back and forth, with one hand on the butt of his pistol and the other on the handle of his dagger.

'It seems he does not understand my messages. It seems that I must explain my position in person.' He thought about this with burgeoning enthusiasm. The discomfort of the drive back to Asmara would be greatly reduced by the superb upholstery and suspension designed by Messrs Rolls and Royce, and would be more than adequately offset by the quasi-civilized amenities of the town. A marble bath, clean laundry, cool rooms with high ceilings and electric fans, the latest newspapers from Rome, the company of the dear and kind young hostesses at the casino – all this was suddenly immensely attractive. Furthermore, it would be an opportunity to supervise the curing and packaging of the hunting trophies he had so far accumulated. He was anxious that the lion skins were correctly handled and the numerous bullet holes were properly patched. The further prospect of

144

reminding the General of his background, upbringing and political expendability also had much appeal.

'Gino,' he bellowed abruptly, and the Sergeant dashed into the tent, automatically focusing his camera.

'Not now! Not now!' The Count waved the camera aside testily. 'We are going back to Asmara for conference with the General. Inform my driver accordingly.'

Twenty-four hours later, the Count returned from Asmara in a mood of bile and thunder. The interview with General De Bono had been one of the low points in the Count's entire life. He had not believed that the General was serious in his threat to remove him from his command and pack him off ignobly back to Rome – until the General had actually begun dictating the order to his smirking aide-de-camp, Captain Crespi.

The threat still hung over the Count's handsome curly head. He had just twelve hours to reach and secure the Wells of Chaldi – or a second-class cabin on the troopship *Garibaldi*, sailing five days later from Massawa for Napoli, had been reserved for him by the General.

Count Aldo Belli had sent a long and eloquent cable to Benito Mussolini, describing the General's atrocious behaviour, and had returned in high pique to his battalion – completely unaware that the General had anticipated his cable, intercepted it and quietly suppressed it.

Major Castelani did not take the order to advance seriously, expecting at any moment the counter-order to be given, so it was with a sense of disbelief and rising jubilation that he found himself actually aboard the leading truck, grinding the last dusty miles through rolling landscape towards the setting sun and the Wells of Chaldi.

The heavy rainfall precipitated by the bulk of the Ethiopian massif was shed from the high ground by millions of cascades and runnels, pouring down into the valleys and the lowlands. The greater bulk of this surface water found its devious way at last into the great drainage system of the Sud marshes and from there into the Nile River, flowing northwards into Egypt and the Mediterranean Sea.

A smaller portion of the water found its way into blind rivers like the Awash, or simply streamed down and sank without trace in the soft sandy soils of the savannah and desert.

One set of exceptional geological circumstances that altered this general rule was the impervious sheet of schist that stretched out from the foot of the mountains and ran in a shallow saucer below the red earth of the plain. Run-off water from the highlands was contained and channelled by this layer, and formed a long narrow underground reservoir stretching out like a finger from the base of the Sardi Gorge, sixty miles into the dry hot savannah.

Closer to the mountains, the water ran deep, hundreds of feet below the earth's surface, but farther out, the slope of the land combined with the raised lip of the schist layer forced the water up to within forty-five feet of the surface.

Thousands of years ago the area had been the grazing grounds of large concentrations of wild elephant. These indefatigable borers for water had detected the presence of this subterranean lake. With tusk and hoof they had dug down and reached the surface of the water. Hunters had long since exterminated the elephant herds, but their wells had been kept open by other animals, wild ass, oryx, camel, and, of course, by man who had annihilated the elephant.

Now the wells, a dozen or more in an area of two or three square miles, were deep excavations into the blood-red earth. The sides of the wells were tiered by narrow worn paths that wound down so steeply that sunlight seldom penetrated to the level of the water.

The water itself was highly mineralized, so that it had a milky green appearance and a rank metallic taste, but nevertheless it had supported vast quantities of life over the centuries. And the vegetation in the area, with its developed root systems, drew sustenance from the deep water and grew more densely and greenly than anywhere else on the dry bleak savannah.

Beyond the wells, in the direction of the mountains, was an area of confused broken ground, steep but shallow wadis and square hillocks so low as to be virtually only mounds of dense red laterite. Over the ages, the shepherds and hunters who frequented the wells had burrowed into the sides of ravine and hillock, so that they were now honeycombed with caves and tunnels.

It was as though nature had declared a peace upon the wells. Here man and animal came together in wary truce that was seldom violated. Amongst the grey-green thorn trees and dense scrub goat and camel grazed in company with gazelle and gerenuk, oryx and greater kudu.

In the hush of noon, the column of four armoured cars came in from the east, and the hum of their engines carried at distance to the multitude that awaited their arrival.

Jake led, as usual, followed by Vicky, then came Gregorius with Sara riding in the turret of his car and the white stallion trailing them on a long lead rein. In the rear rode Gareth. Suddenly Sara shrieked at such a high pitch that her voice carried over the engine noise and she pointed ahead to the low valley filled with green scrub and taller denser trees. Jake halted the column and climbed up into the turret.

Through his binoculars he studied the open forest, and then started as he discerned a horde of moving figures coming headlong on wings of fine pale dust.

147

'My God,' he muttered aloud. 'There must be hundreds of them,' and he felt a stab of uneasiness. They looked anything but friendly.

At that moment, he was distracted by the sound of galloping hooves close by, and Sara came dashing past him. She was mounted bareback on the white stallion, her robes streaming and fluttering in the sun-bright wind. She was shouting with almost hysterical excitement as she galloped to meet the oncoming riders and her behaviour reassured Jake a little. He signalled the column forward once again.

The first ranks came swiftly in dust clouds, on running camels and galloping shaggy horses. Fierce, dark-faced men in billowing robes of dirty white, and a motley of other colours. Urging forward their mounts with wild cries, brandishing the small round bronze and iron studded and bossed war shields, they came racing towards the column. As they approached, they split into two wings and tore headlong past the startled drivers in a solid wall of moving men and animals.

Most of the men were bearded, and here and there some warrior wore proudly a great fluffy headdress of lion mane proclaiming his valour to the world. The manes rippled and waved on the wind as the riders drove by, urging on their mounts with the high 'Looloo' ululations so characteristic of the Ethiopians.

The weapons they carried amazed Gareth, who as a professional dealer recognized twenty different types and makes, each one of them a collector's piece – from the long muzzle-loading Tower muskets with the fancy hammers over percussion caps, through a range of Martini Henry carbines, which fired a heavy lead bullet in a cloud of black powder smoke, to a wide selection of Mausers and Schneiders, Lee-Metfords, and obsolete models from half the arms-manufacturers of the world.

As the riders swept by, they fired these weapons into the air, long spurts of black powder against the evening sky, and the crackle of musketry blended with the fierce ululations of welcome.

After the first wave of riders came another of those on mules and donkeys – moving more slowly but making as much noise and immediately after them came a swarming mob of running, howling foot soldiers, mingled with whom were women and shrieking children, and dozens of yelping dogs, scrawny yellow curs with long whippy tails and ridges of standing hair running down their skeletal backbones.

As the first rank of riders turned, still loolooing and firing into the air, to complete the encirclement of the armoured column, they ran headlong into the following rabble and the entire congregation became a struggling mob of men and animals.

Jake saw a mother with a child under her arm go down under the hooves of a running camel, the child flying from her grip and rolling in the sandy earth. Then he was past, forging ahead through a narrow path in the sea of humanity.

Sara was keeping the path open, leading them in, riding just ahead of Jake's car, laying about her viciously with a long quirt of hippo hide to hold back the mob, while around her wheeled the wildly excited riders still firing their pieces into the air, and dozens of runners pressed in closely, trying to climb aboard the moving cars.

Gradually the press of bodies and animals built up, until at last, following Sara, they moved slowly through the open forest that surrounded the wells into one of the shallow but steeply sided wadis in the broken ground beyond.

Here any further forward movement became impossible. The wadi was choked solidly with humanity, even the steep earthen sides and the ledges above were crowded so closely that unfortunates, pushed by those behind, could no longer keep their position and came tumbling down the sheer sides on to the heads of those in the wadi below. The cries of protest were lost in the general hubbub.

From each of the turrets, the heads of the four drivers appeared timidly, like gophers peering out of their holes. They made helpless signs and expressions at each other, unable to communicate in the uproar.

Sara leaped from the back of the plunging stallion on to the sponson of Jake's car and began raining blows and kicks on those who were still attempting to climb aboard the vehicle. She was enjoying herself immensely, Jake realized, as he noticed the battle lust in her eyes and heard the crack of her whip and the yelps of her victims. He thought of trying to restrain her – and then discarded the idea as being highly dangerous. Instead, he looked about distractedly for some other means to subdue the boisterous welcome and noticed for the first time the entrances to numerous caves in the sides of the wadi.

From a number of these dark openings now poured a body of men, wearing a semblance of uniform – jodhpurs and baggy khaki tunics, their chests crossed with bandoliers of ammunition, putteed calves and bare feet, high turbans bound around their heads and Mauser rifles swinging heartily, the butts used as clubs. They were every bit as enthusiastic as Sara, but considerably more successful in their attempts to quieten the crowd.

'My grandfather's guards,' Sara explained to Jake, still panting and grinning happily from her recent exertions. 'I am sorry, Jake, but sometimes my people get excited.'

'Yeah,' said Jake. 'So I noticed.'

With gun butts rising and falling the guards cleared a space around the four laden vehicles, and the noise dropped in volume until it was equivalent to a medium-sized avalanche. The four drivers climbed warily down and came together in a defensive group in the small stretch of open ground before the caves. Vicky Camberwell placed herself strategically between Jake and Gareth and behind the lanky robed figure of Gregorius – and she felt even more secure when Sara slipped up beside her and took her hand.

'Please do not worry,' she whispered. 'We are all your friends.'

'You could have fooled me, honey.' Vicky smiled back at her, and squeezed the slim brown hand. At that moment a procession emerged from the caves, headed by four coal-black priests of the Coptic Christian Church in their gaudy robes, chanting in Amharic, swinging incense and carrying ornate, if crudely wrought bronze crosses.

Immediately after the priests followed a figure so tall and thin as to appear a caricature of the human shape. A long flowing shamma of yellow and red stripes hung loosely on the gaunt frame. There was the suggestion of legs as long and as thin as those of an ostrich beneath the skirts of the robe as he strode forward, and the man's dark head was completely bald of hair – no beard or eyebrows – just a round glistening pate.

His eyes were completely enclosed in a web of deep wrinkles and fleshy folds of old dried-out skin. The mouth was utterly toothless, so that the jaw seemed to be collapsible, folding the face in half like the bellows of a concertina. He gave an impression of vast age that was offset immediately by the youthful spring in his step and the twinkle in the black birdlike eyes, and yet Gareth realized that he could not be less than eighty years old.

Gregorius hurried forward and knelt briefly for the old man's blessing, while Sara whispered to the group.

'This is my grandfather, Ras Golam,' she explained. 'He speaks no English, but he is a great nobleman and a mighty warrior – the bravest in all Ethiopia.'

The Ras ran a lively eye over the group and selected Gareth Swales, resplendent in thorn-proof tweeds. He leapt forward and, before Gareth could avoid it, enfolded him in an embrace that was redolent of powerful native tobacco, woodsmoke, and other heady odours.

'How do you do?' shouted the Ras, his only words of English.

'My grandfather is a great lover of the English,' explained Gregorius, as Gareth struggled in the Ras's embrace. 'That is why all his sons and grandsons are sent to England.'

'He has a decoration which even makes him an English milord,' Sara told them proudly, and pointed to her grandfather's chest where nestled a star of gaudy enamel and shiny paste chips.

Noticing the gesture, the Ras released Gareth and invited them to admire the decoration, and, on his other breast, a rosette of tricolour silk in the centre of which was a framed miniature of the old Queen Victoria herself.

'Tremendous, old boy – absolutely tremendous,' Gareth agreed, as he re-adjusted the lapels of his jacket and smoothed back his hair.

'When he was a young man, my grandfather did a great service to the Queen – and that is why he is now an English milord,' Sara explained, and then she broke off to listen to her grandfather, and to translate. 'My grandfather welcomes you to Ethiopia, and says that he is proud to embrace such a distinguished English gentleman. He has heard from my father of your fame as a warrior, that you bear the great Queen's medal for courage—'

'Actually, it was Georgie Five's gong,' Gareth demurred modestly.

At that moment, the dignified figure of Lij Mikhael Sagud stepped from the entrance of the cave behind the Ras.

'My father recognizes only one English monarch, my dear Swales,' he explained quietly. 'It is useless to try and convince him that she has passed away.'

He shook hands with all three of them, with a quick word of welcome for Jake and Vicky before turning back to listen to the Ras again.

'My father asks if you have brought your medal – he wishes you to wear it when you and he ride into battle side by side against the enemy,' and Gareth's expression changed.

'Now hold on there, old fellow,' he protested. Gareth had no intention of riding into another battle in his life, but the moment had passed and the Ras was shouting orders to his guard.

In response, they clambered aboard the armoured cars and began unloading the wooden cases of weapons and ammunition which they stacked in the clearing before the caves, beating back the eager crowds that pressed forward.

Now the priests came forward to bless the cars and weapons of war, and Sara took the opportunity to pull Vicky away and lead her unobtrusively to one of the caves.

'My servants will bring you water to bathe,' she whispered. 'You must look beautiful for the feast. Perhaps we will decide which one it will be tonight.'

As night fell, so the entire following of Ras Golam gathered in the main wadi, those ranking highest or with most push managing to find seating in the large central cave while the others filled the valley with row upon row of seated and robed figures. The whole scene was lit by leaping bonfires.

The fires reflected against the night sky with a faint orange glow which Major Luigi Castelani noticed at a distance of twenty kilometres from the Wells.

He halted the column and climbed up on the roof of the leading truck to study this phenomenon, uncertain at first if the light of the fires was some freak afterglow of the sunset, but soon realizing that this was not the case.

He jumped down and snapped at the driver, 'Wait for me,' before striding rapidly back along the long column of tall canvas-covered trucks to where the command car stood at the centre.

'My Colonel.' Castelani saluted the sulking figure of the Count who slumped on the rear seat of the Rolls with one hand thrust into the front of his unbuttoned tunic, much like the defeated Napoleon returning from Moscow. Aldo Belli had not yet recovered from the shock to his pride and self-esteem inflicted by the General. He had temporarily withdrawn from the vulgar world, and he did not even look up as Castelani made his report.

'Do what you think correct in the circumstances,' he muttered without interest. 'Only make certain we have control of the Wells before dawn,' and the Count turned his head away, wondering if Mussolini had yet received his cable.

What Castelani thought correct in the circumstances was to darken the column immediately and put his entire battalion in a state of instant readiness. No lights were to be shown in any circumstances, and a rigorous silence was imposed. The column now advanced at little more than a walking speed, with each driver personally warned that engine noise was not to exceed idling volume. All the men had been alerted and rode now in silence with loaded weapons and tense nerves.

When at last the Eritrean guides pointed out to Castelani the shallow forested valley below them, there was sufficient light from the sliver of silver moon overhead for Castelani to survey the ground with the eye of an old professional. Within ten minutes, he had planned his dispositions, decided where to hold his motor pool and main bivouac, where to site his machine guns, place his mortars and lay his rifle trenches. The Colonel grunted his agreement without even looking up, and quietly the Major gave the orders which would put into effect his plans and keep the battalion working all night.

'And the first man who drops a shovel or sneezes I will strangle with his own guts,' he warned, as he glanced apprehensively at the faint glow that emanated from amongst the low dark hills beyond the Wells.

In the main cave, the air was so thick and warm and moist that it lay upon the company like a wet woollen blanket. In the uneven light of the fires it was impossible to see from one end to the other of the cavernous room, with its rough earthen wall and columns. The restless body of guests and servants flitted through the smoky gloom like wraiths. Every once in a while there would be the terrified bellows of an ox from the wadi outside the main entrance of the cave. The bellows would cease abruptly as the blockman swung his long two-handled sword and the carcass fell with a thud that seemed to reverberate through the cavern. A vast shout of approval greeted the fall of the beast, and a dozen eager assistants flayed the hide, hacked the flesh into bloody strips and piled them on to huge platters of baked clay.

The servants staggered into the cave, bearing the laden platters of steaming, quivering meat. The guests fell upon it, men and women alike, snatching up the bleeding flesh, taking an end between their teeth, pulling it tight with one hand and hacking free a bite-sized piece with a knife grasped in the other. The flashing blade passed a mere fraction from the end of the diner's nose and warm blood trickled unheeded down the chin, as the lump was swallowed with a single convulsive heave of the throat.

Each mouthful was washed down into the belly with a swig of the fiery Ethiopian *tej* – a brew made from wild honey, a liquid the colour of golden amber, with the impact of a charging buffalo bull.

Gareth Swales sat between the old Ras and Lij Mikhael in the place of honour, while Jake and Vicky were a dozen places farther away amongst the lesser notables. In deference to the appetite and tastes of foreigners, they were offered, in place of raw beef, an endless succession of bubbling pots containing the fiery casseroles of beef, lamb, chicken and game that are known under the inclusive title of *wat*. These highly spiced, peppery but delicious concoctions were spooned out on to thin sheets of unleavened bread and rolled into a cigar shape before eating.

Lij Mikhael warned his guests against the *tej* – and instead offered Bollinger champagne, wrapped in wet sacking to lower its temperature. There was also pinch bottle Haig, London Dry Gin, and a vast array of liqueurs – Grand Marnier, yellow and green Chartreuse, Dom Benedictine, and the rest. These incongruous beverages in the desert reminded the guests that their host was wealthy beyond the normal concept of wealth, the lord of vast estates and, under the Emperor, the master of many thousands of human beings.

The Ras sat at the head of the feast, with a war bonnet of lion's mane covering his bald pate. It made a startling, but rather moth-eaten wig – for it was forty years since the Ras had slain the lion, and the ravages of time were apparent.

Now the Ras cackled with laughter as he rolled a sheet

of the unleavened bread, filled with steaming *wat*, into the shape and size of a Havana cigar – and thrust it, dripping juice, into Gareth Swales's unprepared mouth.

'You must swallow it without using your hands,' Lij Mikhael explained hastily. 'It is a game my father enjoys.'

Gareth's eyes bulged, his face turned crimson with lack of air and the bite of chilli sauce. Gulping and gasping and chewing manfully, he struggled to ingest the huge offering.

The Ras hooted merrily, drooling a little saliva from the toothless mouth, his entire face a network of moving wrinkles as he encouraged Gareth with cries of 'How do you do? How do you do?'

At last with his dignity in shreds, red-faced, sweating and panting laboriously, the roll of bread disappeared down Gareth's straining throat. The Ras folded him once more in that brotherly embrace, and Lij Mikhael poured another goblet full of Bollinger for him.

However, Gareth, who did not enjoy being the butt of anyone's joke, freed himself from the Ras, pushed the glass aside and waved one of the servants to him. From the reeking bloody platter he selected a strip of raw beef almost as thick as his wrist and as long as his forearm. Without warning, he thrust one end of it into the Ras's gaping toothless mouth.

'Suck on that, you old bastard,' he shouted, and the Ras stared at him with startled rheumy bloodshot eyes. Then, although he was unable to smile because of the long red strip that hung from his lips like some huge swollen tongue, the Ras's eyes turned to slits in a mask of happy wrinkles. His jaw seemed to unhinge like a python swallowing a goat. He gulped and an inch of the meat shot into his mouth, he gulped again and another inch disappeared. Gareth stared at him as gulp succeeded gulp and swiftly the morsel dwindled in size. Within seconds the Ras's mouth was empty, and he snatched up a bowl of *tej* and drank half a pint of the heady liquor, wiped blood and *tej* from his chin with the skirt of his shamma, belched like an air-locked geyser, then with a falsetto cackle of merriment hit Gareth a resounding crack between the shoulder blades. In the Ras's view, they were now comrades of the soul – both English aristocrats, renowned warriors, and each had eaten from the other's hand.

Gregorius Maryam had anticipated exactly what his grandfather's reaction to his white guests would be. He knew that Gareth's nationality and undoubted aristocratic background would overshadow all else in the Ras's estimation. However, the young prince's feelings for Jake Barton had become close to adulation – and he did not intend that his hero should be ignored. He chose the one subject which he knew would engage his grandfather's full attention. He slipped unnoticed from the din of the overcrowded cave, and when he returned, he carried Jake's stiff crackling lion skin that had by now completely dried out in the hot, dry desert wind.

Although he held it high above his head, the tail brushed the ground on one side and the nose on the other. The Ras, one arm still around Gareth's shoulder, looked up with interest and fired a string of questions at his grandson, as the boy spread the huge tawny skin before him.

The replies made the old man so excited that he leaped to his feet and grabbed his grandson by one arm, shaking him agitatedly as he demanded details – and Gregorius replied with as much animation, his eyes shining as he mimed the charge of the lion, and the act of hurling the bottle and the crushing of its skull.

Comparative silence had fallen over the smoky, dimlit cavern, and hundreds of guests craned forward to hear the details of the hunt. In that silence, the Ras walked down to where Jake sat. Stepping, without looking, into various bowls of food and kicking over a jug of *tej*, he reached the big curly-headed American and lifted him to his feet.

'How do you do?' he asked, with great emotion, tears of admiration in his eyes for the man who could kill a lion with his bare hands. Forty years before, the Ras had broken four broad-bladed spears before he had put a blade in the heart of his own lion.

'Never better, friend,' Jake grunted, clumsy with embarrassment, and the Ras embraced him fiercely before leading him back to the head of the board.

Irritably the Ras kicked one of his younger sons in the ribs, forcing him to vacate the seat on his right hand where he now placed Jake.

Jake looked across at Vicky and rolled his eyes helplessly as the Ras began to ladle steaming *wat* on to a huge white round of bread and roll it into a torpedo that would have daunted a battle cruiser. Jake took a deep breath and opened his mouth wide, as the Ras lifted the dainty morsel the way an executioner lifts his sword.

'How do you do?' he said, and with another hoot of glee thrust it in to the hilt.

The Colonel and all the officers of the Third Battalion were exhausted from long hours of forced march and, by the time they reached the Wells of Chaldi, were anxious only to see their tents erected and their cots made up – after that they were quite content that the Major be left to use his own initiative.

Castelani sited his twelve machine guns in the sides of the valley where they commanded a full arc of fire, and below them he placed his rifle trenches. The men sank the earthworks swiftly and with little noise in the loose sandy soil, and they buttressed their trenches and machine-gun nests with sandbags.

The mortar company he held well back, protected by both rifle trenches and machine-gun nests, from where they could drop their mortar bombs across the whole area of the wells with complete impunity.

While his men worked, Castelani personally paced out distances in front of his defences, and supervised the placing of the painted metal markers, so that his gunners would be able to fire over accurately ranged sights. Then he hurried back to chivvy along the ammunition parties who staggered up in the darkness, slipping in the sandy soil and cursing softly, but with feeling, under the burden of the heavy wooden cases.

All that night he was tireless, and any man who laid down his shovel for a few minutes of rest took the risk of being pounced upon by that looming figure, the stentorian voice restrained to a husky but ferocious whisper, and the rolling swagger tense with suppressed outrage.

At last, the squat machine guns with their thick water-jacketed barrels were lowered down into the new excavations and set up on their tripods. Only after Castelani had checked the traverse of each and sighted down through the high sliding rear-sight into the moonlit valley was he satisfied. The men flung themselves down to rest and the Major allowed the kitchen parties to come up with canteens of hot soup and bags of hard black bread.

Gareth Swales felt bloated with food and slightly bleary with the large quantities of lukewarm champagne which Lij Mikhael had pressed upon him.

On one side, the Ras and Jake had established a rapport that overcame the language barrier. The Ras had convinced himself that as Americans spoke English they were English, and that Jake as a lion-killer was clearly a member of the upper stratum of society – in short a kind of honorary aristocrat. Every time the Ras drained another pint of *tej*, Jake became more socially acceptable – and the Ras had drained many pints of *tej* by this stage.

The atmosphere was indeed so jovial and aflame with bonhomie and camaraderie that Gareth felt emboldened to ask, on behalf of the partnership, the question that had been burning his tongue for the last many hours.

'Toffee, old lad, have you got the money ready for us?'

The Prince seemed not to have heard, but refilled Gareth's glass with champagne, and leaned across to translate one of Jake's remarks for his father, and Gareth had to take his arm firmly.

'If it's all right by you, we'll take our wages and trouble you no more. Ride off into the sunset with violins playing, and all that rot.'

'I'm glad you raised the point.' Toffee nodded thoughtfully, looking anything but glad. 'There are some things we have to discuss.'

'Listen, Toffee old son, there is absolutely nothing to discuss. All the discussing was done long ago.'

'Now, don't upset yourself, my dear fellow.' It was, however, in Gareth's nature to become very agitated when someone who owed him money wanted to discuss things. The usual subject of discussion was how to avoid making payment, and Gareth was about to protest volubly and loudly when the Ras chose that moment to rise to his feet and make a speech.

This caused a certain amount of consternation, for the Ras's legs had been turned by large quantities of *tej* to the consistency of rubber, and it required the efforts of two of his guardsmen to get him to his feet and keep him there.

However, once up, he spoke with clarity and force while Lij Mikhael translated for the benefit of the white guests.

At first, the Ras seemed to wander. He spoke of the first rays of the sun touching the peaks of the mountains, and the feel of the desert wind in a man's face at noon, he reminded them of the sound of the birth cry of a man's first-born child and the smell of the earth turning under the plough. Gradually an attentive silence fell upon his unruly audience, for the old man had still a power and force that demanded complete respect.

As he went on, so a greater dignity invested him; he shrugged off the supporting hands of his guard and seemed to grow in stature. His voice lost the querulous tremor of age and took on a more compelling ring. Jake did not need the Prince's translation to know that he was speaking of man's pride, and the rights of a free man. The duty of a man to defend that freedom with life itself, to preserve it for his sons and their children.

'And now there comes a powerful enemy to challenge our rights as free men. An enemy so powerful, armed with such terrible weapons, that even the hearts of the warriors of Tigre and Shoa shrivelled in their breasts like diseased fruit.'

The old Ras was panting now, and a scanty sweat trickled from under the tall lion headdress and ran down the wrinkled black cheeks.

'But now, my children, powerful friends have come to stand beside us. They have brought to us weapons as powerful as those of our enemies. No longer must we fear.'

Jake realized suddenly what pathetic store the Ras had placed in the worn and obsolete war materials they had brought him. He talked now of meeting the mighty armies of Italy on even terms.

Abruptly, Jake felt a choking sense of guilt. He knew that a week after he left, the four armoured cars would be piles of junk. There was no man in all the Ras's following who could keep their elderly and temperamental engines running.

Even if they were brought into action before the engines expired, they would present a threat only to unsupported infantry. The moment they engaged with Italian armour they would be instantly and hopelessly out-classed. Even the light Italian CV.3 tanks would be immune to the fire of the Vickers guns that the cars mounted, while in return the thin steel of the cars would offer no protection from the 50 mm armour-piercing shell that the enemy fired. There would be no one to explain all this to the Ras and teach him how to achieve the best from the puny weapons he commanded.

Jake visualized the first and probably the last battle that Ras Golam would fight. Scorning manoeuvre and strategy, he would certainly throw in all his force – armoured cars, Vickers machine guns, obsolete rifles and swords – in a single frontal attack. This was the way he had fought all his battles – and the way he would fight the last.

Jake Barton felt his heart go out to the gallant ancient, who stood now shouting a challenge to a modern military power, prepared to defend to the death what was his – and Jake felt a curious sense of recklessness. It was a reaction that he knew well and usually it led him into positions of acute discomfort and danger.

'Forget it,' he told himself firmly. 'It's their war. Take the money and run.' Then suddenly he looked across the dimly lit cave to where Vicky Camberwell sat. She listened to the old Ras with misty eyes, and her expression was enchanted as she leaned her golden head close to the dark curly head of Sara Sagud, not wanting to miss a word of the translation.

Now she saw Jake watching her, and she smiled and nodded vehemently – almost as though she had read his doubts.

'Leave Vicky also?' Jake wondered. 'Leave them all and run with the gold?' He knew that nothing would induce Vicky to leave with them. For her the story was here, her involvement was complete, and she would stay to the end – the inevitable end.

The smart thing was to go, the dumb thing to stay and fight another man's war that was already lost before it had begun; the dumb thing was to stake twenty thousand dollars which was his share of the profits, and all his future plans, the Barton engine, and the factory to build it, against the remote chance of winning a lady who promised to be a lifetime of trouble once she was won.

'I never was a dab hand at doing the smart thing,' Jake thought ruefully, and smiled back at Vicky.

The Ras was suddenly silent, panting with the force of his feelings and the effort of voicing them. His listeners were mesmerized also, staring at the thin-robed figure with its wild lion wig.

The Ras made a commanding gesture and one of his guards handed him the broad two-handed sword, its blade long and naked. The Ras leaned his weight upon it and commanded again, and they carried in the war drums. The Ras's ceremonial drums, passed down to him by his father and his father before him, drums that had beaten at Magdala against Napier, at Adowa against the Italians and at a hundred other battles.

They were as tall as a man's shoulder, elaborately carved of hardwood and covered with rawhide, and the drummers took up their stance with the barrels of their drums held between their knees.

The drum with the deepest bass tone set the rhythm and the lesser drums joined in with the variations and counter-

164

points, a chorus that jarred a man's gut and loosened his brain in his skull.

The old Ras listened to it with his head bowed over the sword, until the rhythm took a hold on him and his shoulders began to jerk and his head came up. With a leap like a white bird taking flight, he landed in the open space before the drummers. The great sword whirled high above his head, and he began to dance.

Gareth took Mikhael Sagud by the sleeve and lifted his voice in competition with the drums, and resumed at the point where he had been interrupted.

'Toffee, you were telling me about the money.'

Jake heard him and leaned across to catch the Prince's reply, but the Prince was silent, watching his father leap and twirl in the intricate and acrobatic dance.

'We have delivered the goods, old chap. And a deal is a deal.'

'Fifteen thousand sovereigns,' said the Prince thoughtfully.

'That's the exact figure,' Gareth agreed.

'A dangerous sum of money,' murmured the Prince. 'Men have been killed for much less.' And they made no reply.

'I think of your safety, of course,' the Prince went on. 'Your safety, and my country's chances of survival. Without an engineer to maintain the cars, and a soldier to teach my men to use the new weapons – we will have wasted fifteen thousand sovereigns.'

'I feel very badly for you,' Gareth assured him. 'I'll eat my heart out for you while I am having dinner at the Cafe Royal, I really will – but truly, Toffee, you should have thought of this long ago.'

'Oh, I did – my dear Swales – I assure you I gave it much thought.' And the Prince turned to smile at Gareth. 'I thought that no one would be foolish enough to take on his person fifteen thousand gold sovereigns in the middle of Ethiopia and then try and get out of the country – without the Ras's personal approval and protection.'

They stared at him.

'Can you imagine the delight of the shifta, the mountain bandits, when they learned that such a rich prize was moving unprotected through their territory?'

'They would know, of course?' murmured Jake.

'I fear that they might be informed.' The Prince turned to him.

'And if we tried to go back the way we came?'

'Through the desert on foot?' the Prince smiled.

'We might use a little of the gold to buy camels,' Jake suggested.

'I fancy you might find camels hard to come by, and somebody might inform the Italians and the French of your movements – to say nothing of the Danakil tribesmen who would slit the throats of their own mothers for a single gold sovereign.'

They watched the Ras send the great sword humming six inches over the heads of the bass drummers, and then turn a grotesque flapping pirouette.

'God!' said Gareth. 'I took you at your word, Toffee. I mean word of honour, and old school—'

'My dear Swales, these are not the playing fields of Eton, I'm afraid.'

'Still, I never thought you'd welsh.'

'Oh, dear me, I am not welshing. You can have your money now – this very hour.'

'All right, Prince,' Jake interrupted. 'Tell us what more you want from us. Tell us, is there any way we get out of here with a safe conduct, and our money?'

The Prince smiled warmly at Jake, leaning to pat his arm. 'Always the pragmatist. No time wasted in tearing the hair or beating the breast, Mr Barton.'

'Shoot,' said Jake.

'My father and I would be very grateful if you would work for us for a six-month contract.'

'Why six months?' demanded Gareth.

'By then all will be lost, or won.'

'Go on,' Jake invited.

'For six months you will exercise your skills for us – and teach us how best to defend ourselves against a modern army. Service, maintain and command the armoured cars.'

'In return?' Jake asked.

'A princely salary for the six months, a safe conduct out of Ethiopia, and your money guaranteed by a London bank at the end of that time.'

'What is fair wages for putting one's head on the butcher's block?' Gareth asked bitterly.

'Double – another seven thousand pounds each,' said the Prince without hesitation, and the men on each side of him relaxed slightly and exchanged glances.

'Each?' asked Gareth.

'Each,' agreed Lij Mikhael.

'I only wish I had my lawyer here to draw up the contract,' said Gareth.

'Not necessary,' Mikhael laughed, and shook his head and drew two envelopes from his robes. He handed one to each of them.

'Bank-guaranteed cheques. Lloyds of London. Irrevocable, I assure you – but post-dated six months ahead. Valid on the first of February next year.'

The two white men examined the documents curiously. Carefully Jake checked the date on the bank draft – 1st February, 1936 – and then read the figure – fourteen thousand pounds sterling only – and he grinned.

'The exact amount – the precise date.' He shook his head admiringly. 'You had it all figured out. Man, you were thinking weeks ahead of us.'

167

'Good God, Toffee,' Gareth intoned mournfully. 'I must say I am appalled. Utterly appalled.'

'Does that mean you refuse, Major Swales?'

Gareth glanced at Jake, and a flash of agreement passed between them. Gareth sighed theatrically. 'Well, I must say that I did have an appointment in Madrid. They've got themselves this little war they are working on, but—' and here he studied the bank draft again, 'but one war is very much like another. Furthermore, you have given me some fairly powerful reasons why I should stay on.' Gareth withdrew the wallet from his inside pocket and folded the draft into it. 'However, that doesn't alter the fact that I am utterly appalled by the way this whole business has been conducted.'

'And you, Mr Barton?' Lij Mikhael asked.

'As my partner has just remarked — fourteen thousand pounds isn't exactly peanuts. Yes, I accept.'

The Prince nodded, and then his expression changed, became bleak and savage.

'I must urge you most cogently not to attempt to leave Ethiopia before the expiry of our agreement — justice is crude but effective under my father's administration.'

At that moment the gentleman under discussion lifted the sword high above his head and then drove the point deep into the earth between his feet. He left it there, the blade shivering and gleaming in the firelight, and staggered wheezing and cackling to his place between Jake and Gareth.

He flung a skinny old arm around each of them and greeted them with a hug and an affectionate cry of 'How do you do?', and Gareth cocked a speculative eye at him.

'How would you like to learn to play gin rummy, old son?' he asked kindly. Six months was a lot of time to while away and there might yet be further profit in the situation, he thought.

The sound of the drums woke Count Aldo Belli from a deep, untroubled sleep. He lay and listened to them for a while, to the deep monotonous rhythm like the pulse of the earth itself, and the effect was lulling and hypnotic. Then suddenly the Count came fully awake and the adrenalin poured hotly into his bloodstream. A month before leaving Rome he had attended a screening of the latest Hollywood release, *Trader Horn*, an African epic of wild animals and bloodthirsty tribesmen. The sound of tribal drums had been skilfully used on the sound track to heighten the sense of menace and suspense, and the Count now realized that out there in the night the same terrible drums were beating.

He came out of his bed in a single bound with a roar that woke those in the camp who were still asleep. When Gino rushed into the tent, he found his master standing stark-naked and wild-eyed in the centre of his tent with the ivory-handled Beretta in one hand and the jewelled dagger clutched in the other.

The instant the drums began beating, Luigi Castelani hurried back to the bivouac, for he knew exactly what reaction to expect from his Colonel. He arrived to find that the Count was fully uniformed, had selected a bodyguard of fifty men and was on the point of embarking in the waiting Rolls. The engine was running and the driver was as eager to leave as his august passenger.

The Count was not at all pleased to see the bulky figure of his Major come hurrying out of the darkness with that unmistakable swaggering gait. He had hoped to get clear before Castelani could intervene, and now he immediately went on the offensive.

'Major, I am returning to Asmara to report in person to the General,' shouted Aldo Belli, and tried to reach the Rolls, but the Major was too nimble for him and interposed his bulk and saluted.

'My Colonel, the defences of the wells are now complete,' he reported. 'The area is secure.'

'I shall report that we are being attacked in overwhelming force,' cried the Count, and tried to duck around Castelani's right side, but the Major anticipated the move and jumped sideways to keep belly to belly.

'The men are dug in, and in good spirits.'

'You have my permission to withdraw in good order under the enemy's bloodthirsty assault.' The Count attempted to lull the man with the prospect of escape, and then lunged to the left to reach the Rolls – but the Major was swift as a mamba, and again they faced each other. The entire officer corps of the Third Battalion, hastily dressed and alarmed by the drums in the night, had assembled to watch this exhibition of agility as the Count and Castelani jumped backwards and forwards like a pair of game cocks sparring at each other. Their sentiments were heavily on the side of their Colonel, and they would have enjoyed nothing more than the spectacle of the retreating Rolls. They would then have been free to follow in haste.

'I do not believe the enemy is present in any force.' Castelani's voice was raised to a level where the Count's protests were completely drowned. 'However, it is essential that the Colonel takes command in person. If there is to be a confrontation, it will involve a value judgement.' The Major pressed forward a step at a time, until his chest was an inch from the Colonel's and their noses almost touched. 'We are not formally at war. Your presence is essential to reinforce our position.'

The Colonel was pressed to the point where he had no choice but to fall back a pace, and the watching officers sighed sadly. It was an act of capitulation. The contest of wills was over – and although the Count continued to protest weakly, the Major worked him away from the Rolls the way a good sheep dog handles its flock.

'It will be dawn in an hour,' said Castelani, 'and as soon as it is light, we shall be in a position to evaluate the situation.'

At that moment the drums fell silent. Up the valley in the caves, the Ras had at last finished his dance of defiance, and to the Count the silence was cheering. He threw one last wistful look at the Rolls, and then let his gaze wander to the fifty heavily armed men of his bodyguard – and took a little more heart.

He squared his shoulders and drew himself erect, throwing back his head.

'Major,' he snapped. 'The battalion will stand firm.' He turned to his watching officers, all of whom tried to fade into insignificance and avoid his eyes. 'Major Vito, take command of this detachment and move forward to clear the ground. The rest of you fall in around me.'

The Colonel gave the Major and his fifty stalwarts a respectable lead, so that they might draw any hostile fire, and then, surrounded by a protective screen of his reluctant juniors and prodded forward by Luigi Castelani, he moved cautiously along the dusty path that wound down the slope of the valley to where the battalion's forward elements had been so expertly entrenched.

The most junior of Ras Golam's multitudinous grooms was fifteen years of age. The previous day one of the Ras's favourite mares in his care had snapped her halter rope while he was taking her down to the water. She had galloped out into the desert, and the boy had followed her for the whole of that day and half of the night, until the capricious creature had allowed him to come up with her and grasp the trailing end of the rope.

Exhausted by the long chase and chilled by the cold

night wind, the boy had huddled down on her neck and allowed the mare to pick her own way back to the water holes. He was half asleep, clinging by instinct alone to the mare's mane, when a short while before dawn she wandered into the perimeter of the Italian base.

A nervous sentry had challenged loudly, and the startled animal had plunged into a full run through the outskirts of the camp. Now, fully awake, the boy had clung to the galloping horse, and seen the lines of parked trucks and military tents looming out of the darkness. He had seen the stacked rifles, and recognized the shape of the helmet of another sentry who had challenged again as they passed through the outer lines.

Peering back under his own arm he had seen the flash of the rifle shot and heard the crack of the bullet pass his bowed head, and he urged the horse on with heels and knees.

By the time the groom reached the deep wadi, the Ras's following was at last succumbing to the effects of a full night's festivities. Many of them had drifted away to find a place to sleep, others had merely huddled down in their robes and slept where they had eaten. Only the hardened few still ate and drank, argued and sang, or sat in *tej*-numbed silence about the fires – watching the womenfolk begin to prepare the morning meal.

The boy flung himself off the mare at the entrance to the caves, ducked under the arms of the sentries who would have restrained him and ran into the crowded, smoky and dimly lit interior. He was gabbling with fright and import-ance, the words tumbling over each other and making no sense – until Lij Mikhael caught him by the upper arms and shook him to restore his senses.

Then the story he told made sense, and rang with urgent conviction. Those within earshot shouted it to those further back, and within seconds the story, distorted and garbled,

172

had flashed through the gathering and was running wildly through the whole encampment.

The sleepers awakened, every man armed and every woman and child curious and voluble. They streamed out of the caves and from the rough tents and shelters in the narrow ravines. Without command, moving like a shoal of fish without a leader but with a single purpose, laughing sceptically or shouting speculation and comment and query, brandishing shields and ancient firearms, the women clutching their infants, and the older children dancing around them or darting ahead, the shapeless mob streamed out of the broken ground and down into the saucer-shaped valley of the wells.

In the caves, Lij Mikhael was still explaining the boy's story to the foreigners, and arguing the details and implications with them and his father. It was Jake Barton who realized the danger.

'If the Italians have sent in a unit to grab the wells, then it's a calculated act of war. They'll be looking for trouble, Prince. You'd best forbid any of your men to go down there, until we have sized up the situation properly.'

It was too late, far too late. In the first faint glimmer of dawn, when the light plays weird tricks on a man's eyes, the Italian sentries peering over their parapets saw a wall of humanity swarming out of the dark and broken ground, and heard the rising hubbub of hundreds of excited voices.

When the drumming had begun, many of the blackshirts were huddled below the firing step of their trenches, swaddled in their greatcoats and sleeping the exhausted sleep of men who had travelled all the previous day, and worked all the night.

The non-commissioned officers kicked and pulled them to their feet, and shoved them to their positions along the parapet. From here they peered, befuddled with sleep, down into the valley.

173

With the exception of Luigi Castelani, not a single man in the Third Battalion had ever faced an armed enemy, and now after an infinity of nerve-tearing waiting, at last the experience was upon them in the dark before the dawn when a man's vitality is at its lowest ebb. Their bodies were chilled and their brains unclear. In the uncertain light, the mob that poured into the valley was as numerous as the sands of the desert, each figure as large as a giant and as ferocious as a marauding lion.

It was in this moment that Colonel Aldo Belli, panting with exertion and nervous strain, stepped out of the narrow communication trench on to the firing platform of the forward line of emplacements. The Sergeant in command of the trench recognized him instantly and let out a cry of relief.

'My Colonel, thank God you have come.' And forgetful of rank and position he seized the Count's arm. Aldo Belli was so busy trying to fight off the man's sweaty and importunate clutches that it was some seconds before he actually glanced down into the darkened valley – then his bowels turned to jelly and his legs seemed to buckle under him.

'Merciful Mother of God,' he wailed. 'All is lost. They are upon us.' With clumsy fingers he unbuckled the flap of his holster and as he fell to his knees he drew the pistol. 'Fire!' he screamed. 'Open fire!' And crouching down well below the level of the parapet, he emptied the Beretta straight upwards into the dawn sky.

Manning the Italian parapets were over four hundred combatants; of these over three hundred and fifty were riflemen, armed with magazine-loaded bolt-action weapons, while another sixty men in teams of five serviced the cunningly placed machine guns.

Every man of this force had endured grinding nervous

174

strain, listening to the war drums and now confronted by a sweeping mob of threatening figures. They crouched like dark statues behind their weapons, fingers curled stiffly around the triggers, and squinted over the open sights of rifle and machine gun.

The Count's shriek of command and the crackle of the pistol shots were all that was necessary to snap the paralysing bonds of fear that held them. The firing was started around Aldo Belli's position, by men close enough to hear his command. A long line of muzzle flashes bloomed and twinkled along the forward slope of the valley, and three machine guns opened with them. The tearing sound of their long traversing bursts drowned out the crackle of musketry and their tracer flickered and flew in long white arcs out across the valley to bury itself in the dark moving blot of humanity.

Taken in the flank, the mob broke and surged away towards the dark silence of the far slope of the valley, away from the sheets of bright white tracer and the red rows of rifle fire. Leaving their dead and wounded scattered behind them, they spread like spilled oil across the valley floor.

The silent gunners on the far slope saw them coming, held their fire for a few more confused panic-soured moments, and then, seeing themselves threatened, they opened also. The delay had the effect of allowing the survivors of the first volley to race deeply into the fields of overlapping fire that Castelani had so cleverly planned.

Caught in the open ground, hemmed in by a murderous storm of fire, the forward movement of the mob broke down, and they milled aimlessly, the women shrieking and clutching at their children, the children darting and doubling like a shoal of fish trapped in a tidal pool, some of the warriors kneeling in the open and beginning at last to return fire. The red flashes of the black powder were long and dull and smoky and ineffectual against men in entrenched positions; they served only to intensify the ferocity of the Italian attack.

Now the surge of uncontrolled, panic-stricken humanity slowed and eventually ceased. The unarmed women who still survived gathered their children and covered them with their robes, crouching down over them as a mother hen does with her chicks, and the men crouched also, firing blindly and wildly up the slopes of the valley at the muzzle flashes that were fading now as the sun rose and the light strengthened.

Twelve machine guns, each firing almost seven hundred rounds a minute, and three hundred and fifty rifles poured a sheet of bullets down into the valley. Minute after minute the firing continued, and slowly the light strengthened, unmercifully exposing the survivors in the valley below.

The mood of the attackers changed. From panicky, nervously strung out green militia, they were transformed. The almost drunken elation of victorious attackers gripped them, they were laughing triumphantly now as they served the guns. Their eyes bright with the blood lust of the predator, the knowledge that they could kill without retribution made them bold and cruel.

The miserable popping and flashing of ancient muskets in the valley below them was so feeble, so lacking in menace, that not a man amongst them was still afraid. Even Count Aldo Belli was now on his feet, brandishing his pistol and shouting with a high, girlish hysteria.

'Death to the enemy! Fire! Keep firing!' and cautiously he lifted his head another inch above the parapet. 'Kill them! Ours is the victory!'

The valley floor, as the first rays of sunlight touched it, was covered with thick swathes of the dead and maimed. They lay scattered singly, piled in clumps like mounds of old clothing in a flea market, thrown haphazardly on the pale sandy earth or arranged in neat patterns like fish on the slab.

In the centre of the killing-ground, there was still life and movement. Here and there a figure might leap up and run with robes flapping, and immediately the machine guns would follow it, quick stabbing spouts of dust closing swiftly until they met and held on the running figure, when it would collapse and roll on the sandy earth.

The warriors who still crouched over their ancient rifles, with their dark faces lifted to the slopes, were now providing good practice for the riflemen above them. The Italian officers' voices, high-pitched and excited, called down fire upon them, and swiftly each of these defiants was hit by carefully aimed fire and fell, some of them kicking and twitching.

The firing had lasted almost twenty minutes now, and there were few targets still on offer. The machine guns traversed expectantly, firing short bursts into the heaped carcasses, shattering already mutilated flesh, or tore clouds of dust and flying shale from the rounded lips of the deep water holes, from the cover of which a sporadic fire still popped and crackled.

'My Colonel.' Castelani touched Aldo Belli's arm to gain his attention, and at last he turned wild-eyed and elated to his Major.

'Ha, Castelani, what a victory – what a great victory, hey? They will not doubt our valour now.'

'Colonel, shall I order the cease fire?' and the Count seemed not to hear him.

'They will know now what kind of soldier I am. This brilliant victory will win for me a place in the halls—'

'Colonel! Colonel! We must cease fire now. This is a slaughter. Order the cease fire.'

Aldo Belli stared at him, his face beginning to flush with outrage.

'You crazy fool,' he shouted. 'The battle must be decisive, crushing! We will not cease now – not until the victory is ours.' He was stuttering wildly and his hand shook as he pointed down into the bloody shambles of the valley.

'The enemy have taken cover in the water holes, they must be flushed out and destroyed. Mortars, Castelani, bomb them out.'

Aldo Belli did not want it to end. It was the most deeply satisfying experience of his life. If this was war, he knew at last why the sages and the poets had invested it with such glory. This was man's work, and Aldo Belli knew himself born to it.

'Do you question my orders?' he shrieked at Castelani. 'Do your duty, immediately.'

'Immediately,' Castelani repeated bitterly, and for a moment longer stared stonily into the Count's eyes before he turned away.

The first mortar bomb climbed high into the clear desert dawn, before arcing over and dropping vertically down into the valley. It burst on the lip of the nearest well. It kicked up a brief column of dust and smoke, and the shrapnel whinnied shrilly. The second bomb fell squarely into the deep circular pit, bursting out of sight below ground level. Mud and smoke gushed upwards, and out of the water hole into the open ground crawled and staggered three scarecrow figures with their tattered and dirty robes fluttering like flags of truce.

Instantly the rifle fire and machine-gun fire burst over them, and the earth around them whipped by the bullets seemed to liquefy into a cascade of flying dust, into which they tumbled and at last lay still.

Aldo Belli let out a hoot of excitement. It was so easy and so deeply satisfying. 'The other holes, Castelani!' he screamed. 'Clean them out! All of them!'

Concentrating their fire on one hole at a time, the

mortars ranged in swiftly. Some of the holes were deserted, but at most of them the slaughter was continued. A few survivors of the shimmering bursts of shrapnel staggered out into the open to be cut down swiftly by the waiting machine guns.

The Count was by now so emboldened that he climbed up on the parapet, the better to view the field and watch the mortars fire on the remaining holes, and to direct his machine gunners.

The hole nearest the wadis and broken ground at the head of the valley was the next target, and the first bomb was over, crumping in a tall jump of dust and pale flame. Before the next bomb fell, a woman jumped up over the lip and tried to reach the mouth of the wadi. Behind her she dragged a child of two or three years, a naked toddler with fat little bow legs and a belly like a brown ball. He could not keep up with the mother and lost his footing, so she dragged him wailing along the sandy earth. Straddling her hip and clutched with desperate strength to her breast was another younger infant, also naked, also wailing and kicking frantically.

For several seconds, the running, heavily burdened woman drew no fire, and then a burst from a machine gun fell about her and a bullet struck and severed the arm by which she held the child. She staggered in a circle, shrieking dementedly and waving the stump of the arm like the spout of a garden hose. The next burst smashed through her chest, the same bullets shattering the body of the infant on her hip, and she fell and rolled like a rabbit hit by a shotgun. The guns fell silent again and remained silent while the naked toddler stood up uncertainly.

He began to wail again, standing solidly at last on the fat dimpled legs, a string of blue beads around the tightly bulging belly and his penis sticking out like a tiny brown finger.

From the mouth of the wadi emerged a running horse, a raw-boned and rangy white stallion galloping heavily over the sandy ground with a frail boyish figure lying low along its neck, a black shamma flying out wildly behind. The rider drove the stallion on towards where the child stood weeping, and had almost covered the open ground before the gunners realized what was happening.

The first machine gun traversed on the galloping animal, but this lead-off was stiff and the bullets kicked dust slightly high and behind. Then the horse reached the child and the rider reined in sharply, sending it rearing on its hind quarters, and the rider swung down to make the pick-up.

At that moment, two other machine guns opened up on the stationary target.

Jake Barton realized that there was only one way to prevent a confrontation between the Italian force which had appeared so silently and menacingly at the wells and the undisciplined mob of warriors and camp followers of the Ras's entourage.

There was no chance that he could make himself heard in the hubbub of anxiously raised voices and emotional outbursts of Amharic as the Ras tried to make his view heard above the attempts of fifty of his chieftains and captains to do exactly the same thing.

Jake needed an interpreter and he thrust his way towards Gregorius Maryam, grabbed him firmly by the arm and dragged him out of the cave. It needed considerable force, for Gregorius was as intent as everybody else in having his views and suggestions aired.

Jake was surprised to find how light it was outside the caves, and that the night had passed so swiftly. Dawn was only minutes away, and the dry desert air was sweet and heady after the crowded cave with its smoking fires.

In the light of the camp fires and the pale sky, he saw the mob streaming away down the wadi towards the wells, as happily excited as the crowds at a fairground.

'Stop them, Greg,' he shouted. 'Come on, we've got to stop them,' and the two of them ran forward.

'What is it, Jake?'

'We've got to stop them running into the Eyetie camp.'

'Why?'

'If somebody starts shooting, there will be a massacre.'

'But we are not at war, Jake. They can't shoot.'

'Don't bet on it, buddy boy,' grunted Jake grimly, and his alarm was contagious. Side by side, they caught up with the straggling rear of the column and elbowed and kicked their way through it.

'Back, you bastards,' roared Jake. 'Get back, all of you,' and made the meaning clear with flying fists and feet.

With Gregorius beside him, Jake reached the narrow mouth of the wadi where it debouched into the saucer-shaped valley of the wells. Like the wall of a dam the two of them linked arms and managed to hold the flood of humanity there for a minute or so, but the pressure from those straining forward from the rear threatened to sweep them away, while the mood changed from high-spirited curiosity to angry resentment at this check upon their efforts to join the hundreds of their comrades who had already passed out of the wadi and were streaming out across the open valley.

At the moment when they were swept aside, the firing began out there upon the slopes of the valley and instantly the mob froze and their voices died away. There was no further forward movement, and Jake turned and scrambled up the steep side of the wadi for a better view out into the valley.

From there he watched the slaughter that turned the valley into a charnel house. He watched with a sick fascination that changed slowly, as minute after minute the guns continued their clamour. He felt it become anger and outrage that outweighed all else, so that he was hardly aware of the slim cold hand that sought his, and he glanced down only for an instant at Vicky's golden head at his shoulder, before turning his entire concentration back to the dreadful tragedy being played out before them.

Vaguely he was aware that Vicky was sobbing beside him, and that she had gripped his hand so tightly that the nails were driven deep into his palm. Yet even in his dreadful anger, Jake was studying the ground and marking the Italian positions. On his other hand, Gregorius Maryam was praying softly, his smooth young face turned to a muddy grey with horror and the words of the prayer forced between tight lips like the last breaths of a dying man.

'Oh God,' whispered Vicky in a tight, choked voice, as the mortar bombing began, dropping relentlessly into the depressions where the survivors huddled for shelter. 'Oh God, Jake, what can we do?'

But he did not answer and it went on and on. They were caught in the nightmare of it, powerless in the grip of this horror – watching the mortars continue the hunt, until the woman with her two infants burst out into the open not three hundred yards ahead of them.

'Oh God, oh please Jesus,' whispered Vicky. 'Please don't let it happen. Please make it stop now.'

The guns hunted the woman and they watched her die, and the child rise to its feet and stand lost and bewildered beside the mother's corpse. The thud of galloping hooves sounded in the wadi below them and Gregorius swung around and cried, 'Sara! No!' as the girl rode out, crouched low over the stallion's neck. She rode bare-backed, a tiny dark figure on the big white animal.

'Sara!' Gregorius cried again, and would have followed her, running out alone into that deadly plain, but Jake grabbed his arm and held him easily, though he struggled and cried out again in Amharic.

The girl rode on unscathed through the storm of fire, and Vicky's breathing stopped as she watched. It was impossible that Sara could reach the child and return. It was stupid, so stupid as to make her anger leap even higher – and yet there was something so moving about that frail beautiful child riding out to her death, that it filled Vicky with a sense of her own inadequacy, a sense of great humility – for even in this proud moment, she was aware that she was incapable of such sacrifice.

She watched the stallion rear, and the girl lean out to gather the small brown infant, saw the machine guns find their target at last, and the stallion whinnied and went down in a tangle of flailing hooves, pinning both the girl and the child, while the bullets continued to spurt dust and slap loudly against the still kicking body of the stallion.

Gregorius was still struggling and blabbering his horror, and Jake turned and struck him an open-handed blow across the face.

'Stop that!' Jake snarled, his own anger and outrage making him brutal. 'Anybody who goes out there is going to get his arse shot off.'

The blow seemed to steady Gregorius.

'We have got to get her, Jake. Please, Jake. Let me fetch her.'

'We'll do it my way,' snapped Jake. His face seemed carved from hard brown stone, but his eyes were ferocious and his jaws clamped closed with his anger. Roughly he shoved Gregorius ahead of him down into the wadi, and he dragged Vicky after him. She tried to resist, leaning back against his strength, her head turned towards the plain, and her reluctant feet sliding in the loose earth.

'Jake, what are you doing?' she protested, but he ignored her.

'We'll mount the guns. It won't take long.' He was planning through his rage, as he dragged them back along the wadi to where the cars were parked beyond the caves. Vicky and Gregorius were helpless in the ferocity of his grip, swept along by his strength and his anger.

'Vicky, you will drive for me. I'll serve the gun,' he told her. 'Greg, you drive for Gareth.'

Jake's breathing was shallow and fast with his rage. 'We can only man two cars, one we will use as a diversion – you and Gareth swing south along the back of the ridge and that will keep them busy while Vicky and I pick up Sara and as many of the others as we can find alive.'

The two of them listened to him, and were swept forward with a fresh urgency. As they ran back along the wadi, a final brief storm of machine-gun fire and exploding mortar bombs preceded the deep aching silence which now fell over the desert.

The three of them turned the final bend in the course of the wadi and came upon a scene of utter pandemonium. The ravine was filled solidly with those who had escaped the Italian fire struggling to load their possessions, their tents and bedding, their chickens and children, on to the panicky bellowing camels and the skittering braying mules and donkeys.

Already hundreds of riders were galloping away, climbing the sides of the wadi or disappearing into the labyrinth of broken ground. New widows wailed in the uproar and their grief was catching, the children shrieked and whimpered in sympathy, and over it all hung a blue miasma of smoke from the cooking fires and dust from the trampling hooves and milling feet.

The four cars stood in their solid orderly rank, aloof from the masses of humanity, gleaming in their coats of white paint with the vivid red crosses emblazoned upon their sides.

Jake pushed a way through for them, towering head and shoulders above the throng, and when they reached the nearest car Jake grasped Vicky about the waist and swung her easily up into the sponson. For a moment his expression softened.

'You don't have to come,' he said. 'I guess I went a little mad then, you don't have to drive – Gareth and I will take one car.'

Her face was deathly pale also, and there were deep bruised smears under her eyes from a night without sleep and the horrors of the slaughter. Her tears had dried, leaving dirty smears down her cheeks, but she shook her head fiercely.

'I'm coming,' she said. 'I'll drive for you.'

'Good girl,' said Jake. 'Help Gregorius top up. We will need full fuel tanks. I'll get the Vickers.' He turned away, shouting to Gregorius. 'We'll use Miss Wobbly and Tenastelin – Vicky will help you refuel.'

A detail from the Ras's personal bodyguard were already bringing the wooden cases of weapons and munitions out of the storage cave as Jake arrived. Each case was carried between four straining troopers to where the camels knelt. It was then lifted into the pannier on each side of the hump and hastily lashed down.

'Hey, you lot.' Jake came up with a group carrying a crated Vickers. 'Bring that along this way.' They paused in their labours, not understanding until Jake made unmistakable signs, but at that moment a captain of the guard hurried up to intervene. After one shouted exchange Jake realized that the language barrier was insurmountable. The man was obstinate and time was wasting.

'Sorry, friend,' he apologized. 'But I am in a bit of a hurry,' and he hit him a roundhouse clout that ended the

185

argument conclusively and sent the man flying backwards into the outstretched arms of two of his men.

'Come along.' Jake pushed the guards with the crate towards where the cars stood. The thought of Sara lying out there in the valley was driving him frantic. He imagined her bleeding slowly to death, her bright young blood draining away into the sandy soil – and he hustled the two men forward through the press of animals and human beings.

As he came up, Gregorius was swinging the crank handle on Miss Wobbly and the engine caught and ran smoothly as Vicky eased back the ignition.

'Where is Gareth?' Jake shouted.

'Can't find him,' answered Gregorius. 'We'll have to go in one car,' and then both of them swung round at the familiar bantering laugh. Gareth Swales was leaning nonchalantly against the side of the car, looking as unruffled and calm as ever, his hair neatly combed and the tweed suit as immaculate as if it had just come from his tailor.

'I say,' smiled Gareth, crinkling his eyes against the drift of blue smoke from the cheroot between his lips. 'Big Jake Barton and his two eager ducklings about to take on the entire Italian army.'

Vicky's head appeared in the driver's hatch.

'We've been looking for you,' she shouted furiously.

'Ah,' quoth Gareth lightly. 'We will now hear from the Girl Guides Association.'

'Sara is out there.' Gregorius ran to Gareth. 'We are going to fetch her. You and I will take the one car, Vicky and Jake the other.'

'Nobody is going anywhere.' Gareth shook his head, and Gregorius seized the lapels of his suit and shook them urgently. 'Sara. You don't understand – she's out there! We have to fetch her.'

'I say, old lad, would you mind unhanding me,' murmured

186

Gareth and removed Gregorius' hands from his lapel. 'Yes. We know about Sara, but—'

Vicky yelled from the driver's hatch. 'Leave, him, Gregorius. We don't need anyone who is afraid—' and Gareth straightened up abruptly, his expression grim and his eyes snapping.

'I have been called many things in my life, my dear young lady. Some of them justified, but nobody has ever called me a coward.'

'Well, there is always a first time, buster,' shouted Vicky, her face crimson with anger and streaked with dirt, her blonde hair ruffled and hanging into her eyes – and she pointed one quivering finger at Gareth, 'and for you this is that first time!'

They stared at each other for a moment longer before Lij Mikhael strode between them, his dark face set but commanding.

'Major Swales is acting on my express orders, Miss Camberwell. I have ordered that the cars and all my father's troops will fall back immediately.'

'Good God, man.' Vicky transferred her anger from Gareth to the Prince. 'That's your daughter lying out there.'

'Yes,' said the Prince softly. 'My daughter on the one hand – my country on the other. There is no doubt which I must choose.'

'You're not making sense,' Jake interposed roughly.

'I think I am.' The Prince turned to him and Jake saw the dark torment in the man's eyes. 'I cannot make a hostile move, it's what the Italians are seeking. An excuse to attack in full strength. We must turn the other cheek now, and use this atrocity to win world support.'

'But Sara,' Vicky interrupted. 'We could pick her up in a minute.'

'No.' The Prince lifted his chin. 'I cannot show the

enemy these new weapons of ours. They must remain hidden until the time is right to strike.'

'Sara,' cried Gregorius. 'What of Sara?'

'When these machines and the new guns are safely on their way back to the Sardi Gorge, I shall ride out myself to fetch her body,' said the Prince with a simple dignity. 'But until then my duty must come first.'

'One car,' pleaded Gregorius. 'For Sara's sake.'

'No, I cannot use even one car,' said the Prince.

'Well, I can,' snapped Vicky and her tousled golden head disappeared into the driver's hatch, the engine roared and Miss Wobbly shot forward scattering men and animals before her, and swung in a tight sliding right-hand turn towards the course of the wadi.

Unarmed and alone, Vicky Camberwell was going out to face the machine guns and the mortars, and only one man amongst them acted swiftly enough.

Jake shouldered the Prince aside and sprinted across the circle of the car's turn, coming alongside a moment before it plunged into the narrow ravine. He got a grip on one of the welded brackets abaft the engine cowling, and although his shoulder joint was almost wrenched from its socket, he swung himself up and fell belly down across the sponson.

Clinging grimly on to the leaping, jouncing vehicle, he dragged himself forward until he could peer down the driver's hatch.

'Are you crazy?' he bellowed, and Vicky looked up and gave him a fleeting but angelic grin.

'Yes. How about you?' A heavier impact came up through the chassis of the car and momentarily drove Jake's breath from him so he could not answer. Instead, he clawed his way up the side of the turret, almost losing four fingers as the loose hatch cover slammed closed at another leap of the car.

Using all his strength, Jake lifted it again, and secured

the retaining catch before he scrambled down into the cab. He was only just in time, for at that moment Vicky drove the car at full throttle out into the valley.

The sun was clear of the horizon now, smearing long dark shadows across the golden sands. Dust and smoke from the mortar barrage still drifted in a stately brown cloud over the ridge, and the bodies of the dead were thrown at random across the bare plain. The women's dresses made bright splashes of colour against the monochrome of the desert.

Jake swept a swift glance around the ridge that commanded the plain, and saw that many of the Italian troopers had left their trenches. They wandered in small groups around the edges of the slaughter ground, and their movements were awed and timid – green troops still not hardened to the reality of open wounds and twisted corpses.

They froze in attitudes of surprise as the car burst out of the wadi, and flew on dusty wings towards the nearest water-hole. It took many seconds for them to move, and then they turned and pelted for their earthworks, tiny figures in dark uniforms with legs and arms pumping in frantic haste.

'Turn broadside,' yelled Jake. 'Show them the crosses!' and Vicky reacted swiftly, swinging the car into a tight left-hander that had her up on two wheels, sliding broadside in the sand, displaying to the Italians the huge scarlet crosses on the hull.

'Let me have your shirt,' Jake yelled again. It was the only white cloth they had with them. 'I need a flag of truce!'

'It's all I have on,' Vicky shrieked back. 'I'm bare underneath.'

'You want to be modest and dead?' howled Jake. 'They'll start shooting any moment now.' And she steered with one hand as she unbuttoned her shirt front and leaned forward in the seat to yank the tails out of her skirt. She shrugged out of it and reached up into the turret to hand him the bundled shirt. Each time they hit another bump, Vicky's breasts bounced like rubber balls, a sight that distracted Jake for a hundredth part of a second before chivalry and duty recalled him and he stood high in the turret, arms stretched above his head, streaming the white shirt like a flag, balancing with a sailor's legs against the wild antics of the car.

To the hundreds of men who lined the parapet of the Italian trenches Jake displayed two emotive symbols, the red cross and the white flag, symbols so powerful that even men in the white-hot must of the blood lust hesitated with their fingers still curled about the triggers of the machine guns.

'It's working,' shrieked Vicky, and swung the car on to its original heading, almost throwing Jake from his precarious roost in the turret. He dropped the shirt and clutched wildly at the coamings of the turret, the shirt floating away like a white egret on the wing.

'There she is,' Vicky cried again. The carcass of the white stallion lay dead ahead, as she braked hard and then pulled the car to a standstill beside it, interposing the armoured body of the car between the pile of bodies and the watching Italians on the ridge.

Jake dropped down into the cab and crawled back to open the rear double doors of the car, knocking open the locking handles as he called over his shoulder.

'Keep your hatch battened and don't, for chrissakes, show your head.'

'I'll help you,' Vicky stated boldly.

'The hell you will,' snapped Jake, tearing his eyes off her magnificent chest. 'You'll stay where you are – and keep the engine running.'

The doors flew open and Jake tumbled headfirst out on to the sandy earth. Spitting grit from his mouth, he crawled swiftly to the carcass of the white horse. Close up, the hide was shaggy and flea-bitten, dappled with faint patches of chestnut. On this pale background the bullet holes were like dark red mouths where already the metallic blue flies clustered delightedly. The stallion lay heavily across Sara's lower body, pinning her face down to the earth.

The naked boy child had been hit by one of the hooves as the horse fell. The side of the tiny bald skull had been crushed, a deep indentation above the temple into which a baseball would have fitted neatly. There was no chance that he still lived and Jake transferred his attention to the girl.

'Sara,' he called, and she lifted herself on her elbows, looking back at him from huge terrified dark eyes. Her face was smeared with dust, the skin shaved from one cheek where she had slid against the ground, exposing the pale pink meat from which lymph leaked in clear liquid beads.

'Are you hit?' Jake reached her.

'I don't know,' she whispered huskily, and he saw that the satin of her breeches was soaked with dark blood. He placed both feet against the carcass of the horse and tried to roll it off her legs, but the dead weight of the animal was enormous. He would have to stand, taking his chances with the guns.

Jake came to his feet and felt the cold fingers of fear brush lightly along his spine as he turned his back to the nearest Italian trenches and stooped to the horse.

Crouching with his weight balanced evenly on the balls of both feet, he took the tail and the lower hind leg of the animal; lifting and turning with all his strength, he began to roll the carcass off Sara's legs and pelvis. She cried out in pain, such a sharp high-pitched shriek that he had to stop.

She was praying incoherently in Amharic, weeping slow fat tears of agony that cut runnels through the pale dust on her cheeks.

Jake panted, 'Once more – I'm sorry,' and he braced himself. At that moment Vicky yelled from the car.

'Jake, they are coming! Hurry, oh God, please hurry!'

Jake swung around and ran to the car, peering over the high engine compartment.

With a long plume of pale dust boiling out from behind it, a large open vehicle crowded with armed men was dropping swiftly down towards them from the ridge.

'My God,' grunted Jake, screwing up his eyes against the low blinding rays of the morning sun. 'It can't be!' But even at that range in the dust and bad light, there was no mistaking the gracious and dignified lines of a Rolls-Royce. Jake was seized by a feeling of unreality – that amid all this horror should appear something of such beauty.

'Hurry, Jake.' Vicky's voice spurred him on, and he ran back to the dead horse, seized its hind legs and began wrestling it on to its back with the girl's agonized cries as an accompaniment.

Grunting and straining, Jake lifted the horse by main strength until it was balanced critically along its spine with the legs pointed loosely at the morning sky, and now he could hear the approaching engine-beat of the Rolls and the faint but excited voices of its occupants. He denied the temptation to look around again and, instead, let the carcass flop heavily over on to its other flank, freeing the frail body of the child-woman beneath it.

Still panting with his efforts, Jake dropped on one knee beside her. She was hit in the upper leg, he saw at once, the entry wound was six inches above the knee, and when he felt swiftly for a bone-break, there was another quick flood of dark crimson blood that poured warmly over his fingers and drenched the slick satin of her breeches afresh. Jake found the exit wound in the inside of her thigh, but knew by feel and instinct that it had missed the bone. Still, she was losing blood heavily and he inserted a forefinger into the tear in her breeches and ripped the cloth cleanly to the ankle; he pulled it up exposing her long slim leg to the crutch. The wound was deep and blue in the darkly lustrous flesh, and Jake tore the flapping trouser-leg free and wound one quick turn of it around the thigh above the wound.

Using both arms and the strength of his shoulders he drew the crude tourniquet so tight that the flow of blood was instantly stemmed and he tied the ends of the bandage with two swift turns, and then looked up just as the Rolls-Royce skidded to a violent halt across the front of the armoured car.

There seemed to be a state of utter confusion amongst the occupants of the Rolls, and again Jake felt a sense of unreality. In the front seat, the driver gripped the steering-wheel in one hand and a rifle in the other with white knuckles and fingers that shook like those of a man in fever. His ashen face was shining with the sweat either of some terrible fever or some equally terrible terror. On the seat beside him crouched a small wiry figure with a rifle slung over one shoulder and with a brown wizened monkey face partly obscured by a square black Leica camera with an enormous bellows lens. In the back seat of the Rolls was a large powerfully built man, with a granite face and the level controlled manner of a man of action. A dangerous man, Jake recognized instantly, and he saw that he was a major. He held a rifle in one hand and with the other was trying to help to his feet a smaller, more handsome man in a splendid uniform of elegantly tailored black gaberdine adorned with silver badges and insignia.

On this officer's head, a brimless black helmet with a silver skull and crossbones rode at a jaunty angle, like a pirate in a Christmas pantomime, but the face below it was fixed in the same pale emotion as that of the driver. It became clear to Jake that the last thing this gallant wanted was to be helped to his feet. He was curled up in the corner of the seat in such a way as to offer the smallest possible target, and he slapped petulantly· at the Major's helping hand. Protesting shrilly and brandishing an expensively plated and engraved pistol, it was clear that his presence in the Rolls was by no means voluntary.

Jake stooped over the body of the girl and slipped one arm under her shoulders and the other beneath her knees, careful not to inflict further hurt. Jake stood up with her in his arms while she clung to him like a child.

This action caused the big stern-faced Major to turn all his attention on Jake, to level his rifle at him and call a peremptory order in Italian. It was clearly an order to stand where he was, and, looking into the muzzle of the rifle and into the pale expressionless eyes, Jake knew that the man would shoot without hesitation if he were not immediately obeyed. There was a deadliness, a quiet aura of menace about him that chilled Jake as he stood with the slim warm body in his arms, and he collected his senses and his words.

'I am American,' he said firmly. 'American doctor.' There was no recognition in the Major's expression, but he turned his head and glanced at the officer who stirred receptively, half-rose in his seat, then thought better of it. He sank back again, speaking carefully around the bulk of his Major.

'You are my prisoner,' he cried, his voice unsteady, but his English clear and unaccented. 'I place you in protective custody.'

'You are contravening the Geneva Convention.' Jake tried to make his tone indignant, as he sidled towards the invitingly open rear doors of the car.

'I must inspect your credentials.' The officer was recovering rapidly from his recent indisposition. Fresh colour flooded the classically handsome face, new interest flashed in the dark gazelle eyes, and the smooth baritone voice gained strength and a fine ringing timbre.

'I, Colonel Count Aldo Belli, command you to account to me.' His gaze switched to the huge steel body of the car.

'This is an armoured vehicle of war. You fly false colours, sir.'

As the Count spoke, he realized for the first time that neither the big curly-headed American nor the big old-fashioned vehicle which towered over them was armed. He could clearly see the empty gun-mounting in the turret – and his courage came flooding back. Now at last he leaped to his feet, throwing out his chest, one hand on his hip, the other aiming the pistol at Jake.

'You are my prisoner!' he declaimed once more, then from the corner of his mouth he growled at the front seat, 'Gino, quickly. A shot of me capturing the American.'

'At once, Excellency.' Gino was focusing the camera.

'I protest,' shouted Jake, and sidled another few paces towards the inviting rear doors of the car.

'Stay where you are,' snapped the Count and glanced at Gino. 'All right?' he asked.

'Tell the American to move a little to the right,' Gino replied, still peering into the view-finder.

'A little to the right!' commanded the Count in English, gesturing with the pistol, and Jake obeyed, for it brought him closer to his goal, but he was still shouting his protests.

'In the name of humanity – and the International Red Cross—'

'I shall radio Geneva today,' the Count shouted back, 'to enquire of your credentials.'

'Smile a little, Excellency,' said Gino.

The Count burst into a radiant smile and half-turned towards the camera.

'Then I shall have you shot!' he promised, still smiling.

'If you let this girl die,' yelled Jake, 'it will be the act of a barbarian.'

The smile vanished instantly and the Count scowled darkly. 'And your actions, sir, are those of a spy. Enough talk – surrender yourself.' He lifted the pistol threateningly and aimed at the centre of Jake's chest. Jake felt a chill of despair, as he saw the big Major reinforce the order by sliding the safety catch of his rifle to the 'fire' position and pointing it at Jake's belly.

At this critical moment, the driver's hatch of the armoured car flew open with a clang that startled them all – and Vicky Camberwell rose to view, her blonde hair awry and her cheeks burning with anger.

'I am an accredited member of the American Press Association,' she yelled as loudly as any of them. 'And I assure you that this outrage will be reported to the world in every detail. I warn you that—' There was much more in this vein, and Vicky's anger was such that she could not remain still, she jumped up and down and flung her arms about in wild gesticulations – for the moment completely oblivious of the fact that she was bared to the waist.

Her audience in the Rolls was under no such illusion. Every man of them was a member of a nation whose favourite pastime was the adoration and pursuit of beautiful women, and every one of them considered himself to be the national champion.

As Vicky's bounty wobbled and swung and bounced with agitation, the four Italians gaped half in disbelief and half in delight. The raised weapons sank and were forgotten. The Major attempted to rise to his feet in a gesture of chivalry, but was thrust firmly backwards by the Count. The driver's foot slipped off the clutch and the Rolls bucked violently and the engine stalled. Gino uttered an oath of approval, raised the camera, found the film was expended, swore again and opened the camera without taking his eyes off Vicky, dropped it from clumsy hands, and abandoned it, grinning beatifically at this blonde vision.

The Count began to raise his helmet, remembered he was now a warrior and with his other hand threw out a

Fascist salute, found he was still gripping the pistol and did not have enough hands, so he held his helmet and the pistol to his chest with one hand.

'Madam,' he said, dark eyes flashing, his voice taking on a romantic ring. 'My dear lady—'

At that moment, the Major tried again to rise and the Count shoved him back into the seat once more – while Vicky continued her tirade with no diminution in fervour.

Jake was completely forgotten by the Italians. He took four running steps and dived through the rear doors into the steel cab of the car. He rolled over and dropped Sara into the space for the ammunition bins behind the driver's seat, and in a continuation of the same movement he kicked the doors closed and turned the locking handle.

'Drive!' he shouted at Vicky, although only her backside was visible as she stood on the driver's seat. 'Come on!' and hauled her downwards so that she sat with a thud on the hard leather seat, still shouting abuse at the enemy. 'Drive!' Jake shouted louder still. 'Get us out of here!'

The shocked dismay of the four Italians, as Vicky disappeared abruptly from view like an inverted jack-in-a-box, lasted for many seconds and held them paralysed by disappointment.

Then the armoured car's engine roared and it bounded forward, straight at them; swinging broadside at the last moment, it hit the Rolls only a glancing blow, crumpling the front mudguard and shattering the glass headlamp, before it tore off in its own dust storm towards the broken ground beyond the wells.

Castelani was the first to act; he leaped to the ground and raced to reach the crank handle, shouting at the driver to start the engine. It fired at the first kick and the Major sprang on to the running board.

'Chase them,' he shouted in the driver's ear, brandishing his rifle, and once again the driver sprang the clutch and the Rolls leapt forward with such violence that the Count was tumbled backwards onto the soft leather seat, his helmet sliding forward over his eyes, his polished boots kicking to the skies and his trigger finger tightening involuntarily. The Beretta fired with a vicious crack and the bullet flew an inch past Gino's ear, so that he fell to the floorboards on top of his camera, and whimpered with fright.

'Faster!' shouted the Major in the driver's ear. 'Head them off, force them to turn!' and his voice was louder and more authoritative. He wanted a clean shot at the few vulnerable points in the car's armour – the driver's visor or the open gun-mounting.

'Stop!' screeched the Count. 'I'll have you shot for this.'

Side by side, the two vehicles pitched and lurched together like a team in harness, not ten feet separating them.

Within the armoured car, Vicky's vision through the visor was limited to a narrow arc ahead, and she concentrated on that as she shouted, 'Where are they?'

Jake picked himself out of the corner where he and Sara had been thrown, and crawled towards the command turret. In the Rolls alongside, Castelani braced himself and raised the rifle. Even at that close range, five of his shots struck the thick steel hull with ringing sledgehammer blows and went whining away across the desert spaces. Only one bullet entered the narrow breech of the gun-mounting. Trapped within the hull, it ricocheted amongst the three of them like an angry living thing, splattering them with stinging slivers of lead, and bringing death within inches before it ploughed into the back of the driver's seat.

Jake popped his head out of the turret and discovered the Rolls running hard beside them, the burly Major frantically reloading his empty rifle, and the other passengers bouncing around helplessly.

'Driver!' shouted Jake. 'Hard right!' and felt a quick flush of pride and affection as Vicky responded instantly. She swung the great armoured hull so suddenly that the other driver had no time to respond, the two vehicles came together with a shower of bright white sparks and a thunderous grinding crash.

'Save us, Mother of God!' shrieked the Count. 'We are killed.' The Rolls reeled under the impact, shearing off and losing ground, her paintwork deeply scarred and her whole side dented and torn. Castelani had leaped nimbly into the back seat at the last possible moment, avoiding having his legs crushed by the collision, and now he had reloaded the rifle.

'Closer,' he shouted at the driver. 'Give me another shot at her!' But the Count had at last recovered his balance and pushed his helmet on to the back of his head.

'Stop, you fool.' His voice was clear and urgent. 'You'll kill us all,' and the driver braked with patent relief, smiling for the first time that day.

'Keep going, you idiot,' said Castelani sternly, and placed the muzzle of the rifle to the driver's earhole. His smile switched off, and his foot fell heavily on the pedal again.

'Stop!' said the Count, as he dragged himself up again, adjusted his helmet with one hand and placed the muzzle of the Beretta pistol in the driver's vacant earhole. 'I, your Colonel, command you.'

'Keep going,' growled Castelani. And the driver closed his eyes tightly, not daring to move his head, and roared straight at the ramparts of red earth that guarded the wadi.

In the moment before the Rolls ploughed headlong into a wall of sunbaked earth, the driver's dilemma was resolved for him. Gregorius, for lack of another ally, had appealed to his grandfather's warrior instincts, and despite the vast quantities of *tej* that he had drunk, that ancient had responded nobly, gathering his bodyguard about him and outstripping them in the race down the wadi. Only Gregorius himself kept pace with the tall, gangling figure as he ran down to the plain.

The two of them came out side by side, and found the Rolls and the white-painted armoured car bearing down on them at point-blank range in a storm of dust. It was a sight to daunt the bravest heart, and Gregorius dived for the shelter of the red earth ramparts. But the Ras had killed his lion, and did not flinch.

He flung up the trusty old Martini Henry rifle. The explosion of black powder sounded like a cannon shot, a vast cloud of blue smoke blossomed and a long red flame shot from the barrel.

The windscreen of the Rolls exploded in a silver burst of flying glass splinters, one of which nicked the Count's chin.

'Holy Mary, I'm killed,' cried the Count, and the driver needed nothing further to tip his allegiance. He swung the Rolls into a tight, roaring U-turn and not all of Castelani's threats could deter him. It was enough. He could take no more. He was going home.

'My God,' breathed Jake, as he watched the battered Rolls swinging tightly away, and then gathering speed as it accelerated back towards the ridge, the arms and weapons of its occupants still waving wildly, and their voices raised in loud hysterical argument that faded with distance.

The Ras's cannon boomed again, speeding them on their way, and Vicky slowed the car as they came up to him. Jake reached down and helped the ancient gentleman aboard. His eyes were bloodshot and he smelled like an abandoned brewery, but his wizened old face was crinkled into a wicked grin of satisfaction.

'How do you do?' he asked, with evident relish.

'Not bad, sir,' Jake assured him. 'Not bad at all.'

A little before noon, the formation of armoured cars parked in the open grassland twenty miles beyond the wells. A halt had been called here to allow the straggling mass of refugees that had escaped the slaughter at Chaldi to come up with them, and this was the first opportunity that Vicky had to work on Sara's leg. It had stiffened in the last hour, and the blood had clotted into a thick dark scab. Though Sara made no protest, she had paled to a muddy colour and was sweating in tiny beads across her forehead and upper lip as Vicky cleaned the wound and poured half a bottle of peroxide into it. Vicky sought to distract her as she worked by bringing up the subject of the dead they had left scattered about the water-holes under the Italian guns.

Sara shrugged philosophically. 'Hundreds die every day of sickness and hunger and from the fighting in the hills. They die without purpose or reason. These others have died for a purpose. They have died to tell the world about us—' and she broke off and gasped as the disinfectant boiled in the wound.

'I am sorry,' said Vicky quickly.

'It is nothing,' she said, and they were quiet for a while, then Sara asked, 'You will write it, won't you, Miss Camberwell?'

'Sure,' Vicky nodded grimly. 'I'll write it good. Where can I find a telegraph office?'

'There is one at Sardi,' Sara told her. 'At the railway office.'

'What I write will burn out their lines for them,' promised Vicky, and began to bind up the leg with a linen bandage from the medicine chest. 'We'll have to get these breeches off you.' Vicky inspected the bloodstained and tattered velvet dubiously. 'They are so tight, it's a wonder you haven't given yourself gangrene.'

'They must be worn so,' Sara explained. 'It was decreed by my great-grandfather, Ras Abullahi.'

201

'Good Lord.' Vicky was intrigued. 'What on earth for?'

'The ladies in those days were very naughty,' Sara explained primly. 'And my great-grandfather was a good man. He thought to make the breeches difficult to remove.'

Vicky laughed delightedly.

'Do you think it helps?' she demanded, still laughing.

'Oh no,' Sara shook her head seriously. 'It makes it very hard.' She spoke with the air of an expert, and then thought for a moment. 'They come down quickly enough – it's when you want to get them up again in a hurry – that can be very difficult.'

'Well, the only way we are going to get you out of these now is to cut you loose.' Vicky was still smiling, as she took a large pair of scissors from the medicine chest and Sara shrugged again with resignation.

'They were very pretty before Jake tore them – now it does not matter.' And she showed no emotion as Vicky snipped carefully along the seam and peeled them off her.

'Now you must rest.' Vicky wrapped her naked lower body in a woollen shamma and helped her settle comfortably on one of the thin coir mattresses spread on the floor of the car.

'Stay with me,' Sara asked shyly, as Vicky picked up her portable typewriter and would have climbed out of the rear doors.

'I must begin my despatch.'

'You can work here. I will be very quiet.'

'Promise?'

'I promise,' and Vicky opened the case and placed the typewriter in her lap, sitting cross-legged. She wound a sheet of fresh paper into the machine, and thought for a moment. Then her fingers flew at the keys. Almost instantly, the anger and outrage returned to her and was transferred smoothly into words and hammered out on the thin sheet of yellow paper. Vicky's cheeks flamed with colour and she tossed her head occasionally to keep the tendrils of fine blonde hair out of her eyes.

Sara watched her, keeping very still and silent until Vicky paused to wind a fresh sheet into the typewriter, then she broke the silence.

'I have been thinking, Miss Camberwell,' she said.

'You have?' Vicky did not look up.

'I think it should be Jake.'

'Jake?' Vicky glanced at her, baffled by this sudden shift in thought.

'Yes,' Sara nodded with finality. 'We will take Jake as your first lover.' She made it sound like a group project.

'Oh, we will – will we?' The idea had already entered Vicky's head and was almost firmly rooted, but she baulked instantly at Sara's bold statement.

'He is so strong. Yes!' Sara went on. 'I think we will definitely take Jake,' and with that statement she dashed as low as they had ever been the chances of Jake Barton.

Vicky snorted derisively, and flew at the typewriter once again. She was a lady who liked to make her own decisions.

The river of moving men and animals flowed wedge-shaped across the sparsely grassed and rolling landscape beneath the mountains. Over it all hung a fine mist of dust, like sea fret on a windy day, and the sunlight caught and flashed from the burnished surfaces of the bronze war shields and the lifted lance-tips. Closer came the mass of riders until the bright spots of the silk shammas of the officers and noblemen showed clearly through the loom of the dust cloud.

Standing on the turret of Priscilla the Pig, Jake shaded the lens of his binoculars with his helmet and tried to see beyond the dust clouds, searching anxiously for any pursuit by the Italians. He felt goose-flesh march up his arms and tickle the thick hair at the nape of his neck as he imagined this sprawling rabble caught in a crossfire of modern machine guns, and he fretted for the arrival of their own weapons which were lost somewhere amongst that ragged army.

He felt a touch on his shoulder and turned quickly to find Lij Mikhael beside him.

'Thank you, Mr Barton,' said the Prince quietly, and Jake shrugged and turned back to his scrutiny of the distant plains.

'It was not the correct thing – but I thank you all the same.'

'How is she?'

'I have just left her with Miss Camberwell. She is resting – and I think she will be well.'

They were silent a while longer, before Jake spoke again.

'I'm worried, Prince. We are wide open. If the Italians chase now it will be bloody murder. Where are the guns? We must have the guns.'

Lij Mikhael pointed out on to the left rear flank of the approaching host.

'There,' and Jake noticed for the first time the ungainly shapes of the pack camels, almost obscured by dust and distances, but standing taller than the shaggy little Harari ponies that surrounded them, and lumbering stolidly onwards towards where the cars waited. 'They will be here in half an hour.'

Jake nodded with relief. He began planning how he would arm the cars immediately, so that they could be deployed to counter another Italian attack – but the Prince interrupted his thoughts.

'Mr Barton, how long have you known Major Swales?' Jake lowered the glasses and grinned.

'Sometimes I think too long,' and regretted it, as he noticed the Prince's immediate anxiety.

'No. I didn't mean that. It was a bad joke. I haven't known him long.'

'We checked his record very carefully before—' he hesitated.

'Before tricking him into taking on this commission,' Jake suggested, and the Prince smiled faintly and nodded.

'Precisely,' he agreed. 'All the evidence suggests that he is an unscrupulous man, but a skilled soldier with a proven record of achievement in training raw recruits. He is an expert weapons instructor, with a full knowledge of the mechanism and exploitation of modern weapons.' The Prince paused.

'Just don't get into a card game with him.'

'I will take your advice, Mr Barton.' The Prince smiled fleetingly, and then was serious again. 'Miss Camberwell called him a coward. That is not so. He was acting under my direct orders, as a soldier should.'

'Point taken,' grinned Jake. 'But then I'm not a soldier, only a grease monkey.' But the Prince brushed the disclaimer aside.

'He is probably a better man than he thinks he is,' said Jake, and the Prince nodded.

'His combat record in France is impressive. The Military Cross and three times mentioned in despatches.'

'Yeah, you have me convinced,' murmured Jake. 'Is that what you wanted?'

'No,' admitted the Prince reluctantly. 'I had hoped that you might convince me,' and they both laughed.

'And did you check my record also?' Jake asked.

'No,' admitted the Prince. 'The first time I ever heard of

you was in Dar es Salaam. You and your strange machines were a bonus – a surprise packet.' The Prince paused again, and then spoke so softly that Jake barely caught the words, 'and perhaps the best end of the bargain.' Then he lifted his chin and looked steadily into Jake's eyes. 'The anger is still with you,' he said. 'I can see how strong it is.'

With surprise, Jake realized that the Prince was correct. The anger was in him. No longer the leaping flames that had kindled at the first shock of the atrocity. Those had burned down into a thick glowing bed in the pit of his guts, but the memory of men and women caught by the guns and the mortars would sustain that glow for a long time ahead.

'I think now you are committed to us,' the Lij went on softly, and Jake was amazed at the man's perception. He had not yet recognized that commitment himself; for the first time since he had landed in Africa, he was motivated by something outside himself. He knew that he would stay now, and that he would fight with the Lij and these people as long as they needed him. In an intuitive flash he realized that if these simple people were enslaved, then all of mankind – including Jake Barton – were themselves deprived of a measure of freedom. A line, almost forgotten, imperfectly learned long ago and not then understood surfaced in his memory.

'"No man is an island," – ' he said, and the Lij nodded and continued the quotation.

' – "entire of itself. Any man's death diminishes me, because I am involved in mankind".' The Lij's dark eyes glowed. 'Yes, Mr Barton, John Donne. I think that in you I have been lucky. You are fire, and Gareth Swales is ice. It will work for me. Already there is a bond between you.'

'A bond?' and Jake laughed, a brief harsh bark of laughter, but then stopped and thought about the Prince's words. The man had even greater perception than Jake had at first realized. He had a knack of turning over unrecognized truths.

'Yes. A bond,' said the Lij. 'Fire and ice. You will see.' They were silent for a while, standing high on the steel turret of the car, bare-headed in the sun, each man thinking his own thoughts.

Then the Lij roused himself and turned to point into the west.

'There is the heart of Ethiopia,' he said. 'The mountains.' They both lifted their heads to the soaring peaks, and the great flat-topped Ambas that characterized the Ethiopian highlands.

Each table land was divided from the next by sheer walls of riven rock, blue with distance and remote as the clouds into which they seemed to rise, and by the deep dark gorges that looked to split the earth like the axe-stroke of a giant, plunging thousands upon thousands of feet to the swiftly raging torrents in their depths.

'The mountains protect us. For a hundred miles on each side no enemy may pass.' The Prince swept his arms wide to encompass the curving blue wall of rock that faded both north and south into the smoky distances where they merged with the paler bright blue of the sky.

'But there is the Sardi Gorge.' Jake saw it cleave the wall of mountains, a deep funnel driving into the rock – perhaps fifteen miles across at its widest point, but then narrowing swiftly and climbing steeply towards the distant heights.

'The Sardi Gorge,' the Prince repeated. 'A lance pointed into the exposed flank of the Lion of Judah.' He shook his head and his expression was troubled and once again that haunted, hunted look was in his eyes. 'The Emperor, Negusa Nagast, Haile Selassie, has gathered his armies in the north. One hundred and fifty thousand men to meet the main thrust of the Italians which must come from the north, out of Eritrea and through Adowa. The Emperor's flanks are secured by the mountains – except here at the gorge. This is the only place at which a modern mechanized army might win its way to the high ground. The road up the gorge is steep and rough, but the Italians are engineering masters. Their roadmaking wizardry dates back to the Caesars. If they force the mouth of the gorge, they could have fifty thousand men on the highlands inside of a week.' He punched his fist upward towards the far blue peaks. 'They would be across the Emperor's rear, between him and his capital at Addis Ababa, with the road to the city wide open to them. It would be the end for us – and the Italians know it. Their presence here at the Wells of Chaldi proves it. What we encountered there today was the advance guard of the enemy attack which will come through the gorge.'

'Yes,' Jake agreed. 'It seems that is so.'

'The Emperor has charged me with the defence of the Sardi Gorge,' said the Prince quietly. 'But at the same time he has ordained that the great bulk of my fighting men must join his army which is now gathering on the shores of Lake Tana, two hundred miles away in the west. We will be short of men, so short that without your cars and the new machine guns you have brought to me, the task would be impossible.'

'It isn't going to be a push-over, even with these beaten-up old ladies.'

'I know that, Mr Barton, and I am doing everything in my power to improve the betting in our favour. I am even treating with a traditional enemy of the Harari to form a common front against the enemy. I am trying to put aside old feuds, and convince the Ras of the Gallas to join us in the defence of the Gorge. The man is a robber and a degenerate, and his men are all shifta, mountain bandits, but they fight well and every lance now arms us against the common enemy.'

Jake was conscious of the faith that the Prince was

placing in him; he was being treated like a trusted commander and his newly realized sense of involvement was strengthened.

'An untrustworthy friend is the worst kind of enemy.'

'I don't recognize that quotation?' the Prince enquired.

'Jake Barton, mechanic.' Jake grinned at him. 'Looks like we've got ourselves a job of work. What I want you to do is pick out some of your really bright lads. Ones that I can teach to drive a car — or men that Gareth can use as gunners.'

'Yes. I have already discussed that with Major Swales. He made the same suggestion. I will hand-pick my best for you.'

'Young ones,' said Jake. 'Who will learn quickly.'

The Ras sat crouched like an ancient vulture in the strip of shade thrown by Gareth's car, the Hump; his eyes were narrowed like those of a sniper and he mumbled to himself, drooling a little with excitement. When Gregorius reached out and tried to view the fan of cards that the Ras held secretively to his bosom, his hand was slapped away angrily, and a storm of Amharic burst about him. Gregorius was justly put out of countenance by this, for he was, after all, his grandfather's interpreter. He complained to Gareth, who squatted opposite the Ras holding his own cards carefully against the front of his tweed jacket.

'He does not want me to help him any more,' protested Gregorius. 'He says he understands the game now.'

'Tell him he is a natural.' Gareth squinted around the smoke that spiralled upwards from the cheroot in the corner of his mouth. 'Tell him he could go straight into the salon privé at Monte Carlo.'

The Ras grinned and nodded happily at the compliment, and then scowled with concentration as he waited for Gareth to discard.

'Anyone for the ladies?' Gareth asked innocently as he laid the queen of hearts face up on the inverted ammunition box that stood between them, and the Ras squawked with delight and snatched it up. Then he hammered on the box like an auctioneer and began laying out his hand.

'Skunked, by God!' Gareth's face crumpled in a convincing display of utter dismay and the Ras nodded and twinkled and drooled.

'How do you do?' he asked triumphantly, and Gareth judged that the Christmas turkey was now sufficiently fattened and ready for plucking.

'Ask your venerable grandfather if he would like a little interest on the next game. I suggest a Maria Theresa a point?' and Gareth held up one of the big silver coins between thumb and forefinger to illustrate the suggestion.

The Ras's response was positive and gratifying. He summoned one of his bodyguard, who drew a huge purse of lion skin from out of his voluminous shamma and opened it.

'Hallelujah!' breathed Gareth, as he saw the sparkle of golden sovereigns in the recesses of the purse. 'Your deal, old sport!'

The controlled dignity of the Count's bearing was modelled aristocratically on that of the Duce himself. It was the mien of the aristocrat, of the man born to command. His dark eyes flashed with scorn, and his voice rang with a deep beauty that sent shivers up his own spine.

'A peasant, reared in the gutters of the street. I am

amazed that such a person can have reached a rank such as Major. A person like yourself—' and his right arm shot out with the accusing finger straight as a pistol barrel, 'a nobody, an upstart. I blame myself that I was soft-hearted enough to place you in a position of trust. Yes, I blame myself. That is the reason I have until this time overlooked your impudence, your importunity. But this time you have overreached yourself, Castelani. This time you have refused to obey a direct command from your own Colonel in the face of the enemy. This I cannot ignore!' The Count paused, and a shadow of regret passed fleetingly behind his eyes. 'I am a compassionate man, Castelani – but I am also a soldier. I cannot, in deference to this honoured uniform that I wear, overlook your conduct. You know the penalty for what you have done, for disobeying your superior officer in the face of the enemy.' He paused again, the chin coming up and dark fires burning in his eyes. 'The penalty, Castelani, is death. And so it must be. You will be an example to my men. This evening, as the sun is about to set, you will be led before the assembled battalion and stripped of your badges of rank, of the beloved insignia of this proud command, and then you will meet your just deserts before the rifles of the firing-squad.'

It was a longish speech, but the Count was a trained baritone and he ended it dramatically with arms spread wide. He held the pose after he had finished and watched himself with gratification in the full-length mirror before which he stood. He was alone in his tent, but he felt as though he faced a wildly applauding audience. Abruptly he turned from the mirror, strode to the entrance of the tent and threw back the flap.

The sentries sprang to attention and the Count barked, 'Have Major Castelani summoned here immediately.'

'Immediately, my Colonel,' snapped the sentry, and the Count let the flap drop back into place.

Castelani came within ten minutes and saluted smartly from the entrance of the tent.

'You sent for me, my Colonel?'

'My dear Castelani.' The Count rose from his desk; the strong white teeth contrasted against the dark olive-gold tan, as he smiled with all his charm and went to take the Major's arm. 'A glass of wine, my dear fellow?'

Aldo Belli was enough of a realist to see that without Castelani's professional eye and arm guiding the battalion, it would collapse like an unsuccessful soufflé, or more probably like a dynamited cliff upon his head. Passing sentence of death on the man had relieved the Count's feelings, and now he could feel quite favourably disposed towards him.

'Be seated,' he said, indicating the camp chair opposite his desk. 'There are cigars in the humidor.' He beamed fondly, like a father at his eldest son. 'I would like you to read through this report and to place your signature in the space I have marked.'

Castelani took the sheaf of papers and began to read, frowning like a bulldog and with his lips forming the words silently. After a few minutes, he looked startled and glanced up at Aldo Belli.

'My Colonel, I doubt if it was forty thousand savages that attacked us.'

'A matter of opinion, Castelani. It was dark. No one will ever know for certain how many there were.' The Count waved the objection aside with a genial smile. 'It is merely an informed estimate – read on. You will find I have good things to say of your conduct.'

And the Major read on and blanched.

'Colonel, the enemy casualties were 126 dead, not 12,600.'

'Ah, a slip of the pen, Major, I will correct that before sending it to headquarters.'

'Sir, you make no mention of the enemy possessing an armoured vehicle.'

And the Count frowned for the first time since the beginning of the meeting.

'Armoured vehicle, Castelani, surely you mean an ambulance?'

The encounter with the strange machine was best forgotten, Belli had decided. It reflected no credit on anybody – particularly none upon himself. It would merely add a jarring note to the splendours of his report.

'It would be quite in the normal course of things for the enemy to have some sort of medical service – not worth mentioning. Read on! Read on! Caro mio, you will find that I have recommended you for a decoration.'

General De Bono had summoned his staff to a lunchtime conference to appraise the readiness of the expeditionary force to commence its invasion of the Ethiopian highlands. These conferences were a weekly affair, and the General's staff had not taken long to understand that in exchange for a really superb luncheon, for the reputation of the General's chef was international, they were expected to provide the General with good reasons which he might relay to the Duce for delaying the start of the offensive. The staff had fully entered into the spirit of the game, and some of their offerings had been inspired. However, even their fertile imaginations were now beginning to plough barren land. The Inspector General of the Medical Corps had tentatively diagnosed a straightforward case of gonorrhoea contracted by an infantry man as 'suspected smallpox' and had written a very good scarestory warning of a possible epidemic – but the General was not certain whether it could be used or not. They needed something better than that. They were discussing this now over the cigars and liqueurs, when the door of the dining room was thrown open and Captain Crespi hurried to the head of the table. His face was flushed, and his eyes wild, his manner so agitated that an electric silence fell over the roomful of very senior and slightly inebriated officers.

Crespi handed a message to the General, and he was so disturbed that what was intended as a whisper came out as a strangled cry of outrage.

'The clown!' he panted. 'The clown has done it!'

The General, alarmed by this enigmatic statement, snatched the message and his eyes flew across the sheet before he handed it to the officer beside him and covered his face with both hands.

'The idiot!' he wailed, while the message passed swiftly from hand to hand, and a hubbub of raised voices followed it.

'At least, your Excellency, it is a great victory,' called an infantry commander, and suddenly the entire mood of the assembly changed.

'My planes are ready, General. We await the word to follow up this masterly strategy of yours,' cried the Commander of the Regia Aeronautica, leaping to his feet – and the General uncovered his eyes and looked confused.

'Congratulations, my General,' called an artilleryman, and struggled unsteadily upright, spilling port down the front of his jacket. 'A mighty victory.'

'Oh dear!' murmured De Bono. 'Oh dear!'

'An unprovoked attack by a horde of savages' – Crespi had retrieved the message and read the memorable words of Count Aldo Belli aloud – 'firmly resisted by the courage of the flower of Italian manhood.'

'Oh dear!' said De Bono a little louder, and covered his eyes again.

'Almost fifteen thousand of the enemy dead!' shouted a voice.

'An army of sixty thousand routed by a handful of Fascist sons. It is a sign for the future.'

'Forward to the ultimate victory.'

'We march! We march!'

And the General looked up again. 'Yes,' he agreed miserably. 'I suppose we shall have to now.'

The Third Battalion of the blackshirt 'Africa' regiment was paraded in full review order on the sandy plain above the Wells of Chaldi. The ground was neatly demarcated by the meticulous rows of pale canvas tents and neat lines of white stones. In twenty-four hours, under the goading of Major Castelani, the camp had taken on an air of permanence. If they gave him a day or two more, there would be roads and buildings also.

Count Aldo Belli stood in the back of the Rolls, which, despite the loving attentions of Giuseppe the driver, was showing signs of wear and attrition. However, Giuseppe had parked it with the damaged side away from the parade and he had burnished the good side with a mixture of beeswax and methylated spirits until it shone in the sunlight, and had replaced the shattered windscreen and the broken lamp glass.

'I have here a message received an hour ago which I shall read to you,' shouted the Count, and the parade stirred with interest. 'The message is personal to me from Benito Mussolini.'

'Il Duce. Il Duce. Il Duce,' roared the battalion in unison, like a well-trained orchestra, and the Count lifted a hand to restrain them and he began to read.

215

'"My heart swells with pride when I contemplate the feat of arms undertaken by the gallant sons of Italy, children of the Fascist revolution, whom you command"—' the Count's voice choked a little.

When the speech ended, his men cheered him wildly, throwing their helmets in the air. The Count climbed down from the Rolls and went amongst them, weeping, embracing a man here, kissing another there, shaking hands left and right and then clasping his own hands above his head like a successful prizefighter and crying 'Ours is the victory,' and 'Death before dishonour,' until his voice was hoarse and he was led away to his tent by two of his officers.

However, a glass of *grappa* helped him recover his composure and he was able to pour a warrior's scorn on the radio message from General De Bono which accompanied the paean of praise from Il Duce.

De Bono was alarmed and deeply chagrined to discover that the officer he had judged to be an ineffectual blowhard had indeed turned out to be a firebrand. In view of the Duce's personal message to Belli, he could not, without condemning himself to the political wilderness, order the man back to headquarters and under his protective wing where he could be restrained from any further flamboyant action.

The man had virtually established himself as an independent command. Mussolini had chided De Bono with his failure to go on the offensive, and had held up the good Count's action as an example of duty and dedication. He had directly ordered De Bono to support the Count's drive on the Sardi Gorge and to reinforce him as necessary.

De Bono's response had been to send the Count a long radiogram, urging him to the utmost caution and pleading with him to advance only after reconnaissance in depth and after having secured both flanks and rear.

Had he delivered this advice forty-eight hours earlier, it

would have been most enthusiastically received by Aldo Belli. But now, since the victory at the Wells of Chaldi and the Duce's congratulatory message, the Count was a changed man. He had tasted the sweets of battle honours and learned how easily they could be won. He knew now that he was opposed by a tribe of primitive black men in long night-dresses armed with museum weapons, who ran and fell with gratifying expedition when his men opened fire.

'Gentlemen,' he addressed his officers. 'I have today received a code green message from General De Bono. The armies of Italy are on the march. At twelve hundred hours today,' he glanced at his wrist-watch, 'in just twelve minutes' time, the forward elements of the army will cross the Mareb River and begin the march on the savage capital of Addis Ababa. We stand now at the leading edge of the sword of history. The fields of glory are ripening on the mountains ahead of us – and I, for one, intend that the Third Battalion shall be there when the harvest is gathered in.' His officers made polite, if uncommitted sounds. They were beginning to be alarmed by this change in their Colonel. It was to be hoped that this was rhetoric rather than real intention.

'Our esteemed commander has urged me to exercise the utmost caution in my advance on the Sardi Gorge,' and they smiled and nodded vehemently, but the Count scowled dramatically and his voice rang. 'I will not sit here quiescent, while glory passes me by.' A shudder of unease ran through the assembled officers, like the forest shaken by the first winds of winter, and they joined in only half-heartedly when the Count began to sing 'La Giovinezza'.

Lij Mikhael had agreed that one of the cars might be used to carry Sara up the gorge to the town of Sardi where a Catholic mission station was run by an elderly German doctor. The bullet wound in the girl's leg was not healing cleanly, and the heat and swelling of the flesh and the watery yellow discharge from the wound were causing Vicky the greatest concern.

Fuel for the cars had come down from Addis Ababa on the narrow gauge railway as far as Sardi, and had then been packed down the steeper, lower section of the gorge by mule and camel. It waited for them now at the foot of the gorge where the Sardi River debouched through a forest of acacia trees into a triangular valley, which in turn widened to a mouth fifteen miles across before giving way to the open desert. At the head of the valley, the river sank into the dry earth and began its long subterranean journey to where it emerged at last in the scattered water-holes at the Wells of Chaldi.

Lij Mikhael was going up to Sardi with Vicky's car, for he had arranged to meet the Ras of the Gallas there in an attempt to co-ordinate the efforts of the two tribes against the Italian aggressors, and then an aircraft was being sent down to Sardi from Addis to fly him to an urgent war conference with the Emperor at Lake Tana.

Before he left, he spoke privately with Jake and Gareth, walking with them a short way along the rugged road that climbed steeply up the gorge – following the rocky water course of the Sardi River.

Now they stood together, staring up the track to where it turned into the first steep bend and the river came crashing down beside it in a tall white-plumed waterfall that drifted mist across the surface of the track and induced a growth of dark green moss upon the boulders.

'It's as rough as a crocodile's back here,' said Jake. 'Will Vicky get the car up?'

'I have had a thousand men at work upon it – ever since I knew you were bringing these vehicles,' the Lij told him. 'It is rough, yes, but I think it will be passable.'

'I should jolly well hope so,' Gareth murmured. 'It's the only way out of this lovely little trap into which we have backed ourselves. Once the Eyeties close the entrance to the valley—' and he turned and swept a hand across the vista of plain and mountain that lay spread below them, and then he smiled at the Prince.

'Just the three of us here now, Toffee old boy. Let's hear from you. What exactly do you want from us? What are the objectives you have set for us? Are we expected to defeat the whole bloody army of Italy before you pay us out?'

'No, Major Swales.' The Prince shook his head. 'I thought I had made myself clear. We are here to cover the rear and flank of the Emperor's army. We must expect that eventually the Italians will force their way up this gorge and reach the plateau and the road to Dessie and Addis – we can't stop them, but we must delay them at least until the main engagements in the north are decided. If the Emperor succeeds, the Italians will withdraw here. If he fails, then our task is over.'

'How long until the Emperor fights?'

'Who can tell?'

And Jake shook his head, while Gareth took the stub of his cigar from his mouth and inspected the tip ruefully.

'I'm beginning to think we are being underpaid,' he said. But the Prince seemed not to hear and he went on speaking quietly but with a force that commanded their attention.

'We will use the cars here on the open ground in front of the gorge to the best possible effect, and my father's troops will support you.' He paused, and they all looked down at the sprawling encampment of the Ras's army, amongst the acacia trees. Stragglers were still drifting in across the plain from the rout at the wells, lines of camels and knots of

219

horsemen surrounded by amorphous formations of foot soldiers. 'If the Gallas join us, they can provide another five thousand fighting men that will bring our strength to twelve thousand – or thereabouts. I have had my scouts study the Italian encampment, and they report an effective strength of under a thousand. Even with their armaments, we should hold them here for many days—'

'Unless they are reinforced, which they will be, or bring up armour, which they will do,' said Gareth.

'Then we will withdraw into the gorge – demolishing the road as we go, and resisting at each strong place. We won't be able to use the cars again until we reach Sardi – but there in the bowl of the mountains there is good open ground and room to manoeuvre. It is also the last point at which we can effectively block the Italian advance.' They were silent again and the sound of an engine came up to them. They watched the armoured car reach the foot of the gorge and begin growling and nosing its way upwards, at the pace of a walking man, except where it had to back and lock hard to make one of the steep hairpin bends in the road. The Lij roused himself and sighed with what seemed a deep weariness of the spirit.

'One thing I must mention to you, gentlemen. My father is a warrior in the old style. He does not know the meaning of fear, and he cannot imagine the effect of modern weapons – especially the machine gun – on massed foot soldiers. I trust you to restrain his exuberance.'

Jake remembered the bodies hanging like dirty laundry on the barbed wire of France, and felt the cold tickle run up his spine. Nobody spoke again until the car, still blazoned with its crimson crosses, drew up level with where they stood and they scrambled down the bank to meet it.

Vicky's head appeared in the hatch. She must have found an opportunity to bathe, for her hair was newly washed and shiny and caught behind her head in a silk ribbon. The sun had bleached her hair to a whiter gold, but the peachy velvet of her complexion had been gilded by that same sun to a darker honey colour. Immediately Jake and Gareth moved forward, neither trusting the other to be alone with her for an instant.

But she was brusque, and concerned only with the injured girl who was laid out on the floor of the cab on a hastily improvised bed of blankets and skins. Her leave-taking was off-hand and distracted while the Lij climbed in through the rear doors, and she pulled away again up the steep track followed by a squadron of the Prince's bodyguard looking like a gang of cut-throats on their shaggy mountain ponies, festooned with bandoliers of ammunition and hung with rifles and swords. They clattered away after the car, and Jake watched them out of sight. He felt a sense of deep unease that the girl should be up there in the mountains beyond any help that he could give her. He was staring after the car.

'Put your mind back in your pants,' Gareth advised him cynically. 'You're going to need it for the Eyeties, now.'

From the foot of the gorge to the lip of the bowl of land in which stood the town of Sardi was a few dozen miles across the ground, but the track climbed five thousand feet and it took six hours of hard driving for Vicky to reach it.

The Prince's labour gangs were working upon the track still, groups of dark men in mud-stained shammas, hacking away at the steep banks and piles of boulders that blocked the narrow places. Twice these men had to rope up the car to drag and shove it over a particularly treacherous stretch with the torrent roaring in its bed a hundred feet below and the wheels of the car inches from the crumbling edge of the precipice.

In the middle of the afternoon the sun passed behind the towering ramparts of stone leaving the gut of the gorge in deep shadow, and a clammy chill made Vicky shiver even as she wrestled with the controls of the heavy vehicle. The engine was running very unevenly, and back-firing explosively at the change of atmospheric pressure as they toiled upwards. Also Sara's condition seemed to be worsening rapidly. When Vicky stopped briefly to rest her aching arms and back muscles she found that Sara was running a raging fever, her skin was dry and baking hot and her dark eyes were glittering strangely. She cut short her rest and took the wheel again.

The gorge narrowed dramatically, so the sky was a narrow ribbon of blue high above and the cliffs seemed almost to close jaws of granite upon the labouring car. Although it seemed impossible, the track turned even more steeply upwards so that the big back wheels spun and skidded, throwing out fist-sized stones like cannon balls and scattering the escort who followed closely.

Then abruptly Vicky drove the car over the crest and came out through rocky portals into a wide, gently inclined bowl of open ground hemmed in completely by the mountain walls. Perhaps twenty miles across, the bowl was cultivated in patches, and scattered with groups of the round *tukuls*, the thatch and daub huts of the peasant farmers. Domestic animals, goats and a few milk cows grazed along the course of the Sardi River where the grass was green and lush and thick forests of cedar trees found a precarious purchase along the rocky banks.

The town itself was a gathering of brick-built and white-plastered buildings, whose roofs of galvanized corrugated iron caught the last probing rays of the sun as it came through the western pass.

Here in the west, the mountains fell back, allowing a broad gentle incline to rise the last two thousand feet to the level of the plateau of the highlands. Down this slope, the narrow-gauge railway looped in a tight series of hairpins until it entered the town and ended in a huddle of sheds and stock pens.

The Catholic mission station was situated beyond the town on the slopes of the western rise. It was a sadly dilapidated cluster of tin-roofed daub buildings, grouped around a church built of the same materials. The church was the only building that was freshly whitewashed. As they drove past the open doors, Vicky saw that the rows of rickety pews were empty, but that lighted candles burned upon the altar and there were fresh flowers in the vases.

The church's emptiness and the sorry state of the buildings were a reflection of the massive power of the Coptic Church over this land and its people. There was very little encouragement given to the missionaries of any other faith, but this did not prevent the local inhabitants from taking advantage of the medical facilities offered by the mission.

Almost fifty patients squatted along the length of the veranda that ran the full length of the clinic, and they looked up with minimal interest as Vicky parked the armoured car below them.

The doctor was a heavily built man, with short bowed legs and a thick neck. His hair was cropped close to the round skull and was silvery white, and his eyes were a pale blue. He spoke no English, and he acknowledged Vicky with a glance and a grunt, transferring all his attention to Sara. When two of his assistants rolled her carefully on to a stretcher and carried her up on to the veranda, Vicky would have followed but the Lij restrained her.

'She is in the best hands – and we have work to do.'

The telegraph office at the railway station was closed and locked, but in answer to the Prince's shouts the station master came hurrying anxiously down the track. He recognized Lij Mikhael immediately.

The process of tapping out Vicky's despatch on the telegraph was a long, laborious business, almost beyond the ability of the station master whose previous transmissions had seldom exceeded a dozen words at a time. He frowned and muttered to himself as he worked, and Vicky wondered in what mangled state her masterpiece of the journalistic art would reach her editor's desk in New York. The Prince had left her and gone off with his escort to the official government residence on the outskirts of the village, and it was after nine o'clock before the station master had sent the last of Vicky's despatch – a total of almost five thousand words – and Vicky found that her legs were unsteady and her brain woolly with fatigue when she went out into the utter darkness of the mountain night. There were no stars, for the night mists had filled the basin and swirled in the headlights as Vicky groped her way through the village and at last found the government residence.

It was a large sprawling complex of buildings with wide verandas, whitewashed and iron-roofed, standing in a grove of dark-foliaged casa flora trees from which the bats screeched and fluttered to dive upon the insects that swarmed in the light from the windows of the main building.

Vicky halted the car in front of the largest building and found herself surrounded by silent but watchful throngs of dark men, all of them heavily armed like the Harari she knew, but these were a different people. She did not know why, but she was sure of it.

There were many others camped in the grove. She could see their fires and hear the stamp and snort of their tethered

224

horses, the voices of the women and the laughter of the men.

The throng opened for her and she crossed the veranda and entered the large room which was crowded with many men, and lit by the smoky paraffin lamps that hung from the ceiling. The room stank of male sweat, tobacco and the hot spicy aroma of food and *tej*.

A hostile silence fell as she entered, and Vicky stood uncertainly on the threshold, scrutinized by a hundred dark suspicious eyes, until Lij Mikhael rose from where he sat at the far end of the room.

'Miss Camberwell.' He took her hand. 'I was beginning to worry about you. Did you send your despatch?' He led her across the room and seated her beside him, before he indicated the man who sat opposite him.

'This is Ras Kullah of the Gallas,' he said, and despite her weariness, Vicky studied him with interest.

Her first impression was identical to that she had received from the men amongst the casa flora trees outside in the darkness. There was a veiled hostility, a coldness of the spirit about the man, an almost reptilian aura about the dark unblinking eyes.

He was a young man, still in his twenties, but his face and body were bloated by disease or debauchery so that there was a soft jelly-like look to his flesh. The skin was a pale creamy colour, unhealthy and clammy, as though it had never been exposed to sunlight. His lips were full and petulant, a startling cherry red in colour that ill suited the pale tones of his skin.

He watched Vicky, when the Prince introduced her, with the same dead expression in his eyes, but gave no acknowledgement – though the flat snakelike eyes moved slowly over her body, like loathsome hands, dwelling and lingering on her breasts and her legs, before moving back to Lij Mikhael's face.

225

The pudgy, swollen hands lifted a buck-horn pipe to the dark cherry lips and Ras Kullah drew deeply upon it — holding the smoke in his lungs before exhaling slowly. When Vicky smelled the smoke, she knew the reason for the dead eyes in the Ras's puffy face.

'You have not eaten all day,' said Lij Mikhael, and gave instructions for food to be brought to Vicky. 'You will excuse me now, Miss Camberwell, the Ras speaks no English and our negotiations are still at an early stage. I have ordered a room made ready where you may rest as soon as you have eaten. We shall be talking all the night,' the Lij smiled briefly, 'and saying very little, for a blood feud of a hundred years is what we are talking around.' He turned back to the Ras.

The hot, spicy food warmed and filled the cold hollow place in the pit of Vicky's stomach, and a mug of fiery *tej* made her choke and gasp, but then lifted her spirits and revived her journalist's curiosity so that she could look again with interest at what was happening around her.

The interminable discussion went on between the two men, cautious plodding negotiations between implacable enemies, reluctantly drawn together by a greater danger and a more powerful adversary.

On either side of Ras Kullah sat two young Galla women, pale sloe-eyed creatures, with noble regular features and thick dark hair frizzled out into a stiff round bush that caught the light of the lanterns and glowed along the periphery like a luminous halo. They sat impassively showing no emotion, even when the Ras fondled one or the other of them with the absent-minded caress that he might have bestowed on a lap dog. Only once, as he took a fat round breast in one plump soft paw and squeezed it, the girl winced slightly and Vicky seeing the crimson linen of her blouse dampened in a wet dark patch at the nipple realized that the girl's breast was heavy with milk.

Vicky's artificial sense of well-being was fast fading now, sinking once again under the weight of her weariness, and lulled by the food in her belly, the thick smoky atmosphere and the hypnotic cadence of the Amharic language. She was on the point of excusing herself from the Lij and leaving when there was a disturbance outside the room, and the shrill angry cries of a voice creaking with age and indignation. The room was immediately electric with a charged feeling of expectation, and Ras Kullah looked up and called out querulously.

A youth of perhaps nineteen years of age was dragged into the room and held by two armed guards in the centre of the hastily cleared space before Ras Kullah. His arms were bound with rawhide that cut deeply into the flesh of his wrists, and his face was wet and shiny with the sweat of fear, while his eyes rolled wildly in their sockets.

He was followed by a shrieking crone, a wizened baboon-like figure, swathed in a voluminous black shamma, stiff with filth and greenish with age. Repeatedly she attempted to attack the captive youth, clawing at his face with bony hooked fingers, her toothless old mouth opened in a dark pink-lined pit as she leaped and cavorted before the terrified youth, trying again and again to reach him, while the two guards pushed her away with cheerful guffaws and playful blows, never relinquishing their grip on their prisoner.

The Ras leaned forward to watch this play with suddenly awakening interest, his dark dull eyes taking on a sparkle of anticipation as he asked a question, and the crone flew to him and flung herself full-length before him.

She began to bleat out a long high-pitched plea, attempting at the same time to grasp and kiss the Ras's feet. The Ras giggled with anticipation, kicking away the old woman's hands and occasionally asking a question that was answered either by the guards or the grovelling crone.

227

'Miss Camberwell,' whispered the Prince. 'I suggest that you leave now. This will not be pleasant to watch.'

'What is it?' Vicky demanded, her professional instincts roused. 'What are they doing?'

'The woman accuses the youth of murdering her son. The guards are her witnesses and the Ras is trying the case. He will give judgement in a moment, and the sentence will be carried out immediately.'

'Here?' Vicky looked startled.

'Yes, Miss Camberwell. I urge you to leave. The punishment will be biblical, from the Old Testament which is the centre of the Coptic faith. It will be a tooth for a tooth.'

Vicky hesitated to take the Prince's advice, all human experience was her field – no matter how bizarre, and suddenly it was too late.

Laughingly, the Ras thrust the old woman away again with a kick to the chest that sent her sprawling across the beaten earth floor – and he called a peremptory command to the guards who held the accused youth. Flapping like a maimed black crow upon the floor, the crone set up a wailing shriek of triumph as she heard the verdict, and she tried to regain her feet. The guards guffawed again and began to strip away the condemned man's clothing, tearing it from his body until he stood completely naked except for his bonds.

The crowded room now buzzed with excitement at the coming entertainment, and the doorway and windows were packed with those who had come in from the encampment amongst the casa flora trees. Even the two impassive madonnas who flanked the Ras had become animated, leaning forward to chatter softly to each other, smiling secretly as their dark-moon eyes shone and the full swollen breasts swung heavily under the thin material of their blouses.

The doomed youth was whimpering softly, his head

turning back and forth, as though seeking escape, his naked body slim and finely muscled with dark amber skin that glowed in the lamplight, and his arms bound tightly behind his back. His legs were long and the muscles looked hard and beautifully sculptured, and the dark bush of curls in his groin was dense and crisp-looking. His thick circumcised penis hung limply, seeming to epitomize the man's despair. Vicky tried to tear her eyes away, ashamed to look upon a human being stripped thus of all dignity, but the spectacle was mesmeric.

The old woman hopped and flapped in front of the captive, her wrinkled brown features contorted in an expression of utter malice – and she opened her toothless mouth and spat into his face. The spittle ran down his cheek and dripped on to his chest.

'Please leave now,' Lij Mikhael urged Vicky, and she tried to rise, but it seemed that her legs would not respond.

One of the Galla warriors sitting opposite Vicky drew the narrow-bladed dagger from the tooled leather sheath on his hip. The handle was carved from the horn of a kudu bull and bound with copper wire, the blade was slightly curved and viciously pointed, twice the span of a man's hand in length. He shouted to attract the woman's attention, then sent the weapon skidding across the floor towards her – and she pounced upon it with another gleeful shriek and pranced before the cringing youth, brandishing the knife while the watchers shouted encouragement to her.

The captive began to twist and struggle, watching the knife with the fixed concentration of despair and terror, but the two tall guards held him easily, chuckling like a pair of gaunt ogres, watching the knife also.

The old woman let out one more high-pitched shriek, and leapt at him – the long skinny black arm lunged out, the point of the blade aimed at his heart. The woman's strength was too frail to drive it home, and the point struck bone and glanced aside, skidding around the ribcage, opening a long shallow cut that exposed the white bone in its depths for the instant before blood flooded out between the lips of the wound. A howl of delight went up from the assembled Gallas, and they goaded on the avenger with mocking cries and yips like those of a pack of excited jackals.

Again and again the old woman struck, and the youth kicked and struggled, his guards roaring with laughter and the blood from the shallow wounds flying and sparkling in the lamplight, splattering the old woman's knife arm and speckling her angry screeching face. Her frustration made her blows more wild and feeble.

Unable to penetrate his chest, she turned her attack upon his face. One blow split his nose and upper lip, and the next slashed across his eye, turning the socket instantly into a dark blood-glutted hole. The guards let him fall to the floor.

The old woman leapt upon his chest and, clinging to him like a huge, grotesque vampire bat, she began to saw determinedly at the youth's throat until at last the carotid artery erupted, dousing her robes and puddling the floor on which they rolled together – while the Galla watchers roared their approbation.

Only then could Vicky move; she leapt to her feet and pushed her way through the throng that jammed the doorway and ran out into the cool night. She realized that her blouse was damp with the sweat of nausea and she leaned against the stem of a casa flora tree, trying to fight it, unavailingly; then she doubled over and retched tearingly, choking up her horror.

The horror stayed with her for many hours, denying her the sleep her body craved. She lay alone in the small room that Lij Mikhael had ordered for her, and listened to the drums beating and the shouts of laughter and bursts of singing from the Galla encampment amongst the casa flora trees.

When she slept at last, it was not for long, and then she awoke to a soft tickling movement on her skin and the first fiery itch across her belly. Disgusted by the loathsome touch she threw aside the single blanket and lit the candle. Across the flat smooth plain of her belly, the bites of vermin were strung like a girdle of angry red beads – and she shuddered, her whole body crawling with the thought of it.

She spent what remained of the night huddled uncomfortably on the floor of the armoured car. The mountain cold struck through the steel of Miss Wobbly's hull, and Vicky shivered into the dawn, scratching morosely at the hot lumps across her stomach. Then she filled the growling ache of her empty stomach with a tin of cold corned beef from the emergency rations in the locker under the driver's seat, before driving up the slope of the western pass to the German mission station where she experienced the first lift of spirits since the horrors of the night.

Sara had responded almost miraculously to the treatment she was receiving, and although she was still weak and a little shaky, the fever had abated, and she was once more able to give Vicky the benefit of her vast wisdom and worldly experience.

Vicky sat beside the narrow iron bedstead in the overcrowded ward, while other patients coughed and groaned around her, and held Sara's thin dry hand from which the flesh seemed to have wasted overnight – and poured out to her the horrors still pent up inside her.

'Ras Kullah,' Sara made a moue of disgust. 'He is a degenerate man, that one. Did he have his milch cows with

231

him?' Vicky was for a moment at a loss, until she remembered the two madonnas. 'His men scour the mountains to keep him supplied with pretty young mothers in full milk – ugh!' She shuddered theatrically, and Vicky felt her unsettled stomach quail. 'That and his hemp pipe – and the sight of blood. He is an animal. His people are animals – they have been our enemies since the time of Solomon, and it shames me now that we must have them to fight beside us.' Then she changed the subject in her usual mercurial fashion.

'Will you go down the pass again today?'

'Yes,' Vicky said, and Sara sighed.

'The doctor says that I cannot go with you – not for many days still.'

'I will fetch you, as soon as you are ready.'

'No. No,' she protested. 'It is shorter and easier on horseback. I will come immediately – but until then carry my love to Gregorius. Tell him my heart beats with great fury for him, and he walks through my thoughts eternally.'

'I will tell him,' agreed Vicky, delighted at the sentiment and the choice of words. At that moment a tall young man in a white jacket, with the face of a brown pharaoh and huge dark eyes, came to record Sara's temperature, stooping solicitously over her and murmuring softly in Amharic as he felt for her pulse with delicate finely shaped hands.

Sara was transformed instantly into a languid wanton, with smouldering eyes and pouting lips, but when the orderly left, she was instantly herself again, giggling delightedly as she drew Vicky's head down to whisper in her ear.

'Is he not as beautiful as the dawn? He studies to be a doctor, and goes soon to the University at Berlin. He has fallen in love with me since last night – and as soon as my leg is less painful I shall take him as a lover.' And when she saw Vicky's startled glance, she went on hurriedly, 'But just for a short time, of course. Only until I am well enough to ride back to Gregorius.'

Then Lij Mikhael came, riding with his wild horsemen. They waited outside in the sun while the Prince came into the ward to take farewell of his daughter. His sombre mood lightened momentarily as he embraced Sara, and he saw how well she was recovered. Then he told the two women,

'Yesterday at noon, the Italian army under General De Bono crossed the Mareb River in force and has begun to march on Adowa and Amba Aradam. The wolf is into the sheepfold. There has already been fighting and the Italian aeroplanes are bombing our towns. We are now at war.'

'It is no surprise,' said Sara. 'The only surprise is that they took so long.'

'Miss Camberwell, you must return as swiftly as you can to my father at the foot of the gorge, and warn him that he must be ready to meet an enemy attack.' He drew out a gold pocket watch and glanced at it. 'Within the next few minutes, an aircraft will be landing here to take me to the Emperor. I would be obliged, Miss Camberwell, if you would accompany me to the landing field.'

Vicky nodded, and the Lij went on. 'Ras Kullah's men are assembled there. He has agreed to send fifteen hundred horsemen to join my father, and they will follow you—' He got no further, for Sara intervened hotly.

'Miss Camberwell must not be left alone with those hyenas of Kullah's. They would eat their own mothers.'

The Lij smiled and held up a hand. 'My own bodyguard will ride with Miss Camberwell, under my strict charge to protect her at all times.'

'I do not like it,' pouted Sara, and groped for Vicky's hand.

'I will be all right, Sara.' She stooped and kissed the girl, who clung to her for an instant.

'I will come soon,' whispered Sara. 'Do nothing until I am with you. Perhaps it should be Gareth after all,' and Vicky chuckled.

'You're getting me confused.'

'Yes,' agreed Sara. 'That's why I should be there to advise you.'

L ij Mikhael and Vicky stood side by side on the hull of Miss Wobbly and shaded the sun from their eyes as they watched the aircraft come in between the peaks.

As a pilot Vicky could appreciate the difficulty of the approach, down into the bowl of Sardi, where treacherous down-draughts fell along the cliffs, creating whirlpools of turbulence. The sun had already dispelled the chill of the night making the high mountain air even thinner and more treacherous.

Vicky recognized the aircraft type immediately, for she had trained for her own pilot's licence on a similar model. It was a Puss Moth, a small sky-blue high-winged monoplane, powered by the versatile De Havilland four-cylinder aero engine. It would carry a pilot and two passengers in a tricycle arrangement of seating, the pilot up front in an enclosed cabin under the broad sweep of the wings. Seeing the familiar aircraft reminded her, with a fleeting but bitter pang, of those golden untroubled days before October 1929, before that black Friday of evil reputation. Those idyllic days when she had been the only daughter of a rich man, spoilt and pampered, plied with such toys as motor cars and speed boats and aircraft.

All that had been swept away in a single day. Everything had gone, even that adoring godlike figure that had been her father – dead by his own hand. She felt the chill of it still, the sense of terrible loss, and she turned her thoughts aside and concentrated on the approaching aircraft.

The pilot came in down the western pass under the cliffs, then turned steeply and side-slipped in towards the only piece of open ground in the valley that was free of rocks and holes. It was used as a stockyard, gymkhana ground or polo field as the need arose – and at the moment the ankle-deep grass was providing grazing for fifty goats.

Ras Kullah's horsemen drove the goats from the field at a gallop, and then as the Puss Moth touched down, they wheeled and tore down the field at its wing-tips, firing their rifles into the air and vying with each other to perform feats of horsemanship.

The pilot taxied to where the car stood and opened the side window. He was a burly young white man, with a sun-tanned face and curly hair. He shouted above the engine rumble in an indeterminate colonial accent – Australian, New Zealand or South African, 'Are you Lij Mikhael?'

The Prince shook hands briefly with Vicky before jumping down. With his shamma fluttering wildly in the slipstream from the propeller, he hurried to the aircraft and climbed into the tiny cabin.

The pilot was watching Vicky with a lively interest through the side window and when she caught his eye he pursed his lips and made a circle with thumb and forefinger in the universal sign of approval. His grin was so frank and boyishly open that Vicky had to grin back.

'Room for one more!' he shouted, and she laughed and shouted back,

'Next time, perhaps.'

'It will be a pleasure, lady,' and he gunned the motor and swung away – lining up on the short rough-surfaced runway. Vicky watched the Puss Moth climb laboriously up towards the mountain crests. As the busy buzzing of its engine faded, a feeling of terrible aloneness fell over her and she glanced around apprehensively at the hordes of swarthy horsemen who surrounded the armoured car. Suddenly she realized that not one of all these men could speak her language, and that now there was a small cold cramp of fear at the base of her belly to go with the aloneness.

Almost desperately, she longed for some contact with the world which she knew, rather than these savage horsemen in this land of wild mountains. For an instant she thought of checking the telegraph office for a reply to her despatch, but dismissed the idea immediately. There was no chance that her editor would yet have received, let alone replied to her communication. Now she looked around her and identified the knot of men and horses that comprised Lij Mikhael's bodyguard, but they seemed very little different from the greater mass of Gallas. Little comfort there, and she climbed quickly down into the driver's hatch of the car and engaged the low gear.

She bumped over the rough ground and found the track that led down along the river towards the tall grey stone portals of the gorge. She was aware of the long untidy column of mounted men that followed her closely, but her mind leapt ahead to her arrival at the foot of the gorge, to her reunion with Jake and Gareth. Suddenly those two were the most important persons in her whole existence – and she longed for them, both or either of them, with a strength that showed in the white knuckles of her hands as she gripped the steering-wheel.

The descent of the gorge was a more terrifying experience than the ascent. The steeper stretches fell away before Vicky with the gut-swooping feel of a ski-run, and once the heavy cumbersome car was committed to it, its own weight took charge and it went down bucking and skidding. Even with the brakes locking all four wheels, it kept plunging downwards, with very little steering control transmitted to the front wheels.

A little after noon, Vicky had come more than halfway down the gorge, and she remembered that this final pitch was the truly terrifying part, where the track clung to the precipice high above the roaring river in its rocky bed. Her arms and back were painfully cramped with the effort of fighting the kicking wheel, and sweat had drenched the hair at her temples and stung her eyes. She wiped it away with her forearm, and went at the slope, braking hard the moment that the car began rolling down the thirty-degree incline.

With rock and loose earth kicking and spewing out from under the big wheels, they descended in a heavy lumbering rush, and halfway down Vicky realized that she had no control and that the vehicle was gradually slewing sideways and swinging its tail out towards the edge of the cliff.

She felt the first lurch as one rear wheel dropped slightly, riding out over the hundred-foot drop, and instinctively she knew that in this instant of its headlong career, the car was critically hanging at the extreme edge of its balance. In a hundredth of a second, it would go beyond the point of recovery, and she made without conscious thought a last instinctive grasp at survival. She jumped her foot from the brake pedal, swung the wheel into the line of skid and thrust her other foot down hard on the throttle. One wheel hung over the cliff, the other caught with a vicious jerk as the engine roared at full power, and the huge steel hull jumped like a startled gazelle, and hurled itself away from the cliff edge, struck the far bank of earth and rocky scree and was flung back, miraculously, into its original line of track.

At the bottom of the pitch, the slope eased. Vicky fought the car to a standstill there and dragged herself out of the driver's hatch. She found that she was shaking uncontrollably, and that she had to get to a private place off the track, for in reaction she was close to vomiting and her control of her other bodily functions was shaken by that terrible sliding, bucking ride.

She had left the column of horsemen far behind, and could only faintly hear their voices and the clatter of hooves on the rocky track as she scrambled and clawed her way up the side of the gorge to a thicket of dwarf cedar trees, where she could be alone.

There was a spring of clear sweet water amongst the cedars and when her body had purged itself and she had it under control again, she knelt beside the rocky pool and bathed her face and neck. Using the surface of the shining water as a mirror, she combed her hair and rearranged her clothing.

The reaction to extreme fear had left her feeling light-headed and slightly apart from reality. She picked her way out of the cedar thicket, and down to where the car stood upon the track. The Galla horsemen had arrived and they and their mounts crowded the entire area, back up the track for half a mile, and in a solid mob about the armoured car. Those nearest the car had dismounted, and when she tried to make her way through their ranks they gave her only minimal passage, so that she must brush close to them.

Suddenly she realized with a fresh lunge of fear in her chest that the Harari bodyguard of Lij Mikhael was no longer with her – and she stopped uncertainly and looked about her, trying to find where they were.

An aching silence had fallen on the Gallas, and now she saw that their expressions were tense also. The faces, with their handsome, high-boned features and beaky noses, turned towards her with the predatory expectation of the hunting hawk, and the eyes burned with the same fierce excitement with which they had watched the old crone do her bloody work the previous night.

The Harari, where were the Harari? She looked about her wildly now but could not find a familiar face – and then in the silence she heard the clatter of distant hooves from far down the gorge and she knew without any shade of doubt that they had left her, they had been driven away by the threats of their ancient enemies, who outnumbered them so heavily.

She was alone and she turned to go back, but found that they had closed about her, cutting off her retreat – and now they pressed gradually closer about her, with the same smouldering, gloating expression on every face.

She had to go forward, there was no way back – and she forced herself to walk slowly on towards the car. At each step a tall robed figure stood to block her way. She knew she must show no sign of fear, any show of weakness at all would trigger them, and she had a single brief image of her own pale body spread-eagled upon the rocky earth, plaything for a thousand. She thrust the image firmly aside and walked on slowly. At the last possible instant, each tall figure moved aside, but there was always another beyond to take its place and each time the throng pressed closer upon her. She could feel their heightening expectation, almost smell it in the hot musk of their packed bodies – the change in the faces was there too; they watched her with a growing excitement, teeth grinning, breath shortening and eyes like claws in her flesh.

Suddenly she could go no further; a figure taller and more compelling than any other blocked her path. She had noticed this man before. He was a Gerazmach, a high Galla officer. He wore a shamma of dark blue silk wrapped about his throat and falling to his knees. His hair was fluffed out in a wide halo about the lean, cruel face – and a scar ran down from the outer corner of his eye to the point of his jaw.

He said something to her in a voice that was thick with lust, and she did not understand the words – but the meaning was clear. The crowd around her stirred and she heard the sound of their breathing and felt them press even closer towards her. A man laughed near her, and there was something so ugly in the sound that it struck her like a physical force.

She wanted to scream, to turn and try and claw herself free but she knew that was what they were waiting for. It needed just that provocation and they would hurl themselves upon her. She gathered what was left of her reserves and put it all into her voice.

'Get out of my way,' she said clearly, and the man before her smiled. It was one of the most terrifying things she had ever seen.

Still smiling, he dropped one hand to his groin, opened the fold of his shamma, and made a gesture so obscene that Vicky recoiled, and she felt the scalding blood burn her throat and her cheeks. There was no control in her voice now as she blurted, 'Oh, you swine – you filthy swine,' and the man reached for her, his robe still open. As she shrank back, she felt the others behind her thrust her forward again.

Then another voice spoke. The words were banal but the tone hissed like the sound of a scimitar swung at the cut.

'All right, chaps. That's enough of that nonsense.'

Vicky felt the pressure of bodies about her ease, and she spun around with a sob catching in her throat.

Gareth Swales strolled down the passage that opened for him through the dense press of robed bodies. His whole carriage seemed indolent, and the white open-necked shirt with an I Zingari scarf at the throat was crisp and immaculate – but Vicky had never before seen the expression he wore. The rims of his nostrils were ice-white and his eyes burned with a controlled fury.

She would have flung herself at him, sobbing with relief, but his voice crackled again.

'Steady. We're not out yet,' and she caught herself, lifted her chin and smothered the next sob before it escaped.

'Good girl,' he said, without taking his eyes from the face of the tall Galla in the blue robe, and he kept on walking steadily towards him, taking Vicky's arm as he drew level with her. She felt the strength of his fingers through the thin stuff of her blouse, and it seemed to flow into her, charging her depleted reserves, and the jelly weakness in her legs firmed.

The Galla leader stood his ground as Gareth stepped up to him, and for a space of time that was less than five seconds but seemed to Vicky like a round of eternity, the two men locked gazes and wills. Blazing blue eyes levelled with smouldering black – then suddenly the Galla broke, he glanced aside and shrugged, chuckled weakly, and turned away to talk loudly with the man who stood beside him.

Unhurriedly, Gareth stepped through the gap the man had left and they were at the car.

'Are you well enough to drive?' Gareth asked quietly, as he swung her up on the sponson and she nodded.

'The engine's switched off,' she blurted; they could not risk cranking to start.

'She's on the slope,' said Gareth, turning to face the crowding Gallas and hold them off with his level gaze. 'Roll her to a start.'

As Vicky scrambled into the driver's hatch, Gareth placed a cheroot between his lips, and struck a match with his thumb nail. The little act distracted the hostile pack for an instant, and they watched his hands as he lit the cheroot and blew a long blue feather of smoke towards them.

Behind him, the car began to roll, and Gareth swung himself aboard easily with the cheroot clamped between his teeth and gave the horsemen a mocking salute as the car gathered speed down the slope. Neither of them spoke as they dropped swiftly downwards, two miles in silence.

Then, without taking her eyes off the track ahead, Vicky told Gareth as he stood above and behind her in the turret,

'You weren't even afraid—'

'In a blue funk, old girl – absolute blue funk.'

'And I once called you a coward.'

'Quite right too.'

'How did you get there so fast?'

'I was up there looking for defensive positions – against the jolly old Eyeties. Saw your faithful bodyguard taking off and came to have a look.'

The track ahead of Vicky dissolved in a mist of tears, and she had to hit the brakes hard. Afterwards, she was not sure quite how it happened but she found herself in Gareth's arms, pressing herself to him with all of her strength and shaking violently with her sobs.

'Oh God, Gareth, I don't know what I'll ever do to repay you for this.'

'I'm sure we will think of something,' he murmured, holding her with a practised embrace that was lulling and so wonderfully secure. She felt then that she did not want ever to leave his arms – and she lifted her lips to his and with a mild amazement saw on his face, in the usually mocking blue eyes, such an expression of tenderness as she had never expected was possible.

His lips were another surprise, they were very warm and soft and tasted of man and the bitter aromatic smoke of his cheroots; she had never realized that he was so tall and his body so hard, or his hands so strong. The last sob wracked her body, and then she sighed voluptuously and shuddered softly with the strength of physical awakening more intense than she had ever experienced in her entire life.

For a moment, the journalist in her attempted to analyse the source of this sudden passion, and she knew it as the product of the previous night's sleepless horrors, of fatigue and of the day's terrors. Then she no longer queried it, but let it spread through her whole body.

The encampment of the Ras's army at the foot of the Sardi Gorge sprawled for four miles amongst the acacia forests, a vast agglomeration of living things which murmured softly with life, like a hive of honeybees at midday, and which had already cloaked itself in blue woodsmoke and the myriad odours of human and animal ingestion and excretion.

The camp site that Gareth and Jake had chosen was set apart from the main body, in a denser, shadier patch of acacia, below a tall rocky waterfall where the Sardi River fell the last steep pitch to the plain and formed a dark restless pool in which Vicky could bathe away the filth from her body and from her mind.

It was almost dark when she climbed back to the camp with her wet hair bound in a towel, carrying her wash bag. Gareth was seated upon a log beside the smouldering camp fire. He was watching the steaks of a freshly butchered ox grilling on the coals, and he made room for her on the log beside him and offered her Scotch whisky and lukewarm water in a tin mug, which she accepted gratefully and which tasted as good as anything she had ever drunk.

In silence they sat together, almost but not quite touching, and watched the swift coming of the African night. They were alone, and the faint voices from the main encampment below them seemed only to emphasize this aloneness.

Jake, the old Ras and Gregorius had taken out two of the armoured cars and a camel patrol on a reconnaissance back towards the Wells of Chaldi. In the same exercise, Jake was to train the new gunners in the use of the Vickers machine guns. Gareth, as the military expert, had been left to survey the gorge and to judge the ground for defence in the event of a forced retreat up the gorge – under Italian pressure. He had been doing this when he had come across Vicky and the Galla horsemen.

Sitting now beside the fire, under a sky that was suddenly very black and half-obscured by the mountains that towered over them, Vicky was aware of a feeling of complete acceptance, an Arabic kismet of the spirit, as though fate had arranged this moment and the effort of avoiding it was too great.

They were alone, and that was how it was meant to be. The deep physical arousal and feeling of utter commitment that she had experienced earlier, on their escape from the threatening horde of Gallas, still lingered – still filled her body and her conscious mind with an ethereal glow.

She ate a little of the grilled meat, hardly tasting it, not looking at the man beside her, but staring dreamily at the brilliant diamond-white sparkle of the stars above the dark peaks, yet fully and electrically aware of him – of the nearness of him, so close that although they were still not touching she could feel the warmth emanating from his body upon her arm like the caress of a desert wind. She could almost feel his eyes as he watched her quietly. His gaze was so compelling that at last she could no longer pretend not to be aware of it, and she turned her head and met his eyes steadily.

The ruddy glow of the coals enhanced the clean regular planes of his face, and gilded the red gold of his hair. In that moment, she believed he was the most beautiful human being she had ever seen – and it required an effort to tear her eyes away from him.

As she stood up and walked away she felt her heart hammering within her chest, like a wild animal trying to escape its cage, and she heard the roar of blood in her own ears.

The interior of her tent was lit softly by the firelight

through the canvas, and she did not light the lamp, but undressed slowly in the semi-darkness and dropped her clothing carelessly across the folding chair beside the entrance. Then she lay down upon the narrow cot, and the woollen blanket was rough against the naked skin of her buttocks and back. Each breath was an effort now, and she lay rigidly with her hands clenched at her sides – almost afraid, almost exultant – her head propped on the single pillow and staring down at her body, aware of it as never before. Watching, with a sense of wonder, how each breath changed the shape of her heavily rounded breasts and how the nipples firmed slowly and thrust out, darkening perceptibly until they were so tight and hard that they pained her exquisitely.

She heard the crunch of his footsteps approach the tent, and her breathing jammed, and she thought with a small shock that she might suffocate and die. Then the flap of the tent swung open, and he stooped through and stood tall, letting the flap fall closed behind him.

Instinctively she covered herself, one arm folding across her chest and the other hand spreading protective fingers over the mound of fine fluff at the base of her belly.

He stood silently, outlined against the fire glow on the canvas, and she began to breathe again, quick and shallow. It seemed that he stood there for ever, silent and watchful, and she felt the skin of her arms and thighs prickle with goose-flesh at the slow steady scrutiny. Then he unbuttoned his shirt and let it slide to the earth. The fire glow flickered on his finely muscled arms, they rippled with a red gold sheen, like wet marble, as he moved.

He came at last to her bed and stood over her, and she wondered that the body of a man could be so slim and supple, with such lovely line and balance – then she remembered how she had once stood before the statue of Michelangelo's David with just the same depth of awe.

She lifted the hands that covered her own body, reached up like a supplicant, and drew him down upon herself.

She woke once during the night, and the fire had died away outside the tent, but a bright white moon had sailed up over the mountains and it glowed now with a silvery light through the canvas above them, striking down directly upon them.

The strange white light divested Gareth's sleeping face of all colour. It was pale now, like that of a statue or of a corpse – and Vicky experienced a sudden revulsion of feeling. There was a small dull weight at the back of her mind. When she examined it closely, she found that it was guilt – and she experienced a mild anger at a society that had burdened her with that guilt. That she could not enjoy a man, that her body could not be used as nature had intended without this backlash of emotion.

She raised herself on one elbow, careful not to disturb the man beside her, and she studied his face – pondering this new sense of guilt, and exploring her feelings for him. Slowly she realized that the two were bound inextricably together.

There was no real depth to her feelings for Gareth Swales, she had been carried along on a treacherous tide of fatigue and reaction from fear and horror. The guilt she had experienced was a consequence of this lack of substance, and she felt suddenly confused and sad.

She lay back beside the long fine length of his body, but now she had moved slightly, so that they no longer touched. She knew that after love, all animals are sad, but she thought that there was more to her feelings than that.

Suddenly, without really knowing why, she thought of Jake Barton – and the depth and cold of her sadness deepened. It was long before she slept again, but then she slept late and the morning sunlight was striking through the canvas and outside there was the sound of engines and many voices.

She sat up hurriedly, still half asleep, clutching the rough blanket to her breast, confused and owl-eyed, to discover that she was alone upon the cot – and all that remained of the night was the indentation and warmth of Gareth's body upon the blanket beside her, and the swollen aching feeling deep within her where he had been.

W hen Vicky threw on her clothes hurriedly and, still tying her hair, went out into the sunlight, she was just in time to witness the arrival of a sorry procession.

In the lead was Jake's car, Priscilla the Pig. No longer glossy white and blazoned with the insignia of the International Red Cross, it was painted instead a sandy tan colour with patches of darker camouflage in an earthy brown to break up the outline of the big angular hull and turret. The thick barrel of a Vickers machine gun protruded belligerently from the mounting.

Above the turret fluttered the tricoloured green, yellow and red pennant of Ethiopia and below that the dark blue field and golden lion of the Ras's household standard – and everything was covered with a thick coating of fine red dust.

Close behind the Pig, and attached to her by a stout towline, came Tenastelin – Gregorius's car – similarly daubed with dull camouflage paint and flying the standards of Ethiopia and Ras, and with her gun ports filled with lethal hardware. However, despite the warlike trappings, the machine had an air of dejection as it was dragged ignobly into the camp and from its rear end came a frightful grinding clatter that brought Gareth Swales hurrying half-dressed from his tent, with an angry question to shout as Jake's head appeared in the driver's hatch.

'What the hell happened?' and Jake's face was red and scowling with outrage.

'That old—' and at a loss for a suitable expletive, he indicated with a jerk of his thumb the Ras, who sat proudly in the turret of the crippled car, showing no remorse whatsoever, but beaming fondly and toothlessly on Gareth. 'Not content with firing off a thousand rounds of Vickers ammunition, he kicked Gregorius out of the driver's seat and gave us a demonstration that would have looked good at Indianapolis!'

'Oh my God!' groaned Gareth.

'How do you do?' shouted the Ras cheerily, acknowledging the applause.

'Why didn't you stop him?' demanded Gareth.

'Stop him! Jesus, have you ever tried to stop a charging rhinoceros! I chased him halfway to the coast before I caught him—'

'What's the damage?'

'He's stripped the gearbox, and burned out the clutch – he may have thrown a con rod – but I haven't gotten up enough courage to look yet.'

Jake climbed wearily from the driver's hatch, raising his dust goggles. Red dust had sifted into the thick mop of his curls and clung in the stubble of his beard, and the protected skin around his eyes was pale and naked-looking, giving him an innocent wide-eyed expression. He began beating the dust out of his trousers and shirt, still berating the happily grinning Ras.

'The old bastard is as happy as a pig in a mud wallow. Look at his face. Reconnaissance in force! It was more like a bloody circus.'

At that moment, Jake noticed Vicky for the first time, and the scowl disappeared miraculously, to be replaced by an expression of such transparent delight that she felt her guilt return swiftly and deeply, so that it gave her a cold sick feeling in the pit of her stomach.

'Vicky!' Jake called. 'God, I was worried about you!'

Vicky was able to purge a little of the feeling of guilt by busying herself at the cooking fire, in a fine show of domesticity, and she served the men with griddle cakes and grilled steaks, the last of the potatoes they had brought with them and a pan full of the pigeon-sized eggs laid by the scrawny native fowls. The camp table was set out under the acacias, in the dappled early-morning sunlight, and as Vicky worked at the fire, Jake reported the results of the reconnaissance.

'Once the Ras had tired of firing the Vickers, shooting up every tree and rock we passed, and we were just about out of ammunition, we were able to circle out northwards, keeping the speed down to avoid dust, and we found a good piece of ground from which to observe the road from Massawa to the Wells. There was a bit of traffic, transports mostly with motorized escort, but we couldn't stay too long as the Ras, God bless his friendly little soul, wanted to continue his target practice on them. We had a job stopping him. So I pulled back and we came in towards the Wells from the west again.' Jake paused to sip at the mug of coffee, and Gareth turned to Vicky as she squatted, rosy-faced, over the cooking fire.

'How's breakfast coming along, my dear?' he said. It was not the words nor the endearment, but rather the proprietorial tone, that made Jake glance sharply at Vicky. The tone Gareth had used was that which a man uses to his own woman. For a second, Vicky held Jake's glance, and then she turned busily back to her cooking, and Jake dropped his eyes thoughtfully at the steaming mug in his hands.

'How close did you get?' Gareth asked easily. He had noticed the silent exchange between Vicky and Jake – and he was relaxed and contented, lolling back in the camp chair and rolling a cheroot between his fingers.

'I left the cars in the broken ground, and went in on foot. Didn't want to take the Ras too close. I was able to watch the Eyetie position for a couple of hours. They have dug in well, and I saw gun positions with a good field of fire placed along the ridge. They are in a hell of a defensive position – and it would be crazy to attack them there. We will have to wait for them to come to us.'

Vicky brought the food to them, and as she leaned across Gareth he touched her bare upper arm in a casual caress. She drew back quickly and went to fetch the pan of eggs. Jake had noticed the gesture, yet his voice was even and unruffled as he went on,

'I wanted to circle out and to figure the chances of attacking their positions from the rear, but that was when the old Ras got bored and gave us a demonstration of hell-driving. My God, I'm hungry.' Jake filled his mouth with food, and then asked in a muffled voice, 'How did you get on, Gary?'

'There is good defensive ground in the gorge. I have the construction gangs digging positions in the slopes. We should be able to give a good account, if the Eyeties try to force their way through.'

'Well, we have got scouts watching them. Gregorius picked a hundred of his best men for the job. We will know as soon as they begin to move from the Wells, but I would like to know how much time we have before they move. Every day will give us more time to prepare, to decide on our tactics, and train the Harari – teach them how to fight with modern weapons—'

Vicky came back to the camp table and sat down.

'You haven't got time,' she said. 'No time at all.'

'What does that mean?' Jake looked up.

'The Italians crossed the Mareb yesterday at noon. They crossed in force, and they have begun bombing the towns and the roads. It's war now. It's begun.'

Jake whistled softly.

'Hey ho! Here we go!' he said, and then turned to Gareth. 'You'd best be the one who tells the Ras. You are the only one who can control him.'

'I'm touched by your faith,' murmured Gareth mildly.

'I have a pretty good idea what the Ras's reaction will be. He'll want to rush straight out there and start throwing punches. He's likely to get his whole tribe wiped out. You've got to calm him down.'

'How do you suggest I do that – give him a shot of morphine or hit him over the head?'

'Get him into a gin-rummy game,' suggested Jake maliciously. He scooped the last of the egg into his mouth and stood up from the table still chewing. 'Good chow, Vicky – but I reckon I'd better have a look at the damage the Ras did to Tenastelin. See if we can get her running again for the Eyeties to shoot at.'

For two hours, Jake worked alone on Tenastelin, rigging the block and tackle from one of the main branches of the big acacia tree and loosening the bolts to lift out the entire gearbox. Twenty yards away, Vicky sat at the table in front of her tent, and hammered out her next despatch on the little portable typewriter. Both of them were very much aware of each other as they worked, but their behaviour was elaborately unconcerned and they each made a show of concentrating all their attention on their separate tasks.

At last, Jake strained on the tackle and the dismembered

gearbox lifted jerkily off its seating and swayed, dripping grease from the acacia branch. Jake stood back and wiped his hands on a lump of cotton waste soaked in gasoline.

'Coffee break,' he said, and went to the fire. He poured two mugs full of black coffee and took them to where Vicky sat.

'How are you doing?' he asked, glancing at the page in her typewriter. 'Pulitzer stuff, is it?'

Vicky laughed, as she accepted the mug of coffee. 'Prizes never go to the best man.'

'Or to those who really want them,' agreed Jake, sitting down opposite her, and she felt a flare of annoyance that he had turned the conversation so neatly.

'Damn you, Jake Barton. I don't have to answer to you – or to anybody,' she said softly.

'Right,' he said. 'Quite right. You're a big girl now – but just remember that you're playing with the big boys. And some of them play very rough.'

'Is there any charge, counsellor?' She looked up at him defiantly, and then she saw the look in his eyes and the anger shrivelled within her.

'I don't want to fight with you, Vicky,' he said softly. 'That's the last thing in the world I want to do.' He swallowed the last of his coffee. 'Well,' he said, 'back to work.'

'You give up easily, don't you?' Vicky didn't realize she had spoken until the words were out, and then she wanted them back – but Jake cocked an eye at her, and he grinned that big boyish grin of his.

'Giving up?' Now he laughed aloud. 'Oh, lady! If you believe that then you do me wrong – a grave injustice.' And he moved slowly towards where she sat and stood over her. The laughter faded from his voice and from his eyes as he spoke in a new husky tone.

'You really are very lovely.'

'Jake.' She held his eyes. 'I wish I could explain – but I just don't understand myself.' He touched her cheek and stooped down to her. 'No, Jake, please don't—' she said and made no effort to avoid his lips, but before they touched hers, there was the urgent sound of galloping hooves, coming up through the forest.

The two of them drew slowly apart, still watching each other's eyes and Gregorius Maryam rode into the camp on a shaggy little mountain pony.

'Jake,' he called, sliding down off the saddle. 'It's war! It's begun! The Italians have crossed the Mareb. Gareth has just told my grandfather.'

'The timely messenger,' murmured Vicky, but her voice was a little shaky, and her smile lopsided.

'I've come to help you fix my car, Jake. We must be ready to fight,' called Gregorius, and tossed his reins to the servant who followed him. 'Let's get to work. There is little time – my grandfather has called all his commanders to a war council at noon. He wants you there.'

Gregorius turned away and hurried to the gutted hulk of Tenastelin. For a moment longer Jake stood over Vicky, and then he shrugged with resignation.

'Just remember,' he threatened her mildly, 'I don't give up,' and he followed Gregorius.

An hour later they had stripped the gearbox and spread its component parts on a sheet of clean canvas. Jake rocked back on his heels.

'Well, grandpappy has cooked his goose,' he said, and Gregorius apologized solemnly.

'He is a very impetuous gentleman, my grandfather.'

'It's getting on towards noon.' Jake stood up. 'Let's go down and hear what next he has in store for us, that impetuous gentleman.'

T he Ras's encampment was set a little apart from the main body of his army, and housed only his personal entourage. There were at least two acres of hastily erected *tukuls*, made of sapling frames covered with a range of material from thatch to flattened paraffin cans. Through this encampment wandered the naked snotty-nosed children and the Ras's multitudinous female retainers, together with goats, mangy dogs, donkeys, and camels.

The Ras's tent was set up in the centre of this community. It was a large marquee, patched so often that little of the original canvas was visible. His bodyguard was grouped protectively at the entrance.

Beyond the Ras's tent was a large area of open sandy ground, almost completely covered by rank upon rank of patiently squatting warriors.

'My God,' exclaimed Jake. 'Everyone gets to the war council.'

'It's the custom,' explained Gregorius. 'All may attend, but only the commanders may speak.'

To one side, separated from the Harari troops by a small space of beaten earth and centuries of rankling hostility, were the Galla contingent, and Vicky pointed them out to Jake.

'Pretty bunch,' he murmured. 'With allies like that, who needs enemies?'

Gregorius led them directly to the Ras's tent, and the guards stood aside for them to enter. The interior was dark and hot, redolent with the smell of the rank native tobacco and spiced food. At the far end of the tent, a knot of silent men squatted in a tense circle about two figures – the Ras, swathed in dark woollen robes, and Gareth Swales in a light silk shirt and white flannels.

For a moment Jake thought that the two central figures were deeply immersed in planning the strategy and defence of the Sardi Gorge – then he saw the neat piles of pasteboard spread out on the golden Afghanistan rug between them.

'My God,' said Jake. 'He took me at my word.' Gareth looked up from the fan of cards he held in his right hand.

'Thank God.' His face showed obvious relief. 'I only wish it had been an hour earlier.'

'What's the trouble.'

'This old bastard is cheating,' said Gareth, with barely suppressed outrage quivering in his voice. 'He has caught me for almost two hundred quid this morning. I'm utterly appalled, I must say. They obviously have no scruples, these people—' and here Gareth glanced at Gregorius, 'no offence meant, of course. But I must admit I am staggered.'

And the Ras nodded and grinned happily, his eyes sparkling with triumph, as he waved Jake and Vicky to a seat on a pile of cushions beside him.

'If he's cheating – don't play with him,' suggested Vicky, and Gareth looked pained.

'You don't understand, old girl. I haven't been able to figure how he's doing it. He's invented a method new to science and the gambling halls of the world. He might be an absolutely unscrupulous old rogue, but he must be some sort of genius as well. I've just got to keep on playing with him until I work out his system.' Gareth's doleful expression became radiant. 'My God, when I do – Monte Carlo here I come!' He discarded a six of spades. The Ras leapt upon it with a cackle of triumph and began laying out his hand.

'Oh my God,' groaned Gareth. 'He's done it again.'

The tense group of counsellors and elders around the game exploded in a delighted burst of cheers and felicitations, and the Ras acknowledged their congratulations like a victorious prizefighter. Grinning and snuffling he leaned across the rug and with a loud cry of 'How do you do!' he punched Gareth's arm playfully, and Gareth winced and massaged the limb tenderly.

'He does that every time he wins. He's got a touch like a demented blacksmith – I'm black and blue.'

'How do you do!' cried the Ras again, louder than before, and he shaped up to punch once more, but Gareth hastily produced his purse, and the Ras relaxed.

'He keeps punching until I pay.' Gareth counted out the coins, while the Ras and his followers watched in heavy-breathing concentration, which only broke into smiles and laughter again when the pile of coins in front of Gareth reached the stipulated amount. 'No credit in this game,' Gareth explained, as he shoved the money across. 'Cash on the nail, or you get your arm broken. This old bastard – ' Gareth glanced again at Gregorius, ' – no offence, of course. But this old bastard wouldn't trust his own mother, probably with good reason. I'm absolutely appalled! I've met some shockers in my time – but this chap takes the biscuit.' There was a deep respect in Gareth's tone, which changed to mild alarm as the Ras gathered the cards preparatory to the next deal, and he turned to Gregorius.

'Please explain to your dear grandfather that, though I'd be delighted to accommodate him at a future date, I do think he should now concentrate a little of his skills on confounding the common enemy. The armies of Italy are waiting.'

Reluctantly, the Ras laid the cards aside and, with a sharp speech in Amharic, put the war council into session, then immediately turned to Jake Barton.

'My grandfather wishes to know the state of his armoured squadron. He is impressed with the cars, and is certain that they can be used to great advantage.'

'Tell him that he has wrecked a quarter of his armoured squadron. We've got three runners left.'

The Ras showed no remorse at this rebuke, but turned to his commanders and launched into a long vivid account of his exploits as a driver, his wide gestures describing the speed and dash of his evolutions. The account was punctuated by loyal exclamations of wonder from his officers, and it was some minutes before he turned back to Jake.

'My grandfather says that three of these wonderful machines will be enough to send the Italians running back into the sea.'

'I wish I shared his confidence,' remarked Gareth, and Jake went on,

'There is one other small problem, we are short of crews – drivers and gunners – for the cars. We'll need a week or two to train your men.'

The Ras interrupted fiercely, almost as though he had understood Jake, and there was a fierce murmur of agreement from his commanders.

'My grandfather intends to attack the Italian positions at the Wells of Chaldi. He intends to attack immediately.'

Jake glanced at Gareth, who rolled his eyes to the heavens. 'Give him the word, old son,' he said, but Jake shook his head.

'It'll come better from you.'

Gareth drew a deep breath and launched into a long explanation as to the suicidal futility of a frontal attack, even with armoured support, against guns dug into a commanding position.

'The Italians must advance. That is when our chance will come.'

It took all Gareth's eloquence to make the Ras agree, albeit reluctantly, to wait for the enemy to make the first move, to watch with his forward scouts for the moment when the Italians left their fortified positions above the Wells and moved out into the open grassland where they would be more vulnerable.

Once the Ras had agreed, scowling and muttering, to cool his ardour that long, then Jake could take over from Gareth and suggest the tactics that might best be employed.

'Please tell your grandfather that we come back to my original warning – we do not have crews for all three cars.'

'I can drive,' interrupted Vicky Camberwell, suddenly aware that she was being squeezed out of consideration.

Gareth and Jake exchanged glances again, and were both instantly in complete agreement, but it was Gareth who spoke for them.

'It's one thing acting as a ferry driver, and another as a combatant, my dear. You are here to write about the fighting, not get mixed up in it.'

Vicky flashed a scornful glance at him and turned to Jake.

'Jake,' she began.

'Gareth's right.' He cut her short. 'I agree with that – all the way.' Vicky subsided angrily, knowing there was no profit in arguing now – not accepting their lordly decrees, but willing to bide her time. She listened quietly as the discussion flowed back and forth. Jake explained how the cars should be used to shock the enemy and punch open the Italian defences so that the Ethiopian cavalry could stream through and exploit the disordered infantry.

The Ras's scowls smoothed away, and an unholy grin replaced them. His eyes glowed like black coals in their beds of dark wrinkled flesh, and when at last he gave his orders, he spoke with the ringing and final authority of a royal warrior that brooked no further argument.

'My grandfather decrees that the first attack will be made upon the enemy as soon as they advance beyond the caves of Chaldi. It will be made by all the horsemen of both Harari and Galla, and led by two armoured cars. The infantry, the Vickers guns and one armoured car will be held in reserve here at the Sardi Gorge.'

'What about the crews for the cars?' asked Jake.

'You and I, Jake, in one car, and in the other car Major

Swales will be the driver and my grandfather will be the gunner.'

'I can't believe it's happening to me,' groaned Gareth. 'That old bastard is stark raving bloody mad. He's a menace to himself and everyone within a fifty-mile range.'

'Including the Italians,' agreed Jake.

'It's all very well for you to grin like that – you won't be locked up in a tin can with a maniac. Gregorius, tell him—'

'No, Major Swales.' Gregorius shook his head, and his expression was remote and frosty. 'My grandfather has given his orders. I will not translate your objections – though if you insist I will give him an exact translation of what you have just said about him.'

'My dear chap.' Gareth held up his hands in a gesture of capitulation. 'I count it an honour to be selected by your grandfather – and my remarks were made in fun, I assure you. No offence, old chap, no offence at all.' And he watched helplessly, as the Ras picked up the pack of playing cards and began to deal the next hand.

'I just hope the jolly old Eyeties get a move on. I can't afford much more of this.'

M ajor Luigi Castelani saluted from the entrance of the tent.

'As you ordered, my Colonel.'

Count Aldo Belli nodded to him in the full-length mirror a brief acknowledgement before he switched his attention back to his own image.

'Gino,' he snapped. 'Is that a mark on the toecap of my left boot?' and the little sergeant dropped to his knees at the Count's feet and breathed heavily on the boot, dulling the glossy surface before polishing it lovingly with his own sleeve. The Count glanced up and saw that Castelani still lingered in the entrance. His expression was so lugubrious and doom-laden that the Count felt his anger return.

'Your face is enough to sour the wine, Castelani.'

'The Count knows my misgivings.'

'Indeed,' he thundered. 'I have heard nothing but your whines since I gave my orders to advance.'

'May I point out once more that those orders are in direct—'

'You may not. Il Duce, Benito Mussolini himself, has placed a sacred trust upon me. I will not fail that trust.'

'My Colonel, the enemy—'

'Bah!' Scorn flashed from the dark, heavily fringed eyes. 'Bah, I say. Enemy, you say – savages, I say. Soldiers, you say – rabble, say I.'

'As my Colonel wishes, but the armoured vehicle—'

'No! Castelani, no! It was not an armoured vehicle, but an ambulance.' The Count had truly convinced himself of this. 'I will not let this moment of destiny slip through my fingers. I refuse to creep about like a frightened old woman. It is not in my nature, Castelani, I am a man of action – of direct action. It is in my nature to spring like a leopard at the jugular vein of my enemy. The time of talking is over now, Castelani. The time for action is upon us.'

'As my Colonel wishes.'

'It is not what I wish, Castelani. It is what the gods of war decree, and what I – as a warrior – must obey.'

There did not seem a reply to this and the Major stood silently aside as the Count swept out of the tent, with chin upheld, and with a firm, deliberate tread.

Castelani's strike force had been ready since dawn. Fifty of the heavy troop transporters made up a single column, and he had spent most of the night deliberating on the order of march.

His final disposition was to leave a full company in the fortified position above the Wells of Chaldi, under the command of one of the Count's young captains. All other troops had been included in the flying column which was to drive hard on the gorge, seize the approaches and fight its way up to the highlands.

In the van, Castelani had placed five truck-loads of riflemen, and immediately behind them were the machine-gun sections, which he knew he could bring into action within minutes. Another twenty truck-loads of infantry followed them – ten in the extreme rear. Under his eye and hand, he had placed his field artillery.

In the event of the column running into real trouble, he was relying on the infantry to buy him the precious time needed to unlimber and range his Howitzers. Under their protective muzzles, he was mildly confident that he could extricate the column from any predicament into which the Count's newfound courage and vaunting visions of glory might lead them – mildly, but not entirely, confident.

Beside each stationary truck the driver and crew were sprawling on the sandy earth, bareheaded, tunics unbuttoned and cigarettes lit. Castelani threw back his head, inflated his lungs and let out a bellow that seemed to echo against the clear high desert sky.

'Fall in!' and the sprawling figures scrambled into frenzied activity, grabbing weapons and adjusting uniforms as they formed ragged ranks beside each truck.

'My children,' said Aldo Belli, as he began to pace down the line. 'My brave boys,' and he looked at them, not really seeing the misbuttoned tunics, the stubble on their chins, nor the hastily pinched-out cigarettes behind the ears. His vision was misted with sentiment, his imagination dressed them in burnished breastplates and horse-tail plumes.

'You are thirsty for blood?' the Colonel asked, and threw back his head and laughed a reckless carefree laugh. 'I will give you buckets of it,' he said. 'Today you will drink your fill.'

The men within earshot shuffled their feet and glanced uneasily at each other. There was a definite preference for Chianti amongst them.

The Count stopped before a thin rifleman, still in his teens, with a dark shaggy mop of hair hanging out from under his helmet.

'Bambino,' said the Count, and the youth hung his head and grinned in sickly embarrassment. 'We will make a warrior out of you today,' and he embraced the boy, then held him off at arm's length and studied his face. 'Italy gives of her finest, none are too young or too noble to be spared sacrifice on the altar of war.' The boy's ingratiating grin changed swiftly to real alarm.

'Sing, bambino, sing!' cried the Count, and himself opened 'La Giovinezza' in his soaring baritone while the youth quavered uncertainly below him. The Count marched on, singing, and reached the head of the column as the song ended. He nodded to Castelani, too breathless to speak, and the Major let out another bull bellow.

'Mount up!'

The formations of black-shirted troopers broke up into confused activity as they hurried to the cumbersome trucks and climbed aboard.

The Rolls-Royce stood in pride of place at the head of the column, Giuseppe sitting ready at the wheel with Gino beside him, his camera at the ready.

The engine was purring, the wide back seat packed with the Count's personal gear – sports rifle, shotgun, travelling rugs, picnic hamper, straw wine carrier, binoculars, and ceremonial cloak.

The Count mounted with dignity and settled himself on the padded leather. He looked at Castelani.

'Remember, Major, the essence of my strategy is speed and surprise. The lightning blow, swift and merciless, delivered by the steel hand at the enemy's heart.'

Sitting beside the driver in the rear truck of the column, eating the dust of the forty-nine trucks ahead, and already beginning to sweat freely in the oven heat of the steel cab, Major Castelani inspected his watch.

'Mother of God,' he growled. 'It's past eleven o'clock. We will have to move fast if we—'

At that moment, the driver swore and braked heavily, and before the truck had come to a halt, Castelani had leapt out on to the running board and climbed high on to the roof of the cab.

'What is it?' he shouted to the driver ahead.

'I do not know, Major,' the man shouted back.

Ahead of them the entire column had come to a halt, and Castelani braced himself for the sound of firing – certain that they had run into an ambush. There was confused shouting of question and comment from the drivers and crews of the stranded convoy, as they climbed down and peered ahead.

Castelani focused his binoculars, and at that moment the sound of gunfire carried clearly across the desert spaces, and the swift order to deploy his field guns was on Castelani's lips as he found the Rolls-Royce in the lens of his binoculars.

The big automobile was out on the left flank, racing through the scrubby grass, and in the back seat the Count was braced with a shotgun levelled over the driver's head. Even as Castelani watched, a flock of plump brown francolin burst from the grass ahead of the speeding Rolls, rising steeply on quick wide wings. Long blue streamers of gunsmoke flew from the muzzles of the shotgun, and two of the birds exploded in puffs of soft brown feathers, while the survivors of the flock scattered away, and the Rolls came to a halt in a skidding cloud of dust.

Castelani watched Gino, the little Sergeant, jump from the Rolls and run to pick up the dead birds and carry them to the Count.

'Porco Dio!' thundered the Major, as he watched the Count pose for the camera, still standing in the rear of the Rolls, holding the dangling feathered brown bodies and smiling proudly into the lens.

T here was a rising feeling of despondency and alarm in the Ras's army. Since the middle of the morning, through a day of scalding heat and unrelenting boredom, they had waited.

The scouts had reported the first forward movement of the Italian force at ten o'clock that morning, and immediately the Ras's forces had moved forward into their carefully prepared positions.

Gareth Swales had spent days selecting the best possible ground in which to meet the first Italian thrust, and each contingent of the wild Ethiopian cavalry had been carefully drilled and properly cautioned as to the sequence of ambush and the necessity of maintaining strict discipline.

The chosen field was situated between the horns of the mountains, in the mouth of the funnel formed by the debouchment of the Sardi Gorge. It was obvious that this was the only approach route open to the Italians, and it was nearly twelve miles wide.

The attackers must be led in close to the southern horn of the funnel, where the Vickers machine guns had been sited on the rocky slopes, and where a minor water course had chiselled its way down to the plain. The water course was dry now, and it meandered out into the plain for five miles before vanishing, but it was deep and wide enough to conceal the large contingents of Harari and Galla horsemen.

This mass of cavalry had been waiting all day, squatting beside their mounts in the sugar-white sand of the river bed. The two separate factions had been diplomatically separated. The Harari were placed at the head of the trap, nearest the rocky slope of the mountain with the Vickers gunners hidden on their flank in strong posts amongst the rocks. The Galla, under the scar-faced Gerazmach in the blue shamma, were grouped farther out on the open plain at a point where the dry water course turned sharply and angled out towards the arid grassland.

Here in the bend, the banks were still steep enough to conceal fifteen hundred mounted men. These, with almost three thousand of the Ras's own cavalry, formed a formidable offensive army – especially if thrown in unexpectedly on a confused and unbalanced enemy. The mood of the Ethiopians, ever sanguinary, was aggravated by the many hours of enforced inactivity, crouching without cover from the blinding sun on a white sand bed which reflected its rays like a mirror. The horses were already distressed by the heat and lack of water – while the men were murderous.

Gareth Swales had contrived a net, using the natural wide curve of the water course, into which he hoped to lure the Italian column. Two miles farther out in the plain, beyond where he now stood on the turret of the Hump, a fold of ground concealed the small band of mounted men who were to provide the bait. They had been waiting there since the scouts had first reported the Italian movement early that morning. Like everybody else they must by this time be restless, bored and thoroughly uncomfortable. Gareth wondered that this huge amorphous body of undisciplined,

265

independent, spirited hillsmen had so long maintained cohesion. He would not have been surprised if by this stage half of them had lost interest and had set off homewards.

The only person who was occupied and seemed happy enough was Jake Barton, and Gareth lowered his binoculars and regarded what he could see of him with irritation. The front upper half of that gentleman was completely hidden within the engine compartment of Priscilla the Pig, and only his legs and backside protruded. The muffled strains of 'Tiger Rag' whistled endlessly added to Gareth's irritation.

'How are you coming along there?' he called, merely to stop the music, and Jake's tousled head emerged, one cheek smeared with black oil.

'I think I've found it,' he said cheerfully. 'A lump of muck in the carb,' and he wiped his hands on the lump of cotton waste that Gregorius handed him. 'What are the Eyeties up to?'

'I think we've got a small problem, old son,' Gareth murmured softly, turning once more to resume his vigil, and his expression for once was serious and concerned. 'I must admit that I banked on the old Latin dash and swagger to bring them charging down here without a backward glance.'

Jake came across from his car and clambered up beside Gareth. The two armoured cars were parked at the extreme end of the curved water course, just before it lost its identity and vanished into the limitless sea of grass and rolling sandy hills. Here the banks of the river were only just enough to cover the hulls of the two cars, but they left the turrets partially exposed. A light cover of cut thorn branches made them inconspicuous, while allowing them to act as observation posts for the crews.

Gareth handed Jake his binoculars. 'I think we've got ourselves a really wily one here. This Italian commander isn't rushing. He's coming on nice and slow, taking his time.' Gareth shook his head worriedly. 'I don't like it at all.'

'He's stopped again,' Jake said, watching the distant dust cloud that marked the position of the advancing column. The dust cloud shrivelled, and subsided.

'Oh my God!' groaned Gareth, and snatched the binoculars. 'The bastard is up to something, I'm sure of it. This is the seventh time the column has halted – and for no apparent reason at all. The scouts can't work it out – and nor can I. I've got a nasty hollow feeling that we are up against some sort of military genius, a modern Napoleon, and it's making me nervous as hell.'

Jake smiled and advised philosophically, 'What you really need is a soothing game of gin. The Ras is waiting for you.' As if on cue, the Ras looked up brightly and expectantly from the ammunition box set in the small strip of shade under the hull. He had laid out a pattern of playing cards on the lid which he had been studying. His bodyguard were grouped behind him. They also looked up expectantly.

'They've got me surrounded,' groaned Gareth. 'I'm not sure which one is the most dangerous – that old bastard down there, or that one out there.'

He raised the binoculars again and swept the long horizon below the mountains. There was no longer any sign of dust.

'What the hell is he up to?'

I n fact this seventh halt called by Count Aldo Belli was to be the briefest of the day, and yet one of the most unavoidable.

It was in fact an occasion of the utmost urgency, and while the Count's portable commode was hastily unloaded from the truck carrying his personal gear, he twisted and wriggled impatiently on the back seat of the Rolls while Gino, the batman, tried to comfort him.

'It is the water from those wells, Excellency,' he nodded sagely.

Once the commode had been set up, with a good view of the distant mountains before it, a small canvas tent was raised around it to hide the seat from the curious gaze of five hundred infantry men.

The job was completed, only just in time, and a respectful and expectant hush fell over the entire column as the Count climbed carefully down from the Rolls and then dashed like an Olympic athlete for the small lonely canvas structure and disappeared. The silence and expectation lasted for almost fifteen minutes – and was shattered at last by the Count's shouts from within the tent.

'Bring the doctor!'

Five hundred men waited with all the genuine suspense of a movie audience, speculation and rumour running wildly down the column until it reached Major Castelani. Even he, convinced as he was that he had seen it all, could not believe the cause of this fresh delay, and he went forward to investigate.

He arrived at the tent to find the Count and his medical advisers crowded around the commode and avidly discussing its contents. The Count was pale, but proud, like a new mother whose infant is the centre of attention. He looked up as Castelani appeared in the doorway, and the Major recoiled slightly as, for a moment, it seemed the Count might invite him to join in the examination.

He saluted hastily, taking another step backwards.

'Has your Excellency orders for me?'

'I am an ill man, Castelani,' and the Count struck a pose, drooping visibly, his head lolling weakly. Then slowly he drew back his shoulders, and his chin came up. A wan but brave smile tightened his lips. 'But that is of no account. We advance, Castelani. Onwards! Tell the men I am well. Hide the truth from them. If they know of my illness, they will despair. They will panic.'

Castelani saluted again. 'As you wish, my Colonel.'

'Help me to the car, Castelani,' he ordered, and reluctantly the Major took his arm. The Count leaned heavily upon him as they crossed to the Rolls, but he smiled gallantly at his men and waved to the nearest of them.

'My poor brave boys,' he muttered. 'They must never know. I will not fail them now.'

'What the hell is happening out there?' fretted Gareth Swales, glancing up anxiously at Jake on the turret of the car above him.

'Nothing!' Jake assured him. 'No sign of movement.'

'I don't like it,' reiterated Gareth morosely, and his expression hardly altered as the Ras let out one of his triumphant cries and began laying out his cards.

'I don't like that either,' he said again, and reached for his wallet before the Ras reminded him. While the Ras shuffled and dealt the next hand, he continued his conversation with Jake.

'What about Vicky? Nothing from that quarter either?'

'Not a peep,' Jake assured him.

'That's another thing I don't like. She took it too calmly. I expected her to put in an appearance long ago – despite my orders.'

'She won't be coming,' Jake assured him, raising the binoculars again and sweeping the empty horizon.

'I wish I was that confident,' muttered Gareth, picking up his cards. 'I've been expecting to see her car driving up at any minute. It isn't like her to sit meekly in camp, while the action is going on out here. She's a front-ranker, that one. She likes to be right there when anything is happening.'

'I know,' Jake agreed. 'She had that mean look in her eye when she agreed to stay at the gorge. So I just made sure she wasn't going to use Miss Wobbly. I took the carbon rod out of the distributor.'

Gareth began to grin. 'That's the only good news I've had today. I had visions of Vicky Camberwell arriving in the middle of a fire fight.'

'Poor bloody Italians,' observed Jake, and they both laughed.

'Sometimes you surprise me. Do you know that?' said Gareth, and he drew a cheroot from his breast pocket and tossed it up to where Jake stood. 'Thanks for looking after what is mine,' he said. 'I appreciate that.'

Jake bit the tip off the cigar, and gave him a quizzical look as he flicked a match across the rough steel of the turret and held the flame in his cupped hands to burn off the sulphur.

'They are all mavericks until somebody puts a brand on them. That's the law of the range, old buddy,' he answered, and lit the cigar.

Vicky Camberwell had selected five full-grown men from the Ras's camp attendants, rewarded each with a silver Maria Theresa dollar, and worn each of them down to the fine edge of exhaustion. One after the other, they had taken hold of Miss Wobbly's crank handle and turned it like a squad of demented organ-grinders – while Vicky shouted encouragement and threats at them from the driver's hatch, her eyes blazing and cheeks fiery with frustration.

After an hour of this she was convinced that sabotage

had been employed to keep her safely out of the way, and she began to check out Miss Wobbly's internal organs. She was one of those unusual women who liked to know how things worked, and throughout her life had plagued a long series of mechanics, boyfriends and instructors with her questions. It was not enough for her to switch on a machine and steer it. She had made herself an excellent driver and pilot, and in the process she had acquired a fair idea of the workings of the internal combustion engine.

'All right, Mr Barton – let's find out what you've done,' she muttered grimly. 'Let's start on the fuel system.'

She rolled up her sleeves and tied a scarf firmly around her hair. Her five hefty helpers watched with awe as she approached the engine compartment and lifted the cowling, and then they crowded forward to get a good view and offer their advice. She had to beat them back and shoo them away before she could begin work, but then she was completely absorbed in her task, and in half an hour had checked and tested the fuel system, making sure that gasoline was travelling freely from the tank along the lines to carburettor and cylinders, and that the pump was functioning smoothly.

'Right, now let's check out the electrics,' she muttered to herself, and turned irritably as an insistent hand tugged at her belt, breaking her concentration.

'Yes, what is it?' Her expression changed, lighting up happily as she saw who it was.

'Sara!' She embraced the girl. 'How on earth did you get here?'

'I escaped, Miss Camberwell. It was so boring in the hospital. I had my father's men bring a horse for me and I climbed out of the window and rode down the gorge.'

'What about your friend – the young doctor?' Vicky demanded, still holding the girl and surprised by the strength of her affection for her.

'Oh, him!' Sara's voice held a world of scorn and contempt. 'He was the most boring thing in the hospital. Doctor! Ha! He knows nothing about how a body works – I had to try and teach him, and that was no fun.'

'And your leg?' she asked. 'How is your leg?'

'It is nothing – almost well.' Sara tried to dismiss the injury – but Vicky saw that she was drawn and haggard. The long, rough ride down the gorge must have taxed her, and as Vicky led her tenderly to a seat in the shade of the acacias, she favoured the injured leg heavily.

'I heard there is going to be a battle. That's really why I came. I heard the Italians are advancing—' She looked round her brightly, seeming to thrust her pain and weariness aside. 'Where are Jake and Gareth? Where is Gregorius? We must not miss the battle, Miss Camberwell.'

'That's what I am working on.' Vicky's smile faded. 'They have left us behind.'

'What!' Sara's bright look became bellicose and then outraged as Vicky explained how they had been edged out.

'Men! You cannot trust them,' fumed Sara. 'If they aren't trying to tip you on your back, then it's something worse. We aren't going to let them do it, are we?'

'No,' Vicky agreed. 'We are most certainly not.'

With Sara beside her, it was impossible to continue her work on the armoured car, for the girl made up for a total ignorance of the mechanism by an unbounded curiosity and when Vicky should have been inspecting the magneto, she found instead that she was looking closely at the back of Sara's head which had been interposed. After she had forcibly elbowed her aside for the sixth time, she asked with exasperation,

'Do you know how to fire a Vickers machine gun?'

'I am a mountain girl,' boasted Sara. 'I was born with a gun in one hand and a horse between my legs.'

'Or what have you,' murmured Vicky, and the girl grinned impishly.

'But have you ever fired a Vickers?'

'No,' admitted Sara reluctantly, and then brightened. 'But it won't take me long to find out how it works.'

'There!' Vicky indicated the thick water-jacketed barrel that protruded from the turret. 'Go ahead.'

When Sara scrambled awkwardly on to the sponson, still favouring the leg, Vicky could return to her inspection. It was another half hour before she exclaimed,

'He has taken the carbon rod out of the distributor. Oh, the sneaky swine.'

Sara's head popped out of the turret. 'Gareth?' she asked.

'No,' answered Vicky. 'Jake.'

'I didn't expect it of him.' Sara climbed down beside Vicky to inspect the damage.

'They're all the same.'

'Where has he hidden it?'

'Probably in his own pocket.'

'What are we going to do?' Sara wrung her hands anxiously. 'We'll miss the battle!'

Vicky thought a moment and then her expression changed. 'In my bag, in the tent, is an Ever-Ready flashlight. There is also a leather cosmetic case. Bring them both to me, please.'

One of the flashlight dry-cell batteries, split open by the curved blade of the dagger from Sara's belt, yielded a thick carbon rod from its core, and Vicky shaped it carefully with the nail-file from her cosmetic case, until it slipped neatly into the central shaft of the distributor – and the engine fired at the first swing of the crank.

'You are really very clever, Miss Camberwell,' said Sara, with such patent and solemn sincerity that Vicky was deeply touched. She smiled up at the girl who stood above the driver's seat, her head and shoulders in the turret and her knees braced against the back of the driver's seat.

'Think you can work that gun yet?' she asked, and Sara nodded uncertainly and placed her slim dark hands on the clumsy mahogany pistol grips, standing on tiptoe to squint through the sights.

'Just take me to them, Miss Camberwell.'

Vicky let out the clutch and swung the car in a tight lock out from under the acacia trees and on to the steep rocky track which led to the wide open grassland in the funnel of the mountains.

'I am very angry with Jake,' declared Sara, clutching wildly for support as the car pounded and thumped over the rough track. 'I did not expect him to behave that way – hiding the carbon rod. That is more like Gareth. I am disappointed in him.'

'You are?'

'Yes, I think we should punish him.'

'How?'

'I think Gareth should be your lover,' Sara stated firmly. 'I think that is how we will punish Jake.'

In between wrestling with the heavy steering, and dancing her feet over the steel pedals of brake and clutch, Vicky thought about what Sara had said. She thought also of Jake's broad rangy shoulders, and thickly muscled arms – she thought about his mop of curly hair and that wide boyish grin that could change so quickly to a heavy frown. Suddenly she realized how very much she wanted to be with him, and how she would miss him if he were gone.

'I must thank you for sorting out my affairs for me,' she called to the girl in the turret. 'You have a knack.'

'It's a pleasure, Miss Camberwell,' Sara called back. 'It is just that I understand these things.'

As the afternoon wore on, so thunderheads of cloud formed upon the mountains in the west. They soared into a sky of endless sapphire blue, smoothly rounded masses of silver that rolled and swirled with a ponderous majesty, swelling high and darkening to the colour of ripening grapes and old bruises.

Yet over the plain the sky was open, clear and high, and the sun burned down and heated the earth so that the air above it shimmered and danced, distorting vision and distance. At one moment the mountains were so close that it seemed they reached to the heavens and they must topple upon the small group of men crouched in the shade of the two concealed armoured cars; at the next they seemed remote and miniaturized by distance.

The sun had heated the hulls of the cars so that the steel would blister skin at a touch – and the men who waited, all of them except Jake Barton and Gareth Swales, crawled like survivors of a catastrophe beneath the hulls, seeking relief from the unrelenting sun.

The heat was so intense that the gin rummy game had long been abandoned, and the two white men panted like dogs, the sweat drying instantly on their skins and crusting into a thin film of white salt crystals.

Gregorius looked to the mountains, and the clouds upon them, and he said softly, 'Soon it will rain.' He looked up to where Jake Barton sat like a statue on the turret of Priscilla the Pig. Jake had swathed his head and upper body in a white linen shamma to protect it from the sun and he held the binoculars in his lap. Every few minutes, he would lift them to his eyes and make one slow sweep of the land ahead before slumping motionless again.

Slowly the shadows crept out from the hulls of the cars, the sun turned across its zenith and gradually lost its white glare, its rays toned with yellows and reds. Once again, Jake lifted the binoculars and this time paused midway in his automatic sweep of the horizon. In the lens the familiar dun feather of the distant cloud once again wavered softly at the line where pale earth and paler sky joined.

He watched it for five minutes, and it seemed that the dust cloud was fading – shrivelling, and that the shimmering pillars of heat-distorted air were rising, screening his vision.

Jake lowered the glasses and a warm flood of sweat broke from his hairline, trickled down his forehead into his eyes. He swore softly at the sting of salt and wiped it away with the hem of the linen shamma. He blinked rapidly, and then lifted the glasses again – and felt his heart jump in his chest and the prickle of rising hair on the nape of his neck.

The freakish currents and whirlpools of heated air cleared suddenly, and the dust cloud that minutes before had seemed remote as the far shores of the ocean was now so close and crisply outlined against the pale blue white sky that it filled the lens. Then his heart jumped again – below the rolling spreading cloud he could make out the dark insect shapes of many swiftly moving vehicles. Suddenly the viscosity of the air changed again, and the shapes of the approaching column altered – becoming monstrous, looming through the mist of dust – closer, every second closer and more menacing.

Jake shouted, and Gareth was beside him in an instant.

'Are you crazy?' he gasped. 'They'll overrun us in a minute.'

'Get started,' Jake snapped. 'Get the engines started,' and slid down into the driver's hatch. There was a flurry of sudden frantic movement around the cars. The engines were cranked into reluctant life, surging and missing and back-firing as the volatile fuel turned to vapour in the heat and starved the engines.

The Ras was lifted into the turret of Gareth's car by half a dozen of his men at arms, and installed behind the Vickers gun. Their job accomplished, his men were leaving him and hurrying to mount their ponies when the Ras let out a series of shrieks in Amharic and pointed at the empty cave of his own mouth, devoid of teeth and big enough to hibernate a bear.

There was a brief moment of consternation, until the senior and eldest man at arms produced a large leather-covered box from his saddle bag and hurried with it to kneel humbly on the sponson of the car and proffer the open box to the Ras. Mollified, the Ras reached into the box and brought out a magnificent set of porcelain teeth, big and white and sharp enough to fit in the mouth of a Derby winner, complete with bright red gums.

With only a short struggle he forced the set into his mouth, and then snapped them like a brook trout rising to the fly, before peeling back his lips in a death's head grin.

His followers cooed and exclaimed with admiration, and Gregorius told Jake proudly,

'My grandfather only wears his teeth when he is fighting or pleasuring a lady,' and Jake spared a brief glance from the advancing Italian army to admire the dazzling dental display.

'Makes him look younger, not a day over ninety,' he gave his opinion, and revved the engine, carefully manoeuvring the car into a hull-down position below the bank from where he could keep the Italians under observation. Gareth brought the other car up alongside and grinned at him from the open hatch. It was a wicked grin, and Jake realized that the Englishman was looking forward to the coming clash with anticipation.

It was no longer necessary to use binoculars. The Italian column was less than two miles distant, moving swiftly on a course that was carrying it parallel to the dry river-bed, beyond the curved horns of the ambush into the open unprotected funnel of flat land between the mountains. Another fifteen minutes at this rate of advance and it would have turned the Ethiopian flank and would be able to drive without resistance to the mouth of the gorge – and Jake knew better than to hope to be able to reorganize the rabble of cavalry once their formations were shattered. Instinctively he knew that they would fight like giants as long as the tide carried them forward, but any retreat would become a rout, and they would race for the hills like factory workers at five o'clock. They were accustomed to fighting as individuals, avoiding setpiece battles, but snatching opportunity as it was offered, swift as hawks, but giving instantly before any determined thrust by an enemy.

'Come on!' he muttered to himself, pounding his fist against his thigh impatiently, and with the first stirring of alarm. Unless the bait was offered within the next few moments—

Because they fought as individuals, each man his own general, and because the art of ambush and entrapment came as naturally to the Ethiopian as the feel of a rifle in his hand, Jake need not have fretted.

Seeming to rise from the flat scorched earth under the wheels of the leading Italian vehicles, a small galloping knot of horsemen flitted across the heat-tortured earth, seeming to float above it like a flock of dark birds. Their shapes wavering and indistinct, wrapped in pale streamers of dust, they cut back obliquely across the Italian line of march, running hard for the centre of the hidden Ethiopian line.

Almost instantly a single vehicle detached itself from the head of the column and headed on a converging course with the flying horsemen. Its speed was frightening, and it closed so swiftly that the squadron of cavalry was forced to veer away, forced to edge out towards where the two armoured cars were hidden.

Behind the single speeding vehicle the Italian column lost its rigid shape. The front half of it swung away in a long untidy line abreast in pursuit of the horsemen. These were all larger, heavier vehicles, with high, canvas-covered cupolas, and their progress was ponderous and so slow that they could not gain perceptibly on the galloping horses.

However, the smaller faster vehicle was gaining rapidly and Jake stood higher to give himself a better view as he refocused the binoculars. He recognized instantly the big open Rolls-Royce tourer that he had last seen at the Wells of Chaldi. Its polished metalwork glittered in the sunlight, its low rakish lines enhancing the impression of speed and power, as the dust boiled out from behind its spinning rear wheels with their huge flashing central bosses.

Even as he watched, the Rolls braked and skidded broadside, coming to a halt in a furiously billowing cloud of dust. A figure tumbled from the rear seat.

Jake watched the man brace himself over the sporting rifle and the spurt of gunsmoke from the muzzle as he fired seven shots in quick succession, the rifle kicking up abruptly at the recoil and the thud thud of the discharge reaching Jake only seconds later.

The horsemen were drawing swiftly away from the Rolls, but neither the changing range nor the dust and mirage affected the marksman. At each shot a horse went down, sliding against the earth, legs kicking to the sky – or plunging and rolling, as it struggled to regain its legs, falling back at last and lying still.

Then the rifleman leaped aboard the Rolls again, and the pursuit was continued, gaining swiftly on the survivors, the heavy phalanx of trucks and troop transports lumbering on behind it – the whole mass of horses, men and machines rolling steadily deeper into the killing-ground that Gareth Swales had so carefully surveyed and laid out for them.

'The bastard!' whispered Jake, as he watched the Rolls skid to a standstill once more. The Italian was taking no chances of approaching the horsemen closely. He was standing well off, out of effective range of their ancient weapons, and he was picking them off one at a time, in the leisurely fashion of a shotgunner at a grouse shoot – in fact, the whole bloody episode was being played out in the spirit of the hunt. Even at the range of almost a thousand yards, Jake seemed able to sense the blood passion of the Italian marksman, the man's burning urge to kill merely for the sake of inflicting death, for the deep gut thrill of it.

If they intervened now, cutting into the flank of the widespread and disordered column, they might save the lives of many of the frantically fleeing horsemen. But the Italian column was not yet fully enmeshed in the trap that had been laid. Swiftly, Jake traversed the glasses across the dust-swirling and heat-distorted plain – and for the first time he noticed that a dozen trucks of the Italian rearguard had not joined the mad, tear-arse, helter-skelter stampede after the Ethiopian horsemen. This small group had halted, seemingly under some strict control, and now they had been left two miles behind the roaring, dusty avalanche of heavy vehicles. Jake could spare no more attention to this group, for now the slaughter was being continued, the wildly flying horsemen being cut down by the crack rifleman from the Rolls.

The temptation to intervene now overwhelmed Jake. He knew it was not the correct tactical moment, but he thought, 'The hell with it, I'm not a general, and those poor bastards out there need help.'

He shoved his right foot down hard on the throttle and the engine bellowed, but before he could pull forward and run at the bank, he was forestalled by Gareth Swales. He had been watching Jake, and the play of emotion over his face was plain to read. At the moment he revved the engine, Gareth swung the front end of the Hump across his bows, blocking him effectively.

'I say, old chap, don't be an idiot,' Gareth called across the narrow space. 'Calm the savage breast, you'll spoil the whole show.'

'Those poor—' Jake shouted back angrily.

'They've got to take their chances.' Gareth cut him short. 'I told you once before your sentimental old-fashioned ideas would get us both into trouble.'

At this stage the argument was drowned by the Ras. He was standing tall in the turret above Gareth. He had armed himself with the broad, two-handed war sword, and now the excitement became too much for him to bear longer in silence. He let out a series of shrill ululating war cries, and swung the sword in a great hissing circle around his head – both the silver blade and his brilliant set of teeth catching the sun and flashing like semaphores.

He punctuated his shrill war cries with wild kicks at his driver, urging him in heated Amharic to have at the enemy, and Gareth ducked and twisted out of the way of his flying feet.

'A bunch of maniacs!' protested Gareth as he dodged. 'I've got myself mixed up with a bunch of maniacs!'

'Major Swales!' shouted Gregorius, unable to stay out of the argument a moment longer. 'My grandfather orders you to advance!'

'You tell your grandfather to—' but Gareth's reply was cut short as a foot caught him in the ribs.

'Advance!' shouted Gregorius.

'Come on, for chrissake,' yelled Jake.

'Yaahooo!' hooted the Ras, and swung around in the turret to wave on his men at arms. They needed no further invitation. In a loose mob, they spurred their ponies past the stymied cars and, brandishing their rifles above their heads, robes streaming in the wind like battle ensigns, they lunged up the steep bank into the open and galloped furiously on to the flank of the scattered Italian column.

'Oh my God,' sighed Gareth. 'Every man a bloody general—'

'Look!' shouted Jake, pointing back down the course of

281

the dry river-bed, and they all fell abruptly silent at the spectacle.

It seemed as though the very earth had opened, disgorging rank upon rank of wildly galloping horsemen. Where a moment before the sweep of land below the mountains had been empty and silent, now it swarmed with men and horses, hundreds upon hundreds of them, dashing headlong upon the lumbering Italian column.

The dust hung over it all, rolling forward like the fog off a winter sea, shrouding the sun, so that horses and machines were dark infernal shapes below the sombre clouds, and the ruddy sun glinted dully on the steel of rifle and sword.

'That does it,' Gareth agreed bitterly, and reversed his car to clear Jake's front, before swinging away, engine roaring and the wheels spinning for purchase in the steep loose earth of the river-bank.

Jake turned wide of the other car and took the bank at an angle to lessen the gradient, and the two cumbersome machines burst out into the plain, wheel to wheel.

Before them was the open flank of massed soft-skinned vehicles, as tempting a target as they had ever been offered in their long and warlike careers. The two iron ladies swept forward together, and it seemed to Jake that there was a new tone to the deep engine note – as though they sensed that once again they were fulfilling the true reason for their existence. Jake glanced quickly at the Hump as she sailed along beside him. Her angular steelwork, with its flat abrupt surfaces from which rose the tall turret, still gave her the ugly old-maidish silhouette, but there was a new majesty in the way she plunged forward – her bright Ethiopian colours fluttered gaily as a cavalry pennant and the high thin-rimmed wheels spurned the sandy earth like the hooves of a thoroughbred. Beneath him, Priscilla drove forward as gamely, and Jake felt a warm flood of affection for his two old ladies.

'Have at them, girls!' he shouted aloud, and Gareth Swales, head protruding from the driver's hatch of the Hump, turned towards him. There was a freshly lit cheroot clamped in the corner of his mouth, seeming to have sprouted there miraculously of its own accord, and Gareth grinned around it.

'*Noli illegitimi carborundum!*' Jake caught the words faintly above the roar of wind and motor, then turned his full attention back to controlling the racing machine, and bringing her as swiftly as possible into the gaping breach in the Italian line.

Abruptly the pattern of movement ahead of him changed. The exultantly pursuing Italian warriors had realized belatedly that the roles had been neatly switched.

T he Count picked up the horseman in the sight, and led off just a touch, a hair's breadth, for the Mannlicher was a high-velocity rifle and the range was not more than a hundred metres.

He saw the hit clearly, the man lurched in the saddle and sprawled forward over the horse's neck, but he did not fall. The rifle dropped from his hands and cartwheeled across the earth, but the man clung desperately to the horse's mane while quick crimson spread across the shoulder of his dirty white robe.

The Count fired again, aiming for the junction of the horse's neck and shoulder, and saw the jarring impact spin the animal off its feet, so that it fell heavily upon its wounded rider, crushing the air from his lungs in a short high wail.

The Count laughed, wild with excitement. 'How many, Gino? How many is that?'

'Eight, my Colonel.'

'Keep counting. Keep counting,' he urged, as he swung the rifle, seeking the next target, peering eagerly over the open vee sight. Then suddenly he froze, the rifle barrel wavering and sinking to point at his glossy toecaps. His lower jaw unhinged and slowly sank, as if in sympathy with the rifle barrel. His recent affliction, forgotten in the excitement of the chase; returned suddenly with a force that turned his bowels to water and his legs to rubber.

'Merciful Mary!' he whispered.

The entire horizon was moving, an unbroken line from one edge of his vision to the other. It took him many seconds to assimilate what he was seeing, to realize that instead of fifteen horsemen, there were suddenly thousands upon thousands, and that rather than running before him they were now moving towards him at a velocity which he would not have believed possible. As he stared, he saw rank upon rank of the enemy seemingly rising from the very earth ahead of him, and rushing towards him through a curtain of fine pale dust. He saw the lowering sun glint red as blood upon the naked blades, and the drumming of galloping hooves sounded like the thunder of a giant waterfall. Yet faintly through the thunder, he heard the blood-freezing war shrieks of the horsemen.

'Giuseppe,' he gasped. 'Take us away from here – fast! Very fast.' This was the sort of appeal that went directly to the driver's heart. He spun the big car so nimbly that the Count's considerably weakened legs collapsed and he fell backwards onto the leather seat.

Spread over a front of a quarter of a mile behind and on each side of the Rolls came thirty of the dun-coloured Fiat troop-carriers. Despite their most fervent efforts, they had lost ground steadily to the thrusting Rolls and they now lumbered along almost a thousand yards behind. However, the excitement of the chase had affected the occupants and they had climbed up on the cabs and cupolas, and hung there hooting and yelling as they watched the sport, like runners at a fox hunt.

This solid phalanx of vehicles, advancing almost wheel to wheel over the rough ground, at a speed which would have horrified the manufacturers, was suddenly faced with the urgent necessity of reversing its headlong career without any loss of speed.

The drivers of the two leading trucks whose need was most critical solved the problem by spinning the wheels to hard lock, one left and the other right, and they came together radiator to radiator at a combined speed in excess of sixty miles per hour. In a roaring cloud of steam, splintering glass and rending metal, their cargoes of black-shirted infantry men were scattered like wheat upon the earth, or impaled on various metal projections of the vehicle bodies. The trucks, inextricably locked into each other, settled slowly on their shattered suspensions, and no sooner had the dust begun to drift away than there was a belly-shaking thump as the contents of their shattered fuel tanks ignited in a tall volcanic spout of flame and black smoke.

The other vehicles managed to reverse their courses without serious collision and streamed away into their own dust-clouds, pursued by a horde of galloping, gibbering cavalry.

Count Aldo Belli could not bring himself to glance back over his shoulder, certain that he would find a razor-edged sword swishing inches from his cringing rear, and he leaned over his driver, spurring him to greater speed by beating on his unprotected head and shoulders with a fist clenched like a hammer.

'Faster!' shouted the Count, his fine baritone rising to an uncertain contralto. 'Faster, you idiot – or I will have you shot!' and he hit the driver again behind one ear, experiencing a small spark of relief as the Rolls overtook the rear vehicles in the disordered herd of fleeing trucks.

Now at last he judged it safe to look back, and his relief was more intense when he realized that the Rolls was easily capable of out-running a mounted man. He experienced a warm flood of returning courage.

'My rifle, Gino,' he shouted. 'Give me my rifle.' But the Sergeant was trying to focus his camera on the pursuing horde, and the Count hit him a blow over the top of his head.

'Idiot. This is war,' he bellowed. 'And I am a warrior – give me my rifle!'

Giuseppe, the driver, hearing him, reluctantly decided that he was expected to slow the Rolls to give the Count an opportunity to follow his warlike intentions – but at the first diminution of speed, he received another lusty crack on the centre of his pate and the Count's voice went shrill again.

'Idiot,' he screeched. 'Do you want to get us killed? Faster, man, faster!' and with unbounded relief the driver pushed his foot flat on the throttle and the Rolls leapt forward again.

Gino was down on his hands and knees at the Count's feet, and now he came up with the Mannlicher in his hands and handed it to the Count.

'It's loaded, my Count.'

'Brave boy!' The Count braced himself with the rifle held at his hip, and looked about for something to shoot at. The Ethiopian cavalry had fallen well behind at this stage, and the Rolls had overtaken most of the troop-carriers – they were between the Count and the enemy. The Count was considering ordering Giuseppe to work his way out on to the flank, and thus give him an open field of fire – weighing the pleasure of shooting down the black riders at a respectable range against any possible physical danger to himself – and he turned on his precarious perch in the back seat to look out in that direction.

He stared incredulously at what he saw. Two great

humpbacked shapes were sailing in across the open grassland. They looked like two deformed camels, coming on swiftly with a curious loping progress that was at once comical and yet dreadfully menacing.

The Count stared at them uncomprehendingly, until with a sudden jolt of shock and a new warm flood of adrenalin into his bloodstream, he realized that the two strange vehicles were moving fast enough and at such an angle as to cut off his retreat.

'Giuseppe!' he shrieked, and hit the driver with the butt of the Mannlicher. It was not a heavy blow, it was meant merely to attract his attention, but Giuseppe had already taken much punishment and was by now lightly concussed. He clung to the wheel with white knuckles and roared on directly into the path of the new enemy.

'Giuseppe!' shrieked the Count again, as he suddenly recognized the gaily coloured flashes on the turret of the nearest machine, and at the same instant saw the thick stubby cylindrical shape that protruded ahead of it. It was fluted vertically and at the far end a short pipelike muzzle thrust out of the heavy water-jacket.

'Oh, merciful Mother of God!' he howled as the machine altered course slightly and the muzzle of the Vickers machine gun pointed directly at him.

'You fool!' he shrieked at Giuseppe, hitting him again. 'Turn! You idiot, turn!'

Suddenly through the tears of pain, the singing in his ears, and the blinding terror that gripped him, Giuseppe saw the huge camel-like shape looming up ahead of him and he spun the wheel again – just as the muzzle of the Vickers erupted in a fluttering pillar of bright flame and the air all around them was torn by the hiss and crack of a thousand bull whips.

Major Castelani stood on the cab of his truck, and peered disapprovingly through his binoculars into the distant clouds of rolling dust where confused movement and shadowy indistinguishable shapes flitted without seeming purpose or pattern.

It had required all of his presence and authority to restrain the ten trucks which carried the artillery men and towed their field pieces, to keep them under his personal command and to prevent them joining in the wildly enthusiastic rush after the small contingent of Ethiopian horsemen.

Castelani was about to give the order to mount up and cautiously follow the Count's charge into history and glory, when he raised the binoculars again – and it seemed that the pattern of dust-obscured movement out there had altered. Suddenly he saw the unmistakable shape of a Fiat transport emerge from the dust bank, and move ponderously back towards him. Through the glasses the men who clung to the canvas roof were all staring back in the direction from which they were coming at speed.

He panned the glasses slowly and saw another truck lumber out of the dust-mist headed back towards him. One of the soldiers on its roof was aiming and firing his rifle back into the obscuring clouds and his comrades, clinging to the roof about him, were frozen in attitudes of trepidation and alarm.

At that moment, Castelani heard something which he recognized instantly, his skin prickling at the distant ripping tearing sound. The sound of a British Vickers machine gun. His eye sought the direction, turning swiftly to the right flank of the extended Italian column which seemed now to be rushing back towards him in confused and completely disordered retreat.

He picked up the tall hump-backed shape instantly, standing high on the open plain, coming in fast with the strange bounding motion of a rocking horse, cutting boldly into the flank of the mass of soft-skinned Italian transports.

'Unlimber the guns,' shouted Castelani. 'Prepare to receive enemy armour.'

The Vickers machine guns in the turrets of the two armoured cars had ball-type mountings. The barrels could be elevated or depressed, but they could not traverse more than ten degrees to left or right, this being the limit of the ball mountings' turn. The driver had of necessity to act as gun-layer, swinging the entire vehicle to aim the gun, or at least bring it within the limited traverse of the mounting.

The Ras found this frustrating beyond all enduring. He would select a target, and shout in perfectly clear and coherent Amharic to his driver. Gareth Swales, not understanding a word of it, had already selected another target and was doing his best to line up on it while the Ras delivered a series of wild kicks at his kidneys to register his royal right of refusing to engage it.

The consequence of this was that the Hump wove a crazy, unpredictable course through the Italian column, spinning off at sudden tangents as the two crew members shouted bitter recriminations at each other, almost ignoring the sheets of rifle fire that thundered upon the steel hull from point-blank range, like hail on a galvanized roof.

Priscilla the Pig, on the other hand, was doing deadly execution. She had missed her first burst fired at the speeding Rolls, and it had ducked away behind the screen of dust and bucking trucks. Now, however, Jake and Gregorius were working with all the precision and mutual understanding that had developed between them.

'Left driver, left, left,' called Gregorius, peering down the open sights of the Vickers at the truck that roared and bounced along a hundred yards ahead of them.

'All right, I'm on him,' shouted Jake, as the vehicle appeared in the narrow field of his visor. This was a perforated steel plate that allowed only forward vision – but once Jake had the truck centred, he followed its violent efforts to dislodge him, closing in rapidly until he was twenty yards behind it.

The back of the truck was packed with black-shirted infantry men. Some of them were directing wild but rapid rifle fire at the pursuing car, the bullets clanging and whining off the hull, but most of them clung white-faced to the sides of the truck and stared back with stricken eyes as the armoured death carrier bore down inexorably upon them.

'Shoot, Greg!' called Jake. Even through the cold anger that gripped him, he was pleased that the boy had obeyed his orders and held his fire until this moment. There would be no wastage now, at so short a range every round ripped into the Italian truck, tearing through canvas, flesh, bone and steel at the rate of seven hundred rounds a minute.

The truck swerved violently and its front end collapsed; it went over broadside, crashing over and over, flinging the men high in the air, the way a spaniel throws off the droplets from its back as it leaps from water to land.

'Driver, right,' called Gregorius immediately. 'Another truck, right, a little more right – that's it, you're on.' And they roared in pursuit of another panic-stricken load of Italians.

A hundred yards away on their flank the Hump scored its first success. Gareth Swales was no longer able to accept the indignity of the Ras's flying feet, and his frenzied and completely unintelligible commands. He left the controls of the racing car to swing an angry punch at the Ras.

'Cut that out, old chap,' he snapped. 'Play the game — I'm on your side, damn it.'

The car, no longer under control, jinked suddenly. Almost side by side with them sped a Fiat truck, filled with Italians, and the driver had not yet realized that there was another enemy apart from the pursuing hordes of Ethiopian horsemen. His head was twisted around over his shoulder at an impossible angle, and he drove by instinct alone.

The two uncontrolled vehicles came together at an acute angle and at the top of their combined speeds. Steel met steel in a storm of sparks and they staggered away from the blow, both of them veering over steeply. For a moment it seemed that the Hump would go over; she teetered at the extreme end of her centre of gravity and then came back on to all four wheels with a crash that threw the men inside her unmercifully against her steel sides, before racing on again with Gareth wrestling at the wheel for control.

The Fiat truck was lighter and stood higher; the armoured car had caught her neatly under the cab and she did not even waver, but flipped over on her back, all four wheels still spinning as they pointed at the sky, and the cab and canvas-covered hood were torn away instantly, the men beneath them smeared between steel and hard earth.

It was all too much for the Ras. He could no longer contain his frustration at being enclosed in a hot metal box from which he could see almost nothing, while all around hundreds of his hated enemies were escaping with complete impunity. He flung open the hatch of the turret and stuck out his head and shoulders, yipping shrilly with bloodlust, frustration, anger and excitement.

At that moment, an open sky-blue and glistening black Rolls-Royce tourer flashed across the front of the Hump. In the rear seat was an Italian officer bedecked with the glittering insignia of rank — instantly Gareth Swales and the

Ras were in perfect accord once again. They had found a target eminently acceptable to both of them.

'I say, tally-ho!' cried Gareth, to be answered by a bloodcurdling 'How do you do!' like the crowing of an enraged rooster from the turret above him.

Count Aldo Belli was in hysterics, for the driver seemed to have lost all sense of direction; now more than just a little concussed, he had turned at right angles across the line of flight of the Italian column. This was as hazardous as running an ocean liner at full speed through a field of icebergs – for the rolling dust-clouds had reduced visibility to less than fifty feet, and out of this brown fog the lumbering troop-carriers appeared without warning, the drivers in no fit condition to take evasive action, all looking back over their shoulders.

Ahead of them, two more monstrous shapes appeared out of the dust; one was an Italian truck and the other was one of the cumbersome camel-backed vehicles with the Ethiopian colours splashed upon its hull and a Vickers machine gun protruding from its turret.

Suddenly the armoured car swerved and crashed heavily into the side of the truck, capsizing it instantly and then swerving back towards the Rolls. It came so close, towering over them so threateningly, that it entered even Giuseppe's limited field of vision.

The effect was miraculous. Giuseppe shot bolt upright in his seat and, with the touch of an inspired Nuvolari, brought the Rolls round on two wheels, cutting finely across the armoured bows just at the moment that the hatch of the turret flew open and a wizened brown face, filled with the largest, whitest and most flashing teeth the Count had ever seen, popped out of the turret and emitted a war cry so shrill and heart-chilling that the Count's bowels flopped over like a stranded fish.

As the barrel of the Vickers swung on to the Rolls, the Ethiopian gunner ducked down into the turret, and the barrel elevated slightly until the Count found himself staring stupidly into its dark round aperture – but Giuseppe had been watching also in the driving mirror, and now he spun the wheel and the Rolls flashed aside like a mackerel before the driving charge of the barracuda. The blast of shot from the Vickers tore down its left side lifting a storm of dirt and pebbles in spurting fountains high into the air.

The armoured car swung heavily to follow the Rolls' manoeuvre, the leaping dust fountains swinging with it, closing in mercilessly. However, Giuseppe, faced with the prospect of death, hit the brakes so hard that the Count was catapulted forward, howling protests, to hang over the front seat, his ample black-clad buttocks pointing at the heavens and his glistening boots kicking wildly as he fought for balance.

The sheet of bullets from the swinging Vickers passed mere inches ahead of the Rolls, and Giuseppe swung the wheel to hard opposite lock, released the brakes and trampled hard on the throttle. The Rolls kicked over hard, wheels spinning for purchase, then bounded ahead with such impetus that the Count was thrown backwards again, crashing into a sitting position on the rear leather seat, his helmet falling over his eyes.

'I'll have you shot,' he gasped, as he struggled weakly to adjust the helmet. Giuseppe was too busy to hear him. His duck and swerve had beaten the Ethiopian gunner, and the superior speed of the Rolls was carrying it swiftly out of harm's way. Just a few more seconds – then the ancient but splendidly toothed head of the gunner appeared once more in the turret, and the bows of the armoured car and the questing muzzle of the Vickers swung back. The gunner dropped back behind the gun and the roaring clatter of bullets sounded high above the bellow of straining engines. Once again, the dust storm of bullets tore up the earth, swinging rapidly towards the Rolls.

Slightly ahead of the two vehicles, another growling, labouring troop-carrier loomed out of the dust on a parallel course with them, but travelling at only half the speed under its heavy load of terrified troopers.

Giuseppe touched the wheel, swaying out slightly away from the stream of bullets, then he swung hard the opposite way and as the armoured car turned to follow him he ducked neatly behind the troop-carrier, screened by its high unstable bulk from the deadly machine gun. The Ethiopian kept firing.

As the solid hose of fire tore through the canvas hood of the truck, ripping and shredding the men crowded shoulder to shoulder beneath it, the Rolls was pulling away swiftly in its lee. Suddenly, it was out of the dust clouds into the crystal desert air, with a vista of open land stretching away to the horizon – a horizon which was the passionate destination of every man in the Rolls. The lumbering troop-carriers were left behind, and the Rolls could make a clean run of it. The way the Count felt at that moment, they would only stop once he was safely into his defensive positions above the Wells of Chaldi.

Then quite suddenly, he was aware of the guns on the open plain ahead of him. They were drawn up neatly in spaced-out triangular batteries, three vees of three guns each, with the gunners grouped about them and the long fat barrels covering the approaching mass of fleeing vehicles. There was a parade-ground feeling of calm and good order about them that made the Count blubber with relief after the nightmare from which he had just emerged.

'Giuseppe, you have saved us,' he sobbed. 'I am going to give you a medal.' The threat of capital punishment made a few minutes earlier was forgotten. 'Drive for the guns, my brave boy. You have done good work – and you'll find me grateful.'

At that moment, emboldened by talk of safety, Gino lifted himself from the floorboards where he had been resting these last few minutes. He looked cautiously over the rear of the Rolls, and what he saw caused him to let out a single strangled cry and to drop once more into his original position on the floor.

Behind them the Ethiopian armoured car had burst out of the dust clouds and was bounding determinedly after them.

The Count took one look also, and immediately resumed his encouragement of Giuseppe, beating on his head with a fist like a judge's gavel.

'Faster, Giuseppe!' he shrieked. 'If he kills us, I'll have you shot.' And the Rolls raced for the protection of the guns.

'Steady now!' intoned Major Castelani gravely, trying by the tone of his voice to quiet their nerves.

'Steady, my lads. Hold your fire. Hold your fire.

'Remember your drill,' he said. 'Just remember your range drill, soldier.' He paused a moment beside the nearest gun-layer, lifting his binoculars and sweeping the field ahead.

The dust cloud was rolling rapidly towards them, but all the action was confused and indistinct.

'You are loaded with high explosive?' the Major asked quietly, and the gun-layer gulped nervously and nodded.

'Remember, the first shot is the only one you can aim with care. Make it count.'

'Sir.' The man's voice was unsteady, and Castelani felt a stab of anger and contempt. They were all unblooded boys, unsteady and nervous. He had been forced to push them to their places and put the trails of the guns in their hands.

He turned abruptly, and strode to the next battery.

'Steady now, lads. Hold your fire until it counts.'

They turned strained, pale faces to him; one of the layers looked as though he would burst into tears at any moment.

'The only thing you have to be afraid of is me,' growled Castelani. 'Let one of you open fire before I give the order – and you'll—'

A cry interrupted him, as one of the loaders stood up and pointed out on to the field.

'Take that man's name,' snapped Castelani, and turned with dignity, making a show of polishing the lens of his binoculars on his sleeve before raising them to his eyes.

Colonel Count Aldo Belli was leading his men back so enthusiastically that he had outstripped them by half a mile, and every moment was widening the gap. He was driving directly at the centre of the artillery batteries, and he was standing tall in the back seat of the Rolls, with both arms waving and gesticulating as though he was being attacked by a swarm of bees.

Even as Castelani watched, from out of the brown curtains of dust beyond the Rolls burst a machine that he recognized instantly, despite its new camouflage paint and the unfamiliar weapon in the turret. It did not need the gay pennant that flew above it to identify his enemy.

'Very well, lads,' he said quietly. 'Here they come. High explosive, and wait for the order. Not a moment before.'

The speeding armoured car fired, a long tearing ripping burst. Much too long, Castelani thought with grim satisfaction. That gun would be overheating, and they could expect a jam. An experienced gunner laid down short, spaced bursts of fire – the enemy were green also, Castelani decided.

'Steady, lads,' he snapped, watching his men stir restlessly at the sound of gunfire and exchange nervous glances.

The car fired again, and he saw the fall of shot around the Rolls, kicking up swift jumping spurts of dust and earth – another long ripping hail of fire. That ended abruptly and was not repeated.

'Ha!' snorted Castelani, with satisfaction. 'She has jammed.' His wavering gunners would not have to receive fire. It was good. It would steel them, give them confidence to shoot, without being shot at.

'Steady now. All steady. Not long to wait. Nice and steady now.' His voice lost its jagged, emery-paper tone and became soothing and crooning like a mother at the cradle. 'Wait for it, lads. Easy now.'

The Ras did not understand what had happened, why the gun remained silent, despite all the strength of both his hands on pistol grip and triggers. The long canvas belt of ammunition still drooped from the bins and fed into the breech of the Vickers – but it no longer moved.

The Ras swore at the gun, such an oath that, had he hurled it at another man, would have led immediately to a duel to the death, but the gun remained silent.

Armed with his two-handed battle sword, the Ras climbed half out of the turret and brandished it about his head.

It is doubtful if he would have realized what three batteries of modern 100 mm field guns would have looked like from the business end, or, if he had recognized them, whether they would have daunted his determined pursuit of the fleeing Rolls. As it was, his reason and vision were clouded with the red mists of battle rage. He did not see the waiting guns.

Below him, Gareth Swales leaned forward in the driver's seat peering short-sightedly through the visor, which narrowed his field of vision and partially obscured it as though he was looking through the perforated bottom of a kitchen colander. His eyes were swimming from the cordite smoke, the engine fumes and the dust-motes – so that he blinked rapidly as he concentrated all his efforts in following the speeding ethereal shape of the Rolls. He did not see the waiting guns.

'Shoot, damn you,' he shouted. 'We are going to lose him.' But above him the Vickers was silent, and from his seat low down in the hull, the slight fold of ground so carefully chosen by Major Castelani half-hid the batteries. He raced towards them, drawn on inexorably by the fleeting shape of the Rolls dancing elusively ahead of him.

'Good.' Castelani allowed himself a bleak little smile as he watched the enemy vehicle come on steadily. Already it was within comfortable range for an experienced gunner, but he knew it must be half as close again before his own crews could make any certainty of their practice.

The Rolls, however, was a mere two hundred metres in front of the guns, and coming on at a speed that could not have been less than sixty miles an hour. Three terrified and chalky faces were turned towards him in dreadful appeal and three voices were raised in loud cries for succour. The Major ignored them and swiftly turned his professional eye back to the enemy. He found it was still two thousand metres out across the plain but closing satisfactorily. He was on the point of uttering another reassurance to his edgy gunners, when the Rolls roared through the narrow gap in the centre of his batteries.

The Count had at that moment temporarily found his feet and replaced his helmet on his head. Standing on the high platform of the Rolls, his voice, powered with adrenalin and shrill with terror, carried clearly to every gunner.

'Open fire!' shrieked the Count. 'Open fire immediately – or I will have you all shot!' and then, realizing that they should be encouraged to remain at their posts and cover his withdrawal, he reached frantically for inspiration and flung over his shoulder one rousing 'Death before dishonour!' before the Rolls bore him away, still at sixty miles an hour, towards the long distant horizon.

The Major lifted his voice in a great bugling bellow to countermand the order, but even his lungs were no match for the thunderous volley of nine field guns fired in as close to unison as they had never been in training. Each gunner took his Colonel at his literal word when he said 'immediately' and such refinements as laying and aiming were forgotten in the dire urgency of firing as furiously and as fast as possible.

In the circumstances, it was nothing short of a miracle that one high-explosive shell found a mark. This was a Fiat troop-carrier which emerged at that moment from the dust clouds a quarter of a mile behind the Ethiopian armoured car. The shell was fused to a thousandth of a second delay; it went in through the radiator, shattered the engine block, disintegrated the driver, then burst in the midst of the group of terrified infantrymen huddled under the canvas hood. The engine and front wheel of the truck kept going forward for a few seconds before beginning to roll and bounce over the irregular ground – the rest of the truck and twenty men went straight upwards, fifty feet in the air like a troupe of maniacal acrobats.

Only one other shell came close to hitting the enemy. It burst ten yards in front of the Hump, emptying in a towering pillar of flame and yellow earth, and gouging a deep round crater, four feet across, into which the speeding car plunged.

The Ras, whose head was protruding from the turret, and

whose mouth and eyes were wide open, had all three of these body apertures filled with flying sand from the explosion – and his war whoops were cut off abruptly, as he choked for breath and tried frantically to wipe his streaming eyes.

Gareth also had his vision abruptly closed by the pillar of flame and sand, and he drove blindly into the shell crater. The impact threw him out of his seat, and the steering-wheel hit him in the chest, driving the wind out of his lungs before snapping off short at the floorboards.

With another bound, the Hump bounced jauntily out of the shell crater with streamers of dust and shell smoke swirling about her. She was hanging over on one side with her springs snapped off by the jolt, and her front wheels locked firmly to one side, yet her engine still bellowed at full power and she went into a tight right-hand circle, around and around like a circus animal.

Wheezing for breath, Gareth dragged himself back into the driver's seat, only to find that there was no longer a steering column and that the throttle had jammed at the fully open position. He sat there for long seconds, shaking his head to clear it, and struggling desperately for breath, for the hull was filled with dust and smoke.

Another shell, bursting somewhere close beside the hull, roused him from the stupors of shock, and he reached up, unlatched the driver's hatch and stuck his head out into the open air. At what seemed like point-blank range, three full batteries of Italian field guns were firing at him.

'Oh my God!' he gasped painfully, as another volley of high explosive erupted around the rapidly circling car, the blast jarring his eyeballs and rattling his teeth in his head. 'Let's go home!' he said and began to hoist himself out of the narrow hatch-way. His feet came clear of the steel flooring of the hull only just in time to save every bone below his knees in both legs from being shattered into small fragments.

Two thousand yards away across the plain Major Castelani was fighting for control against the panic that the Count had instilled in his gunners. They were loading and firing with such single-minded passion that all the other refinements of gunnery were completely forgotten. The layers were no longer making a pretence of seeking a target, but merely jerking the lanyard at the very moment the breech block clanged shut.

Castelani's bellows made no impression on the half-deafened and almost completely dazed gunners. The Count's last injunction to death had shattered their nerves completely and they were all of them beyond reason.

Castelani dragged the nearest layer from his seat behind the gun shield, and prised open the man's death grip on the lanyard. Cursing bitterly at the quality of the men under his command, he pedalled the traverse and elevating handles of the gun with a smooth expert action. The thick barrel dropped and swung until the insect speck of the armoured car loomed suddenly large in the magnifying prism of the gunsight. It was tearing in a crazy circle, clearly out of control, and Castelani picked up the rhythm of its circle and hit the lanyard with a short hard jerk of the wrist. The barrel flew back, arrested at last by the hydraulic pistons of the shock absorber, and the fifteen-pound cone-shaped steel shell was hurled on an almost flat trajectory across the plain.

It was aimed fractionally low. It passed inches below the tall shuttered bows of the car, between the two front wheels, and struck the earth directly below the driver's compartment.

The released energy of the blast was deflected by the earth's surface up into the soft underbelly of the hull. It blew the engine block off its seating, tore off the big front wheels like wings from a roast chicken, and stove in the steel floor of the hull with a great Thor's hammer stroke.

If Gareth Swales's feet had been in contact with the steel floor of the hull, the shock would have been transmitted directly into the bones of his feet and legs, and he would have suffered that dreadful but characteristic wound of the tankman – below the knees his legs would have been transformed into bags of shattered bone.

He was, however, suspended half in and half out of the driver's hatch with both legs kicking frantically in the air, and the shock of the blast came up like carbon dioxide in a bottle of freshly opened champagne. He was the cork and he was shot out of the hatch, still kicking.

The effect on the Ras was the same. He came out of the turret, propelled high by the blast – and he met Gareth at the top of his trajectory. The two of them came down to earth simultaneously, with the Ras seated between Gareth's shoulder blades, and the wonder of it was that neither of them was impaled upon the war sword which went with them and finally pegged deep into the earth six inches from Gareth's ear as he lay face down and feebly tried to dislodge the Ras from his back.

'I warn you, old chap,' he managed to gasp. 'One day you are going to go too far.'

The sound of oncoming engines, many of them and all roaring in high revolutions, made Gareth's efforts to dislodge the Ras more determined. He sat up spitting sand and blood from his crushed lips, and looked up to see the remaining Italian transports bearing down on them like the starting grid of the Le Mans Grand Prix.

'Oh my God!' gasped Gareth, his scattered wits reassembling hastily, and he crawled frantically into the shattered and still smoking carcass of the Hump, beginning to shrink down out of sight before he realized that the Ras was no longer with him.

'Rassey, you stupid old bastard – come back,' he shouted despairingly. The Ras, once again armed with his trusty broadsword, was staggering out on unsteady stork's legs, stunned by the shell burst but still fighting mad, and there was no doubting his intentions. He was going to take on the entire motorized column single-handed, and as he hurried to meet them, shouting a challenge, he loosened up with a few hissing two-handed cuts with the sword.

Gareth had to duck under the swinging blade, going in low in a flying rugby tackle, to bring the old warrior down in an untidy heap.

He dragged him, still shouting and struggling furiously, under cover of the broken steel hull, just as the first Italian truck roared past them. The pale-faced occupants paid them not the slightest attention – they were intent on one thing only and that was following their Colonel.

'Shut up!' growled Gareth, as the Ras tried to provoke them with some of the foulest oaths in the Amharic language. Finally he had to hold the Ras down, wrap his shamma around his head, and sit on it – while the Italian Fiats thundered past, and the rolling clouds of dust spread over them as though driven by the khamsin.

Once through the dust and confused stampede of trucks, Gareth thought he glimpsed the hump-backed shape of Priscilla the Pig, and he released the Ras for a moment to wave and shout, but the car disappeared almost instantly, hard on the trail of a lumbering Fiat, and Gareth heard the short crashing burst of the Vickers clearly, even above the thunder of many engines.

Then suddenly they were all past, streaming away, the engine sounds fading, the dust settling – and then there was another sound, faint yet but growing with every second.

Although most of the Harari and Galla horsemen had long ago given up the pursuit in favour of the more enjoyable and profitable occupation of looting the capsized and damaged Italian trucks, a few hundred of the more hardy souls still flogged on their foundering mounts.

This thin line of horsemen came sweeping forward, ululating and casually cutting down the Italian survivors from the destroyed trucks who fled before them on foot.

'All right, Rassey.' Gareth unwound the shamma from around his head. 'You can come out now. Call your boys up, and tell them to get us out of here.'

In the few moments of respite while the main body of motorized infantry came through the batteries, Major Castelani hurried from gun to gun, lashing with tongue and cane until he had contained the infectious panic of his gunners and had them under his hand again. Then out of the dust clouds, appearing at short pistol range as suddenly as a ghost ship, but with the Vickers machine gun in its turret crackling wickedly and the muzzle blast flickering in an angry throbbing red glow, was a second Ethiopian armoured car.

It was enough to destroy the semblance of control that Castelani had forced heavy-handedly upon the gun crews. As the armoured car swung across their line at point-blank range, raking the exposed guns with a withering burst of machine-gun fire, the loaders dropped their ready shells and almost knocked the layers from their seats in their anxiety to get behind the armoured shield of the gun. They all huddled there with their heads well down. The driver of the armoured car, after that one rapid pass down the front of the batteries, swung the vehicle abruptly back into the screen of dust. Jake had been just as startled by the encounter as were the gunners; at one moment he had been joyously tearing along after a fat wallowing Fiat, and at the next he had emerged from a cloud of dust to be confronted by the gaping muzzles of the big guns.

'My God, Greg,' Jake shouted up at the boy in the turret. 'We nearly ran right into them.'

'Volleyed and thundered – do you remember the poem?'

'Poetry, at a time like this?' growled Jake, and he gave Priscilla the throttle.

'Where are we going?'

'Home, and the sooner the quicker. That's a powerful argument they are pointing at us.'

'Jake—' Gregorius began to protest, when there was a bang and a flash that glowed briefly even through the shrouds of dust, and close beside the high turret passed a 100 mm shell. The air slammed against their eardrums and the shriek of it made both of them flinch violently, the air stank of the electric sizzle of its passing, and it burst half a mile beyond them in a tall tower of flame and dust.

'Do you see what I mean?' asked Jake.

'Yes, Jake – oh yes, indeed.'

As he spoke, the dust clouds that had covered them so securely now subsided and drifted aside, exposing them unmercifully to the attentions of the Italian guns, but revealed also was another tempting target. The Ethiopian cavalry were still coming on, and after a few futile volleys had burst around the tiny elusive shape of the speeding car, Castelani resigned himself to the limitations of his gunners and switched targets.

'Shrapnel,' he bellowed. 'Load with shrapnel fuse for air burst.' He hurried along the battery, repeating the order to each layer, emphasizing his orders with the cane. 'New target. Massed horsemen. Range two thousand five hundred metres, fire at will.'

The Ethiopian ponies were small shaggy beasts, bred for

sure-footed ascent of mountain paths, rather than sustained charges across open plains – they had, moreover, been pastured for weeks now on the dry sour grass of the desert, and in consequence their strength was by this time almost expended.

The first shrapnel burst fifty feet above the heads of the leading riders. It popped open like a gigantic pod of the cotton plant, blooming with sudden fearsome splendour against the milky blue sky. It bloomed with a crack as though the sky had shattered, and instantly the air was filled with the humming, hissing knives of flying shrapnel.

A dozen of the ponies went down under the first burst, pitching forward abruptly over their own heads and flinging their riders free. Then the sky was filled with the deadly cotton balls, and the continuous crack of the bursts sent the ponies wheeling and the riders crouching low on their withers or swinging out of the saddle to hang low under the bellies of their mounts. Here and there a braver soul would kick his feet free of the stirrups and pick up a dismounted comrade on each of the leathers, the gallant little ponies labouring under their triple burdens. Within seconds, the entire Ethiopian army – its single remaining armoured vehicle and all its cavalry – were in a retreat every bit as headlong as that of the motorized Italian column which was still on its way back to the Wells of Chaldi. The field was left entirely to Castelani's artillery – and the stranded crew of the Hump.

From the shelter of the shattered hull, Gareth Swales watched his hopes of quick rescue fading rapidly in the shape of the dwindling cavalry.

'Don't blame them, not really,' he told the Ras, and then he looked across at the speeding armoured car. Priscilla the Pig was rapidly overhauling the cavalry.

'Him I do,' he muttered. 'He saw us – I know he did.' There had been a moment when Priscilla the Pig had passed within a quarter of a mile of them, had in fact turned directly towards them for a few moments. 'Do you know something, Rassey old fellow, I do believe we are being set up for a couple of Patsys.' He glanced at the Ras, who lay beside him like an old hunting dog that has been worked too hard; his chest laboured like a blacksmith's bellows, and his breathing whistled shrilly in his throat.

'Better take those choppers out of your mouth, old chap – or else you're going to swallow them. The fighting's over for the day. Take it nice and easy now. We've got a long walk home tonight.'

And Gareth Swales transferred all his attention back to the disappearing car.

'Big-hearted Jake Barton is leaving us here – and going home to spoon up the honey. Who was the chap that David pulled the same trick on? Come on, Rassey, you are the Old Testament expert – wasn't it Uriah the Hittite?' He shook his head sadly. Gareth was already ready to believe the worst. 'I take it very much amiss, Rassey, I can tell you. Probably have done exactly the same myself, mind you – but I do take it amiss coming from a fine upright citizen like Jake Barton.'

The Ras had not listened to a word of it. He was the only man in the two armies for whom the battle had not ended. He was just having a short rest, as behove a warrior of his advanced years. Now, with a single bound, he was on his feet again, snatching up his sword and heading directly for the centre of the Italian batteries. Gareth was taken completely off balance, and the Ras had covered fifty yards of the necessary two thousand to the enemy positions before Gareth could overtake him.

It was unfortunate that one of the Italian gun-layers had his binoculars focused on the derelict hull of the Hump at that moment. The belligerence of the Italian gunners was in inverse proportion to the number and proximity of the enemy and all of them were giddy with elation at the total and unexpected victory that had dropped into their laps.

The first shell dropped close beside the broken hull of the Hump, as Gareth caught up with the Ras. Gareth stooped and picked up a rounded stone, about the size of a cricket ball.

'Frightfully sorry, old chap,' he panted, as he cupped the stone in his right hand. 'But we really can't go on like this.'

He made allowance for the brittle old bone of the Ras's skull, and with the stone he tapped him carefully, almost tenderly, above the ear, on the polished black bald curve of the Ras's pate.

As the Ras dropped, Gareth caught him, one arm under his knees and the other around the shoulders, as though he were a sleeping child. The shells were falling heavily about him as Gareth ran back for cover, carrying the Ras's unconscious form across his chest.

Jake Barton heard the crumping explosion of the shells, and shouted up at Gregorius,

'What are they shooting at now?'

Gregorius climbed higher out of the turret and peered back. The crushed hull of the Hump would have been unnoticed at that range, just another speck like a clump of camel-thorn or an amorphous pile of black rock. Indeed, both men had looked at it fifty times in the last few minutes without recognizing it, but the shell bursts, which began to leap about it in fleeting graceful ostrich feathers of dust and smoke, drew Gregorius's eye immediately.

'My grandfather!' he cried anxiously. 'They have been hit, Jake.'

Jake swung the car and halted it, clambering out of the hatch, blowing dust from the lens of his binoculars and then focusing them. The picture of the destroyed car leaped into close-up and he recognized instantly the two distant figures, one in tailored tweeds, the other in flowing robes and swirling skirts; the two of them were locked together breast to breast and for an unbelieving moment Jake thought they were doing a Strauss waltz in the midst of an artillery barrage. Then he saw Gareth lift the Ras off the ground and stagger with him to the shelter of the overturned car.

'We must rescue them, Jake,' Gregorius exclaimed passionately. 'They will be killed out there, if we do not.'

Perhaps it was the telepathic transfer of Gareth Swales's suspicions, but Jake experienced the sudden guilty prick of temptation. At that moment he knew he loved Vicky Camberwell, and there was an easy way to clear the field.

'Jake!' Gregorius called again, and suddenly Jake felt himself so sickened by his own treacherous thoughts that there was a hollow nauseous feeling in the centre of his gut, and he felt the swift flow of saliva from under his tongue.

'Let's go,' he said, and dropped down into the driver's hatch. He swung Priscilla the Pig in a tight skidding turn and ran straight for the forest of shell-bursts.

They drew no fire, the Italians were concentrating on the stationary target – and they seemed to be making better practice as they figured the range. It was a matter of seconds before the Hump took a direct hit, and Jake pressed the throttle flat to the floorboards, but Priscilla the Pig chose this moment to show her true nature. He felt her baulk, and the note of her engine changed momentarily, missing and stuttering, power falling off – then suddenly she picked up again and roared onwards at full power.

'Good little darling.' Jake peered ahead through the visor, and swung slightly out to the left, to come in under cover of the Italians' own shell-bursts and the capsized hull of the Hump.

A shell burst directly ahead, and Jake weaved the big car expertly around the gaping smoking crater, pulled in sharply and spun around to a sliding halt, facing back the way he had come, ready for a quick pull-away. He was hard up under cover of the destroyed hull, partially screened from the Italians, and ten paces from where Gareth Swales was sitting holding the Ras's frail body on his lap.

'Gary!' yelled Jake, sticking his head out of the hatch, and Gareth looked up at him with a startled unbelieving expression. He had been so deafened by shell-bursts that he had not realized that Jake had come back for him. Jake had to shout again.

'Come on, damn you to hell,' and this time Gareth moved with alacrity. He picked up the Ras like a bundle of dirty laundry and ran with him to the car. A shell burst so close that it almost knocked him off his feet, and stones and clouds of earth splattered against the armoured steel.

However, Gareth kept his feet and handed up the Ras to the willing hands and loving care of his grandson.

'Is he all right?' Greg demanded anxiously.

'Hit by a stone, he'll be all right,' Gareth grunted, and leaned for an instant against the side of the car, his breathing sobbing painfully in his throat, his hair and moustache thick with white dust, and the sweat cutting deep wet runnels down his filth-caked cheeks.

He looked up at Jake. 'I thought you weren't coming back,' he croaked.

'It crossed my mind.' Jake reached down and took his hand. He boosted him up the side of the car, and Gareth held his hand for a second longer than was necessary, squeezing slightly.

'I owe you one, old son.'

'I'll call on you,' Jake grinned.

'Any time. Any time at all.'

At that moment, Priscilla the Pig roared heroically, then abruptly backfired in opposition to the Italian shell-bursts. Her engine spluttered, surged, farted despairingly, and then fell silent—

'Oh, you son of a bitch!' said Jake with great and passionate feeling. 'Not now!'

'Reminds me of a girl I knew in Australia—'

'Later,' Jake told him. 'Get on the crank handle.'

'My pleasure, old boy,' and a near miss burst beside them and knocked him off his precarious perch on the sponson. Gareth picked himself up and dusted his lapels fastidiously as he limped to the crank handle.

After a full minute at the handle, spinning it like a demented organ-grinder with no effect at all, Gareth fell back panting again.

'I say, old chap, I'm a bit bushed,' and they changed places quickly.

Jake stooped over the crank handle, ignoring the tempest of bursting shells and swirling dust clouds, and the thick muscles in his arm writhed as he spun the crank.

'She's dead,' Gareth shouted after another minute. Jake persevered, his face turning darkly red and the veins in his throat swelling into thick blue cords – but at last even he released the handle with disgust and stepped back gasping.

'The tool kit is under the seat,' he said.

'You aren't going to do your handyman act here and now?' Incredulously Gareth made a wide gesture that took in the bloody battlefield, the Italian guns and the bursting shells.

'You've got a better idea?' Jake asked brusquely, and Gareth looked about him forlornly, suddenly straightening his slumping shoulders, the droop of his mouth lifting into that eternally jaunty grin.

'Funny you should ask, old son. It just so happens—' and like a conjurer he indicated the apparition that appeared suddenly out of the curtains of leaping dust and fuming cordite.

Miss Wobbly slammed to a dead stop beside them and

311

both hatches flew open. Sara's dark head appeared in one and Vicky's golden one in the other.

Vicky leaned across towards Jake, cupping her hands to her mouth as she shouted in the storm of shellfire,

'What's wrong with Priscilla?'

And Jake gasped, still red-faced and sweating. 'She's thrown one of her fits.'

'Grab the tow rope,' Vicky instructed. 'We'll pull you out.'

The Ethiopian camp swarmed with victorious swaggering warriors; their laughter was loud and their voices boastful. Admiring womenfolk, who watched them from the cooking fires, were preparing the night's feast. The big, black iron pots bubbled with a dozen varieties of *wat*, and the smell of spices and meat lay heavily on the evening cool.

Vicky Camberwell bent over her typewriter, seated under the flap of her tent, and her long supple fingers flew at the keys as the words tumbled from her – describing the courage and fighting qualities of a people who, armed only with sword and horse, had routed a modern army equipped with all the most fearsome weapons of war. When she was in literary flight, Vicky sometimes overlooked small details that might detract from the dramatic impact of her story – the fact that the biblical warriors of Ethiopia had been supported by armoured cars and Vickers machine guns were details of this type, and she ignored them as she ended,

'But how much longer can these proud, simple and gallant people continue to fight off the greedy lusting hordes of a modern Caesar intent on Empire? A miracle happened here today on the plains of Danakil, but the age of miracles is passing and it is clear even to those who have thrown in

312

their lot with this fair land of Ethiopia that she is doomed – unless the sleeping conscience of a civilized world is aroused, unless the voice of justice rings out clearly, calling to the tyrant – Hands off, Benito Mussolini!'

'That's wonderful, Miss Camberwell,' said Sara, leaning over to read the last words as they tapped out on the roller of the machine. 'It makes me want to cry, it's so sad and beautiful.'

'I'm glad you like it, Sara. I wish you were my editor.' Vicky stripped the page from the machine and checked it swiftly, crossing out a word and inking in another before she was satisfied, and she folded the despatch into a thick brown envelope and licked the flap.

'Are you sure he is reliable?' she asked Sara.

'Oh, yes, Miss Camberwell, he is one of my father's best men.' Sara took the envelope and handed it to the warrior who had been waiting an hour outside the tent, squatting at the head of his saddled horse.

Sara spoke to him with great fire and passion, and the man nodded vehemently as she exhorted him and then flung himself into the saddle and dashed away towards the darkening mouth of the gorge, where the smoky blue shadows of evening were enfolding the harsh cliffs and jagged peaks of the mountains.

'He will be at Sardi before midnight. I have told him not to pause along the way. Your message will go on to the telegraph at dawn tomorrow morning.'

'Thank you, Sara dear.' Vicky rose from the camp table and as she covered her typewriter, Sara eyed her speculatively. Vicky had bathed and changed into the one good dress she had brought with her, a light Irish linen in a pale blue, cut with a fashionably low waist and skirt that covered her knees but displayed rounded calves and the narrow delicately shaped ankles which gleamed in their sheaths of fine silk stockings.

'Your dress is pretty,' said Sara softly, 'and your hair is so soft and yellow.' She sighed. 'I wish I were beautiful like you are. I wish I had a lovely white skin like you.'

'And I wish I had a beautiful golden skin like yours,' Vicky countered swiftly, and they laughed together.

'Are you dressed like that for Gareth? He will love you very much when he sees you. Let us go and find him.'

'I've got a better idea, Sara. Why don't you go and find Gregorius. I am sure he is looking for you.'

Sara thought about that for a moment, torn between duty and pleasure.

'Are you certain you'll be all right on your own, Miss Camberwell?'

'Oh, I think so – thank you, Sara. If I get into trouble I'll call you.'

'I'll come right away,' Sara assured her.

Vicky knew exactly where she would find Jake Barton, and she came up silently beside the tall steel hull and watched for a while as he worked, completely absorbed and totally oblivious of her presence. She wondered how she had been so blind as not to have seen him properly before, not to have seen beneath the boyish freshness the strength and quiet assurance of a full mature man. It was an ageless face, and she knew that even when he was an old man the illusion of youth and freshness would remain with him. Yet there was an intensity in the eyes, a steely purpose in the heavy line of the jaw that she had never noticed before. She remembered the dream of his that he had told her – the factory building his own engine – and in a clairvoyant flash she knew that he had the determination and the strength to make it become reality. Suddenly she longed to share it with him, and knew that their two dreams could be placed together, his engine and her book, they could be created together, each gathering strength from the other, pooling their determination and their creative reserves. She thought it would be worth while to share both dreams with a man like Jake Barton.

'Perhaps being in love allows one to see more clearly,' she thought, as she watched him with secret pleasure. 'Or perhaps it simply makes it easy to kid yourself,' and she felt annoyance that her natural cynicism should overtake her now.

'No,' she decided. 'It's not make believe. He is strong and good – and he'll stay that way,' and immediately she thought that perhaps she was trying too hard to convince herself. Unbidden, the memory of the night she had spent so recently with another man flooded back to her, and for a moment she found herself confused and uncertain. She tried to thrust the memory firmly aside, but it nagged at her, and she found herself comparing two men, remembering the wanton and wicked delights she had known, and doubting wistfully that she might ever recapture them.

Then she looked closer at the man she thought she loved, and saw that although his arms were thick and dark with hair, and his hands were large and heavy-knuckled, yet the thick spatulate fingers worked with an almost sensuous skill and lightness, and she tried to imagine them moving on her skin – and the image was so clear and voluptuous that she shuddered and drew in her breath sharply.

Immediately Jake looked up at her, the surprise in his eyes changing instantly to pleasure, and that slow warm smile spreading over his face as he ran his eyes swiftly from the top of her silken head down to the silken ankles.

'Hello, haven't I met you somewhere before?' he asked, and she laughed and pirouetted, flaring the dress.

'Do you like it?' she asked. He nodded silently and then asked,

'Are we going somewhere special?'

'The Ras's feast, didn't you know?'

'I'm not sure I can stand another of his feasts, I don't

315

know which is more dangerous – an Italian attack or that liquid dynamite he serves.'

'You'll have to be there – you're one of the heroes of the great victory,' and Jake grunted and returned his attention to Priscilla the Pig's internal processes.

'Have you found the trouble?'

'No.' Jake sighed with resignation. 'I've taken her to pieces and put her together again – and I can't find a thing.' He stood back, shaking his head and wiping his greasy hands on a wad of cotton waste. 'I don't know. I just don't know.'

'Have you tried starting her again?'

'No point in that – not until I find and cure the trouble.'

'Try,' said Vicky, and he grinned at her.

'It's no use – but to humour you.'

He stooped to the crank handle, and Priscilla fired at the first swing, caught and ran smoothly, purring like a great hump-backed cat in front of the fire.

'My God.' Jake stepped back and stared in amazement. 'There's just no logic to it.'

'She's a lady,' Vicky explained. 'You know that – and there isn't necessarily logic in the way a lady behaves.'

He turned to face her directly and grinned at her, such a knowing expression in his eyes that she felt herself flushing. 'I'm beginning to find that out,' he said, and stepped towards her, but she raised both hands protectively.

'You'll put grease on this dress—'

'If I were to bath first?'

'Bath,' she ordered. 'And then we'll talk again, mister.'

In the last few minutes of daylight, a rider had come down the gorge, clattering and sliding on the rough footing, and then hitting the level ground and galloping into the Ras's camp on a blown and lathered horse.

Sara Sagud took the message he carried, came flying up to the cluster of tents under the flat-topped camel-thorn trees and burst into Vicky Camberwell's tent waving the folded cablegram, without dreaming of announcing her entrance.

Vicky was deep in a bearlike enfolding embrace into which Jake Barton had taken her moments before, and the interruption came just as Vicky was abandoning herself to the pleasure of the moment. Jake towered over her, freshly scrubbed and smelling of carbolic soap, with his hair still wet and newly combed. Vicky broke out of his arms and turned furiously to the girl.

'Oh!' exclaimed Sara, with the natural interest and fascination of a born conspirator discovering a fresh intrigue. 'You are busy.'

'Yes, I am,' snapped Vicky, cheeks aflame with embarrassment and confusion.

'I'm sorry, Miss Camberwell. But I thought this message must be important—' and Vicky's irritation faded, as she saw the cablegram. 'I thought you would want it.' Vicky snatched it from her, broke the seal and read avidly. Her anger faded as she read, and she looked up with shining eyes at Sara.

'You were right – thank you, my dear,' and she spun back to Jake, dancing up to him and flinging both arms around his neck, laughing and gay.

'Hey,' Jake laughed with her, holding her awkwardly in front of the girl, 'What's this all about?'

'It's from my editor,' she told him. 'My story about the attack at the Wells was an international scoop. Headlines around the world – and there is to be an emergency session of the League of Nations.'

Sara snatched the cable form back from her, and read it as though by right.

'This is what my father believed you could do for us, Miss Camberwell – for our land and our people.' Sara was weeping, fat oily tears breaking from the dark gazelle eyes and clinging in her long lashes. 'Now the world knows. Now they will come to save us from the tyranny.' The girl's faith in the triumph of good over evil was childlike, and she pulled Vicky from Jake's arms and embraced her in his stead. 'Oh, you have given us a chance again. We will always be grateful to you.' Her tears smeared Vicky's cheek, and she drew back, sniffing wetly, and wiped her own tears from Vicky's face with the palm of her hand. 'We will never forget you,' she said, and then smiled through the tears. 'We must go and tell my grandfather.'

They found it impossible to convey to the Ras the exact nature of this new advancement of the Ethiopian cause. He was very hazy in his exact understanding of the role and importance of the League of Nations, or the power and influence of the international press. After the first few pints of *tej* he had made sure in his own mind that in some miraculous fashion the great Queen of England had espoused their cause, and that the armies of Great Britain would soon join him in the field. Both Gregorius and Sara spoke to him at great length, trying to explain his error, and he nodded and grinned benevolently at them but remained completely unshaken in his conviction, and ended by embracing Gareth Swales, making a long rambling speech in Amharic, hailing him as an Englishman and a comrade in arms. Then, before the speech ended, the Ras fell suddenly and dramatically asleep in mid-sentence, falling face forward into a large bowl of mutton *wat*. The day's battle, the excitement of learning of his new and powerful ally, and the large quantities of *tej* were too much for him, and four of his bodyguard lifted him from the bowl and carried him snoring loudly to his household tent.

'Do not worry,' Sara told his guests. 'My grandfather will not be gone for long – after a small rest he will return.'

'Tell him not to put himself out,' murmured Gareth Swales. 'I for one have seen about enough of him for one day.'

The glow of the bonfires turned the sky ruddy and paled the moon that sailed above the mountain peaks. It shone on the steel and polished wood of the huge pile of captured weapons, rifles and pistols and ammunition bandoliers, that were heaped triumphantly in the open space before the royal party.

The sparks from the fires rose straight upwards into the still night and the laughter and voices of the guests became more unrestrained as the *tej* gourds circulated.

Farther along the valley, also within the acacia grove, the Gallas of Ras Kullah were celebrating the victory also, and there was the occasional faint outburst of drunken shouts and a fusillade of shots from captured Italian rifles.

Vicky sat between Gareth and Jake. She had not arranged it so, and if given the choice would have sat alone with Jake, but Gareth Swales had not been as easily discouraged as she had believed he might.

Sara came from her place beside Gregorius. Crossing the squatting circle of feasting guests, she knelt on the pile of leather cushions beside Vicky, pushing herself in between Gareth and the girl and she leaned close to Vicky, an arm around her shoulder and her lips touching her ear.

'You should have told me,' she accused her sadly. 'I did not know that you had decided on Jake first. I would have advised you—'

At that instant a sound carried from the camp of the

Gallas to where they sat. It was muted by distance and almost obscured by the closer hubbub of the feasting Harari – yet the terrible heart-stopping quality of it pierced Vicky so that she gasped and clutched Sara's wrist.

Beside her Jake and Gareth had stiffened and were listening also, their heads turned to catch the sound that rose and died in a long-drawn-out rending sob.

'You have not handled them correctly, Miss Camberwell.' Sara went on speaking, as if she had heard nothing.

'Sara, what is it – what was that?' Vicky shook her arm urgently.

'Ah!' Sara made a gesture of disdain and contempt. 'That fat pervert Ras Kullah has come down from his hiding-place. Now that we have won the victory, he has come to enjoy the booty. He arrived an hour ago with his fat milch cows and now he feasts and entertains himself.'

The sound came again. It was inhuman, a terrible high-pitched screech that tore across Vicky's nerves. It rose higher and higher, until Vicky wanted to cover her ears with both hands. At the instant that it seemed her nerves must snap, the sound was cut off abruptly.

A listening silence had fallen upon the revelling throng around the bonfires, and the silence persisted for a few seconds longer after the scream had ended, then there was a murmur of comment and here and there a burst of careless, cruel laughter.

'What is it, damn it, Sara, what are they doing?'

'Ras Kullah is playing with the Italians,' Sara said quietly, and Vicky realized that she had thought no further of the prisoners taken that day from the routed Italian column.

'Playing, Sara? What do you mean?'

And Sara spat like an angry cat, a gesture of utter disgust. 'They are animals, those beasts of Ras Kullah. They will make sport of them all night, and in the morning they will cut away their man's things,' she spat again. 'Before they can marry, they must take a man's things – what do you call them, the two things in the little sac?'

'Testicles,' said Vicky hoarsely, almost choking on the word.

'Yes,' agreed Sara. 'They must kill a man and take his testicles to the bride. It is their custom, but first they will make sport with the Italians.'

'Can't we stop them?' Vicky asked.

'Stop them?' Sara looked amazed. 'They are only Italians, and it is the Galla custom.'

Again came that cry, and again there was complete silence from the revellers. It climbed high into the silent desert air, shriek upon shriek, so that it seemed impossible that it could come from a human lung, and their souls cringed at the dimensions of suffering which could give vent to that pinnacle of agonized sound.

'Oh God! Oh God!' whispered Vicky, and she lifted her eyes from Sara's face to that of Gareth Swales who sat beyond her.

He was silent and still, his face turned half away from her, so that she saw the godlike profile, perfect and cold. As the cry of agony died away, he leaned forward, took a burning twig from the fire and lit the long black cheroot between his white teeth.

He drew deeply and held the smoke, then let it trickle out through his nostrils. Then he turned deliberately to Vicky.

'You heard what the lady said. It's the custom.' He spoke to Vicky, but the remark was addressed to Jake Barton, and his eyes flicked mockingly to him, a half-smile on his lips. The two men held each other's eyes, unblinking and expressionless.

The cry of agony came again – but this time weaker, the aching ringing tone reduced to a sobbing echo on the dark night.

Jake Barton rose to his feet, coming erect with one fluid movement, and in a continuation of the same movement he crossed to the piles of captured Italian weapons. He stooped and picked up an officer's automatic pistol, a 7 mm Beretta, still in its polished leather holster, and he un-buckled the flap and drew the weapon, discarding the leather holster and waist belt. He checked the loaded magazine and then, with a slap of his palm, thrust it back into the recessed butt, pumped the slide to throw a round into the breech, flicked the safety-catch across and slipped the pistol into the pocket of his breeches.

Without looking again at any of the others, he strode away, disappearing beyond the firelight into the darkness, in the direction of the Galla encampment.

'I told him a long time ago that sentimentality is an old-fashioned luxury – an expensive one in this age, and especially in this place,' murmured Gareth, and inspected the ash of his cheroot.

'They will kill him if he goes in there alone,' said Sara in a completely matter-of-fact tone. 'They will be hungry for more blood and they'll kill him.'

'Oh, I don't know it's as bad as that,' Gareth demurred.

'Oh, yes. They'll kill him,' said Sara, and turned back to Vicky. 'Are you going to let him go? They are only Italians,' she pointed out. For a moment, the two women stared at each other, and then Vicky leaped to her feet and went after Jake, the blue linen swirling gracefully around her legs and the firelight playing like liquid bronze gold on her hair as she ran.

She caught up with Jake at the perimeter of the Galla encampment, and she fell in beside him, taking two quick steps to each of his strides.

'Go back,' he said softly, but she did not reply and skipped to keep up with him.

'Do what I say.'

'No, I'm coming with you.'

He stopped and swung to face her, and she lifted her chin defiantly, throwing back her shoulders and drawing herself up to her full height so that she came to his shoulder.

'Listen to me—' he began, and then stopped as the tortured being cried again in the night, and it was a blubbering incoherent sound, half moan, half sob – followed almost immediately by the throaty roar of many hundred voices, the blood roar of a hunting pack, deep and savage.

'That's what it will be like.' His head was turned away from her to listen and his eyes were haunted.

'I'm coming,' she said stubbornly, and he did not reply, but broke away and hurried forward towards the glowing reflection of the Galla fires which turned the branches of the camel-thorns to high cathedral roofs of ruddy light over the encampment.

There were no sentries posted, and they passed unnoticed through the horse lines and the hastily thatched *tukuls* and leather tents, coming suddenly into the centre of the camp where the fires were burning and the Gallas were assembled, a huge dark circle of squatting figures; the firelight bronzed their eager hawk features, and the whole assembly hummed with the charged tension that always holds the spectators at a blood spectacle. Jake remembered it from a prize fight in Madison Square Garden and again from a cock fight in Havana.

The blood lust was running high, and they growled like an animal pack.

'That is Ras Kullah,' whispered Vicky, tugging at Jake's sleeve, and he glanced across the open arena of beaten earth.

Kullah sat on a pile of carpets and cushions, a silk shawl striped in a dozen brilliant colours was draped across his head and shoulders, masking his soft smooth face with shadow – but the firelight caught his eyes and made them glitter with a peculiarly feverish fury.

One of his fat ivory-coloured hands was clenched in his lap, while his other arm was cast around the waist of the woman who sat beside him, and his hand kneaded and worked her yielding flesh. The hand seemed to have life of its own, and it moved, pale and obscene, like a huge slug pulsing softly as it devoured the swollen ripe fruits of the woman's bosom.

Beyond the fires, on the far side of the circle of open earth a group of three Italian soldiers were clustered fearfully, their faces shiny white with sweat and terror in the firelight, and their hands bound behind their backs. They had been stripped to their breeches, and the exposed skin of their backs and arms was welted and bruised where they had been beaten and abused. Their naked feet were swollen and bloody; clearly they had been forced to march thus for long distances across the harsh stony earth. Their dark eyes, huge with horror, were fastened on the spectacle that was being enacted on the open stage of bare earth in the limelight of the fires.

Vicky recognized the woman as one of Ras Kullah's favourites whom she had last seen that night at the rest house of Sardi. Now she knelt, heavy-breasted and intent on her work. The round madonna face was alight with an almost religious ecstasy, the full lips parted and the dark sloe eyes glowing like those of a priestess at some mystic rite. However, more prosaically the sleeves of her shamma were drawn up in businesslike fashion above the elbows like those of a butcher, and her hands were bloody to the wrists. She held the thin curved dagger like a surgeon, and its silver blade was dull and red in the firelight.

The thing over which she worked still wriggled and moved convulsively against its bonds, still breathed and sobbed, but it was no longer recognizable as a man. The knife had stripped away all resemblance – and now as the waiting crowd growled and swayed and sighed, the woman worked doggedly at the base of the disembowelled belly, cutting and tugging, so that the victim screamed again, but feebly – and the woman leapt to her feet and held aloft the mutilated handful she had cut free.

She did a triumphant circuit of the arena, holding her prize high, laughing, dancing on shuffling swaying feet, and the blood trickled down her raised forearm and dripped from the crook of her elbow.

'Stay close,' Jake said softly, but Vicky had never heard that tone in his voice before. She tore her horrified gaze from the spectacle, and saw that his face was stern and drawn, his jaw clenched hard and his eyes terrible.

He drew the pistol from his pocket, and held it against his thigh, his arm hanging loosely at his side, and he moved swiftly, thrusting his way through the press of bodies with such strength that he cleared a path for her to follow him.

Every single Galla was concentrating with all his attention on the dancing woman, and Jake reached Ras Kullah before any of them realized his presence.

Jake took the soft thick upper arm in his left hand, his fingers digging deeply into the putty-soft flesh, and he jerked him to his feet and held him dangling off-balance, swinging him face to face, and he pressed the muzzle of the Beretta into his upper lip, just under the wide nostrils.

They stared at each other, Ras Kullah cringing away from Jake's blazing eyes, and then whimpering at the pain of the fingers cutting into his flesh and fear of the steel muzzle bruising his upper lip.

Jake assembled the few words of Amharic he had learned from Gregorius.

'The Italians,' he said softly. 'For me.'

Ras Kullah stared at him, seeming not to hear – then he

said one word and the men nearest them swayed forward, as though to intervene.

Jake screwed the muzzle of the pistol into Ras Kullah's lip, twisting and smearing the soft flesh against his teeth so that the skin tore and blood sprang swiftly.

'You die,' said Jake, and the man shrilled a denial to his warriors. They drew back reluctantly, fingering their knives and watching with smouldering eyes for their opportunity. The woman with the bloody hands sank to her haunches and a great waiting silence gripped the assembly. They squatted in complete stillness, all their faces turned towards Jake and Ras Kullah. In the silence, the broken bleeding thing beside the fire cried out again, a long-drawn-out breathy sound that tore at Jakes nerves and made his expression ferocious.

'Tell your men,' he said, his voice thick and grating with his anger. Ras Kullah's voice quavered, high as a young girl, and the warriors who guarded the three half-naked prisoners shuffled uncertainly and exchanged glances.

Jake ground the steel fiercely into Ras Kullah's face, and his voice squeaked urgently as he repeated the order. Reluctantly, the guards prodded the prisoners forward in a forlorn terrified group.

'Take his dagger,' Jake said quietly to Vicky, without removing his gaze from Ras Kullah's eyes. Vicky stepped close beside the Ras and gripped the hilt of the weapon on the embroidered belt around his sagging paunch. It was worked in beaten gold and set with crudely cut amethysts, but the blade was brilliant and the edge keen.

'Cut them loose,' said Jake, and in the dangerous moments while she was away from his side, he increased the brutal pressure on the pistol barrel. Ras Kullah stood with his head cocked at an impossible angle, the lips drawn back from his teeth in a fixed snarl and his eyes rolling in their sockets until the whites showed, and the tears of pain poured freely down his cheeks, glinting in the firelight like dew on the yellow petals of a rose.

Vicky cut the rawhide bindings at the Italians' wrists and elbows, and they massaged the circulation back into their arms, huddling together, their pale faces still smeared with dirt and dried blood and their eyes terrified and uncomprehending.

Quickly, Vicky crossed back to Jake and stood close beside him. Somehow there was safety and security when she was near to him. She stayed beside him as Jake forced Ras Kullah, step by step, across the open ground to where the maimed, half-destroyed thing still moved weakly and drew each agonized breath of air with a bubbling sigh.

Jake stooped slightly away from Ras Kullah, but still holding him, and Vicky saw the compassion alter the fierce expression in his eyes for a moment. She did not realize what he was going to do until he dropped the pistol from Ras Kullah's face, and extended his arm at full stretch.

The crack of the pistol was sharp and cutting in the stillness, and the bullet hit the mutilated Italian in the centre of his forehead, leaving a dark blue hole in the gleaming white skin of the brow. His eyelids fluttered like the wings of a dying dove, and the arched straining body sagged and relaxed. A long gusty sigh came up the tortured throat, the sigh a man might make at the very edge of sleep – and then he was still.

Without another look at the man to whom he had given peace, Jake lifted the pistol to Ras Kullah's face again, and with fresh pressure on his arm he forced him to turn and walk slowly back.

With a curt inclination of the head, he signalled the three Italians to move. They went first, moving slowly, still shrinking together, then Vicky followed them, one hand for comfort reaching back to touch Jake's shoulder. Jake held Ras Kullah twisted off balance, and forced him step by step

327

onwards. He knew they must not hurry, must not show weakness, for the flimsy bonds which held the Gallas frozen would snap at the least strain, and they would be upon them in a pack, bearing them down under the press of bodies, and hacking and tearing them to pieces.

Pace after slow steady pace, they moved forward. Time and again their way was blocked by sullen groups of tall dark Gallas, who stood shoulder to shoulder, fingering their weapons, then Jake twisted the muzzle of the pistol into Ras Kullah's soft skin. The man cried out and reluctantly the way opened, the dark warriors moving aside just sufficiently to let them pass, and then falling in behind them and following closely, so closely the leaders were always within arm's length.

Once they were clear of the pack, Jake could increase the pace and he moved steadily up the path through the camel-thorn, shepherding the terrified Italians ahead of him and dragging Ras Kullah bodily along.

'What are we going to do with them?' Vicky asked breathlessly. 'We can't keep Kullah at gun point much longer.'

Jake did not answer; he did not want the closely following Gallas to hear the uncertainty in his voice, yet he didn't want the girl to show signs of fear.

She was right, of course, the Gallas followed them now with an implacable malevolence, pressing closely in an avenging throng that filled the darkness.

'The cars—' said Jake, as inspiration came to him. 'Get them into one of the cars.'

'And then?'

'One thing at a time,' growled Jake. 'Let's get them into the car first.'

And they moved steadily up the path, the Gallas pressing them more closely. One of the tall cloaked figures jostled Jake roughly, trying him, beginning to push harder, and Jake moved smoothly, swinging his weight across and swivelling a quarter of a turn. It was so swift that the Galla could not avoid the blow; even if he had seen it, he was hemmed in and constrained by the press of his comrades' bodies.

Jake hit him with a forearm chop, and the barrel of the pistol caught him in the mouth, snapping off his front teeth cleanly from the upper gum, and the shock of the blow was transferred directly through the frontal sinuses to the brain. The man dropped without a sound and was immediately hidden from view by the men who stumbled over him as they followed. But they did not press so hard now, and Jake switched the pistol back to Ras Kullah's head. The entire incident was over before Kullah could cry out or squirm in the punishing grip that had bruised and twisted his upper arm.

Jake shifted his grip again, forcing the man farther off balance, and hustled him on more urgently. Ahead of them, through the trees, he could make out the ugly humped shapes of the cars, silver grey in the moonlight and silhouetted by the dying ash heaps of the camp fires.

'Vicky, we'll use Miss Wobbly. I'm not taking a chance on Priscilla starting first kick,' he grated. 'Use the driver's hatch. Don't worry about anything else but getting behind that wheel.'

'What about the prisoners?'

'Do what you're told, don't argue, damn it.' They were within twenty feet of the car now, and he told her, 'Now, go, fast as you can.'

She darted away, reaching the high side of Miss Wobbly before any of the Gallas could intervene and she went up it with a single agile bound.

'Close down,' Jake shouted after her, and felt a quick lift of relief as the hatch clanged shut. The Gallas growled like the wolf-pack denied its prey – and they swarmed forward, pressing hard and surrounding the car.

Jake fired a single shot in the air, and Ras Kullah screamed a command. The Gallas drew back fractionally and fell into a sullen silence.

'Vicky, can you hear me?' Jake called, as he shepherded the Italian prisoners close in against the hull.

Her voice was muffled and remote from behind the steel plate as she acknowledged.

'The rear doors,' he told her urgently. 'Get them open – but not before I tell you.' He pushed the Italians around towards the rear of the car, but it was slow work, for they were confused and stupid with terror.

'Now,' Jake shouted and knocked impatiently against the hull with the pistol. The lock grated and the doors swung outwards, and came up against the packed bodies outside.

'Goddamn it,' growled Jake, and got his shoulder to one leaf of the door. He shoved it open, knocking down two of the closest Gallas and in the same movement boosted one of the Italians through the opening into the dark interior of the car. In a panicky scramble, the other two followed him and Jake swung the door closed on them and put his back flat against it, and heard the bolts shot closed on the inside, facing the hating dark faces, and the surging press of their hundreds of bodies. Voices were raised at the rear of the crowd and violence was seconds away – they had seen most of their prey escape, and it needed little more to trigger the mob reflex.

Jake found he was panting as though he had run a long way, and his heart pounded, so that he could feel it jump against his rib cage – but he held Ras Kullah, changing his grip from the pudgy upper arm to the thick wiry bush of his hair, twining his fingers deeply into the stiff, dark halo at the back of his skull and twisting the head so that Ras Kullah faced his men. With the other hand Jake thrust the pistol deeply into the aperture of the man's earhole.

'Speak to them, sweetlips.' He made his voice vicious

330

and menacing. 'Otherwise I'm going to push this piece right out through the other ear.'

Ras Kullah understood the tone, if not the words, and he gabbled out a few hysterical words of Amharic; the front warriors drew back a pace and Jake slid slowly along the hull, keeping his back to the steel and Ras Kullah pinned helplessly by his hair to cover his front. The crowd moved with them, keeping station with them, their faces glowering in the moonlight, cruel and angry, balancing critically on the pinnacle of violence. A voice rang out from the darkness, an authoritative voice urging action, the crowd growled, and Ras Kullah whimpered in Jake's grip.

The sound of Ras Kullah's terror warned Jake that they would be frustrated no longer, the moment was upon them.

'Vicky, are you ready to start?' he called urgently, and her voice was just audible.

'Ready to start.'

He felt the fixed crank handle catch him in the back of the legs, and at that instant a woman's voice shrilled and echoed through the grove of camel-thorn trees. In that heart-stopping ululation of the blood trill, the invocation to violence that the heart of the African warrior cannot resist, the sound struck the jostling press of Gallas like a whip-stroke and their bodies convulsed and their voices rose in an answering blood roar.

'Oh Jesus, here they come,' thought Jake, and put all his strength into the arm and shoulder that took Ras Kullah between the shoulder blades and hurled him forward into the front rank of his own men. He crashed into them, bringing down half a dozen of them in a sprawling tangle over which the next rank tumbled and fell.

Jake turned swiftly and stooped to the crank handle. He had chosen Miss Wobbly for this moment, knowing that she was the most gentle and well-intentioned of all the cars. He would have trembled to put the same trust in Priscilla –

331

and as it was, even she coughed and hesitated at the first swing.

'Please, my darling, please,' Jake pleaded desperately, and at the next swing of the handle she hacked, choked and fired – then suddenly she was running sweetly. Jake jumped for the sponson, just as a great two-handed sword swung down at him from on high.

He heard the hiss of the blade, passing like the flight of a bat in the darkness, and he ducked under it. The sword struck the steel hull of the car and sprayed a fiery burst of sparks, and Jake rolled and fired the Beretta as the Galla raised the sword to swing again.

He heard the bullet slog into flesh, a meaty thump, and the man collapsed backwards, the sword spinning from his hand as he went down – but from every direction, robed figures were swarming up the hull of the car, like safari ants over the carcass of a helpless scarab beetle, and the roar of voices was a storm surf of anger.

'Drive, Vicky – for God's sake, drive,' he yelled, and slammed the pistol over the woolly head of a Galla as it rose beside him. The man fell away and the engine bellowed, the car bounded forward with a jerk that threw most of the Gallas from the hull, and Jake was himself thrown half clear, snatching at one of the welded brackets as he went over and saving himself from falling into the swarming pack of Gallas – but the pistol dropped out of his hand as he clung grimly to his precarious hold.

Miss Wobbly, under Vicky's thrusting foot, roared into the thick wall of men ahead of her and few of them had a chance to avoid her charge. Their bodies went down before her, thudding against the frontal plate of the car, their blood roar changing swiftly to yells and shrieks of consternation as they scattered away into the darkness and the car burst free of the press and tore on down the slope.

Jake dragged himself back on board and steadied himself

against the turret, as he rose to his knees. Beside him a Galla clung like a tick to the back of an ox, wailing in terror while his shamma swirled over his head in the stream of racing air. Jake put one foot against the man's raised buttocks and thrust hard. The man shot head first over the side of the speeding car, and hit the earth with a crunch that was audible even above the roaring engine.

Jake crawled back along the heaving, violently rocking hull and with fist and foot he threw overside one at a time her deck cargo of terrified Gallas. Vicky took the car down the slope under full throttle, weaving wildly through the trees of the grove and at last out on to the open moonlit plain.

Here at last, by pounding with his fist on the driver's hatch, Jake managed to arrest Vicky's wild drive, and she braked the car to a cautious halt.

She came out through the hatch and embraced him with both arms wound tightly around his neck. Jake made no attempt to avoid the circle of her arms, and a silence settled over them disturbed only by their breathing. They had both almost forgotten about their prisoners in the pleasure of the moment, but were reminded by the scuffling and muttering in the depths of the car. Slowly they drew apart, and Vicky's eyes were soft and lustrous in the moonlight.

'The poor things,' she whispered. 'You saved them from that—' and words failed her as she remembered the one they had been too late to save.

'Yes,' Jake agreed. 'But what the hell do we do with them now?'

'We could take them up to the Harari Camp – the Ras would treat them fairly.'

'Don't bet money on it.' Jake shook his head. 'They are all Ethiopians – and their rules of the game are different from ours. I wouldn't like to take a chance on it.'

'Oh Jake, I'm sure he wouldn't allow them to be—'

'Anyway,' Jake interrupted, 'if we handed them over to the Harari, Ras Kullah would be there the next minute demanding them back for his fun – and if they didn't agree, we'd all be in the middle of a tribal war. No, it won't do.'

'We'll have to turn them loose,' said Vicky at last.

'They'd never make it back to the Wells of Chaldi.' Jake looked to the east, across the brooding midnight plain. 'The ground out there is crawling with Ethiopian scouts. They would have their throats slit before they'd gone a mile.'

'We'll have to take them,' said Vicky, and Jake looked sharply at her.

'Take them?'

'In the car – drive out to the Wells of Chaldi.'

'The Eyeties would love that,' he grunted. 'Have you forgotten those flaming great cannons of theirs?'

'Under a flag of truce,' said Vicky. 'There is no other way, Jake. Truly there isn't.'

Jake thought about it silently for a full minute and then he sighed wearily.

'It's a long drive. Let's get going.'

They drove without headlights, not wanting to attract the attention of the Ethiopian scouts or the Italians, but the moon was bright enough to light their way and define the ravines and rougher ground with crisp black shadows, although occasionally the wheels would crash painfully into one of the deep round holes dug by the aardvarks, the nocturnal long-nosed beasts which burrowed for the subterranean colonies of termites.

The three half-naked Italian survivors huddled down in the rear compartment of the car, so exhausted by fear and the day's adventures that they passed swiftly into sleep, a sleep so deep that neither the noisy roar of the engine within the metal hull nor the bouncing over rough ground could disturb them. They lay like dead men in an untidy heap.

Vicky Camberwell climbed down out of the turret to escape the flow of cool night air, and squeezed into the space beside the driver's seat. For a while she spoke quietly with Jake, but soon her voice became drowsy and finally dried up. Then slowly she toppled sideways against him, and he smiled tenderly and eased her golden head down on to his shoulder and held her like that, warm against him in the noisy hull, as he drove on into the eastern night.

The Italian sentries were sweeping the perimeter of their camp at regular intervals with a pair of powerful anti-aircraft searchlights, probably in anticipation of a night attack by the Ethiopians, and the glow of the beams burned up in a tall white cone of light into the desert sky. Jake homed in upon it, gradually reducing his throttle setting as he closed in. He knew that the engine beat would carry many miles in the stillness, but that at lower revs it would be diffused and impossible to pinpoint.

He guessed he was within two or three miles of the Italian camp when in confirmation that the sentries had heard his approach, and that after their recent experiences they were highly sensitive to the sound of a Bentley engine, a star shell sailed upwards a thousand feet into the sky and burst with a fierce blue-white light that lit the desert like a stage for miles beneath it. Jake hit the brakes hard, and waited for the shell to sink slowly to earth. He did not want movement to attract attention. The light died away and left the night blacker than before, but beside him the abrupt change of motion had woken Vicky and she sat up groggily, pushing the hair out of her eyes and muttering sleepily.

'What is it?'

'We are here,' he said, and another star shell rose in a high arc and burst in brilliance that paled the moon.

'There.' Jake pointed out the ridge above the Wells of Chaldi. The dark shapes of the Italian vehicles were laagered in orderly lines, clearly silhouetted by the star shell. They were two miles ahead. Suddenly there was the distant ripping sound of a machine gun, a sentry firing at shadows, and immediately after, a scattered fusillade of rifle shots which petered out into a sheepish silence.

'It seems that everybody is awake, and jumpy as hell,' Jake remarked drily. 'This is about as close as we can go.'

He crawled out of the driver's seat and went back to where the prisoners were still piled upon each other like a litter of sleeping puppies. One of them was snoring like an asthmatic lion, and Jake had to put his boot amongst them to stir them back to consciousness. They came awake slowly and resentfully, and Jake swung open the rear doors and pushed them out into the darkness.

They stood dejectedly, clasping their naked trunks in the chill of the night and peering about them fearfully to discover what new unpleasantness awaited them. At that instant another star shell burst almost overhead, and they exclaimed and blinked owlishly without immediate comprehension as Jake made shooing gestures, trying to drive them like a flock of chickens towards the ridge.

Finally Jake grabbed one of them by the scruff of the neck, pointed his face at the ridge and gave him a shove that sent him tottering the first few paces. Suddenly the man recognized his own camp and the lines of big Fiat trucks in the light of the star shell. He let out a heartfelt cry of relief and broke into a shambling run.

The other two stared for a moment in disbelief and then set out after him at the top of their speed. When they had gone twenty yards, one of them turned back and came to Jake, seized his hand and pumped it vigorously, a huge smile splitting his face; then he turned to Vicky and covered both her hands with wet noisy kisses. The man was weeping, tears streaming down his cheeks.

'That's enough of that,' growled Jake. 'On your way,

friend,' and he turned the Italian and once more pointed him at the horizon and helped him on his way.

The unaffected joy of the released Italians was contagious. Jake and Vicky drove back in a high good mood, laughing together secretly in the dark and noisy hull of the car. They had covered half of the forty miles back to the Sardi Gorge, and behind them the lights of the Italian camp were a mere suggestion of lesser darkness low on the eastern horizon, but still their mood was light and joyous and at some fresh sally of Jake's Vicky leaned across to kiss him on the soft pulse of his throat beneath his ear.

As if of her own accord, Miss Wobbly's speed bled away and she rocked to a gentle standstill in the centre of a wide open area of soft sandy soil and low dark scrub.

Jake earthed the magneto, and the engine note died away into silence. He turned in the seat and took Vicky fully in his arms, crushing her to him with sudden strength that made her gasp aloud.

'Jake!' she protested, half in pain, but his lips covered hers, and her protests were forgotten at the taste of his mouth.

His jaw and cheeks were rough with new beard, the same strong wiry growth of dark hair which curled out of his shirt front, and the man smell of him was like the taste of his mouth. She felt the softness of her own body crave the hardness of his and she pressed herself to him, finding pleasure in the pain of contact, in the bruising pressure of his mouth against her lips.

She knew she was arousing emotions that soon would be beyond either of their control, and the knowledge made her reckless and bold. The thought occurred to her that she had it in her power to drive him demented with passion, and the idea aroused her further, and immediately she wanted to exercise that power.

She heard his breathing roaring in her ears, then realized that it was not his – it was her own, and each gust of it seemed to swell her chest until it must burst.

It was so cramped in the cockpit of the car, and their movements were becoming wild and unrestrained. Vicky felt restricted and itching with constraint. She had never known this wildness before, and for a fleeting instant she remembered the skilful, gentle minuet of formal movements which had been her loving with Gareth Swales, and she compared it to this stormy meeting of passions; then the thought was borne away on the flood, on the need to be free of confinement.

Outside the car, the chill of the desert night prickled the skin of her back and flanks and thighs, and she felt the fine golden hairs come erect on her forearms. He flapped out the bed-roll and spread it on the earth. Then he returned to her, and the heat of his body was a physical shock. It seemed to burn with all the pent-up fires of his soul, and she pressed herself to it with complete abandon, delighting in the contrast of his burning flesh and the cool desert breeze upon her bare skin.

Now at last there was nothing to prevent the range of her hands and she knew they were cold as ghost fingers on him, delighting to hear his gasp again at their touch. She laughed then, a hoarse throaty chuckle.

'Yes.' She laughed again, as he lifted her easily and dropped to his knees on the bed-roll, holding her against his chest.

'Yes, Jake.' She let the last restraint fly. 'Quickly, quickly – my darling.'

It was a raging, a roaring of all her senses. It was an aching, tumultuous storm that ended at last – and afterwards the vast hissing silence of the desert was so frightening that she clung to him like a child and found to her amazement

338

that she was weeping – the tears scalded her eyes and yet were as icy as the touch of frost upon her cheeks.

General De Bono's first cautious but ponderous thrust across the Mareb River, into Ethiopia, met with a success that left him stunned.

Ras Muguletu, the Ethiopian commander in the north, offered only token resistance – then withdrew his forty thousand men southwards to the natural mountain fortress of Amba Aradam. Unopposed, De Bono drove the seventy miles to Adowa and found it deserted. Triumphantly he erected the monument to the fallen Italian warriors – and thereby expunged the stain of defeat from the arms of Italy.

The great civilizing mission had begun. The savage was being tamed, and introduced to the miracles of modern man – amongst them the aerial bomb.

The Royal Italian Air Force ranged the skies above the towering Ambas, reporting all troop movements and swooping down to bomb and machine-gun any concentrations.

The Ethiopian forces were confused and scattered under their tribal commanders. There were half a dozen breaches in their line that a forceful commander could have exploited – indeed even General De Bono sensed this and made another convulsive leap forward as far as Makale. However, here he stopped appalled at his own audacity, stunned by his own achievement.

Ras Muguletu was skulking on Amba Aradam with his forty thousand, while Ras Kassa and Ras Seyoum were struggling to move the great unwieldy masses of their two armies through the mountain passes to link up with the army of the Emperor on the shores of Lake Tana.

They were disordered, vulnerable, ripe to be cut down like wheat — and General De Bono closed his eyes, covered his brow with one hand and turned his head aside. History would never accuse him of recklessness and impetuosity.

'FROM GENERAL DE BONO COMMANDER OF THE ITALIAN EXPEDITIONARY FORCE AT MAKALE TO BENITO MUSSOLINI PRIME MINISTER OF ITALY HAVING CAPTURED ADOWA AND MAKALE I CONSIDER MY IMMEDIATE OBJECTS HAVE BEEN ATTAINED STOP IT IS NOW VITALLY NECESSARY TO CONSOLIDATE THESE SUCCESSES TO FORTIFY MY POSITION AGAINST ENEMY COUNTER ATTACK AND TO SECURE MY LINES OF SUPPLY AND COMMUNICATIONS.'

'FROM BENITO MUSSOLINI PRIME MINISTER OF ITALY MINISTER OF WAR TO GENERAL DE BONO OFFICER COMMANDING THE ITALIAN EXPEDITIONARY FORCE IN AFRICA HIS MAJESTY WISHES AND I COMMAND YOU TO ADVANCE WITHOUT HESITATION ON AMBA ARADAM AND BRING THE MAIN BODY OF THE ENENMY TO BATTLE AS SOON AS POSSIBLE STOP REPLY TO ME.'

'FROM GENERAL DE BONO TO THE PRIME MINISTER OF ITALY GREETINGS AND FELICITATIONS I WISH TO POINT OUT TO YOUR EXELLENCY THAT THE OBJECTIVE AMBA ARADAM IS TACTICALLY UNDESIRABLE ... THE TERRAIN FAVOURS AMBUSH ... CONDITION OF ROADS VERY POOR ... TRUST MY JUDGEMENT ... URGE YOUR EXCELLENCY TO RECONSIDER AND TO TAKE COGNIZANCE OF THE FACT THAT THE MILITARY SITUATION MUST TAKE PRECEDENCE OVER ALL POLITICAL CONSIDERATION.'

'FROM BENITO MUSSOLINI TO MARSHAL DE BONO PREVIOUSLY OFFICER COMMANDING THE ITALIAN EXPEDITIONARY FORCE IN AFRICA HIS MAJESTY ORDERS ME TO CONVEY HIS FELICITATIONS ON YOUR ELEVATION TO THE RANK OF MARSHAL OF THE ARMY AND TO THANK YOU FOR THE IMPECCABLE EXECUTION OF YOUR DUTY IN RECAPTURING ADOWA STOP WITH THE ATTAINMENT OF THIS OBJECTIVE I CONSIDER THAT YOUR MISSION IN EASTERN AFRICA HAS BEEN COMPLETED STOP YOU HAVE EARNED THE GRATITUDE OF THE NATION BY YOUR OBVIOUS MERITS AS A SOLDIER AND YOUR STEADFAST DISCHARGE OF YOUR DUTY AS A COMMANDER STOP YOU ARE REQUESTED TO HAND OVER YOUR COMMAND TO GENERAL PIETRO BADOGLIO ON HIS IMMINENT ARRIVAL IN AFRICA..'

MMarshal De Bono accepted both his promotion and his recall with such good grace that it could have been mistaken, by an uninformed observer, for profound relief. His departure for Rome was completed with such despatch as to avoid by a hair's breadth the semblance of indecorous haste.

General Pietro Badoglio was a fighting soldier. He had staffed the headquarters before Adowa, although he had played no part in that débâcle, and he was a veteran of Caporetto and Vittorio Veneto. He believed that the purpose of war was to crush the enemy as swiftly and as ruthlessly as was possible, with the use of any weapon at his disposal.

He came ashore at Massawa with a furious impatience, angry with everything he found, and impatient of the policies and concepts of his predecessor – although in truth seldom had an incoming commander been handed such an enviable strategic situation.

He inherited a huge, well-equipped army with a buoyant morale, in a commanding tactical position and backed by a magnificent network of communications and a logistics inventory that was alpine in proportions.

The small but magnificently equipped airforce of the expedition was flying unopposed over the Amba mountains, observing all troop movements and pouncing immediately on any Ethiopian concentrations. During one of the first dinners at the new headquarters, Lieutenant Vittorio Mussolini, the younger of the Duce's two sons, one of the dashing Regia Aeronautica aces, regaled his new C-in-C with accounts of his sorties over the enemy highlands – and Badoglio, who had not had close aerial support in any of his previous campaigns, was delighted with this new and deadly weapon. He listened transfixed to the young flier's descriptions of the effect of aerial bombardment – particularly an account of an attack on a group of three hundred or more

342

enemy horsemen led by a tall, dark-robed figure. The young Mussolini told him,

'I released a single hundred-kilo bomb from an altitude of less than a hundred metres, and it fell precisely in the centre of the galloping horsemen. They opened like the petals of a flowering rose, and the dark-robed leader was thrown so high by the blast that he seemed to almost touch my wing-tip as I passed. It was a spectacle of great beauty and magnificence.'

Badoglio was happy that his new command included young men with such fire in their veins, and he leaned forward in his seat at the head of the table to peer down over the glittering silver and sparkling leaded crystal at the flier in his handsome blue uniform. The classical features and dark curly head of hair were the artist's conception of young Mars. Then he turned to the airforce Colonel who sat beside him.

'Colonel, what is the opinion of your young men in the Regia Aeronautica? I have heard much argument for and against – but I would be interested to have your opinion. Should we use the nitrogen mustard?'

'I think I speak for all my young men.' The Colonel sipped his wine and glanced for confirmation at the young ace who was not yet twenty years of age. 'I think the answer must be yes, we must use every weapon available to us.'

Badoglio nodded. The thinking agreed with his own, and the next morning he ordered the canisters of mustard gas shipped from the warehouses of Massawa, where De Bono had been content to let them lie, and despatched them to every airfield where flights of the Regia Aeronautica were based. Thousands upon thousands of the wild tribesmen of Ethiopia would come to know the corrosive dew when later they endured bombardment by artillery and aerial attack with a stoicism greater than most European troops were able to muster – yet they could never come to terms with this terrible substance that turned the open pastures of their mountain fastness to fields of terror. Barefoot, as most of them were, they were pathetically vulnerable to the silent insidious weapon that flayed the skin from their bodies, and then stripped the living flesh from the bone.

This single decision was one of many made that day by the new commander, and signalled the change from De Bono's bumbling, but not unkindly civilizing invasion, to the new concept of total war – war with only one objective.

Mussolini had wanted a hawk, and he had chosen well.

The hawk stood in the centre of the lofty second-storey headquarters office at Asmara. He was too consumed with furious impatience to sit at the wide desk, and when he paced the tiled floor, his heels cracked on the ceramic like drum beats. The elasticity of his stride was that of a man far younger than sixty-five.

He carried his head low on boxer's shoulders, thrusting his chin forward – a heavy chin below a big shapeless round nose, a short-cropped grey moustache and a wide hard mouth.

His eyes were deep sunken into dark cavities, like those of a corpse, but their glitter was alive and aware as he worked swiftly through the lists of his divisional and regimental commanders, assessing each by one criterion only, 'Is he a fighting man?'

Too often the answer was 'no', or at the least uncertain, so it was with a fierce pleasure that he recognized one who was without question a hard-fighting man on whom he could rely.

'Yes,' he nodded vehemently. 'He is the only field commander who has displayed any initiative, who has made any attempt to come to grips with the enemy.' He paused to lift his reading glasses to his eyes and glance again at the reports he held in his other hand. 'He has fought one decisive action, inflicting almost thirty thousand casualties without loss himself. That in itself is an achievement that seems to have gone without suitable recognition. The man should have had a decoration, the order of St Maurice and St Lazarus at the least. Good men must be singled out and rewarded. Look at this – this is typical! When he was aware that the enemy had armoured resources, he was soldier enough to lure that armour into a baited trap, to lead it skilfully and with cool courage on to his entrenched artillery. It was a bold and resourceful stroke for an infantry commander to make – and it deserved to succeed. If only his artillery commander had been a man of equally steely nerves, he would have succeeded in luring the entire enemy armoured column to its total destruction. It was no fault of his that the artillery lost their nerve and opened fire prematurely.'

The General paused to focus his reading glasses on the large glossy photographic print which depicted Colonel Count Aldo Belli standing like a successful big game hunter on the carcass of the Hump. The shattered hull was pierced by shot and in the background lay half a dozen corpses in tattered shammas. These had been collected from the battlefield and tastefully arranged by Gino to give the photograph authenticity. Against his better judgement and his strong instincts of survival, Count Aldo Belli had returned to make these photographic records only after Major Castelani had assured him that the enemy had deserted the field. The Count had not wasted too much time about it, but had his photographs taken, urging Gino to haste, and when it had been done he had returned swiftly to his fortified position above the Wells of Chaldi and had not moved from there since. However, the photographs were an impressive addendum to his official report of the action.

Now Badoglio growled like an angry old lion. 'Despite the incompetence of his junior officers, and there my heart aches for him, this man has wiped out half the enemy armour – as well as half the opposing army.' He hit the report fiercely with his reading glasses. 'The man's a fire-eater, no question about it. I know one when I see one. A fire-eater. This kind of example must be encouraged – good work must be rewarded. Send for him. Radio him to come in to headquarters immediately.'

A s far as Count Aldo Belli was concerned, the campaign had come upon a not unpleasant hiatus. The camp at the Wells of Chaldi had been transformed by his engineers from an outpost of hell into a rather pleasant refuge, with functional amenities, such as ice-making machines and a water-borne sewerage system. The defences were now of sufficient strength to give him a feeling of security. The engineering as always was of the highest quality with extensive covered earthworks, and Castelani had laid out carefully over-lapping fields of fire, and barbed-wire defences in depth.

The hunting in the area was excellent by any standards, with game drawn to the water in the Wells from miles around. The sand-grouse in the evenings filled the heavens with the whistle of their wings, and wheeled in great dark flocks across the setting sun, affording magnificent sport. The bag was measured in grain bags of dead birds.

In the midst of this pleasantly relaxed atmosphere, the new commanding officer's summons exploded like a 100-kilo aerial bomb. General Badoglio's reputation had preceded him. He was a notorious martinet, a man who could not be sidetracked from single-minded purpose by excuse or fabrication. He was insensitive to political influence or power considerations – so much so that it was rumoured that he would have crushed the very Fascist movement itself with force if the issue had been put into his hands back in 1922. He had an almost psychic power to detect subterfuge, and to place a finger squarely on malingerers or lack-guts. They said his justice was swift and merciless.

The shock to the Count's system was considerable. He had been singled out from thousands of brother officers to face this ogre's wrath – for he could not convince himself that the small deviations from reality, the small artistic licences contained in his long, illustrated reports to De Bono had not been instantly discovered. He felt like a guilty schoolboy summoned to dire retribution behind the closed doors of the headmaster's study. The shock hit him squarely in the bowels, always his weak spot, bringing on a fresh onslaught of the malady first caused by the waters of Chaldi Wells, from which he had believed himself completely cured.

It was twelve hours before he could summon the strength to be helped by his concerned underlings into the Rolls-Royce – and to lie wan and palely resigned upon the soft leather seat.

'Drive on, Giuseppe,' he murmured, like an aristocrat giving the order to the driver of the tumbril.

On the long hot dusty drive into Asmara, the Count lay without interest in his surroundings, without even attempting to marshal his defence against the charges he knew he must soon face. He was resigned, abject – his only solace was the considerable damage he would do this upstart, ill-bred peasant, once he returned to Rome, as he was certain he was about to. He knew that he could ruin the man politically – and it gave him a jot of sour pleasure.

Giuseppe, the driver, knowing his man as he did, made the first stop outside the casino in Asmara's main street. Here, at least, Count Aldo Belli was treated as a hero, and he perked up visibly as the young hostesses rushed out on to the sidewalk to welcome him.

Some hours later, freshly shaven, his uniform sponged and pressed, his hair pomaded, and buoyed up on a fragrant cloud of expensive eau de cologne, the Count was ready to face his tormentor. He kissed the girls, tossed back a last glass of cognac, laughed that gay reckless laugh, snapped his fingers once to show what he thought of the peasant who now ran this army, clenched his buttocks tightly together to control his fear and marched out of the casino into the sunlight and across the street into the military head-quarters.

His appointment to meet General Badoglio was for four o'clock and the town hall clock struck the hour as he marched resolutely down the long gloomy corridor, following a young aide-de-camp. They reached the end of the corridor and the aide-de-camp threw open the big double mahogany doors and stood aside for the Count to enter.

His knees felt like boiled macaroni, his stomach gurgled and seethed, the palms of his hands were hot and moist, and tears were not far behind his quivering eyelids as he stepped forward into the huge room with its lofty moulded ceiling.

He saw that it was filled with officers from both the army and the airforce. His disgrace was to be made public, then, and he quailed. Seeming to shrivel, his shoulders slumping, his chest caving and the big handsome head drooping, the Count stood in the doorway. He could not bear to look at them, and miserably he studied his gleaming toecaps.

Suddenly, he was assailed by a strange, a completely alien sound – and he looked up startled, ready to defend himself against physical attack. The roomful of officers were applauding, beaming and grinning, slapping palm to palm – and the Count gaped at them, then glanced quickly over his shoulder to be certain there was no one standing behind him, and that this completely unexpected welcome was being directed at him.

When he looked back he found a stocky, broad-shouldered figure in the uniform of a general advancing upon him. His face was hard and unforgiving, with a fierce grey moustache over the grim trap of his mouth and glittering eyes in deep dark sockets.

If the Count had been in command of his legs and his voice, he might have run screaming from the room, but before he could move the General seized him in a grip of iron, and the moustache raking his cheeks was as rank and rough as the foliage of the trees of the Danakil desert.

'Colonel, I am always honoured to embrace a brave man,' growled the General, hugging him close, his breath smelling pleasantly of garlic and sesame seed, an aroma that blended in an interesting fashion with the fragrant clouds of the Count's perfume. The Count's legs could no longer stand the strain, they almost collapsed under him. He had to grab wildly at the General to prevent himself falling. This threw both of them off balance, and they reeled across the ceramic floor, locked in each other's arms, in a kind of elephantine waltz, while the General struggled to free himself.

He succeeded at last, and backed away warily from the Count, straightening his medals and reassembling his dignity – while one of his officers began to read out a citation from a scroll of parchment and the applause faded into an attentive silence.

The citation was long and wordy, and it gave the Count time to pull his scattered wits together. The first half of the citation was lost to him in his dreamlike state of shock, but then suddenly the words began to reach him. His chin came up as he recognized some of his own composition, little verbal gems from his combat reports – 'Counting only duty dear, scorning all but honour' – that was his own stuff, by the Virgin and Peter.

He listened now, with all his attention, and they were

349

talking about him. They were talking of Aldo Belli. His caved chest filled out, the high colour flooded back into his cheeks, the turmoil of his rebellious bowels was stilled, and fire flashed in his eye once more.

By God, the General had realized that every phrase, every word, every comma and exclamation mark of his report was the literal truth – and the aide-de-camp was handing the General a leather-covered jewel box, and the General was advancing on him again – albeit with a certain caution – and then he was looping the watered silk ribbon over his head so that the big enamelled, white cross with its centre star of emerald green and sparkling diamantine, dangled down the front of the Count's tunic. The order of St Maurice and St Lazarus (military division) of the third class.

Keeping well out of his clutches, the General pecked each of the Count's flushed cheeks and then took a hasty step backwards to join in the applause – while the Count stood there puffed with pride, feeling that his heart might burst.

'You will have that support now,' the General assured him, scowling heavily to hear how his predecessor had grudged the Count sufficient force to win his objectives. 'I pledge it to you.'

They were seated now, just the three of them – General Badoglio, his political agent and the Count – in the smaller private study adjoining the large formal office. Night had fallen outside the shuttered windows and the single lamp was hooded to throw light down on the map spread on the table top, and leave the faces of the three men in shadow.

Cognac glowed in the leaded crystal glasses and the big ship's decanter on its silver tray, and the blue smoke from the cigars spiralled up slow and heavy as treacle in the lamplight.

'I will need armour,' said the Count without hesitation. The thought of thick steel plate had always attracted him strongly.

'I will give you a squadron of the light CV.3s,' said the General, and made a note on the pad at his elbow.

'And I will need air support.'

'Can your engineers build a landing-strip for you at the Wells?' The General touched the map to illustrate the question.

'The land is flat and open. It will present no difficulty,' said the Count eagerly. Planes and tanks and guns, he was being given them all. He was a real commander at last.

'Radio to me when the strip is ready for use. I will send in a flight of Capronis. In the meantime, I will have the transport section convoy in the fuel and armaments – I shall consult the staff at airforce, but I think the 100-kilo bombs will be most effective. High explosive, and fragmentation.'

'Yes, yes,' agreed the Count eagerly.

'And nitrogen mustard – will you have use for the gas?'

'Yes, oh yes, indeed,' said the Count. It was not in his nature to refuse bounty, he would take anything he was offered.

'Good.' The General made another note, laid aside his pencil, and then looked up at the Count. He glowered so ferociously that the Count was startled and he felt the first nervous stir in his belly again. He found the General terrifying, like living on the slopes of a temperamental Vesuvius.

'The iron fist, Belli,' he said, and the Count realized with relief that the scowl was directed not at him, but at the enemy. Immediately the Count assumed an expression every bit as bellicose and menacing. He curled his lip and he spoke, just below a snarl.

351

'Put the blade at the enemy's throat, and drive it home.'

'Without mercy,' said the General.

'To the death,' agreed the Count. He was on his home ground now, and only just hitting his stride; a hundred bloodthirsty slogans sprang to mind – but, recognizing his master, the General changed the snowballing conversation adroitly.

'You are wondering why I have put such importance on your objectives. You are wondering why I have given you such powerful forces, and why I have set such store on you forcing the passage of the Sardi Gorge and the road to the highlands.'

The Count was wondering no such thing, right now he was busy coining a phrase about wading through blood, and he accepted the change of theme reluctantly, and arranged his features in a politely enquiring frame.

The General waved his cigar expansively at the political agent who sat opposite him.

'Signor Antolino.' He made the gesture and the agent sat forward obediently so that the lamplight caught his face.

'Gentlemen.' He cleared his throat, and looked from one to the other with mild brown eyes behind steel-framed spectacles. He was a thin, almost skeletal figure, in a rumpled white linen suit. The wings of his shirt collar were off-centre of his prominent Adam's apple and the knot of the knitted silk tie had slid down and hung at the level of the first button. His head was almost bald, but he had grown the remaining hairs long and greased them down over the shiny freckled plover-egg scalp.

His moustache was waxed into points, but stained yellow with tobacco, and he was of indefinite age – over forty and under sixty – with the dark malarial yellow tan of a man who has lived all his life in the tropics.

'For some time we have been concerned to design an

appropriate form of government for the captured – ah – the liberated territories of Ethiopia.'

'Come to the point,' said the General abruptly.

'It has been decided to replace the present Emperor, Haile Selassie, with a man sympathetic to the Italian Empire, and acceptable to the people—'

'Come on, man,' Badoglio cut in again. Verbal backing and filling were repugnant to him. He was a man of action rather than words.

'Arrangements have been completed after lengthy negotiation, and I might add the promise of several millions of lire, that at the politically opportune moment a powerful chieftain will declare for us, bringing all his warriors and his influence across to us. This man will in due course be declared Emperor of Ethiopia and will administer the territory under Italy.'

'Yes, yes. I understand,' said the Count.

'The man governs part of the area which is the direct objective of your column. As soon as you have seized the Sardi Gorge and entered the town of Sardi itself, this Chief will join you with his men and, with appropriate international publicity, be declared King of Ethiopia.'

'The man's name?' asked the Count, but the agent would not be hurried.

'It will be your duty to meet with this Chief, and to synchronize your efforts. You will also make the promised payment in gold coin.'

'Yes.'

'The man is an hereditary Ras by rank. He is presently commanding part of the army that opposes you at Sardi. However, that will change—' said the agent, and produced a thick envelope from the briefcase beside his chair. It was sealed with the wax tablet and the embossed eagles of the Department of Colonial Affairs. 'Here are your written orders. You will sign for them, please.'

He inspected the Count's signature suspiciously, then, at last satisfied, went on in the same dry disinterested voice.

'One other matter. We have identified one of the white mercenaries fighting with the Ethiopians – those mentioned by you as being reported by the three of your men captured by the enemy and subsequently released.'

The agent paused and drew on his almost dead cigar, puffing up the tip to a bright healthy glow.

'The woman is a notorious *agent provocateur*, a Bolshevik with radical and revolutionary sympathies. She poses as a journalist, employed by an American newspaper whose sentiments have always been strongly anti-Empire. Already some of this woman's biased inflammatory writings have reached the outside world. They have been a severe embarrassment to us at the Department—'

He drew again on the cigar, and spoke again through the billowing cloud of smoke.

'If she is taken, and I hope that you will place priority on her capture, she is to be handed over immediately to the new Ethiopian Emperor-designate, you understand? You are not to be involved, but you will not interfere with the Ras's execution of the woman.'

'I see.' The Count was becoming bored. This political nitpicking was not the type of thing which would hold his attention. He wanted to show the young lady hostesses at the Casino the great cross which now hung around his neck and thumped on his chest each time he moved.

'As for the white man, the Englishman, the one responsible for the brutal shooting of an Italian prisoner of war in front of witnesses, he has been declared a murderer and a political terrorist. When you capture him, he is to be shot out of hand. That order goes for all other foreigners serving under arms with the enemy troops. This type of thing must be put down sternly.'

'You can rely on me,' said the Count. 'There will be no quarter for the terrorists.'

A s General Pietro Badoglio moved forward to Amba Aradam, there were some minor brushes while the Italian General deployed his men for the major stroke. At Abi Addi and Tembien he received advance warning of the fighting qualities of his enemy, barefoot and armed with spear and muzzle-loading gun. As he wrote himself,

'They have fought with courage and determination. Against our attacks, methodically carried out and covered by heavy machine-gun fire and artillery barrage, their troops have stood firm, and then engaged in furious hand-to-hand fighting; or they have moved boldly to counter-attack, regardless of the avalanche of fire that had immediately fallen upon them. Against the organized fire of our defending troops, their soldiers – many of them armed only with cold steel – attacked again and again, pushing right up to our wire entanglements and trying to beat them down with their great swords.'

Brave men, perhaps, but they were brushed aside by the huge Italian war machine. Then at last Badoglio could come at Ras Muguletu, the war minister of Ethiopia, with his entire army waiting like an old lion in the caves and precipitous heights of the natural mountain fortress of Amba Aradam.

He loosed his full might against the old chieftain, the big three-engined Capronis roared in, wave after wave, to drop four hundred tons of bombs upon the mountain in five days of continuous raids, while his artillery hurled fifty thousand heavy shells, arcing them up from the valley into the ravines and deep gorges until the outline of the mountain was shrouded in the red mist of dust and cordite fumes.

Up to now, the time of waiting had passed pleasantly enough for Count Aldo Belli at the Wells of Chaldi. The addition to his forces had altered his entire way of life. Together with the magnificent enamelled cross around his neck, they had added immeasurably to his prestige and correct sense of self-importance.

For the first few weeks he never tired of reviewing and manoeuvring his armoured forces. The six speedy machines, with their low rakish lines and moulded turrets, intrigued him. Their speed over the roughest ground, bouncing along on their spinning tracks, delighted him. They made wonderful shooting-brakes, for nothing held them up, and he conceived the master strategy of using them for game drives.

A squadron of light CV.3 tanks, in extended line abreast, could sweep a thirty-mile swathe of desert, driving all game before them, down to where the Count waited with the Mannlicher. It was the greatest sport of his hunting career.

The scope of this activity was such that even in the limitless spaces of the Danakil desert, it did not pass unnoticed.

Like their Ras, the Harari warriors were men of short patience. Long inactivity bored them, and daily small groups of horsemen, followed by their wives and pack donkeys, drifted away from the big encampment at the foot of the gorge, and began the steep rocky ascent to the cooler equable weather of the highlands, and the comforts and business of home. Each of them assured the Ras before departure of a speedy return as soon as they were needed – but nevertheless it irked the Ras to see his army dwindling and dribbling away while his enemy sat invulnerable and unchallenged upon the sacred soil of Ethiopia.

Tensions in the encampment were running with the strength and passion of the ground-swell of the ocean, when storms are building out beyond the horizon.

Caught up in the suppressed violence, in the boiling pot of emotion, were both Gareth and Jake. Each of them had used the lull to set his own department in order.

Jake had gone out under cover of night behind a screen of Ethiopian scouts to the deserted battlefield, where he had stripped the carcass of the Hump. Working by the light of a hooded bull's-eye lantern, and assisted by Gregorius, he had taken the big Bentley engine to pieces, small enough for the donkey packs – and lugged it all home to the encampment below the camel-thorn trees. Using the replacements, he had rebuilt the engine of Tenastelin ruined by the Ras in his first flush of enthusiasm. Then he had stripped, over-hauled and reassembled the other two cars. The Ethiopian armoured forces were now a squadron of three, all of them in as fine fettle as they had been for the past twenty years.

Gareth, in the meantime, had selected and trained Harari crews for the Vickers guns, and then exercised them with the infantry and cavalry, teaching the gunners to lay down sheets of covering fire. Foot soldiers were taught to advance or retreat in concert with the Vickers.

Gareth had also found time to complete the survey of the retreat route up the gorge, mark each of his defensive positions, and supervise the digging of the machine-gun nests and support trenches in the steep rocky sides of the gorge. An enemy advancing up the twisting hairpin track would come under fire around each bend of the road, and would be open to the steam-roller charge of the foot warriors from the concealed trenches amongst the lichen-covered rocks above the track.

The track itself had been smoothed, and the gradients altered to allow the escape of the armoured cars once the position on the plains was forced by the overwhelming build-up of Italian forces. Now all of them waited, as ready as they could be, and the slow passage of time eroded all their nerves.

It was, then, with a certain relief that the scouts who were keeping the Italian fortifications under day and night surveillance reported back to the Ras's war council that a host of strange vehicles that moved at great speed – without the benefit of either legs or wheels – had arrived to swell the already formidable forces arrayed against them, and that these vehicles were daily engaged in furious activity, from sun-up to sun-down, racing in circles and aimless sweeps across the vast empty spaces of the plains.

'Without wheels,' mused Gareth, and cocked an eyebrow at Jake. 'You know what that sounds like, don't you, old son?'

'I'm afraid I do.' Jake nodded. 'But we'd better go and take a look.'

Half a moon in the sky gave enough light to show up clearly the deeply torn runnels of the steel tracks, like the spoor of gigantic centipedes in the soft fluffy soil.

Jake squatted on his haunches, and regarded them broodingly. He knew now that what he had dreaded was about to happen. He was going to have to take his beloved cars and match them against tracked vehicles with heavier armour, and revolving turrets, armed with big-bored, quick-firing guns. Guns that could crash a missile into his frontal armour, through the engine block, through the hull compartment and any crew members in its path, then out through the rear armour with sufficient velocity still on it to do the same again to the car behind.

'Tanks,' he muttered. 'Bloody tanks.'

'I say, an eagle scout in our midst,' murmured Gareth, sitting comfortably up in the turret of Priscilla the Pig. 'A tenderfoot might have thought those tracks were made by a dinosaur – but you can't fool old hawk-eye Barton, son of the Texas prairies,' and he reached out to stub his cheroot against the side of the turret, an action which he knew would annoy Jake intensely.

Jake grunted and stood up. 'I'm going to buy you an ashtray for your next birthday.' His voice was brittle. It did not matter that his beloved cars might be shot at by rifle, machine gun and now by cannon – that they had been scarred by flying gravel and harsh thorn. The deliberate crushing of burning tobacco against the fighting steel annoyed him, as he knew it was meant to.

'Sorry, old son.' Gareth grinned easily. 'Slipped my mind. Won't happen again.'

Jake swung up the side of the car and dropped into the driver's seat. Keeping the engine noise down to a low murmur, a sound as sweet and melodious in his ears as a Bach concerto, he let Priscilla move away across the moon-gilded plain.

When Jake and Gareth were alone like this, out on a reconnaissance or working together in the gorge, the dagger of rivalry was sheathed and their relationship was relaxed and comforting, spiced only by the mild needling and jostling for position. It was only in Vicky Camberwell's physical presence that the knife came out.

Jake thought about it now, thought about the three of them as he did a great deal each day. He knew that, after that magical night when he and Vicky had known each other on the hard desert earth, she was his woman. It was too wonderful an experience to have shared with another human being for it not to have marked and changed both of them profoundly.

Yet in the weeks since then there had been little opportunity for reaffirmation – a single stolen afternoon by a tall mist-smoking waterfall in the gorge, a narrow ledge of black rock, cool with shadow and green with soft beds of moss, and screened from prying eyes by the overhang of the precipice. The moss had been as soft as a feather bed, and afterwards they swam naked together in the swirling cauldron of the pool, and her body had been slim and pale and lovely through the dark water.

Then again, he had watched her with Gareth Swales – the way she laughed, or leaned close to him to listen to a whispered comment, and the mock-modest shock at his outrageous sallies, the laughter in her eyes and on her lips. Once she touched his arm, a thoughtless gesture while in conversation with Gareth, a gesture so intimate and possessive that Jake had felt the black jealous anger fill his head.

There was no cause for it, Jake knew that. He could not believe she was fool enough or so naive as to walk into the obvious web that Gareth was weaving – she was Jake's woman. What they had done together, their loving was so wonderful, so completely once in a lifetime, that it was not possible she could turn aside to anyone else.

Yet between Vicky and Gareth there was the laughter and the shared jokes. Sometimes he had seen them together, standing on a rock-promontory above the camp or walking in the grove of camel-thorn trees, leaning towards each other as they talked. Once or twice they had both been absent from the camp at the same time – for as long as a complete morning. But it meant nothing, he knew that. Sure, she liked Gareth Swales. He could understand that. He liked Gareth also – more than liked, he realized. It was, rather, a deep comradely feeling of affection. You could not but be drawn by his fine looks, his mocking sense of the ridiculous, and the deep certainty that below that polished exterior and the overplayed role of the foppish rogue was a different, a real person.

'Yeah.' Jake sardonically grinned in the darkness, steering the car south and east around the sky glow that marked the Italian fortifications at the Wells. 'I love the guy. I don't trust him, but I love him – just as long as he keeps the hell away from my woman.'

Gareth stooped out of the turret at that moment and tapped his shoulder.

'There is a ravine ahead and to the left. It should do,' he said, and Jake swung towards it and halted again.

'It's deep enough,' he gave his opinion.

'And we should be able to see across to the ridge and cover all the ground to the east once the sun comes up.' Gareth pointed to the glow of the Italian searchlights and then swept his arm widely across the open desert beyond. 'That looks like where they hold their fun and games every day. We should get a grandstand view from here. We'd better get under cover now.'

They intended to spend the whole of that day observing the activity of the Italian squadron, pulling out again under cover of darkness, so Jake reversed Priscilla gingerly down the steep slope of the ravine, backing and filling carefully, until she was in a hull-down position below the bank – with just the top of her turret exposed – but facing back towards the west with her front wheels at a point in the bank which she could climb handily, if a quick start and a fast escape were necessary.

He switched off the engine, and the two of them armed themselves with machetes and wandered about in the open, hacking down the small wiry desert brush and then piling it over the exposed turret, until from a hundred yards it blended into the desert landscape.

Jake spilled gasoline from one of the spare cans into a

361

bucket of sand, then placed the bucket in the bottom of the ravine and put a match to it. They crouched over the primitive stove, warming themselves against the desert chill, while the coffee brewed. They were silent, thawing out slowly, each thinking his own thoughts.

'I think we've got a problem,' said Jake at last, as he stared into the fire.

'With me that condition goes back as far as I can remember,' Gareth agreed politely. 'But apart from the fact that I am stuck in the middle of a horrible desert, with savages and bleeding hearts for company, with an army of Eyeties trying to kill me, broke except for a post-dated cheque of dubious value, not a bottle of the old Charlie within a hundred miles, and no immediate prospect of escape – apart from that, I'm in very good shape.'

'I was thinking of Vicky.'

'Ah! Vicky!'

'You know that I am in love with her.'

'You surprise me.' Gareth grinned devilishly in the flickering firelight. 'Is that why you have been mooning around with that soppy look on your face, bellowing like a bull moose in the mating season? Good Lord, I would never have guessed, old boy.'

'I'm being serious, Gary.'

'That, old son, is one of your problems. You take everything too seriously. I am prepared to offer odds of three to one that your mind is already set on the ivy-covered cottage, bulging with ghastly brats.'

'That's the picture,' Jake cut in sharply. 'It's that serious, I'm afraid. How do we stand?'

Gareth drew two cigars from his breast pocket, placed one between Jake's lips, lit a dry twig from the fire and held it for him. The mocking grin dropped from his lips and his voice was suddenly thoughtful, but the expression in his eyes was hard to read in the uncertain firelight.

'Down in Cornwall, there's a place I know. A hundred and fifty acres. Comfortable old farm house, of course. I'd have to do it up a bit, but the cattle sheds are in good nick. Always did fancy myself as the country squire, bit of hunting and shooting in between tilling the earth and squirting the milk out of the cows. Might even run to three or four brats, at that. With fourteen thousand quid, and a whacking great mortgage bond, I could just about swing it.'

They were both silent then, as Jake poured the coffee and doused the fire, and squatted again facing Gareth.

'It's that serious,' Gareth said at last.

'So there isn't going to be a truce? No gentlemen's agreement?' Jake murmured into his mug.

'Tooth and claw, I'm afraid,' said Gareth. 'May the best man win, and we'll name the first brat after you. That's a promise.'

They were silent again, each of them lost in his own thoughts, sipping at the mugs and sucking on their cheroots.

'One of us could get some sleep,' said Jake at last.

'Spin you for it.' Gareth flipped a silver Maria Theresa dollar, and caught it neatly on his wrist.

'Heads,' said Jake.

'Tough luck, old son.' Gareth pocketed the coin and flicked out the coffee grounds from his mug. Then he went to spread his blanket on the sandy ravine bottom, under Priscilla the Pig's chassis.

Jake shook him gently in the dawn, and cautioned him with a touch on the lips. Gareth came swiftly awake, blinking his eyes and smoothing back his hair with both hands, then rolling to his feet and following Jake quickly up the side of Priscilla's hull.

The dawn was a silent explosion of red and gold and

brilliant apricot that fanned out across half the eastern sky, touched the high ground with fire but left the long grey-blue shadows smeared across the low places. The crescent of the sinking moon low on the western horizon was white as a shark's tooth.

'Listen,' said Jake, and Gareth turned his head slightly to catch the tremble of sound in the silence of the dawn.

'Hear it?'

Gareth nodded, and lifted his binoculars. Slowly he swept the distant sun-touched ridges.

'There,' said Jake sharply, and Gareth swung the glasses in the direction of Jake's arm.

Some miles off, a string of dark indefinite blobs were moving through one of the depressions in the gently undulating terrain. They looked like beads on a rosary; even in the magnifying lens of the glasses they were too far off and too dimly lit to afford details.

They watched them, following the almost sinuous line as it snaked across their front – until the leading blob drew the line up the gentle slope of ground. As it reached the crest, it was struck with startling suddenness by the low golden sun. In the still cool air there was no distortion, and the dramatic side-lighting made every detail of its low profile clear and crisp.

'CV.3 cavalry tanks,' said Gareth, without hesitation. 'Fifty-horse-power Alfa engines. Ten centimetres of frontal armour and a top speed of eighteen miles an hour.' It was as though he were reading the specifications from a catalogue, and Jake remembered that these were part of his stock-in-trade. 'There's a crew of three, driver, loader gunner and commander – and it looks as though they are mounting the fifty-mm Spandau. They are accurate at a thousand yards and the rate of fire is fifteen rounds a minute.'

As he was speaking the leading tank dropped from sight over the reverse slope of the ridge, followed in quick succession by the five others – and their engine noise droned away into silence.

Gareth lowered his glasses and grinned ruefully. 'Well, we are a little out of our class. Those Spandaus are in fully revolving turrets. We are out-gunned all to hell.'

'We are faster than they are,' said Jake hotly, like a mother whose children had been scorned.

'And that, old son, is all we are,' grunted Gareth.

'How about a bite of breakfast? It's going to be a long hard day to sit out before it's dark enough to head for home.'

They ate tinned Irish stew, heated over the bucket, and smeared on thick spongy hunks of unleavened bread, washed down by tea, strong and sweet with condensed milk and lumpy brown sugar. The sun was well up before they finished.

Jake belched softly. 'My turn to sleep,' he said, and he curled up like a big brown dog in the shade under the hull.

Gareth tried to make himself comfortable against the turret and keep watch out across the open plain, where the mirage was already starting to quiver and fume in the rising heat. He congratulated himself comfortably on his choice of shift; he'd had a good few hours' sleep in the night, and now he had the comparative cool of the morning. By the time it was Jake's turn on watch again, the sun would be frizzling, and Priscilla's hull hot as a wood stove.

'Look out for Number One,' he murmured, and took a leisurely sweep of the land with the glasses. There was no way that an Italian patrol could surprise them here. He had selected the stake-out with a soldier's eye for ground, and he congratulated himself again, as he slumped in relaxation against the turret and lit a cheroot.

'Now,' he thought. 'Just how do you take on a squadron of cavalry tanks, without artillery, minefields or armour-piercing guns – ?' and he let his mind tease and worry the problem. A couple of hours later he had decided that there were ways, but all of them depended on having the tanks come in at the right place, from the right direction at the right time. 'Which, of course, is an animal of a completely different breed,' and that took a lot more thought. Another hour later he knew there was only one way the Italian armoured squadron could be made to co-operate in its own destruction. 'The jolly old donkey and the carrot trick again,' he thought. 'Now all we need is a carrot.' Instinctively he looked down at where Jake lay curled. Jake had not moved once in all the hours, only the deep soft rumble of his breathing showed he was still alive. Gareth felt a prickle of irritation that he should be enjoying such undisturbed rest.

The heat was a heavy oppressive pall, pressing down upon the earth, beating like a gong upon Gareth's head. The sweat dried almost instantly upon his skin, leaving a rime of salt crystals, and he screwed up his eyes as he swept the horizon with the glasses.

The glare and the mirage had obscured the horizon, blotted out even the nearest ridges behind a shifting throbbing curtain of hot air that seemed thick as water, swirling and spiralling in wavering columns and sluggish eddies.

Gareth blinked his eyes, and shook the drops of sweat from his eyebrows. He glanced at his watch. It was still another hour until Jake's shift, and he contemplated putting his watch forward. It was distinctly uncomfortable up on the hull in the sun, and he glanced again at the sleeping form in the shade.

Just then he caught a sound on the thick heated air, a soft quiver of sound, like the hive murmur of bees. There was no way in which to tell the direction of the sound, and Gareth crouched attentively, straining for it. It faded and returned, faded and returned again, but this time stronger and more definite. The configuration of the land and the flawed and heat-faulted air were playing tricks on the ear.

Suddenly the volume of sound climbed swiftly, becoming a humming growl that shook in the heat.

Gareth swung the glasses to the east; it seemed to emanate from the whole curve of the eastern horizon, like the animal growl of the surf.

For an instant the glare and swirling mirage opened enough for him to see a huge darkly distorted shape, a grotesque lumbering monster on four stilt-like legs, seeming as tall as a double-storey building. Then the mirage closed down again swiftly, leaving Gareth blinking with doubt and alarm at what he had seen. But now the growl of sound beat steadily in the air.

'Jake,' he called urgently, and was answered by a snort and a changed volume of snore. Gareth broke off a branch from the layer of camouflage and tossed it at the reclining figure. It caught Jake in the back of the neck and he came angrily awake, one fist bunched and ready to punch.

'What the hell—' he snarled.

'Come up here,' called Gareth.

'I can't see a damned thing,' muttered Jake, standing high on the turret and peering eastwards through his glasses. The sound was now a deep drumming growl, but the wall of glare and mirage was close and impenetrable.

'There!' shouted Gareth.

'Oh my God!' cried Jake.

The huge shape leaped out at them suddenly. Very close, very black and tall, blown up by distortion and mirage to gargantuan proportions. Its shape changed constantly, so at one moment it looked like a four-masted ship under a full suit of black sails – then it altered swiftly into a towering black tadpole shape that wriggled and swam through the soupy air.

'What the hell is it?' Gareth demanded.

'I don't know, but it's making a noise like a squadron of Italian tanks and it's coming straight at us.'

The Captain who commanded the Italian tank squadron was an angry, disgruntled and horribly disillusioned man – a man burdened by a soul-corroding grudge.

Like so many officers of the cavalry tradition, the *arme blanche* of the army, he was a romantic, obsessed by the image of himself as a dashing, reckless warrior. The dress uniform of his regiment still included skin-tight breeches with a scarlet silk stripe down the outside of the leg, soft black riding boots and silver spurs, a tightly fitting bum-freezer jacket encrusted with thick gold lace and heavy epaulets, a short cloak worn carelessly over one shoulder and a tall black shako. This was the picture he cherished of himself – all élan and swagger.

Here he was in some devil-conceived, god-cursed desert, where day after day he and his beloved fighting machines were sent out to find wild animals and drive them in on a set point, where a mad megalomaniac waited to shoot them down.

The damage it was doing his tanks, the grinding wear on tracks running hard over rough terrain and through diamond-hard abrasive sand, was as nothing compared to the damage his pride was suffering.

He had been reduced to nothing but a gamekeeper, a beater, a peasant beater. The Captain spent much of each day at the very edge of tears, the tears of deep humiliation. Every evening he protested to the mad Count in the strongest possible terms and the following day found him once more pursuing wild animals over the desert.

So far the bag had consisted of a dozen lions and wild dogs, and many scores of large antelope. By the time these were delivered to where the Count waited, they were almost exhausted, lathered with sweat, and with a froth of saliva drooling from their jaws, barely able to trot after the long chase across the plains.

The condition of the game detracted not at all from the

Count's pleasure. Indeed, the Captain had been given specific orders to run the game hard so that it came to the guns docile and winded. After his alarming experience with the beisa oryx, the Count was not eager to take foolhardy risks. An easy shot and a good photograph were his yard-sticks of the day's sport.

The greater the bag, the greater the pleasure – and the Count had enjoyed himself immensely since the arrival of the tanks. However, the wastes of the Danakil desert could not support endless quantities of animal life, and the bag had fallen off sharply in the last few days as the herds were scattered and annihilated. The Count was displeased. He told the Captain of tanks so forcibly, adding to the man's discontent and sense of grudge.

The Captain of tanks found the old bull elephant standing alone, like a tall granite monument, upon the open plain. He was enormous, with tattered ears like the sails of an ancient schooner, and tiny hating eyes in their webs of deep wrinkles. One of his tusks was broken off near the lip, but the other was thick and long and yellow, worn to a blunt-rounded tip at the end of its curve.

The Captain stopped his tank a quarter of a mile from where the elephant stood, and examined him through his binoculars while he got over the shock of his size – then the Captain began to smile, a wicked twist of the mouth under his handsome moustache, and his dark eyes sparkled.

'So, my dear Colonel, you want game, much game,' he whispered. 'You will have it. I assure you.'

He approached the elephant carefully from the east, crawling the tank in gingerly towards the animal, and the old bull turned and watched them come. His ears were spread wide and his long trunk sucked and coiled into his mouth as he tested the air, breathing it onto the olfactory glands in his top lip as he groped for the scent of this strange creature.

He was a bad-tempered old bull, who had been harried and hunted for thousands of miles across the African continent, and beneath his scarred and creased old hide were the spear-heads, the potlegs fired from muzzle-loading guns, and the jacketed slugs from modern rifled firearms. All he wanted now in his great age was to be left alone – he wanted neither the demanding company of the breeding cows, the importunate noisy play of the calves, nor the single-minded pursuit of the men who hunted him. He had come into the desert, to the burning days and coarse vegetation to find that solitude, and now he was moving slowly down to the Wells of Chaldi, water which he had last tasted as a young breeding bull twenty-five years before.

He watched the buzzing growling things creeping in towards him, and he tasted their rank oily smell, and he did not like it. He shook his head, flapping his ears like the crash of canvas taking the wind on a new tack, and he squealed a warning.

The growling humming things crept closer and he rolled his trunk up against his chest, he cocked his ears half back and curled the tips – but the tank Captain did not recognize the danger signals and he kept on coming.

Then the elephant charged, fast and massive, the fall of his huge pads thumping against the earth like the beat of a bass drum, and he was so fast, so quick off the mark that he almost caught the tank. If he had he would have flicked it over on its back without having to exert all his mountainous strength. But the driver was as quick as he, and he swung away right under the outstretched trunk, and held his best speed for half a mile before the bull gave up the pursuit.

'My Captain, I could shoot it with the Spandau,' urged the gunner anxiously. He had not enjoyed the chase.

'No! No!' The Captain was delighted.

'He is a very angry, dangerous and ferocious animal,' the gunner pointed out.

'*Si!*' the Captain laughed happily, rubbing his hands together with glee. 'He is my very special gift to the Count.'

After the fifth approach by the tanks, the old bull grew bored with the unrewarding effort of chasing after them. With his belly rumbling protestingly, his stubby tail twitching irritably, and the musk from the glands behind his eyes weeping in a long, wet smear down his dusty cheeks, he allowed himself to be shepherded towards the west by the following line of cavalry tanks – but he was still a very angry elephant.

'You're not going to believe this,' said Gareth Swales softly. 'I'm not even sure I believe it myself. But it's an elephant, and it's leading a full squadron of Eyetie tanks straight to us.'

'I don't believe it,' said Jake. 'I can see it happening – but I don't believe it. They must have trained it like a bloodhound. Is that possible, or am I going crazy?'

'Both,' said Gareth. 'May I suggest we get ready to move. They are getting frightfully close, old son.'

Jake jumped down to the crank handle, while Gareth dropped into the driver's hatch and swiftly adjusted the ignition and throttle setting.

'All set,' he said, glancing anxiously over his shoulder. The great elephant was less than a thousand yards away. Coming on steadily, in that long driving stride, a pace between a walk and a trot that an elephant can keep up for thirty miles without check or rest.

'You might hurry it up, at that,' he added, and Jake spun the crank. Priscilla made no response, not even a cough to encourage Jake as he wound the crank frantically.

After a full minute, Jake staggered back gasping, and doubled over with hands on his knees as he sucked for air.

'This bloody infernal machine—' Gareth began, but Jake straightened up with genuine alarm.

'Don't start swearing at her, or she'll never start,' he cautioned Gareth, and he stooped to the crank handle again. 'Come along now, my darling,' he whispered, and threw his weight on the crank.

Gareth took another quick glance over his shoulder. The bizarre procession was closer, much closer. He leaned out of the driver's hatch and patted Priscilla's engine-cowling tenderly.

'There's my love,' he crooned. 'Come along, my beauty.'

The Count's hunting party sat out in collapsible camp chairs under the screens, double canvas to protect them from the cruel sun. The mess servants served iced drinks and light refreshments, and a random breeze that flapped the canvas occasionally was sufficient to keep the temperature bearable.

The Count was in an expansive mood, host to half a dozen of his officers, all of them dressed in casual hunting clothes, armed with a selection of sporting rifles and the occasional service rifle.

'I think we can rely on better sport today. I believe that our beaters will be trying harder, after my gentle admonitions.' He smiled and winked, and his officers laughed dutifully. 'Indeed, I am hoping—'

'My Count. My Count.' Gino rushed breathlessly into the tent like a frenzied gnome. 'They are coming. We have seen them from the ridge.'

'Ah!' said the Count with deep satisfaction. 'Shall we go down and see what our gallant Captain of tanks has for us this time?' And he drained the glass of white wine in his hand, while Gino rushed over to help him to his feet, and then backed away in front of him, leading him to where Giuseppe was hastily removing the dust covers from the Rolls.

The small procession, headed by the Count's Rolls-Royce, wound down the slope of the low ridge to where the blinds had been sited in a line across the width of the shallow valley. The blinds had been built by the battalion engineers, dug into the red earth so as not to stand too high above the low desert scrub. They were neatly thatched, covered against the sun, with loopholes from which to fire upon the driven game. There were comfortable camp chairs for those long waits between drives, a small but well-stocked bar, ice in insulated buckets, a separate screened latrine – in fact all the comforts to make the day's sport more enjoyable.

The Count's blind was in the centre of the line. It was the largest and most luxuriously appointed, situated so that the great majority of driven game would bunch upon this point. His junior officers had earlier learned the folly of exceeding the Colonel's personal bag or of firing at any animal which was swinging across their front towards the Count. The first offender in this respect had found himself reduced from Captain to Lieutenant, and no longer invited to the hunt, and the second was already back in Massawa writing out requisition forms in the quartermaster's division.

Gino handed the Count from the Rolls, and helped him down the steps into the sunken shelter. Giuseppe saluted and climbed back into the Rolls, swung away and bumped back up the ridge and over the skyline.

The Count settled himself comfortably in the canvas chair. With a sigh, he unbuttoned the front of his jacket, and accepted the damp face cloth that Gino handed him. While the Count wiped the film of sweat from his forehead with the cool cloth, Gino opened a bottle of Lacrima Cristi from the ice bucket and placed a tall frosted crystal glass of the wine on the folding table at the Count's elbow. Next, he loaded the Mannlicher with shiny new brass cartridges from a freshly opened packet.

The Count tossed the cloth aside and leaned forward in his chair to peer through the loophole in front of him, out across the shimmering plain where the small dark desert scrub danced in the heat.

'I have a feeling we shall have extraordinary sport today, Gino.'

'I hope so indeed, my Count,' said the little sergeant and stood to attention behind his chair with the loaded Mannlicher held at the ready across his chest.

'Come on, darling,' croaked Jake, sweat dripping from his chin on to his shirt front as he stooped over the crank handle and spun it for the hundredth time. 'Don't let us down now, sweetheart.'

Gareth scrambled up on to the sponson of Priscilla and took a long despairing glance back over the turret. He felt something freeze in his belly, and his breath caught. The elephant was a hundred paces away, coming directly down on top of them at a loose shambling walk, the great black ears flapping sullenly and the little piggy eyes alight with malevolence.

Right behind it, fanned out on each side, pressing closely on the great beast's heels, came the full squadron of Italian tanks. The sun glittered on the smoothly rounded frontal armour, and caught the bright festival flutter of their cavalry pennants. From each hatch protruded the black-helmeted head of the tank commander. Through the binoculars Gareth could make out the individual features of each commander, they were that close.

Within minutes they would be overrun, and there was no chance that they could escape detection. The elephant was leading the Italians directly to the ravine, and their scanty camouflage of scrub branches would not stand scrutiny at less than a hundred yards.

They could not even protect themselves, the Vickers machine gun was pointed away from the approaching enemy, and the limited traverse of the ball mounting was not sufficient to bring it to bear. Gareth was engulfed suddenly by a black and burning rage for the stubborn piece of machinery beneath his feet. He took a vicious heartfelt kick at the steel turret.

'You treacherous bitch,' he snarled, and at that moment the engine fired and, without preliminary gulping and popping, roared angrily.

Jake bounded up the side of the hull, droplets of sweat flying from his sodden hair, red-faced as he gasped at Gareth.

'You've got the gentle touch.'

'With all women there is the psychological moment, old son,' Gareth explained, grinning with relief as he scrambled into the turret and Jake dropped behind the controls.

Jake gunned the motor, and Priscilla threw off her covering of cut thorn branches. Her wheels spun in the loose sand of the ravine, blowing up a cloud of red dust, and she tore up the steep bank and lunged out into the open – directly under the startled outstretched trunk of the elephant.

The old bull had by this stage suffered provocation sufficient to take him to the edge of a blind, black rage. It needed only this new buzzing frightfulness to launch him over the edge. The leisurely pace that he had set up until now left his mountainous strength and endurance untouched, and now he trumpeted, a ringing ear-splitting challenge that rolled across the vast silences of the desert like the trumpet of doom. His ears curled back against his skull and with his trunk coiled against his chest, he crashed forward into a terrible ground-shaking charge.

His speed over the broken ground was greater than that of Priscilla the Pig, and he bore down upon her like a cliff of grey granite – huge, menacing and indestructible.

The Captain of tanks had been shepherding the old elephant along gently. He did not want him to tax his strength. He wanted to deliver to his commanding officer an animal in the peak of its anger and destructive capabilities.

He was sitting up in his turret, chuckling and shaking his head with anticipation and growing delight, for the hunter's lines were only a mile or so ahead – when suddenly, directly ahead of him, the ground erupted and an armoured car roared out in a cloud of red dust. It was of a model that the Captain had seen only in illustrated books of military history – like an apparition out of the remote past.

It took him some seconds to believe what he was seeing, then with a jarring impact on his already highly strung nerve ends, he recognized the enemy colours that the ancient machine was flying.

'Advance!' he screamed. 'Squadron, advance!' and he groped instinctively at his side for his sword. 'Engage the enemy.'

On each side of him his tanks roared forward, and for want of a sword, the Captain tore his helmet off and waved it over his head.

'Charge!' he screamed. 'Forward into battle!' Now at last he was not a mere game-beater. Now he was a warrior leading his men into action. His excitement was so contagious and the dust thrown up by the car, the elephant and the steel tracks so thick, that the first two tanks did not even see the fifteen-foot-deep sheer-sided ravine. Running side by side, they went into it at the top of their speed – and were destroyed effectively as though they had been demolished by a 100-kilo aerial bomb, the riding wheels ripped away by the impact and the heavy steel tracks flying loose and snaking viciously into the air like living angry cobras. The revolving turrets were torn from their seatings, neatly bisecting the men at the waist, who stood in the hatches, as though with a gigantic pair of scissors.

Clinging to the rim of his own turret and peering backwards, Gareth saw the two machines disappear into the earth, and the great leaping towers of dust that rose high into the air to mark their destruction.

'Two down,' he shouted.

'But another four to go,' Jake shouted back grimly, fighting Priscilla over the rough earth. 'And how about that jumbo?'

'How indeed!'

The elephant, goaded on by the roar of engines and crash of steel behind and by the buzzing bouncing car ahead of it, was making incredible speed over the broken scrubby plain.

'He's right here with us,' Gareth told Jake anxiously. So close was the great beast that Gareth had to look up at it, and he saw the thick grey trunk uncoiling from its chest and reaching out to pluck him from the turret.

'As fast as you like, old son, or you'll have him sitting on your head.'

'I have told that idiot not to run the game down on the guns so hard,' snapped the Count petulantly. 'I have told him a dozen times, have I not, Gino?'

'Indeed, my Count.'

'Run them hard at the beginning, then bring them in gently for the last mile or so.' The Count took an angry gulp at his glass. 'The man is a fool, an insufferable fool – and I can't abide fools around me.'

'Indeed not, my Count.'

'I shall send him back to Massawa—' the rest of the threat trailed away, and the Count sat suddenly upright, the canvas chair creaking under his weight.

'Gino,' he murmured uneasily. 'There is something very strange taking place out there.'

Both of them peered anxiously out through the rifle slots in the thatched wall of the blind at the billowing dust-clouds that raced down upon them with quite alarming speed.

'Gino, is it possible?' asked the Count.

'No, my Count,' Gino assured him, but without any true conviction. 'It is the mirage. It is not possible.'

'Are you certain, Gino?' The Count's voice took on a strident edge.

'No, my Count.'

'Nor am I, Gino. What does it look like to you?'

'It looks like—' Gino's voice choked off. 'I do not like to say, my Count,' he whispered. 'I think I am going mad.'

At that moment the Captain of tanks, whose efforts to catch up with the fleeing armoured car and stampeding elephant were unavailing, opened fire with the 50 mm Spandau upon them. More accurately, he opened fire in the general direction of the rolling dust-cloud which obscured his forward vision, and through which he caught only occasional glimpses of beast and machine. To confound further the aim of his gunner, the range was rapidly increasing, the manoeuvres with which the armoured car was trying to throw off the close pursuit of the elephant were violent and erratic, and the cavalry tank itself was plunging and leaping wildly over the rough ground.

'Fire!' shouted the Captain. 'Keep firing,' and his gunner sent half a dozen high-explosive shells screeching low over the plain. The other tanks heard the banging of their

378

Captain's cannon and immediately and enthusiastically followed his example.

One of the first shells struck the thatched front wall of the blind in which the Count and Gino cowered in horrified fascination. The flimsy wall of grass did not trigger the fuse of the shell so there was no explosion, but nevertheless the high-velocity shell passed not eighteen inches from the Count's left ear, with a crack of disrupted air that stunned him, before exiting through the rear wall of the blind and howling onwards to burst a mile out in the empty desert.

'If the Count no longer needs me—' Gino snapped a hasty salute and before the Count had recovered his wits enough to forbid it, he had dived through the shell hole in the rear wall of the blind and hit the ground on the far side, already running.

Gino was not alone. From each of the blinds along the line leapt the figures of the other hunters, the sound of their hysterical cries almost drowned by the roar of engines, the trumpeting of an angry bull elephant and the continuous thudding roar of cannon fire.

The Count tried to rise from his chair, but his legs betrayed him and he managed only a series of convulsive leaps. His mouth gaped wide in his deathly pale face, but no sound came out of it. The Count was beyond speech, almost beyond movement – just the strength for one more desperate heave, and the chair toppled forward, throwing the Count face down upon the sunken earth floor of the blind, where he covered his head with both arms.

At that instant, the armoured car, still under full throttle, came in through the front wall. The thatched blind exploded around it, but the impetus of the car's charge was sufficient to carry it in a single leap over the dugout. The spinning wheels hurled inches over the Count's prostrate form, showering him with a stinging barrage of sand and loose gravel. Then it was gone.

The Count struggled to sit up, and had almost succeeded when the huge enraged form of the bull elephant pounded over the blind. One of its great feet struck the Count a glancing blow on the shoulder and he screamed like a bandsaw and once again flung himself flat on the floor of the dugout – while the elephant pounded onwards towards the far horizon, still in pursuit of the flying car.

The earth shook beneath the approach of another heavy body, and the Count flattened himself to the floor of the dugout – deafened, dazed and paralysed with terror, until the commander of tanks stood over him and asked solicitously,

'Was the game to your liking, my Colonel?'

Even after Gino returned and helped the Count to his feet, dusted him down and helped him into the back seat of the Rolls, the threats and insults still poured from the Count's choked throat in a high-pitched stream.

'You are a degenerate and a coward. You are guilty of dereliction of duty, of gross irresponsibility. You allowed them to escape, sir – and you placed me in deadly peril—' They eased the Count down on the cushions of the Rolls, but as the car pulled away he jumped up to hurl a parting salvo at the Captain of tanks.

'You are an irresponsible degenerate, sir – a coward and a Bolshevik – and I shall personally command your firing squad—' His voice faded into the distance as the Rolls drew away up the ridge in the direction of the camp, but the Count's good arm was still waving and gesticulating as they crossed the skyline.

380

The elephant followed them far out across the desert, long after the pursuing tank squadron had been left behind and abandoned the chase. The old bull lost ground steadily over the last mile or so, until at last he also gave up and stood swaying with exhaustion but still shaking out his ears and throwing up his trunk in that truculent, almost human gesture of challenge and defiance.

Gareth saluted him with respect as they drew away and left him, like a tall black monolith, out on the dry pale plains. Then he lit two cheroots, crouching down into the turret out of the wind, and passed one down to Jake in the driver's compartment.

'A good day's work, old son. We pranged two of the godless ones, and we have put the others in the right frame of mind.'

'How's that again?' Jake puffed gratefully at the cheroot.

'Next time those tankmen lay eyes on us, they'll not stop to count consequences, but they'll be after us like a pack of long dogs after a bitch.'

'And that's a good thing?' Jake removed the cheroot from his mouth to ask incredulously.

'That's a good thing,' Gareth assured him.

'Well, you could have fooled me.' He drove on for a few more minutes in silence towards the mountains, then shook his head bemusedly.

'Pranged? What the hell kind of word is that?'

'Just thought of it this minute,' Gareth said. 'Expressive, what?'

The Count lay face down upon his cot; he wore only a pair of silk shorts, of a pale and delicate blue, embroidered with his family coat of arms.

His body was smooth and pale and plump, with that sleek well-fed sheen which takes a great deal of money, food and drink to nourish. On the pale skin his body hair was dark and curly and crisp as newly picked lettuce leaves. It grew in a light cloud across his shoulders, and then descended his back to disappear at last – like a wisp of smoke – into the cleft of his milky buttocks that showed coyly above the waist-band of his shorts.

Now the smoothness of his body was spoiled by the ugly red abrasions and new purple bruises which flowered upon his ribs and blotched his legs and arms.

He groaned with a mixture of agony and gratification as Gino knelt over him, his sleeves rolled up to the elbows, and worked the liniment into his shoulder. His dark sinewy fingers sank deeply into the sleek pale flesh, and the stench of liniment stung the eyes and nostrils.

'Not so hard, Gino. Not so hard, I am badly hurt.'

'I am sorry, my Colonel,' and he worked on in silence while the Count groaned and grunted and wriggled on the bed under him.

'My Colonel, may I speak?'

'No,' grunted the Colonel. 'Your salary is already liberal. No, Gino, already I pay you a prince's ransom.'

'My Colonel, you do me wrong. I would not speak of such a mundane subject at this time.'

'I am delighted to hear it,' groaned the Count. 'Ah! There! That spot! That's it!'

Gino worked on the spot for a few seconds. 'If you study the lives of the great Italian Generals – Julius Caesar and—' Gino paused here while he searched his mind and more recent history for another great Italian General; the silence stretched out and Gino repeated, 'Take Julius Caesar, as an example.'

'Yes?'

'Even Julius Caesar did not himself swing the sword. The truly great commander stands aside from the actual battle. He directs, plans, commands the lesser mortals.'

'That is true, Gino.'

'Any peasant can swing a sword or fire a gun – what are they but mere cattle?'

'That is also true.'

'Take Napoleon Bonaparte, or the Englishman Wellington.' Gino had abandoned his search for the name of a victorious Italian warrior within the last thousand years or so.

'Very well, Gino, take them?'

'When they fought, they themselves were remote from the actual conflict. Even when they confronted each other at Waterloo, they stood miles apart like two great chess masters, directing, manoeuvring, commanding—'

'What are you trying to say, Gino?'

'Forgive me, my Count, but have you not perhaps let your courage blind you, have not your warlike instincts, your instinct to tear the jugular from your enemy . . . have you not perhaps lost sight of a commander's true role – the duty to stand back from the actual fighting and survey the overall battle?'

Gino waited with trepidation for the Count's reaction. It had taken him all his courage to speak, but even the Count's wrath could not outweigh the terror he felt at the prospect of being plunged once more into danger. His place was at the Count's side; if the Count continued to expose them both to all the terrors and horrors of this barren and hostile land, then Gino knew that he could no longer continue. His nerves were trampled, raw, exposed, his nights troubled with dreams from which he woke sweating and trembling. He had a nerve below his left eye that had recently begun to twitch without control. He was fast reaching the end of his nervous strength. Soon something within him might snap.

'Please, my Count. For the good of all of us you must curb your impetuosity.'

He had touched a responsive chord in his master. He had voiced precisely the Count's own feelings, feelings which had over the last few weeks' desperate adventures become deep-seated convictions. He struggled up on one elbow, lifted his noble head with its anguished brow and looked at the little sergeant.

'Gino,' he said. 'You are a philosopher.'

'You do me too much honour, my Count.'

'No! No! I mean it. You have a certain gutter wisdom, the perceptions of the streets, a peasant philosopher.'

Gino would not himself have put it quite that way, but he bowed his head in acquiescence.

'I have been unfair to my brave boys,' said the Count, and his whole demeanour changed, becoming radiant and glowing with good will, like that of a reprieved prisoner. 'I have thought only of myself – my own glory, my own honour, recklessly I have plunged into danger, without reckoning the cost. Ignoring the terrible risk that I might leave my brave boys without a leader – orphans without a father.'

Gino nodded fervently. 'Who could ever replace you in their hearts, or at their head?'

'Gino.' The Count clapped a fatherly hand to his shoulder. 'I must be less selfish in the future.'

'My Count, you cannot know how much pleasure it gives me to hear it,' cried Gino, and he trembled with relief as he thought of long, leisurely days spent in peace and security

384

behind the earthworks and fortifications of Chaldi camp. 'Your duty is to command!'

'Plan!' said the Count.

'Direct!' said Gino.

'I fear it is my destiny.'

'Your God-given duty.' Gino backed him up, and as the Count sank down once more upon the cot, he fell with renewed vigour upon the injured shoulder.

'Gino,' said the Count at last. 'When last did we speak of your wages?'

'Not for many months, my Count.'

'Let us discuss it now,' said Aldo Belli comfortably. 'You are a jewel without price. Say, another hundred lire a month.'

'The sum of one hundred and fifty had crossed my mind,' murmured Gino respectfully.

T he Count's new military philosophy was received with unbounded enthusiasm by his officers, when he explained it to them that evening in the mess tent, over the liqueurs and cigars. The idea of leading from the rear seemed not only to be practical and sensible, but downright inspired. This enthusiasm lasted only until they learned that the new philosophy applied not to the entire officer cadre of the Third Battalion, but to the Colonel only. The rest of them were to be given every opportunity to make the supreme sacrifice for God, country and Benito Mussolini. At this stage the new philosophy lost much popular support.

In the end, only three persons stood to benefit from the rearrangement – the Count, Gino and Major Luigi Castelani.

The Major was so overjoyed to learn that he now had what amounted to unfettered command of the battalion that for the first time in many years he took a bottle of *grappa* to his tent that evening, and sat shaking his head and chuckling fruitily into his glass.

The following morning's burning, blinding headache that only *grappa* can produce, combined with his new freedom, made the Major's grip on the battalion all the more ferocious. The new spirit spread like a fire in dry grass. Men cleaned their rifles, burnished their buttons and closed them to the neck, stubbed out their cigarettes and trembled a little – while Castelani rampaged through the camp at Chaldi, dealing out duties, ferreting out the malingerers and stiffening spines with the swishing cane in his right hand.

The honour guard that fell in that afternoon to welcome the first aircraft to the newly constructed airfield were so beautifully turned out with polished leather and glittering metal, and their drill was so smartly performed, that even Count Aldo Belli noticed it, and commended them warmly.

The aircraft was a three-engined Caproni bomber. It came lumbering in from the northern skies, circled the long runway of raw earth, and then touched down and raised a long rolling storm of dust with the wash of its propellers.

The first personage to emerge from the doorway in the belly of the silver fuselage was the political agent from Asmara, Signor Antolino, looking more rumpled and seedy than ever in his creased, ill-fitting tropical linen suit. He raised his straw panama in reply to the Count's flamboyant Fascist salute, and they embraced briefly – the man stood low on the social and political scale – before the Count turned to the pilot.

'I wish to ride in your machine.' The Count had lost interest in his tanks, in fact he found himself actively hating them and their Captain. In sober mood he had refrained from executing that officer, or even packing him off back to Asmara. He had contented himself with a full page of scathing comment in the man's service report, knowing that this would destroy his career. A complete and satisfying vengeance, but the Count was finished with tanks. Now he had an aircraft. So much more exciting and romantic.

'We will fly over the enemy positions,' said the Count, 'at a respectable height.' By which he meant – out of rifle shot.

'Later,' said the political agent, with such an air of authority that the Count drew himself up in a dignified manner, and gave the man a haughty stare before which he should have quailed.

'I carry personal and urgent orders from General Badoglio's own lips,' said the agent, completely unaffected by the stare.

The Count's stiffly dignified mien altered immediately.

'A glass of wine, then,' he said affably, and took the man's arm, leading him to the waiting Rolls.

'The General stands now before Amba Aradam. He has the main concentration of the enemy at bay upon the mountain, and under heavy artillery and aerial bombardment. At the right moment he will fall upon them – and the outcome cannot be in doubt.'

'Quite right,' nodded the Count sagely; the prospect of fighting a hundred miles away to the north filled him with the reflected warmth of the glory of Italian arms.

'Within the next ten days, the broken armies of the Ethiopians will be attempting to withdraw along the road to Dessie and to link up with Haile Selassie at Lake Tana – but the Sardi Gorge is like a dagger in their ribs. You know your duty.'

The Count nodded again, but warily. This was much closer to home.

'I have come now to make the final contact with the Ethiopian Ras who will declare for us, the Emperor-designate of Ethiopia – our secret ally. It is necessary to co-ordinate our final plans, so that his defection will cause the greatest possible confusion amongst the ranks of the enemy, and his forces can be best deployed to support your assault up the gorge to Sardi and the Dessie road.'

'Ah!' the Count made a sound which signified neither agreement nor dissent.

'My men, working in the mountains, have arranged a meeting with the Emperor-designate. At this meeting we will make the promised payment that secures the Ras's loyalty.' The agent made a moue of distaste. 'These people!' and he sighed at the thought of a man who would sell his country for gold. Then he dismissed the thought with a wave of his hand. 'The meeting is fixed for tonight. I have brought one of my men with me who will act as a guide. The place arranged is approximately eighty kilometres from here and we will move out at sundown – which will give us ample time to reach the rendezvous before the appointed hour of midnight.'

'Very well,' the Count agreed. 'I will place transport at your disposal.'

The agent held up a hand. 'My dear Colonel, you will be the leader of the delegation to meet the Ras.'

'Impossible.' The Count would not so swiftly abandon his new philosophy. 'I have my duties here – to prepare for the offensive.' Who knew what new horrors might lurk out in the midnight wastes of the Danakil?

'Your presence is essential to the success of the negotiations – your uniform will impress the—'

'My shoulder, I am suffering from an injury which makes

388

travel most inconvenient – I shall send one of my officers. A Captain of tanks, the uniform is truly splendid.'

'No.' The agent shook his head.

'I have a Major – a man of great presence.'

'The General expressly instructed that you should lead the delegation. If you doubt this, your radio operator could establish immediate contact with Asmara.'

The Count sighed, opened his mouth, closed it again, and then regretfully abandoned his vow to remain within the perimeter of Chaldi camp for the duration of the campaign.

'Very well,' he conceded. 'We will leave at sundown.'

The Count was not about to plunge recklessly into danger again. The convoy which left Chaldi that evening in the fiery afterglow of the sunset was led by two CV.3 cavalry tanks, then followed four truck-loads of infantry, and behind them the remaining two tanks made up a formidable rearguard.

The Rolls was sandwiched neatly in the centre of this column. The political agent sat on the seat beside the Count, with his feet firmly on the heavy wooden case on the floorboards. The guide that the agent had produced from the fuselage of the Caproni was a thin, very dark Galla, with one opaque eyeball of blue jelly caused by tropical ophthalmia which gave him a particularly villainous cast of features. He was dressed in a once-white shamma that was now almost black with filth, and he smelled like a goat that had recently fought a polecat. The Count took one whiff of him and clapped his perfumed handkerchief to his nose.

'Tell the man he is to ride in the leading tank – with the Captain,' and a malicious expression gleamed in his dark eyes as he turned to the Captain of tanks. 'In the tank, do you hear? On the seat beside you in the turret.'

They drove without lights, jolting slowly across the moon-silver plains under the dark wall of the mountains. There was a single horseman waiting for them at the rendezvous, a dark shape in the darker shadows of a massive camel-thorn. The agent spoke with him in Amharic and then turned back to the Count.

'The Ras suspects treachery. We are to leave the escort here and go on alone with this man.'

'No,' cried the Count. 'No! No! I refuse – I simply refuse.' It took almost ten minutes of coaxing, and the repeated mention of General Badoglio's name, to change the Count's stance. Miserably, the Count climbed back into the Rolls, and Gino looked sadly at him from the front seat as the unescorted, terribly vulnerable car moved out into the moonlight, following the dark wild horseman on his shaggy pony.

In a rocky valley that cut into the towering bulk of the mountains, they had to abandon the Rolls and complete the journey on foot. Gino and Giuseppe carrying the wooden case between them, the Count with a drawn pistol in his hand, they staggered on up the treacherous slope of rocks and scree.

In a hidden saucer of rock, around the rim of which were posted the shadowy, hostile figures of sentries, was a large leather tent. Around it were tethered scores of the wild, shaggy ponies – and the interior was lit by smoky paraffin lamps and crowded with rank upon rank of squatting warriors. Their faces were so black in the dim light that only the whites of their eyes and the gleam of their teeth showed clearly.

The political agent strode ahead of the Count, down the open aisle, to where a robed figure reclined on a pile of cushions under a pair of lanterns. He was flanked by two women, still very young, but full-blown – heavy-breasted, and pale-skinned, dressed in brilliant silks, both of them wearing crudely wrought silver jewellery dangling from their ears and strung about their long graceful necks. Their eyes were dark and bold, and at another time and in different circumstances the Count's interest would have been intense. But now his knees felt rubbery, and his heart thumped like a war drum. The political agent had to lead him forward by the arm.

'The Emperor-designate,' whispered the agent, and the Count looked down on the bloated, effeminate dandy who lolled upon the cushions, his fat fingers covered with rings and his eyelids painted like those of a woman. 'Ras Kullah, of the Gallas.'

'Make the correct reply,' instructed the Count, his voice hoarse with strain, and the Ras eyed the Count with apprehension as the agent made a long flowery speech. The Ras was impressed with the imposing figure in its sinister black uniform. In the lamplight, the insignia glittered and the heavy enamelled cross on its ribbon of watered silk blinked like a beacon. The Ras's eyes dropped to the jewelled dagger and ivory-handled pistol at the Count's belt, the weapons of a rich and noble warrior – and he looked up again into the Count's eyes. They also glittered with an almost feverish fanatical light, the Count's regular features were flushed angrily and a murderous scowl furrowed his brow. He breathed like a fighting bull. The Ras mistook the signs of fatigue and extreme fear for the warlike rage of a berserker. He was impressed and awed.

Then his attention was drawn irresistibly away from the Count, as Gino and Giuseppe staggered into the tent, sweating in the lamplight, and bowed over the heavy chest they carried between them. Ras Kullah hoisted himself into

391

a kneeling position, with his soft paunch bulging forward under the shamma and his eyes glittering like those of a reptile.

With an abrupt command, he cut short the agent's speech, and beckoned the two Italians to him. With relief they deposited the heavy chest before the Ras, amid a hubbub of voices from the dark mass of watchers. They pressed forward eagerly, the better to see the contents of the chest, as the Ras prised open the clips with the jewelled dagger from his belt, and lifted the lid with his fat pale hands.

The chest was closely packed with paper-wrapped rolls, like white candles. The Ras lifted one and slit the paper cover with the point of his dagger. There was a silent explosion of flat metal discs from the package. They cascaded into the Ras's ample lap, glittering golden and bright in the lantern light, and he cooed with pleasure, scooping a handful of the coins. Even the Count, with his own vast personal fortune, was impressed by the contents of the chest.

'By Peter and the Virgin,' he muttered.

'English sovereigns,' the agent affirmed. 'But not a high price for a land the size of France.'

The Ras giggled and tossed a handful of coins to his nearest followers, and they fought and squabbled over the coins on their hands and knees. Then the Ras looked up at the Count and patted the cushions, grinning happily, motioning him to be seated, and the Count responded gratefully. The long walk up the valley and his fevered emotions had weakened his legs. He sank down on the cushions and listened to the long list of further demands that the Ras had prepared.

'He wants modern rifles, and machine guns,' translated the agent.

'What is our position?' asked the Count.

'Of course we cannot give them to him. In a month's

time, or a year, he may be an enemy not an ally. You cannot be certain with these Gallas.'

'Say the correct thing.'

'He wants your assurance that the female *agent provocateur* and the two white brigands in the Harari camp are delivered to him for justice as soon as they are captured.'

'There is no reason against this?'

'Indeed, it will save us trouble and embarrassment.'

'What will he do with them – they are responsible for the torture and massacre of some of my brave lads?' The Count was recovering his confidence, and the sense of outrage returned to him. 'I have eye-witness accounts of the terrible atrocities committed on helpless prisoners of war. The wanton shooting of bound prisoners – justice must be done. They must meet retribution.'

The agent grinned without mirth. 'I assure you, my dear Count, that in the hands of Ras Kullah they will meet a fate far more terrible than you would imagine in your worst nightmares,' and he turned back to the Ras and said in Amharic, 'You have our word on it. They are yours to do with as you see fit.'

The Ras smiled, like a fat golden cat, and the tip of his tongue ran across his swollen purple lips, from one corner of his mouth to the other.

By this time, the Count had recovered his breath, and realized that contrary to all his expectations the Ras was friendly and that he was not in imminent danger of having his throat slit and his personal parts forcibly removed, the Count regained much of his aplomb.

'Tell the Ras that I want from him, in exchange, a full account of the enemy's strength – the number of men, guns and armoured vehicles that are guarding the approaches to the gorge. I want to know the enemy's order of battle, the exact location of all his earthworks and strong points – and particularly I want to be informed of the positions occupied by the Ras's own Gallas at the present time. I want also the names and ranks of all foreigners serving with the enemy—' He went on ticking off the points one at a time on his fingers, and the Ras listened with growing awe. Here was a warrior, indeed.

'We have to bait the trap,' said Gareth Swales. He and Jake Barton squatted side by side in the shade cast by the hull of Priscilla the Pig. Gareth had a short length of twig in his right hand, and he had been using it to draw out his strategy for receiving the renewed thrust by the Italians.

'It's no good sending horsemen. It worked once, it's not going to work again.'

Jake said nothing, but frowned heavily at the complicated designs that Gareth had traced on the sandy earth.

'We have conditioned the tank commander. The next look he gets at an armoured car, and he's going to be after it like—'

'Like a long dog after a bitch,' said Jake.

'Exactly,' Gareth nodded. 'I was just going to say that myself.'

'You already did,' Jake reminded him.

'We'll send out one car – one is enough – and hold another in reserve – here.' Gareth touched the sand map. 'If anything goes wrong with the first car—'

'Like a high-explosive shell between the buttocks?' Jake asked.

'Precisely. If that happens the second car pops in like this and keeps them coming on.'

'The way you tell it, it sounds great.'

'Piece of cake, old son, nothing to it. Trust the celebrated Swales genius.'

'Who takes the first car?' Jake asked.

'Spin you for it,' Gareth suggested, and a silver Maria Theresa appeared as if by magic in his hand.

'Heads,' said Jake.

'Oh, tough luck, old son. Heads it is.' Jake's hand was quick as a striking mamba. It snapped closed on Gareth's wrist and held his hand in which the silver coin was cupped.

'I say,' protested Gareth. 'Surely you don't believe that I might—' and then he shrugged resignedly.

'No offence,' Jake assured him, turned Gareth's hand towards him and examined the coin cupped in his palm.

'Lovely lady, Theresa,' murmured Gareth. 'Lovely high forehead, very sensual mouth – bet she was a real goer, what?'

Jake released his wrist, and stood up, dusting his breeches to cover his embarrassment.

'Come on, Greg. We'd better get ready,' he called across to where the young Harari was supervising the preparations taking place on the higher ground above where the cars were parked.

'Good luck, old son,' Gareth called after them. 'Keep your head well down.'

Jake Barton sat on the edge of Priscilla's turret with his long legs dangling into the hatch, and he looked up at the mountains. Only their lower slopes were visible, rising steeply into the vast towering mass of cloud that rose sheer into the sky.

The cloud mass bulged, swelling forward and spilling with the slow viscosity of treacle down the harsh ranges of rock. The mountains had disappeared, swallowed by the cloud monster, and the soft mass heaved like a belly digesting its prey.

For the first time since they had entered the Danakil, the sun was obscured. The cold came off the clouds in gusts, touching Jake with icy fingers of air, so that the gooseflesh pimpled his muscular forearms and he shivered briefly.

Gregorius sat beside him on the turret, looking up also at the silver and dark blue of the thunderheads.

'The big rains will begin now.'

'Here?'

'No, not down here in the desert, but upon the mountains the rain will fall with great fury.'

For a few moments longer, Jake stared up at the pinnacles and glaring slopes of grandeur and menace, then he turned his back upon them and swept the rolling tree-dotted plains to the eastward. As yet, there was no sign of the Italian advance that the scouts had reported, and he turned again and focused his binoculars on the lower slopes of the gorge at the point from which Gareth would signal the enemy's movements to him. There was nothing to be seen but broken rock and the tumbled slopes of scree and rubble.

He dropped his scrutiny lower to where the last small dunes of red sand lapped like wavelets against the great rock reef of the mountains. There were wrinkles in the surface of the plain, sparsely covered with the pale seared desert grasses, but in their troughs thick coarse bush had taken root. The bush was tall and dense enough to hide the hundreds of waiting Harari who lay patiently, belly down, under its cover. Gareth had worked out the method of dealing with the Italian tanks, and it was he who had sent Gregorius up the gorge to the village of Sardi with a gang of a hundred men and fifty camels. Under Greg's direction, they had torn up the rails from the shunting yard of the railway station, packed the heavy steel rails on to the camels and brought them down the perilous path to the desert floor.

Gareth had explained how the rails were to be used, split his force into gangs of twenty men each and exercised them with the rails until they were as efficient as he could hope for. All that was needed now was for Priscilla the Pig to lead the Italian tanks into the low dunes.

Without armour, Gareth estimated they could hold the Italians for a week at the mouth of the gorge. His order of battle placed the Harari on the left and centre, in good positions that interlocked with those of the Galla on the right flank. The Vickers guns had lanes of fire laid down that would make any infantry assault by the Italians suicidal without armoured cover.

They would have to blast their way into the gorge with artillery and aerial bombardment. It would take them a week at the least – that is, if they could dissuade Ras Golam from attacking the Italians, a task which promised to be difficult, for the old Ras's fighting blood was coursing through his ancient veins.

Once they forced the mouth of the gorge and drove the Ethiopian forces into its gut, they had another week's hard pounding to reach the top and the town of Sardi – provided once again that the Ras could be restrained in the role of defender.

Once the Italians broke out of the head of the gorge, the armoured cars could be flung in to hold them for a day or two more, but when they were expended, it was all over. It was an easy drive for the Italians through the rolling highlands on to the Dessie road, to close the jaws of the trap – hopefully after the prey had fled.

Gareth had reported all this to Lij Mikhael, contacting him by telegraph at the Emperor's headquarters on the shores of Lake Tana. The Prince had telegraphed back the Emperor's gratitude and assurances that within two weeks the destiny of Ethiopia would be decided.

'HOLD THE GORGE FOR TWO WEEKS AND YOUR DUTY WILL BE FULLY DISCHARGED STOP

397

YOU WILL HAVE EARNED THE GRATITUDE OF THE EMPEROR AND ALL THE PEOPLES OF ETHIOPIA.'

A week here on the plains, but it all depended on this first encounter with the Italian armour. Gareth's and Jake's observations, backed up by those of the scouts, placed the total number of surviving Italian tanks at four. They must take them out at a single stroke, the whole defence of the gorge pivoted on this.

Jake found that he had been day-dreaming, his mind wandering over the problems they faced and the chances they must take. It took Gregorius's hand on his shoulder to rouse him.

'Jake! The signal.'

Quickly he looked back at the slope of the mountains, and he did not need the binoculars. Gareth was signalling with a primitive heliograph he had contrived with the shaving-mirror from his toilet bag. The bright flashes of light pricked Jake's eyeballs even at that range.

'They are coming in across the valley, line abreast. All four tanks, supported by motorized infantry.' Jake read the signal, and jumped into the driver's hatch while Gregorius slid down the side of the hull and ran to the crank handle.

'That's my darling.' Jake thanked Priscilla, as the engine spluttered busily into life, and then he called up to Gregorius as he climbed into the turret above him. 'I'll warn you every time I turn to engage.'

'Yes, Jake.' The boy's eyes burned with the fire of his anger, and Jake grinned.

'As bad as his grandpappy.' He let in the clutch. They gathered speed swiftly and flew over the crest of the rise, and behind them rolled a long billow of dust, proclaiming their whereabouts to all the world.

The line of Italian tanks was coming straight in, a mile and a half out on their flank.

'Engaging now,' shouted Jake.

'Ready.' Gregorius was crouched over the Vickers in the turret, straining it to the limit of its traverse, ready to fire at the very instant the gun could bear.

Jake put the wheel over hard, and Priscilla swung towards the distant dark beetle shapes of the Italian armour, sailing jauntily right into their teeth.

Above Jake the Vickers roared, and the spent cartridges spewed down into the hull, ringing and pinging against the steel sides, while the sudden acrid stink of burned cordite made Jake's eyes sting and flood with tears.

Through blurred eyes he watched the electric white tracer arc out across the open ground, and fall about the leading tank. Even at that range, Jake made out the tiny spurting fountains of dust and dirt kicked up by the hose of bullets.

'Good lad,' grunted Jake; it was accurate shooting from the bouncing, bounding car at extreme range. Of course, it could do no damage to the thick steel armour of the CV.3, but it would certainly startle and anger the crew, goad them into retaliation.

As he thought it, Jake saw the turret of the tank traverse around as the commander called the target. The stubby barrel of the Spandau foreshortened rapidly, and then disappeared. Jake was looking directly down the muzzle.

He counted slowly to three, it would take that long for the gunner to get on to him, then he yelled,

'Disengaging!' and flung Priscilla hard over, so that she came up on two wheels, ungainly and awkward as she swung away from the enemy line. From the corner of his eye Jake saw the glow of the muzzle flash, and almost instantly afterwards heard the crack of passing shot.

'Son of a gun – that was close!' he muttered, and reached up to throw the hatch and visor open. There was no point in closing down, these Spandaus could penetrate any point of the car's hull as though it were made of *papier mâché* – and Jake would need a good and unlimited view during the next desperate minutes.

Running parallel to the Italian line, he looked across and saw that all four tanks were firing now, and they were bunching, each tank turning towards him as he raced across their front, losing their rigid pattern of advance in their eagerness to keep Priscilla under fire.

'Come along,' muttered Jake. 'Three balls for a dollar, gentlemen, every throw a coconut!' It was too close to the truth to be funny, but he grinned nevertheless. 'Jake Barton's famous coconut shy.'

A shell burst close alongside, showering sand and gravel into the open hatch. They were ranging in on him now, it was time to confuse the range again.

He spat sand from his mouth and yelled, 'Engaging!'

Priscilla spun handily towards the Italian line, and went bounding in towards them with that prim rocking action, her ugly old silhouette grim and uncompromising as the visage of a Victorian matron.

They were close, horribly frighteningly close, so that Jake could hear the Vickers bullets hammering against the black carapace of the leading tank. Gregorius had picked out the formation leader by his command pennant, and was concentrating all his fire upon him.

'Good thinking,' grunted Jake. 'Get the bastard's blood up.' As he spoke, there was a thunderous clank close beside his head, as though a giant had swung a hammer against the steel hull, and the car reeled to the blow.

'We've taken a hit,' Jake thought desperately, and his ears buzzed from the impact and there was the hot acrid stench of burned paint and hot metal in his nostrils. He swung the wheel over and Priscilla responded as handsomely as ever, turning sharply away from the Italian line.

Jake stood up in his compartment, sticking his head out into the open and he saw immediately how lucky they had been. The shell had struck one of the brackets he had welded on to the sponson to carry the arms crates. It had torn the bracket away, and dented the hull, leaving the metal glowing with the heat of the strike – but the hull was intact, they had not been penetrated.

'Are you all right, Greg?' he yelled as he dropped back into his seat.

'They are following, Jake,' the boy called down to him, ignoring the hit. 'They are after us – all of them.'

'Home and mother – here we come,' Jake said, and turned directly away from them, once again changing the range and aim of the Italian gunners abruptly.

Shot burst close, driving the air in upon their eardrums, and making them both flinch involuntarily.

'We are pulling too far ahead, Jake,' called Greg, and Jake glancing up saw that he had his hatch open and his head out.

'Lame bird,' Jake decided reluctantly. If they outstripped the Italians too rapidly, there was a danger they would abandon the chase.

Another shell burst close alongside, covering them with a veil of pale dust, and Jake faked a hit, cutting back the throttle so that their speed bled off, and he swung Priscilla into an erratic broken pattern of flight, like a bird with a broken wing.

'They're gaining on us now,' Greg reported gleefully.

'Don't sound so damned happy about it,' Jake muttered, but his voice was lost in the whine and crack of passing shot.

'They're still coming,' howled Greg. 'And they're still shooting.'

'I noticed.' Jake peered ahead, still flinging the car mercilessly from side to side. The ridge of the first dune was half a mile ahead, but it seemed like an hour later that he felt the earth tilt up under him and they went slithering and skidding up the slip-face of the dune and crashed over the crest into safety.

Jake swung Priscilla into a broadside skid, like a skier performing a christy, bringing her to an abrupt halt in the lee of the dune and then he backed and manoeuvred up until he was in a hull-down position behind the sand, with only the turret exposed.

'That's it, Jake,' cried Greg delightedly, as he found his Vickers would bear again. He crouched over it, and fired short crisp bursts at the four black tanks that roared angrily towards them across the plain.

From the stationary position behind the dune, Gregorius made every burst of fire sweep the oncoming hulls, driving the Latin tempers of the crews into frenzy, like the sting of a tsetse fly on the belly of a bull buffalo.

'That's about close enough,' decided Jake, judging the charge of enemy armour finely. They were less than five hundred yards off now and already they were dropping shell close around the tiny target afforded by the car's turret. 'Let's get the hell out of here.'

He swung Priscilla hard and she plunged down the side of the dune into the trough. As she crashed through the dense dark scrub, Jake caught a glimpse of the men lying in wait under the screen of vegetation. They were stripped to loin-cloths, huddled down over the long steel rails, and two of them had to roll frantically aside to avoid being crushed beneath Priscilla's tall, heavily bossed wheels.

The momentum of her charge down the side of the dune carried her up on the second dune with loose sand pouring out in a cloud from her spinning rear wheels. She reached the crest and went over it at speed, dropping with a gut-swooping dive down the far side.

Jake cut the engine before she had come to rest, and he and Gregorius sprang out of the opened hatches and went pelting back up the dune, labouring in the heavy loose footing, and panting as they reached the crest and looked down into the trough at almost the same instant as the four Italian tanks came over the crest opposite them. Their tracks boiling in the loose sand, they came crashing over the top of the dune, and roared down into the trough.

They tore into the thick bank of scrub, and immediately the bush was alive with naked black figures. They swarmed around the monstrous wallowing hulls like ants around the bodies of shiny black scarab beetles.

Twenty men to each steel rail, using it like a battering ram, they charged in from each side of every tank, thrusting the end of the rail into the sprocketed jockey wheels of the tracks.

The rail was caught up immediately, and with the screech of metal on metal was whipped out of the hands of the men who wielded it – hurling them effortlessly aside. To an engineer, the sound that the machines made as they tore themselves to pieces was like the anguish of living things, like that terrible death squeal of a horse.

The steel rails tore the jockey wheels out of them, and the tracks sprang out of their seating on the sprockets and whipped into the air, flogging themselves to death in a cloud of dust and torn vegetation.

It was over very swiftly, the four machines lay silent and stalled, crippled beyond hope of repair – and around them lay the broken bodies of twenty or more of the Ethiopians who had been caught up by the flailing tracks as they broke loose. The bodies were torn and shredded, as though clawed and mauled by some monstrous predator.

Those who had survived the savage death of the tanks, hundreds of almost naked figures, swarmed over the stranded hulls, loolooing wildly and pounding on the steel turrets with their bare hands.

The Italian gunners still inside the hulls fired their machine guns despairingly, but there was no power on their traversing gear and the turrets were frozen. The guns could not be aimed. They were blinded also – for Jake had armed a dozen Ethiopians each with a bucket of engine oil and dirt mixed to a thick paste. This they had slapped in gooey handfuls over the drivers' and gunners' visors. The tank crews were helplessly imprisoned and the attackers pranced and howled like demented things. The din was such that Jake did not even hear the approach of the other car.

It stopped on the crest of the dune opposite where Jake stood. The hatches were flung open, and Gareth Swales and Ras Golam leaped out of the hull.

The Ras had his sword with him, and he swung it around his head as he charged down the slope to join his men around the crippled tanks.

Across the valley that separated them, Gareth threw Jake a cavalier salute, but beneath the mockery, Jake sensed real respect. Each of them ran down into the trough and they met where the gallon cans of gasoline were buried under a fine layer of sand and cut branches.

Gareth spared a second to punch Jake lightly on the shoulder.

'Hit the beggars for six, what? Good for you,' and then they stooped to drag the cans out of the shallow hole, and with one in each hand staggered through the waist-deep scrub to the tank carcasses.

Jake passed a can up to Gregorius who was already perched on the turret of the nearest tank where his grandfather was trying to prise open the turret hatch with the blade of his broad-sword. His eyes flashed and rolled wildly in his wrinkled black head, and a high-pitched incoherent 'Looloo' keened from the mouthful of flashing artificial teeth – for the Ras was transported into the fighting mania of the berserker.

Gregorius hefted the gasoline can up on to the tank's sponson, and plunged his dagger through the thin metal of the lid. The clear liquid spurted and hissed from the rent, under pressure of its own volatile gases.

'Wet it down good!' shouted Jake, and Gregorius grinned and splattered gasoline over the hull. The stink of it was sharp, as it evaporated from the hot metal in a shimmering haze.

Jake ran on to the next tank, unscrewing the cap of the can as he clambered up over the shattered jockey wheels. Avoiding the stationary barrel of the forward machine gun, he stood tall on the top of the turret and splashed gasoline over the hull, until it shone wetly in the sunlight and little rivulets of the stuff found the joints and gaps in the plating and splattered into the interior.

'Get back,' shouted Gareth. 'Everybody back.' He had doused the other steel carcasses and he stood now on the slope of the dune with an unlit cheroot in the corner of his mouth and a box of Swan Vestas in his left hand.

Jake jumped lightly down from the hull, laying a trail of gasoline from the can he carried as he backed up to where Gareth waited.

'Hurry. Everybody out of the way,' Gareth called again. Gregorius was laying a wet trail of gasoline back to Gareth.

'Somebody go get that old bastard out of the way,' Gareth called with exasperation. A single figure pranced and howled and loolooed on the nearest tank, and Jake and Gregorius dropped the empty cans and raced back. Ducking under the swinging arc of the sword, Jake got an arm around the Ras's

405

skinny, bony chest, swung him bodily off his feet and passed him down to his grandson. Between them they carried him away to safety, still howling and struggling.

Gareth struck one of the Swan Vestas and casually lit the cheroot in his mouth. When it was drawing nicely, he cupped the match to let the flame flare brightly.

'Here we go, chaps,' he murmured. 'Guy Fawkes, Guy. Stick him in the eye. Hang him on a lamp post – ' he flicked the burning match on to the gasoline-sodden earth, ' – and leave him there to die.'

For a moment nothing happened, and then with a thump that concussed the air against their eardrums, the gasoline ignited. Instantly the belt of scrub turned to a tall roaring red inferno, and the flames boiled and swirled, leaped and drummed high into the desert air, engulfing the four stranded tanks in sheets of fire that obscured their menacing silhouettes.

The Ethiopians watched from the dunes, awed by the terrible pageant of destruction they had created. Only the Ras still danced and howled at the edge of the flames, the blade of his sword reflecting the red leaping flames.

The hatches of the nearest tank were thrown open, and out into the searing air leaped three figures, indistinct and shadowy through the flames. Beating wildly at their burning uniforms, the tank crew came staggering out on to the slope of the dune.

The Ras flew to meet them, the sword hissing and glinting as it swung. The head of the tank commander seemed to leap from his fire-blackened shoulders, as the blade cut through. The head struck the ground behind him and rolled back down the dune like a ball, while the decapitated trunk dropped to its knees with a fine crimson spray from the neck pumping straight up into the air.

The Ras raced on towards the other survivors, and his

men roared angrily and swarmed forward after him. Jake uttered a horrified oath and started forward to restrain them.

'Easy, old son.' Gareth caught Jake's arm, and swung him away. 'This is no time for one of your boy scout acts.'

From below them rose the ugly blood roar of the destroyers, as they fell upon the survivors of the other tanks, and the Italians' screams cut like a whiplash across Jake's nerves.

'Let's leave them to it.' Gareth drew Jake away. 'Not our business, old boy. The beggars have got to take their own chances. Rules of the game.'

Across the crest of the dune they leaned together against the steel hull of Priscilla. Jake was panting heavily from his exertions and his horror. Gareth found him a slightly crumpled cheroot in the inside pocket of his tweed jacket, and straightened it carefully before placing it between Jake's lips.

'Told you before, your sentimental but endearing ways will get us both into trouble. They'd have torn you to pieces also if you'd gone down there.'

He lit Jake's cheroot.

'Well, old boy—' he changed the subject diplomatically. 'That takes care of our biggest problem. No tanks – no worries, that's an old Swales family motto,' and he chuckled lightly. 'We'll be able to hold them at the mouth of the gorge for another week now. No trouble at all.'

Abruptly the sunlight was obscured, and instantly the temperature dropped sharply. Both of them glanced up involuntarily at the sky, at the gloom and the sudden chill.

In the last hour, the masses of cloud had come slumping down from the mountains, blotting them out completely, and spreading out on to the fringes of the Danakil desert. From this thick, dark mattress of swirling cloud, fine pale streamers of rain were already spiralling down towards the plain. Jake felt a droplet splatter against his forehead and he wiped it away with the back of his hand.

'I say, we're in for a drop or two,' murmured Gareth, and as if in confirmation the deep mutter of thunder echoed down from the cloud-shrouded mountains, and lightning flared sulkily, trapped within the towering cloud masses and lighting them internally with a smouldering infernal glow.

'That's going to make things—' Gareth cut himself off, and both of them cocked their heads.

'Hello, that's decidedly odd.' Faintly on the brooding air, carrying above the mutter of thunder, came the popping of musketry and the sound of machine-gun fire, like the sound of tearing silk, made indistinct and unwarlike by distance and the muting banks of heavy cloud.

'Deuced odd,' Gareth repeated. 'There should not be any firing from there.' It was in their rear, seeming to come from the very mouth of the gorge itself.

'Come on,' snapped Jake, picking his binoculars out of Priscilla's hatch and scrambling through the loose red sand for the crest of the tallest dune.

The cloud and misty streamers of rain obscured the mouth of the gorge, but now the sound of gunfire was continuous.

'That's not just a skirmish,' muttered Gareth.

'It's a full-scale fire fight,' Jake agreed, peering through the binoculars.

'What is it, Jake?' Gregorius came up the dune to where they stood. He was followed by his grandfather – but the old man moved slowly, exhausted and stiff with age and the aftermath of burned-out passions.

'We don't know, Greg.' Jake did not lower the binoculars.

'I don't understand it.' Gareth shook his head. 'Any Italian probe from the south would have run into our positions in the foothills, and from the north it would have run into the Gallas. Ras Kullah is in a pretty strong spot there. We would have heard the fighting. They can't have gone through there—'

'And we are here in the centre,' Jake added, 'they didn't come through here.'

'It doesn't make sense.'

At that moment, the Ras reached the crest. He paused wearily and removed the teeth from his mouth, wrapped them carefully in a kerchief and tucked them away in some secret recess of his shamma. The mouth collapsed into a dark empty pit, and immediately he looked his age again.

Quickly Gregorius explained this new phenomenon to the old man, and while he listened he ran the blade of his sword into the dune between his feet, scrubbing it clean of the clotted black blood in the dry friable sand. He spoke suddenly in his tremulous old man's voice.

'My grandfather says that Ras Kullah is a piece of dried dung of a venereal hyena,' Gregorius translated quickly. 'And he says my uncle, Lij Mikhael, was wrong to treat with him, and that you were wrong to trust him.'

'Now what the hell does that mean?' Jake demanded fretfully, and lifted the binoculars sweeping again towards the mouth of the Sardi Gorge away across the undulating golden plain – then he exclaimed again. 'Damn it to hell, everything is blowing up. That crazy woman! She promised me, she swore on oath that she would keep out of it for once – and now here she comes again!'

Emerging through the curtains of rain, indistinct under the dark rolling mass of cloud, throwing no dust column on the rain-dampened earth, the tiny sand-coloured shape of Miss Wobbly came bowling towards them with its distinctive stately gait. Even at this distance, Jake could make out the dark speck of Sara's head in the hatch of the high, old-fashioned turret.

Jake started to run down the slip-face of the dune to meet the oncoming car.

'Jake!' Vicky screeched above the engine beat, before she came to a halt, her head thrust out of the driver's hatch, her golden hair shaking in the wind and her eyes huge in the pale intense face.

'What the hell are you doing?' Jake shouted back angrily.

'The Gallas,' Vicky screeched. 'They've gone! Every last man of them! Gone!'

She braked hard and tumbled down to the ground so that Jake had to catch and steady her.

'What do you mean – gone?' Gareth demanded, coming up at that moment – and Sara answered him from Miss Wobbly's turret with her dark eyes sparkling hotly.

'They went, like smoke, like the dirty hill bandits they are.'

'The left flank—' Gareth exclaimed.

'Nobody there. The Italians have come through – without firing a shot. Hundreds and hundreds of them. They are at the gorge, they have overrun the camp.'

'Jake, they would have cut off all our own Harari, it would have been a massacre – Sara gave the order, in her grandfather's name, she ordered them to abandon the right flank.'

'Oh, good Christ!'

'They are trying to fight their way back into the gorge now but the Italians are covering the mouth with machine guns. It's terrible, Jake, oh the desert is thick with the dead.'

'We've lost it all. Everything we gained, at a single throw, it's all gone. This was a feint, the tanks were sent to draw us off. The main attack was through the left – but how did they know the Gallas had deserted?'

'As my grandfather says, never trust either a snake or a Galla.'

'Oh Jake, we must hurry.' Vicky shook his arm. 'They'll cut us off.'

'Right,' snapped Gareth. 'We'll have to get back into the

410

gorge and rally them on the first line of defence in the gorge itself – otherwise they'll run straight back to Addis Ababa.' He swung around to Gregorius. 'If we try and take these men,' and he indicated the hundreds of half-naked, unarmed Harari who were now straggling out of the dunes, 'if we try to take them back through the mouth of the gorge, they'll be shot to pieces by the Italian guns. Can they find their own way on foot up the mountain slopes?'

'They are mountain men,' Gregorius answered simply.

'Good. Tell them to work their way back and assemble at the first waterfall in the gorge. That's the rallying point – the first waterfall.' He turned back to the others. 'On the other hand, *we'll* have to use the gorge – the only way to save the cars. We'll rush the mouth in a tight formation – and pray that the Eyeties haven't had a chance to bring up their artillery yet. Let's go!' He grabbed Ras Golam by the shoulder and dragged him, at an awkward run, back towards where they had left their armoured car parked on the crest of the first dune.

'Get back in the car,' Jake instructed Vicky. 'Keep the engine running. We'll bring up the two other cars. I want you in the centre of the line, then go like hell. Don't stop for anything until we are into the gorge. Do you hear me?'

Vicky nodded grimly.

'Good girl,' he said, and would have turned away, but Vicky held his arm and pressed herself to him. She reached up and kissed him full on the lips, her mouth open and wet and soft and sweet.

'I love you,' she whispered huskily.

'Oh my darling, what a hell of a time you picked to tell me.'

'I only just found out,' she explained, and he crushed her fiercely to his chest.

'Oh, that's lovely,' cried Sara from the turret above them. 'That's beautiful.' She clapped her hands delightedly.

'Until later,' whispered Jake. 'Now get out of here!' and he turned her away and pushed her towards the car. He turned himself and ran lightly back into the dunes, with his heart singing.

'Oh, Miss Camberwell, I am so pleased for you.' Sara reached down to help Vicky up on to the hull. 'I knew it was going to be Mr Barton. I picked him for you long ago, but I wanted you to find out for yourself.'

'Sara, my dear. Please don't say any more.' Vicky hugged her briefly before dropping into the driver's hatch. 'Or the whole thing will turn upside down again.'

Ras Golam was so tired and drained that he could move only at a creaking walk up the dune, even though Gareth tried to prod him into a trot. He plodded on up the dune dragging the sword behind him.

Suddenly there was a sound in the sky above them, as though the heavens had been split by all the winds of hell. A rising, rattling shriek that passed and then erupted in a towering column of sand and yellow swirling fumes against the side of the dune ahead of them, fifty paces below the car that was silhouetted upon the crest.

'Guns,' said Gareth unnecessarily. 'Time to go, Grandpa,' and he would have prodded the Ras again, but there was no need. The sound of gunfire had rejuvenated the Ras instantly; he leaped high in the air, uttering that dreadful screech of a challenge and hunting frantically for his teeth in the folds of his shamma.

'Oh no, you don't.' Grimly, Gareth forestalled the next wild suicidal charge by grabbing the Ras and dragging him protestingly towards the car. The Ras had tasted blood now, and he wanted to go in on foot with the sword – the way a real warrior fights – and he was frantically searching the open horizons for the enemy, as Gareth towed him away backwards.

The next shell burst beyond the crest, out of sight in the trough.

'The first one under, and the second over,' muttered Gareth, struggling to control the Ras's wild lunges. 'Where does the next one go?'

They had almost reached the car when it came in, arcing across the wide lion-coloured plain, through the low grey cloud, howling and rattling the heavens; it plunged down at an acute angle, going in through the thin plating behind the turret of the car, and it burst against the steel floor of the cab.

The car burst like a paper bag. The entire turret was lifted from its seating and went high in the air in a flash of crimson flame and sooty smoke.

Gareth dragged the Ras down on to the sand and held him there while scraps of flying steel and other debris splattered around them. It lasted only seconds and the Ras tried to rise again, but Gareth held him down while the shattered hull of the car brewed up into a fiery explosion of burning gasoline and the Vickers ammunition in the bins began popping and flying like fireworks.

It lasted a long time, and when at last the crackle of ammunition died away, Gareth lifted his head cautiously; immediately another belt caught and rattled away with white tracer flying and spluttering, forcing them flat again.

'Come on, Rassey,' sighed Gareth at last. 'Let's see if we can beg a ride home.' At that moment, the ugly, well-beloved shape of Priscilla the Pig roared abruptly over the crest of the dune and slewed to a halt above them.

'God,' Jake shouted from the driver's hatch. 'I thought you were in it when she blew. I came to pick up the pieces.'

Dragging the Ras, Gareth climbed up the side of the tall hull.

'This is becoming a habit,' Gareth grunted. 'That's two I owe you.'

'I'll send you an account,' Jake promised, and then ducked instinctively as the next shell came shrieking in to burst so close that dust and smoke blew into their faces.

'I get this strange feeling we should move on now,' suggested Gareth mildly. 'That is, if you have no other plans.' Jake sent the car plunging steeply down the face of the dune, turning hard as he hit the firmer earth of the plain and setting a running course for where the mouth of the gorge was hidden by the smoky writhing curtains of cloud and rain.

Vicky Camberwell saw them coming and she swung Miss Wobbly and gunned her on to a parallel course. Wheel to wheel, the two elderly machines bounded across the flat land, and the rain began to crackle against the steel hulls in minute white bursts that blurred their outlines as the next Italian shell burst fifty feet ahead of them, forcing them to swerve to avoid the fuming crater.

'Can you see where the battery is?' yelled Jake, and Gareth answered him, clinging to one of the welded brackets above the hatch, rain streaming down his face and soaking the front of his white shirt.

'They are in the ground that the Gallas deserted, they've probably taken over the trenches I dug with such loving care.'

'Could we have a go at them?' Jake suggested.

'No we can't, old son. I sited those positions myself. They're tight. You just keep going for the gorge. Our only hope is to get into the second line of positions that I have prepared at the first waterfall.' Then he shook his head sorrowfully, screwing up his eyes against the stinging rain-drops. 'You and this crazy old bastard,' he turned his head to the Ras beside him, 'you'll be the death of me, you two will.'

414

The Ras grinned happily at him, convinced that they were charging into a battle again, and deliriously happy at the prospect.

'How do you do?' he cackled, and punched Gareth's shoulder gleefully.

'Could be better, old boy,' Gareth assured him. 'Could be a lot better,' and they both ducked as the next shell came howling low over their heads.

'Those fellows are improving,' Gareth observed mildly.

'God knows they've had plenty of practice recently,' Jake shouted, and Gareth rolled his eyes upwards to the heavy bruised cloud banks.

'Let there be rain,' he intoned, and instantly the thunder cracked and the clouds lit internally with a brilliant electric burst of light. The splattering drops increased their tempo, and the air turned milky with slanting drumming lances of rain.

'Amazing, Major Swales. I would not have believed it,' said Gregorius Maryam from the turret above Gareth's head, and his voice was hushed with awe.

'Nothing to it, my lad,' Gareth disclaimed. 'Just a direct line to the top.'

Rain filled the air in a white teeming fog, so that Jake had to screw up his eyes against the driving needles, and his black curls clung in a sodden mass to his scalp.

Rain wiped out the mountains and the rocky portals of the gorge, so that Jake steered by instinct alone. It roared against the racing steel hull, and closed down visibility to a circle of twenty yards. The Italian shellfire stopped abruptly, as the gunners were unsighted.

Rain pounded every inch of exposed skin, striking with a force that stung painfully, snapping against their faces with a jarring impact that made the teeth ache in their jaws, and sent them crouching for what little cover there was on the exposed hull.

415

'Good Lord, how long does this go on for?' protested Gareth, and he spat the sodden butt of his cheroot over the side.

'Four months,' shouted Gregorius. 'It rains for four months now.'

'Or until you tell it to stop.' Jake grinned wryly, and glanced across at the other machine.

Sara waved reassuringly from the turret of Miss Wobbly, her face screwed up against the driving raindrops and the thick mane of hair plastered to her shoulders and face. Icy rain had soaked the silken shamma she wore and it clung transparently to her body, and her fat little breasts showed through as though they were naked, bouncing to each exaggerated movement of the car.

Suddenly the mist of rain ahead of them was filled with hurrying figures, all of them clad in the long sodden shammas of the Harari; carrying their weapons, they were running and staggering forward through the rain towards the mouth of the gorge.

Gregorius shouted encouragement to them as they sped past, and then translated quickly.

'I have told them we will hold the enemy at the first waterfall – they are to spread the word.'

And he turned back to shout again when suddenly with a startled oath Jake braked and swung the car violently to avoid a pile of human bodies strewn in their path.

'This is where the Italian machine-gunners caught them,' Sara yelled across the gap, and as if in confirmation there came the tearing ripping sound of the machine guns off in the rain mist.

Jake threaded the car past the piles of bodies and then looked around to make sure Vicky was following.

'Now what the hell!' He realized they were alone. 'That woman. That crazy woman,' and he braked, slammed Priscilla into reverse and roared back into the fog until the dark shape of Miss Wobbly loomed up again.

'No,' said Gareth. 'I can't bear it.'

Vicky and Sara were out of the parked car, hurrying amongst the piles of bodies, stooping over a wounded warrior and between them dragging him upright and thrusting him through the open rear doors of the cab. Others, less gravely wounded, were limping and crawling towards the machine, and dragging themselves aboard.

'Come on, Vicky,' Jake yelled.

'We can't leave them here,' she yelled back.

'We've got to get to the waterfall,' he tried to explain. 'We've got to stop the retreat.' But he might not have spoken, for the two women turned back to their task.

'Vicky!' Jake shouted again.

'If you help – it won't take so long,' she called obstinately, and Jake shrugged helplessly before climbing down out of the hatch.

Both cars were crammed with dreadfully wounded and dying Harari, and the hulls were thick with those who still had strength to hold on, before Vicky was satisfied.

'We've lost fifteen minutes.' Gareth glanced at his pocket watch in the rain that still poured down with unabated fury. 'And that could be enough to get us all killed, and lose us the gorge.'

'It was worth it,' Vicky told him stubbornly, and ran to her car. Again the heavily burdened machines ground on towards the mountain pass, and now they had to ignore the pitiful appeals of the wounded they passed. They lay in huddles of rags soaked with rain and diluted pink blood, or they crawled painfully and doggedly on towards the mountains, lifting brown, agonized faces and pleading, clawlike hands as the two machines roared past in the mist.

Once a freak gap in the rain opened visibility to a mile

around them, and a pale shaft of watery sunlight slanted down to strike the cars like a stage light, glistening on the wet steel hulls. Immediately the Italian machine guns opened on them from a range of a mere two hundred yards, and the bullets cut into the clinging mass of humanity, knocking a dozen of them shrieking from their perch before the rain closed in again, hiding them in its soft white protective bosom.

They ran into the main camp below the gorge, and found that it was plunged into terrible confusion. It had been heavily shelled and machine-gunned, and then the rain had turned it all into a deep muddy soup of broken *tukuls*, flattened tents, and scattered equipment.

Dead horses and human corpses were half buried in the mud, here and there a terrified dog or a lost child scurried through the rain.

Spasmodic fighting was still taking place in the rocky ground around the camp, and they caught glimpses of Italian uniforms on the slopes and muzzle-flashes in the gloom. Every few seconds a shell would howl in through the rain and cloud and burst with sullen fury somewhere out of sight.

'Head for the gorge,' shouted Gareth. 'Don't stop here,' and Jake took the path that skirted the grove of camel-thorns, the direct path that passed below and out of sight of the fighting on the slopes, crossed the Sardi River and plunged into the gaping maw of the gorge.

'My men are holding them,' Gregorius shouted proudly. 'They are holding the gorge. We must go to their aid.'

'Our place is at the first waterfall.' Gareth raised his voice for the first time. 'They can't hold here – not when the Eyetie brings up his guns. We've got to get set at the first waterfall to have a chance.' He looked back to where the other car should have been following them, and he groaned.

'No! Oh, please God, no.'

'What is it?' Jake's head popped out of the driver's hatch with alarm.

'They've done it again.'

'Who – ?' But Jake need not have asked. The following car had swung off the direct track, and was now storming up through the rain-blurred camel-thorn trees, heading for the old tented camp in the grove, and only incidentally running directly into the area where the heavy fighting was still rattling and crackling in the rain.

'Catch her,' Gareth said. 'Head her off.' Jake swung off the track and went zigzagging up through the grove with the rear wheels spinning and spraying red mud and slush. But Miss Wobbly had a clear start and a straight run up the secondary track directly into the enemy advance; she disappeared amongst the trees and curtains of rain.

Jake brought the car bellowing out into the camp to find Miss Wobbly parked in the open clearing. The tents had been flattened and the whole area trodden and looted, cases of rations and clothing burst open and soaked with rain; the muddy red canvas of the tents hung flapping in the trees or lay half buried.

From the turret, Sara was firing the Vickers into the trees of the grove, and answering fire whined and crackled around the car. Jake glimpsed running Italian figures, and turned the car so that his own gun would bear.

'Get into them, Greg,' he yelled, and the boy crouched down behind the gun and fired a long thunderous burst that tore shreds of bark off the trees and dropped at least one of the running Italians. Jake lifted himself out of the driver's hatch, and then froze and stared in disbelief.

Victoria Camberwell was out of the armoured car, plodding around in the soup of red mud, oblivious to the gunfire that whickered and crackled about her.

'Vicky!' he cried in despair, and she stooped and snatched

419

something out of the mud with a cry of triumph. Now at last she turned and scampered back to Miss Wobbly, crossing a few feet in front of Jake.

'What the hell—' he protested.

'My typewriter and my toilet bag,' she explained reasonably, holding her muddy trophies aloft. 'One has got my make-up in it, and I can't do my job without the other,' and then she smiled like a wet bedraggled puppy.

'We can go now,' she said.

The track up the gorge was crowded with men and animals, toiling wearily upwards in the icy rain. The pack animals slipped and slithered in the loose footing. Gareth's relief was intense when he saw the bulky shapes of the Vickers strapped to the humpy backs of a dozen camels, and the cases of ammunition riding high in the panniers. His men had done their work and saved the guns.

'Go with them, Greg,' he ordered. 'See them safely up to the first waterfall,' and the boy jumped down to take command, while the two cars ploughed on slowly through the sea of humanity.

'There's no fight left in them,' said Jake, looking down into the dispirited brown faces, running with rainwater and shivering in the cold.

'They'll fight,' answered Gareth, and he nudged the Ras. 'What do you say, Grandpa?' The Ras grinned a weary toothless grin, but his wet clothing clung to the gaunt old frame like the rags of a scarecrow, as Jake brought the car round the slippery, glassy hairpin bend below the first waterfall.

'Pull in here,' Gareth told him, and then scrambled down beside the hull, drawing the Ras down with him.

'Thanks, old son.' He looked up at Jake. 'Take the cars up to Sardi, and get rid of these—' He indicated the sorry cargo of wounded. 'Try and find a suitable building for a hospital. Leave that to Vicky – it'll keep her out of mischief. Either that or we'll have to tie her up—' he grinned, and then was serious. 'Try and contact Lij Mikhael. Tell him the position here. Tell him the Gallas have deserted – and I'll be hard pressed to hold the gorge another week. Tell him we need ammunition, guns, medicine, blankets, food – anything he can spare. Ask him to send a train down to Sardi with supplies, and to take out the wounded.'

He paused, and thought for a moment. 'That's it, I think. Do that and then come back, with all the food you can carry. I think we left most of our supplies down there' – he glanced down into the misty depths of the gorge – 'and these fellows won't fight on an empty stomach.'

Jake reversed the car and pulled back on to the track.

'Oh, and Jake, try and find a few cheroots. I lost my entire stock down there. Can't fight without a whiff or two.' He grinned and waved. 'Keep it warm, old son,' he called, and turned away to begin stopping the trudging column of refugees, pushing them off the track towards the prepared trenches that had been dug into the rocky sides of the gorge, overlooking the double sweep of the track below them.

'Come along, chaps,' Gareth shouted cheerfully. 'Who's for a touch of old glory!'

'FROM GENERAL BADOGLIO, COMMANDER IN CHIEF OF THE AFRICAN EXPEDITIONARY FORCE BEFORE AMBA ARADAM, TO COLONEL COUNT ALDO BELLI, OFFICER COMMANDING THE DANAKIL COLUMN AT THE WELLS OF CHALDI.

'THE MOMENT FOR WHICH WE HAVE PLANNED IS

421

NOW AT HAND STOP I CONFRONT THE MAIN BODY OF
THE ENEMY, AND HAVE HAD THEM UNDER CONTINU-
OUS BOMBARDMENT FOR FIVE DAYS. AT DAWN
TOMORROW I SHALL ATTACK IN FORCE AND DRIVE
THEM FROM THE HIGH GROUND BACK ALONG THE
DESSI ROAD. DO YOU NOW ADVANCE WITH ALL DES-
PATCH TO TAKE UP A POSITION ASTRIDE THE DESSIE
ROAD AND STEM THE TIDE OF THE ENEMY'S RETREAT,
SO THAT WE MAY TAKE THEM ON BOTH TINES OF THE
PITCHFORK.'

Forty thousand men lay upon Amba Aradam,
cowering in their trenches and caves. They were the
heart and spine of the Ethiopian armies, and the
man who led them, Ras Muguletu, was the ablest and
most experienced of all the warlords. But he was powerless
and uncertain in the face of such strength and fury as
now broke around him. He had not imagined it could be
so, and he lay with his men, quiescent and stoic. There
was no enemy to confront, nothing to strike out at, for
the huge Caproni bombers droned high overhead and the
great guns that fired the shells were miles below in the
valley.

All they could do was pull their dusty shammas over
their heads and endure the bone-jarring, bowel-shaking
detonations and breathe the filthy fume-laden air.

Day after day the storm of explosive roared around them
until they were dazed and stupefied, deafened and uncaring,
enduring, only enduring – not thinking, not feeling, not
caring.

On the sixth night the drone of the big three-engined
bombers passed overhead, and Ras Muguletu's men, peering

up fearfully, saw the sinister shapes pass overhead, dark against the silver pricking of the stars.

They waited for the bombs to tumble down upon them once more, but the bombers circled above the flat-topped mountain for many minutes and there were no bombs. Then the bombers turned away and the drone of the engines died into the lightening dawn sky.

Only then did the soft insidious dew that they had sown come sifting down out of the still night sky. Gently as the fall of snowflakes, it settled upon the upturned brown faces, into the fearfully staring eyes, on to the bare hands that held the ancient firearms at the ready.

It burned into the exposed skin, blistering and eating into the living flesh like some terrible canker; it burned the eyes in their sockets, turning them into cherry-red, glistening orbs from which the yellow mucus poured thickly. The pain it inflicted combined both the searing of concentrated acid and the fierce heat of live coals.

In the dawn, while thousands of Ras Muguletu's men whimpered and cried out in their consuming agony, and their comrades, bemused and bewildered, tried unavailingly to render aid, in that dreadful moment, the first wave of Italian infantry came up over the lip of the mountain, and they were into the Ethiopian trenches before the defenders realized what had happened. The Italian bayonets blurred redly in the first rays of the morning sun.

The cloud lay upon the highlands, blotting out the peaks, and the rain fell in a constant deluge. It had rained without ceasing for the two days and three nights since the disaster of Amba Aradam. The rain had saved them, it had saved the thirty thousand survivors of the battle from being overtaken by the same fate as had befallen the ten thousand casualties they had left on the mountain.

High above the cloud, the Italian bombers circled hungrily; Lij Mikhael could hear them clearly, although the thick blanket of cloud muted the sound of the powerful triple engines. They waited for a break in the cloud, to come swooping down upon the retreat. What a target they would enjoy if that happened! The Dessie road was choked for a dozen miles with the slow unwieldy column of the retreat, the ragged files of trudging figures, bowed in the rain, their heads covered with their shammas, their bare feet sliding and slipping in the mud. Hungry, cold and dispirited, they toiled onwards, carrying weapons that grew heavier with every painful step – still they kept on.

The rain had hampered the Italian pursuit. Their big troop-carriers were bogged down helplessly in the treacherous mud, and each engorged mountain stream, each ravine raged with the muddy brown rain waters. They had to be bridged by the Italian engineers before the transports could be manhandled across, and the pursuit continued.

The Italian General Badoglio had been denied a crushing victory and thirty thousand Ethiopian troops had escaped him at Aradam.

It was Lij Mikhael's special charge, placed upon him personally by the King of Kings, Haile Selassie, to bring out those thirty thousand men. To extricate them from Badoglio's talons, and regroup them with the southern army – under the Emperor's personal command – upon the shores of Lake Tana. Another thirty-six hours and the task would be accomplished.

He sat on the rear seat of the mud-spattered Ford sedan, huddled into the thick coarse folds of his greatcoat, and although it was warm and lulling in the sedan interior, and although he was exhausted to the point at which his hands and feet felt completely numb and his eyes as though they were filled with sand, yet no thought of sleep entered his mind. There was too much to plan, too many eventualities to meet, too many details to ponder – and he was afraid. A terrible black fear pervaded his whole being.

The ease with which the Italian victory had been won at Aradam filled him with fear for the future. It seemed as though nothing could stand against the force of Italian arms – against the big guns, and the bombs and the nitrogen mustard. He feared that another terrible defeat awaited them on the shores of Lake Tana.

He feared also for the safety of the thirty thousand in his charge. He knew that the Danakil column of the Italian expeditionary force had fought its way into the Sardi Gorge and must by now have almost reached the town of Sardi itself. He knew that Ras Golam's small force had been heavily defeated on the plains and had suffered doleful losses in the subsequent defence of the gorge. He feared that they might be swept aside at any moment now and that the Italian column would come roaring like a lion across his rear cutting off his retreat to Dessie. He must have time, a little more time, a mere thirty-six hours more.

Then again, he feared the Gallas. At the beginning of the Italian offensive they had taken no part in the fighting but had merely disappeared into the mountains, betraying completely the trust that the Harari leaders had placed in them. Now, however, that the Italians had won their first resounding victories, the Gallas had become active, gathering like vultures for the scraps that the lions left. His own retreat from Aradam had been harassed by his erstwhile allies. They hung on his flanks, hiding in the scrub and scree slopes along the Dessie road, awaiting each opportunity to fall upon a weak unprotected spot in the unwieldy slow-moving column. It was classical shifta tactics, the age-old art of ambush, of hit and run, a few throats slit and a dozen rifles stolen, but it slowed the retreat – slowed it drastically while close behind them followed the Italian horde, and across their rear lay the mouth of the Sardi Gorge.

Lij Mikhael roused himself and leaned forward in the seat to peer ahead through the windscreen. The wipers flogged sullenly from side to side, keeping two fans of clean glass in the mud-splattered screen, and Lij Mikhael made out the railway crossing ahead of them where it bisected the muddy rutted road.

He grunted with satisfaction and the driver pushed the Ford through the slowly moving mass of miserable humanity which dogged the road. It opened only reluctantly as the sedan butted its way through with the horn blaring angrily, and closed again behind it as it passed.

They reached the railway level crossing and Lij Mikhael ordered the driver to pull off the road beside a group of his officers. He slipped out bareheaded and immediately the rain dewed on his bushy dark hair. The group of officers surrounded him, each eager to tell his own story, to recite the list of his own requirements, his own misgivings – each with news of fresh disaster, new threats to their very existence.

They had no comfort for him, and Lij Mikhael listened with a great weight growing in his chest.

At last he gestured for silence. 'Is the telephone line to Sardi still open?' he asked.

'The Gallas have not yet cut it. It does not follow the railway line but crosses the spur of Amba Sacal. They must have overlooked it.'

'Have me connected with the Sardi station – I must speak to somebody there. I must know exactly what is happening in the gorge.'

He left the group of officers beside the railway tracks and walked a short way along the Sardi spur.

Down there, a few short miles away, the close members of his family – his father, his brothers, his daughter – were risking their lives to buy him the time he needed. He wondered what price they had already paid, and suddenly, a mental picture of his daughter sprang into his mind – Sara, young and lithe and laughing. Firmly he thrust the image aside and he turned to look back at the endless file of bedraggled figures that shuffled along the Dessie road. They were in no condition to defend themselves, they were helpless as cattle until they could be regrouped, fed and rearmed in spirit.

No, if the Italians came now it would be the end.

'Excellency, the line to Sardi is open. Will you speak?'

Lij Mikhael turned back and went to where a field telephone had been hooked into the Sardi-Dessie telephone line. The copper wires dangled down from the telegraph poles overhead, and Lij Mikhael took the handset that the officer handed him and spoke quietly into the mouthpiece.

B eside the station master's office in the railway yards of Sardi town stood the long cavernous warehouse used for the storage of grain and other goods. The roof and walls were clad with corrugated galvanized iron which had been daubed a dull rusty red with oxide paint.

The floor was of raw concrete, and the cold mountain wind whistled in through the joints in the corrugated sheets. At a hundred places, the roof leaked where the galvanizing had rusted away, and the rain dripped steadily forming icy puddles on the bare concrete floor.

There were almost six hundred wounded and dying men crowded into the shed. There was no bedding or blankets, and empty grain bags served the purpose. They lay in long lines on the hard concrete, and the cold came up through the thin jute bags, and the rain dripped down upon them from the high roof.

There was no sanitation, no bed pans, no running water, and most of the men were too weak to hobble out into the slush of the goods yard. The stench was a solid tangible thing that permeated the clothing and clung in a person's hair long after he had left the shed.

There was no antiseptic, no medicine – not even a bottle of Lysol or a packet of Aspro. The tiny store of medicines at the missionary hospital had long ago been exhausted. The German doctor worked on into each night with no anaesthetic and nothing to combat the secondary infection. Already the stink of putrefying wounds was almost as strong as the other stench.

The most hideous injuries were the burns inflicted by the nitrogen mustard. All that could be done was to smear the scalded and blistered flesh with locomotive grease. They had found two drums of this in the loco shed.

Vicky Camberwell had slept for three hours two days ago. Since then, she had worked without ceasing amongst the long pitiful lines of bodies. Her face was deadly pale in the gloom of the shed, and her eyes had receded into dark bruised craters. Her feet were swollen from standing so long, and her shoulders and her back ached with a dull unremitting agony. Her linen dress was stained with specks of dried blood, and other less savoury secretions – and she worked on, in despair that there was so little they could do for the hundreds of casualties.

She could help them to drink the water they cried out for, clean those that lay in their own filth, hold a black pleading hand as the man died, and then pull the coarse jute sacking up over his face and signal one of the over-worked male orderlies to carry him away and bring in another from where they were already piling up on the open stoep of the shed.

One of the orderlies stooped over her now, shaking her shoulder urgently, and it was some seconds before she could understand what he was saying. Then she pushed herself stiffly up off her knees, and stood for a moment holding the small of her back with both hands while the pain there eased, and the dark giddiness in her head abated. Then she followed the orderly out across the muddy fouled yard to the station office.

She lifted the telephone receiver to her ear and her voice was husky and slurred as she said her name.

'Miss Camberwell, this is Lij Mikhael here.' His voice was scratchy and remote, and she could hardly catch the words, for the rain still rattled on the iron roof above her head. 'I am at the Dessie crossroads.'

'The train,' she said, her voice firming. 'Lij Mikhael, where is the train you promised? We must have medicine – antiseptic, anaesthetic – don't you understand? There are six hundred wounded men here. Their wounds are rotting, they are dying like animals.' She recognized the rising hysteria in her voice, and she cut herself off.

'Miss Camberwell. The train – I am sorry. I sent it to you. With supplies. Medicines. Another doctor. It left Dessie yesterday morning, and passed the crossroads here yesterday evening on its way down the gorge to Sardi—'

'Where is it, then?' demanded Vicky. 'We must have it. You don't know what it's like here.'

'I'm sorry, Miss Camberwell. The train will not reach you. It was derailed in the mountains fifteen miles north of Sardi. Ras Kullah's men – the Gallas – were in ambush. They had torn up the tracks, they have massacred everybody aboard and burned the coaches.'

There was a long silence between them, only the static hissed and buzzed across the wires.

'Miss Camberwell. Are you there?'

'Yes.'

'Do you understand what I am saying?'

'Yes, I understand.'

'There will be no train.'

'No.'

'Ras Kullah has cut the road between here and Sardi.'

'Yes.'

'Nobody can reach you – and there is no escape from Sardi up the railway line. Ras Kullah has five thousand men to hold it. His position in the mountains is impregnable. He can hold the road against an army.'

'We are cut off,' said Vicky thickly. 'The Italians in front of us. The Gallas behind us.'

Again the silence between them, then Lij Mikhael asked,

'Where are the Italians now, Miss Camberwell?'

'They are almost at the head of the gorge, where the last waterfall crosses the road—' She paused and listened intently, removing the receiver from her ear. Then she lifted it again. 'You can hear the Italian guns. They are firing all the time now. So very close.'

'Miss Camberwell, can you get a message to Major Swales?'

'Yes.'

'Tell him I need another eighteen hours. If he can hold the Italians until noon tomorrow, then they cannot reach the crossroads before it is dark tomorrow night. It will give me another day and two nights. If he can hold until noon, he will have discharged with honour all his obligations to me, and you will all have earned the undying gratitude of the Emperor and all the peoples of Ethiopia. You, Mr Barton and Major Swales.'

'Yes,' said Vicky. Each word was an effort.

'Tell him that at noon tomorrow I shall have made the best arrangements I can for your evacuation from Sardi. Tell him to hold hard until noon, and then I will spare no effort to get all of you out of there.'

'I will tell him.'

'Tell him that at noon tomorrow he is to order all the remaining Ethiopian troops to disperse into the mountains, and I will speak to you again on this telephone to tell you what arrangements I have been able to make for your safety.'

'Lij Mikhael, what about the wounded, the ones who cannot disperse into the hills?'

The silence again, and then the Prince's voice, quiet but heavy with grief.

'It would be best if they fell into the hands of the Italians rather than the Gallas.'

'Yes,' she agreed quietly.

'There is one other thing, Miss Camberwell.' The Prince hesitated, and then went on firmly, 'Under no circumstances are you to surrender yourselves to the Italians. Even in the most extreme circumstances. Anything—' he emphasized the word, '*anything* is preferable to that.'

'Why?'

'I have learned from our agents that sentence of death has been passed on you, Mr Barton and Major Swales. You have been declared *agents provocateurs* and terrorists. You are to be handed over to Ras Kullah for execution of sentence. *Anything* would be better than that.'

'I understand,' said Vicky softly, and she shuddered as she thought of Ras Kullah's thick pink lips, and the soft bloated hands.

'If everything else fails, I will send an—' his voice was cut off abruptly, and now there was no hiss of static across the wires, only the dead silence of lost contact.

For another minute Vicky tried to re-establish contact, but the handset was mute and the silence complete. She

431

replaced it on its cradle, and closed her eyes tightly for a moment to steady herself. She had never felt so lonely and tired and afraid in her entire life.

Vicky paused as she crossed the yard to the warehouse, and she looked up at the sky. She had not realized how late it was. There were only a few hours of daylight left – but the cloud seemed to be breaking up. The sombre grey roof was higher, just on the peaks, and there were light patches where the sun tried to penetrate the cloud.

She prayed quietly that it would not happen. Twice during these last desperate days, the cloud had lifted briefly, and each time the Italian bombers had come roaring at low level up the gorge. On both occasions, the terrible damage they had inflicted had forced Gareth to abandon his trenches and pull back to the next prepared position, and a flood of wounded and dying had engulfed them here at the hospital.

'Let it rain,' she prayed. 'Please God, let it rain and rain.'

She bowed her head and hurried on into the shed, into the stench and the low hubbub of groans and wails. She saw that Sara was still assisting at the plain wooden table, inadequately screened by a tattered curtain of canvas, and lit by a pair of Petromax lamps.

The German doctor was removing a shattered limb, cutting below the knee while the young Harari warrior thrashed weakly under the weight of the four orderlies who held him down.

Vicky waited until they carried the patient away and she called to Sara. The two of them went out and stood breathing the sweet mountain air with relief as they leant close together under the overhanging roof of the veranda while Vicky repeated the conversation she had held with Lij Mikhael.

'Then we were cut off. The line just went dead.'

'Yes,' Sara nodded. 'They have cut the wires. It is only a surprise that Ras Kullah did not do so before. The wires cross over the top of Amba Sacal. Perhaps it has taken this long for them to reach it.'

'Will you go down the gorge, Sara, and give the message to Major Swales? I would go down in Miss Wobbly, but there is almost no fuel in the tank, and I have promised Jake not to waste it. We will need every drop later—'

'It will be quicker on horseback anyway,' Sara smiled, 'and I will be able to see Gregorius.'

'No, it won't take long,' Vicky agreed. 'They are very close.'

Both of them paused to listen to the Italian guns. The thumping detonations of the high explosive reverberated against the mountains, close enough to make the ground tremble under their feet.

'Don't you want me to give a message to Mr Barton?' Sara demanded archly. 'Shall I tell him that your body craves—'

'No,' Vicky cut her short, her alarm obvious. 'For goodness sake don't go giving him one of your salacious inventions.'

'What does "salacious" mean, Miss Camberwell?' Sara's interest was aroused immediately.

'It means lecherous, lustful.'

'Salacious,' Sara repeated, memorizing it. 'It's a fine word,' and with gusto she tried it out. 'My body craves you with a great salacious yearning.'

'Sara, if you tell Jake that I said that, I will murder you with my bare hands,' Vicky warned her, laughing for the first time in many days, and her laughter was cut off in mid-flight by the single ringing scream of terror, and the wild animal roar that followed it.

Suddenly the goods yard was filled with racing figures; they poured out of the thick stand of cedar trees that flanked the railway line, and they crossed the tracks in a few leaping bounds. There were hundreds of them and they poured into the warehouse and fell like a pack of wolves on the rows of helpless wounded.

'The Gallas,' whispered Sara huskily, and for a moment they stood paralysed with horror, staring into the gloomy cavern of the shed.

Vicky saw the old German doctor run to meet the Galla wave, with his arms spread in a gesture of appeal, trying to prevent the slaughter. He took the thrust of a broadsword full in the centre of his chest, and a foot of the blade appeared magically from between his shoulder-blades.

She saw a Galla, armed with a magazine-loaded rifle, run down a line of wounded, pausing to fire a single shot at pointblank range into each head.

She saw another with a long dagger in his hand, not bothering even to slit the throat of the Harari wounded, before he jerked aside the covering of coarse jute bags and his dagger swept in a single cutting stroke across the exposed lower belly.

She saw the shed filled with frenzied figures, their sword-arms rising and falling, their gunfire crashing into the supine bodies, and the screams of their victims ringing against the high roof, blending with the high excited laughter and the wild cries of the Galla.

Sara dragged Vicky away, pulling her back behind the sheltering wall of the shed. It broke the spell of horror which had mesmerized Vicky and she ran beside the girl on flying feet.

'The car,' she panted. 'If we can reach the car.'

Miss Wobbly was parked beyond the station buildings under the lean-to of the loco shed where it was protected from the rain. Running side by side, Vicky and Sara turned the corner of the shed and ran almost into the arms of a dozen Gallas coming at a run in the opposite direction.

Vicky had a glimpse of their dark faces, shining with rain and sweat, of the open mouths and flashing wolf-like teeth, the mad staring eyes, and she smelt them, the hot excited animal smell of their sweat.

Then she was twisting away, like a hare jinking out of the track of a hound. A hand clutched at her shoulder, and she felt her blouse tear, then she was free and running, but she could hear the pounding of their feet close behind her, and the crazy loolooing of excitement as they chased.

Sara ran with her, drawing slightly ahead as they reached the corner of the station building. There was the flash and the crack of a rifle-shot out on their left, and the bullet slammed into the wall beside them. From the corner of her eye Vicky saw other running Gallas, racing in from the main road of the village, their long shammas flapping about them as they ran to head them off.

Sara was drawing away from her. The girl ran with the grace and speed of a gazelle, and Vicky could not keep pace with her. She rounded the corner of the station building ten paces ahead of Vicky, and stopped abruptly.

Under the lean-to shelter, the angular shape of Miss Wobbly was wreathed in furious petals of crimson flame, and the black oily smoke poured from her hatches. The Gallas had reached her first. She had clearly been one of their first targets, and dozens of them pranced around her as she burned – and then scattered as the Vickers ammunition in the bins began exploding.

Sara had halted for only a second, but it was long enough for Vicky to reach her.

'The cedar forest,' gasped Sara, a hand on Vicky's arm as they changed direction.

The forest was two hundred yards away across the tracks, but it was dense and dark, covering the broken ground along the river. They raced out into the open, and immediately twenty other Gallas took up the chase, their voices raised in the pack clamour.

The open yard seemed to stretch to eternity as Vicky ran on ahead of the Gallas. The ground was slushy, so that she sank to the ankles with each step, and the clinging red mud sucked one of the shoes off her foot. So she ran on lopsidedly, her feet sliding and her knees turning weak under her.

Sara raced on lightly ahead, leaping the steel railway track, and her feet flying lightly over the muddy ground. The edge of the forest was fifty feet away.

Vicky felt a foot catch as she tried to jump the tracks and she went down sprawling in the mud. She dragged herself to her knees. On the edge of the forest Sara looked back, hesitating, her eyes huge and glistening white in her smooth dark face.

'Run,' screamed Vicky. 'Run. Tell Jake,' and the girl was gone into the dark forest, with only a flicker of her passing like a forest doe.

The butt of a rifle struck Vicky in the side, below the ribs, and she went down with an explosive grunt of pain into the cold red mud. Then there were hands tearing at her clothing, and she tried to fight, but she was blinded by the clinging wet tresses of her hair, and crippled with the pain of the blow. They hoisted her to her feet, and suddenly a new authoritative voice cracked like a whiplash, and the hands released her.

She lifted her head, hunched up over her bruised belly and side. Through eyes blurred with tears and mud, she recognized the scarred face of the Galla Captain. He still wore the blue shamma, sodden now with rain, and the scar twisted his grin, making it seem even more cruel and vicious.

The front edge of the trench had been reinforced with sandbags and screened with brush, and through the square observation aperture the view down the gorge was uninterrupted.

Gareth propped one shoulder against the sandbags and peered down into the gathering gloom. Jake Barton squatted on the firing step beside him and studied the Englishman's face. Gareth Swales's usually immaculate turnout was now red with dried mud, and stained with sweat, rainwater and filth.

A thick golden stubble of beard covered his jaw like the pelt of an otter, and his moustache was ragged and untrimmed. There had been no opportunity to change clothing or bathe in the last week. There were new lines etched deeply into the corners of his mouth, his forehead, and around his eyes, lines of pain and worry, but when he glanced up and caught Jake's scrutiny, he grinned and lifted an eyebrow, and the old devilish gleam was in his eyes. He was about to speak when from below them another shell came howling up through the deep shades of the gorge, and both of them ducked instinctively as it burst in close, but neither of them remarked. There had been hundreds of bursts that close in the last days.

'It's breaking for certain,' Gareth observed instead, and they both looked up at the strip of sky that showed between the mountains.

'Yes,' Jake agreed. 'But it's too late. It will be dark in twenty minutes.'

It would be too late for the bombers, even if the cloud lifted completely. From bitter experience they knew how long it took for the aircraft to reach them from the airfield at Chaldi.

'It will clear again tomorrow,' Gareth answered.

'Tomorrow is another day,' Jake said, but his mind dwelt on the big black machines. The Italian artillery fired smoke markers on to their trenches just as soon as they heard the drone of approaching engines in the open cloudless sky. The Capronis came in very low, their wing-tips seeming to scrape the rocky walls on each side of the gorge. The beat of their engines rose to an unbearable, ear-shattering roar, and they were so close that they could make out the features of the helmeted heads of the airmen in the round glass cockpits.

Then, as they flashed overhead, the black objects detached from under their fuselage. The 100-kilo bombs dropped straight, their flight controlled by the fins, and when they struck, the explosion shocked the mind and numbed the body. In comparison the burst of an artillery shell was a squib.

The canisters of nitrogen mustard were not aerodynamically stable, and they tumbled end over end and burst against the rocky slopes in a splash of yellow, jellylike liquid that sprayed for hundreds of feet in all directions.

Each time the bombers had come one after the other, endlessly hour after hour, they left the defence so broken that the wave of infantry that followed them could not be repelled. Each time they had been driven out of their trenches, to toil back, upwards to the next line of defence.

This was the last line, two miles behind them stood the granite portals that headed the gorge, and beyond them, the town of Sardi and the open way to the Dessie road.

'Why don't you try and get a little sleep,' Jake suggested, and involuntarily glanced down at Gareth's arm. It was swathed in strips of torn shirt, and suspended in a make-

438

shift sling from around his neck. The discharge of lymph and pus and the coating of engine grease had soaked through the crude bandage. It was an ugly sight covered, but Jake remembered what it looked like without the bandage. The nitrogen mustard had flayed it from shoulder to wrist, as though it had been plunged into a pot of boiling water – and Jake wondered how much good the coating of grease was doing it. There was no other treatment, however, and at least it kept the air from the terrible injury.

'I'll wait until dark,' Gareth murmured, and with his good hand lifted the binoculars to his eyes. 'I've got a funny feeling. It's too quiet down there.'

They were silent again, the silence of extreme exhaustion.

'It's too quiet,' said Gareth again, and winced as he moved the arm. 'They haven't got time to sit around like this. They've got to keep pushing – pushing.' And then, irrelevantly, 'God, I'd give one testicle for a cheroot. A Romeo y Juliette—'

He broke off abruptly, and then both of them straightened up.

'Do you hear what I think I hear?' asked Gareth.

'I think I do.'

'It had to come, of course,' said Gareth. 'I'm only surprised it took this long. But it's a long, hard ride from Asmara to here. So that's what they were waiting for.'

The sound was unmistakable in the brooding silence of the gorge, funnelled up to them by the rock walls. It was faint still, but there was no doubting the clanking clatter, and the shrill squeak of turning steel tracks. Each second it grew clearer, and now they could hear the soft growl of the engines.

'That has got to be the most unholy sound in the world,' said Jake.

439

'Tanks,' said Gareth. 'Bloody tanks.'

'They won't get here before dark,' Jake guessed. 'And they won't risk a night attack.'

'No,' Gareth agreed. 'They'll come at dawn.'

'Tanks and Capronis instead of ham and eggs?'

Gareth shrugged wearily. 'That's about the size of it, old son.'

C olonel Count Aldo Belli was not at all certain of the wisdom of his actions, and he thought that Gino was justified in looking up at him with those reproachful spaniel's eyes. They should have been still comfortably ensconced behind the formidable defences of Chaldi Wells. However, a number of powerful influences had combined to drive him forward once again.

Not the least powerful of these were the daily radio messages from General Badoglio's headquarters, urging him to intersect the Dessie road, 'before the fish slips through our net'. These messages were daily more harsh and threatening in character, and were immediately passed on with the Count's own embellishments to Major Luigi Castelani who had command of the column struggling up the gorge.

Now at last Castelani had radioed back to the Count the welcome news that he stood at the very head of the gorge, and the next push would carry him into the town of Sardi itself. The Count had decided, after long and deep meditation, that to ride into the enemy stronghold at the moment of its capture would so enhance his reputation as to be worth the small danger involved. Major Castelani had assured him that the enemy was broken and whipped, had suffered enormous casualties and was no longer a coherent fighting force. Those odds were acceptable to the Count.

The final circumstance that persuaded him to leave the

camp, abandon the new military philosophy, and mov
cautiously up the Sardi Gorge was the arrival of the
armoured column from Asmara. These machines were to
replace those that the savage enemy had so perfidiously
trapped and burned. Despite all the Count's pleading and
blustering, it had taken a week for them to be diverted from
Massawa, brought up to Asmara by train, and then for them
to complete the long slow crossing of the Danakil.

Now, however, they had arrived and the Count had
immediately requisitioned one of the six tanks as his
personal command vehicle. Once he was within the thick
armoured hull, he had experienced a new flood of confidence
and courage.

'Onwards to Sardi, to write in blood upon the glorious
pages of history!' were the words that occurred to him, and
Gino's face had creased up into that spaniel's expression.

Now in the lowering shades of evening, grinding up the
rocky pathway while walls of sheer rock rose on either hand,
seeming to meet the sullen purple strip of sky high above,
the Count was having serious doubts about the whole wild
venture.

He peered out from the turret of his command tank, his
eyes huge and dark and melting with apprehension, a black
polished steel helmet pulled down firmly over his ears, and
one hand gripping the ivory butt of the Beretta so fiercely
that his knuckles shone white as bone china. At his feet,
Gino crouched miserably, keeping well down within the
steel hull.

At that moment a machine gun opened fire ahead of
them, and the sound echoed and re-echoed against the
sheer walls of the gorge.

'Stop! Stop this instant!' shouted the Count at his driver.
The gunfire sounded very close ahead. 'We will make this
battalion headquarters. Right here,' announced the Count,
and Gino perked up a little and nodded his total agreement.

'Send for Major Castelani and Major Vito. They are to report to me here immediately.'

J ake awoke to the pressure of somebody's hand on his shoulder, and the light of a storm lantern in his eyes. The effort of sitting up required all his determination and he let the damp blanket fall and screwed up his eyes against the light. The cold had stiffened every muscle in his body, and his head felt light and woolly with fatigue. He could not believe it was morning already.

'Who is it?'

'It's me, Jake,' and then he saw Gregorius's dark intense face beyond the lamp.

'Take that bloody thing out of my eyes.'

Beside him, Gareth Swales sat up suddenly. Both of them had been sleeping fully dressed upon the same ragged strip of canvas in the muddy bottom of the dugout.

'What's going on?' mumbled Gareth, also stupid with fatigue.

Gregorius swung the lantern aside and the light fell on the slim figure beside him. Sara was shivering with cold and her light clothing was sodden and muddy. Thorn and branches had scored bloody lines across her legs and arms, and ripped the fabric of her breeches.

She dropped on her knees beside Jake, and he saw that her eyes were haunted with terror and horror, her lips trembled uncontrollably, and the slim hand she laid on Jake's arm was cold as a dead man's, but it fluttered urgently.

'Miss Camberwell. They have taken her—' she blurted wildly, and her voice choked up.

'You should stay on here,' Jake muttered, as they hurried up the slope to where Priscilla the Pig was parked half a mile back from the line of trenches. 'There will be a dawn attack, they'll need you.'

'I'm coming on the ride, Jake,' Gareth answered quietly, but firmly. 'You can't expect me to sit here while Vicky—' he broke off. 'Got to keep a fatherly eye on you, old son,' he went on in the old bantering tone. 'The Ras and his lads will have to take their own chances for a while.'

As he spoke, they reached the hulking shape of the armoured car, parked in the broken ground below the head of the gorge. Jake began to drag the canvas cover off the vehicle, and Gareth drew Gregorius aside.

'One way or another, we should be back before dawn. If we aren't, you know what to do. God knows, you've had enough practice these last few days.'

Gregorius nodded silently.

'Hold as long as you can. Then back to the head of the gorge for the last act. Right? It's only until noon tomorrow. We can hold them that long, tanks or no bloody tanks, can't we?'

'Yes, Gareth, we can hold them.'

'Just one other thing, Greg. I love your grandfather like a brother – but keep that old bastard under control, will you. Even if you have to tie him down.' Gareth slapped the boy's shoulder, changed the captured Italian rifle into his good hand and hurried back to the car, just as Jake boosted Sara up the side of the hull and then ran to the crank handle.

Priscilla the Pig ground up the last few hundred yards of steep ground to the head of the gorge, and they passed gangs of Harari working by torchlight. They had been at it in shifts since the previous evening when Jake and Gareth had heard the Italian tanks coming up the gorge.

Although all his concern was with Vicky, yet Gareth noted almost mechanically that the work gang had performed their task well. The anti-tank walls were higher than a man's head and built from the heaviest, most massive boulders that could be carried down from the cliffs. There was only a gap narrow enough to allow the car to pass in the centre of the walls.

'Tell them to close the gap now, Sara. We won't take the car into the gorge again,' Gareth instructed quietly as they went through and she called out to a Harari officer who stood on top of the highest point of the wall; he waved an acknowledgement, and turned away to supervise the work.

Jake took the car through the natural granite gates, and beyond them lay the saucer-shaped valley and the town of Sardi.

It was burning, and at the sight Jake halted the car and they stood on the hull and looked across at the ruddy glow of the flames that lit the underbelly of the clouds, and dimly defined the mountain masses that enclosed the valley.

'Is she still alive?' Jake voiced all their fears, but it was Sara who answered.

'If Ras Kullah was there when they caught her, then she is dead.'

Then silence again, both men staring out into the night, with anger and dread holding them captive.

'But if he was skulking up in the hills, as he usually does, waiting for the attack to succeed before he shows himself,' she spat expressively over the side of the hull, 'then his men would not dare begin the execution, until he was there to watch and enjoy the work of his milch cows. I have heard they can take the skin off a living body working carefully with their little knives, every inch of skin from head to toes, and the body still lives for many hours.'

And Jake shuddered with horror.

'If you're ready, old boy. I think we could move on now,' said Gareth, and with an effort Jake roused himself and dropped back into the driver's hatch.

There seemed to be a suggestion of the false dawn lightening the narrow strip of sky high above the mountains when Gregorius Maryam scrambled back into the frontline treches.

There was activity already amongst the shadowy figures that crowded the narrow dugouts, and one of the Ras's bodyguard carrying a smoky paraffin lantern greeted him with relief.

'The Ras asks for you.' Gregorius followed him down the trench, stepping carefully amongst the hundreds of figures that slept uncaring on the muddy floor.

The Ras sat huddled in a grey blanket, in one of the larger dugouts off the main trench. The open pit had been roofed in with the remnants of one of the leather tents, and a small fire burned smokily in the centre. The Ras was surrounded by a dozen of the officers of his bodyguard, and he looked up as Gregorius knelt quietly before him.

'The white men have gone?' the Ras asked and coughed, a hacking old man's cough that shook his whole frail body.

'They will return in the dawn, before the enemy attack.' Gregorius defended them quickly, and went on to explain the reasons and the change of plans.

The Ras nodded, staring into the flickering fire, and when Gregorius paused, he spoke again in that rasping, querulous tone.

'It is a sign – and I would have it no other way. Too long I have listened to the council of the Englishman, too long I have quenched the fire in my belly, too long I have slunk like a dog from the enemy.'

He coughed again, painfully.

'We have run far enough. The time has come to fight,' and his officers growled angrily in the gloom around him, and swayed closer to listen to his words. 'Go you to your men, rouse them, fill their bellies with fire and their hands with steel. Tell them that the signal will be as it was a hundred years ago, a thousand years ago. Tell them to listen for my war drums,' a suppressed roar of exultation came from their throats, 'the drums will beat up the dawn, and when they cease, that will be the moment.' The Ras had struggled to his feet, and he stood naked above them; the blanket fallen away, and his skinny old chest heaved with the passion of his anger. 'In that moment, I, Ras Golam, will go down to drive the enemy back across the desert and into the sea from which they came. Every man who calls himself a warrior and an Harari will go down with me—' and his voice was lost in the shrill loolooing of his officers, and the Ras laughed, with the high ringing laugh close to madness.

One of his officers handed him a mug of the fiery *tej* and the Ras poured it down his throat in a single draught, then hurled the mug upon the fire.

Gregorius leapt to his feet and laid a restraining hand upon the skinny old arm.

'Grandfather.'

The Ras swung to him, the bloodshot rheumy eyes burning with a fierce new light.

'If you have woman's words to say to me, then swallow them – and let them choke the breath in your lungs, and turn to poison in your belly.' The Ras glared at his grandson, and suddenly Gregorius understood.

He understood what the Ras was about to do. He was a man old and wise enough to know that his world was passing, that the enemy was too strong, that God had turned his back upon Ethiopia, that no matter how brave the heart and how fierce the battle – in the end there was defeat and dishonour and slavery.

The Ras was choosing the other way – the only other way.

The flash of understanding passed between the youth and the ancient, and the Ras's eyes softened and he leaned towards Gregorius.

'But if the fire is in your belly also, if you will charge beside me when the drums fall silent – then kneel for my blessing.'

Suddenly Gregorius felt all care and restraint fall away, and his heart soared up like an eagle, borne aloft by the ancient atavistic joy of the warrior.

He fell on one knee before the Ras.

'Give me your blessing, grandfather,' he cried, and the Ras placed both hands upon his bowed head and mumbled the biblical words.

A warm soft drop fell upon Gregorius's neck, and he looked up startled.

The tears were running down the dark wrinkled cheeks, and dripping unashamedly from the Ras's chin.

Vicky Camberwell lay face down upon the filthy earthen floor of one of the deserted *tukuls* on the outskirts of the burning town. The floor swarmed with legions of lice, and they crawled softly over her skin, and their bites set up a burning irritation.

Her hands were bound behind her back with strips of rawhide rope, and her ankles were bound the same way.

Outside, she could hear the rustle and crackle of the burning town, with an occasional louder crash as a roof collapsed. There were also the shouts and wild laughter of the Gallas, drunk on blood and *tej*, and the chilling sound of the few Harari captives who had been saved from the initial massacre to provide entertainment during the long wait before Ras Kullah arrived in the captured town.

Vicky did not know how long she had lain. Her hands and feet were without feeling, for the rawhide ropes were tightly knotted. Her ribs ached from the blow that had felled her, and the icy cold of the mountain night had permeated her whole body so that the marrow in her bones ached with it, and fits of shivering racked her as though she were in fever. Her teeth chattered uncontrollably and her lips were blue and tight, but she could not move. Any attempt to alter her position or relieve her cramped limbs was immediately greeted with a blow or a kick from the guards who stood over her.

At last her mind blacked out, not into sleep, for she could still dimly hear the din from around the hut, but into a kind of coma in which sense of time was lost, and the acute discomfort of the cold and her bonds receded.

Hours must have passed in this stupor of exhaustion and cold, when she was roused by another kick in her stomach and she gasped and sobbed with the fresh pain of it.

She was aware immediately of a change in the volume of sound outside the hut. There were many hundreds of voices raised in an excited roar, like that of a crowd at a circus. Her guards dragged her roughly to her feet, and one of them stooped to cut the rawhide that bound her ankles, and then straightened to do the same to those at her wrists. Vicky sobbed at the bright agony of blood flowing back into her feet and hands.

Her legs collapsed under her and she would have fallen, but rough hands held her and dragged her forward on her knees towards the low entrance of the hut. Outside, there was a dense pack of bodies that filled the narrow street. Dark menacing figures that pressed forward eagerly as she appeared in the entrance of the hut, and a blood-crazed roar went up from the crowd.

Her guards dragged her forward along the street, and the crowd swarmed forward, keeping pace with her, and the roar of their voices was like the sound of a winter storm.

Hands clutched at her, and her guards beat them away laughingly, and hustled her onwards with her paralysed legs flopping weakly under her. They carried her forward into the goods yards of the railways, through the steel gate, past the mountainous pile of naked mutilated corpses, all that remained of men whom she had helped to nurse.

The yard was lit by the smoky fluttering light of hundreds of torches, and it was only when she was almost up to the warehouse veranda that she recognized the figure that lolled indolently upon his cushions, using the raised concrete ramp as a grandstand from which to direct and watch the execution.

Vicky's terror came rushing back like a black icy flood, and she tried desperately to twist herself free of the clutching hands, but they carried her forward and then lifted her suddenly.

Three of the heavy Galla lances had been set into the soft earth of the yard in the form of a tripod, with the steel lance tips bound firmly at the apex of the pyramid. With a force that she could not resist, her arms and legs were spread, and again she felt the lashing of rawhide at her wrists and ankles.

Her captors fell back in a circle, and she found herself suspended from the tripod of lances like a starfish, and the weight of her body cut the leather straps viciously into her flesh.

She looked up. Directly above her on the concrete ramp sat Ras Kullah. He said something to her in a high piping voice, but she did not understand the words and she could only stare in fascinated terror at his thick, soft lips. The tip of his tongue came out and ran slowly across his lips, like a fat golden cat.

He giggled suddenly and motioned to the two women who flanked him on the cushions. They came down into the yard, with their silver jewellery tinkling and the multi-coloured silk of their robes glowing in the lamplight like the plumage of two beautiful birds of paradise.

As though they had rehearsed their movements, one

went to each side of Vicky as she hung on the tripod of lances. Their faces were serene, remote and lovely as two exotic blooms on the long graceful stems of their necks.

It was only when they reached up to touch her that Vicky saw the little silver knives in their hands, and she wriggled helplessly, her head twisting to watch the blades.

With expert economical movements the two women slit the fabric of Vicky's clothing, from the yoke of her blouse at the throat, down in a single stroke to the hem of her skirt, and the dress fell away like an autumn leaf, and dropped into the mud below her.

Ras Kullah clapped his hands with glee, and the dense pack of dark bodies swayed and growled, pressing a little closer.

With the same unhurried knife strokes, the sheer silk of Vicky's underwear was cut away and discarded, and she hung there naked and vulnerable, unable to cover her pale smooth body, with the long finely sculptured limbs spread and pinioned.

She dropped her head forward so that the golden hair fell forward and covered her face.

One of the Galla women moved around until she faced Vicky directly. She reached out with the little silver knife and touched the point to the white skin just below the base of her throat where a pulse beat visibly like a tiny trapped animal, and slowly, achingly slowly, she drew the blade downwards.

Vicky's whole body convulsed, every limb stiffened and her back arched rigidly so that the shape of the muscle stood out clearly beneath the smooth unblemished skin.

Her head flew back, her eyes wide and staring, her mouth gaping open – and she screamed.

The woman drew the knife on downwards, between the tense straining breasts. The white skin opened to the shallow carefully controlled razor point, and a vivid scarlet line marked the slow track of the blade as it moved on inexorably downwards.

The voice of the crowd rose, a gathering roar like the sound of a storm wind coming from afar, and Ras Kullah leaned forward on his cushions. His eyes shone and the wet pink lips were parted.

Two things happened simultaneously. From the darkness beyond the station buildings, Priscilla the Pig burst out into the torchlit area. Up until that moment when Jake Barton thrust down fully on the throttle, the gentle hum of the engine had been drowned by the animal roar of the crowd.

The heavy steel hull, driven by the full thrust of the old Bentley engine, ploughed into the crowd and went through it like a combine harvester through a field of standing wheat. Without any slackening of speed, it tore a pathway through the dense pack, directly towards the clearing where Vicky hung on the tripod of lances.

At the same moment, Gareth Swales stepped out of the black oblong of the warehouse door, directly behind where Ras Kullah sat.

He had the Italian rifle over the crook of his injured arm, and he fired without lifting the butt to his shoulder.

The bullet smashed into the elbow of the Galla woman's knife arm, and the arm snapped like a twig, the knife flew from the nerveless fingers and the woman shrieked and collapsed into the mud at Vicky's feet.

The second woman swirled, her right hand drew back like the head of a striking adder, and she aimed the knife blade at Vicky's soft white stomach; as she began the stroke that would plunge it hilt-deep, Gareth moved the rifle muzzle fractionally and fired again.

The heavy bullet caught the woman in the exact centre of her golden forehead. The black hole appeared there like a third empty eye socket, and her head snapped backwards as though from a heavy blow.

As she went down, Gareth worked the bolt of the rifle and dropped the muzzle, again only fractionally, but as Ras Kullah twisted around desperately on his cushions, his mouth wide open and a gurgling cry keening from the thick wet lips, the muzzle of the rifle was aimed directly into the pink pit of his throat – and Gareth fired the third shot. It shattered the front teeth in Ras Kullah's upper jaw, before plunging on into his throat and then exiting through the back of the neck. The Ras went over backwards, and flapped and jumped like a maimed frog.

Gareth stepped over him, and jumped down lightly into the yard. A Galla rushed at him with a broadsword held high above his head. Gareth fired again without lifting the rifle, stepped over the body and reached Vicky's side just as Jake Barton swung the car to a skidding halt next to them and tumbled out of the driver's hatch with a Harari dagger in his hand.

In the turret above them, Sara fired the Vickers in a long continuous blast, swinging it back and forth in its limited traverse – and the Galla crowd scattered panic-stricken into the night.

Jake slashed the thongs that held Vicky suspended and she fell forward into his arms.

Gareth stooped and gathered Vicky's torn clothing out of the mud and bundled it under his injured armpit.

'Shall we move on now, old son?' he asked Jake genially. 'I think the fun is over,' and between them they lifted Vicky up the side of the hull.

The drums brought Count Aldo Belli out of a troubled dream-plagued sleep – and he sat bolt upright from his hard couch on the floorboards of the hull, with his eyes wide and staring, and fumbled frantically for his pistol.

'Gino!' he shouted. 'Gino!' and there was no reply. Only that terrible rhythm in the night, pounding against his head so that he thought it might drive him mad. He tried to close his ears, pressing the palms of his hands to them, but the sound came through, like a gigantic pulse, the heartbeat of this cruel and savage land.

He could bear it no longer, and he crawled up inside the hull until he reached the rear hatch of the tank, and thrust his head out.

'Gino!'

He was answered instantly. The little sergeant's head popped up from where he had been cowering in his blankets on the rocky ground between the steel tracks. The Count could hear his teeth clattering in his skull like typewriter keys.

'Send the driver to fetch Major Castelani, immediately.'

'Immediately.'

Gino's head disappeared, and a few moments later appeared again so abruptly that the Count let out a startled cry and pointed the loaded pistol between his eyes.

'Excellency,' squawked Gino.

'Idiot,' snarled the Count, his voice husky with terror. 'I could have killed you, don't you realize I have the reactions of a leopard?'

'Excellency, may I enter the machine?'

Aldo Belli thought about the request for a moment, and then enjoyed a perverse pleasure in refusing.

'Make me a cup of coffee,' he ordered, but when it came he found that the incessant cacophony of drums that filled his head had worked on his nerves to the point where he could not hold the mug steady, and the rim rattled against his teeth.

'Goat's urine!' snapped the Count, hoping that Gino had not noticed the unsteady hand. 'You are trying to poison me,' he accused and tossed the steaming liquid over the side, and at that moment the stocky figure of the Major loomed out of the darkness of the gorge.

'The men are standing to, Colonel,' he growled. 'In another fifteen minutes it will be light enough—'

'Good. Good.' The Count cut him short. 'I have decided that I should return immediately to headquarters. General Badoglio will expect me—'

'Excellent, Colonel,' the Major interrupted in his turn. 'I have received intelligence that large bands of the enemy have infiltrated our lines, and are operating in the rear areas. There is a good chance you might be able to bring them to account.' Castelani, by this time, knew his man intimately. 'Of course, with the small escort that can be spared, it will be a desperate business.'

'On the other hand,' the Count mused aloud, 'I wonder if my heart does not lie here – with my boys? There comes a time when a warrior must trust his heart rather than his head – and I warn you, Castelani, my fighting blood is aroused.'

'Indeed, Colonel.'

'I shall move up immediately,' announced Aldo Belli, and glanced anxiously back into the dark depths of the gorge. His intention was to place his command tank fairly in the centre of the armoured column, protected from both front and rear.

The drumming continued, booming and pounding against his brain until he felt he must scream aloud. It seemed to emanate from the very earth, out of the fierce dark slope of rock directly ahead, and it bounced and reverberated from the rock walls of the gorge, driving in upon him in great hammers of sound.

Suddenly, the Count realized that the darkness was dispersing. He could make out the shape of a stunted cedar tree on the scree slope above his position where, moments before, there had been only black shades. The tree looked like some misshapen monster, and quickly the Count averted his eyes and looked upwards.

Between the mountains the narrow strip of sky was defined, a paler pink light against the black brooding mass of rock. He dropped his gaze and looked ahead, the darkness retreated rapidly, and the dawn came with dramatic African suddenness.

Then the beat of the drums stopped. It was so abrupt, the transition from a pounding sea of sound to the deathly, unearthly silence of the African dawn in the mountains. The shock of it held Aldo Belli transfixed and he peered, blinking like an owl, up the gorge.

There was a new sound, thin and high as the sound of night birds flying, plaintive and weird, an ululation that rose and fell so that it was many moments before he recognized it as the sound of hundreds upon hundreds of human voices.

Suddenly he started, and his chin snapped up. 'Mary, Mother of God,' he whispered, as he stared up the gorge.

It seemed that the rock was rolling down swiftly upon them like a dark fluid avalanche, and the ululation rose, becoming a wild loolooing clamour. Swiftly the light strengthened and the Count realized that the avalanche was a sweeping tide of human shapes.

'Pray for us sinners,' breathed the Count and crossed himself swiftly, and at that instant he heard Castelani's voice, like the bellow of a wild bull, out of the darkened Italian positions.

Instantly the machine guns opened together in a thunderous hammering roar that drowned out all other sound. The tide of humanity seemed no longer to be moving forward; like a wave upon a rock it broke on the Italian guns, and milled and eddied about the growing reef of their own fallen bodies.

The light was stronger now – strong enough for the Count to see clearly the havoc that the entrenched machine guns made of the massed charge of Harari warriors. They fell in thick swathes, dead upon dead, as the guns traversed back and forth. They piled up in banks in front of the Italian positions so that those still coming on had to clamber over the fallen, and when the guns swung back, they too fell building a wall of bodies.

The Count's terror was forgotten in the fascination of the spectacle. The racing figures coming down the narrow gorge seemed endless, like ants from a disturbed nest. Like fields of moving wheat, and the guns reaped them with great scythe-strokes and piled them in deep windrows.

Yet here and there, a few of the racing figures came on, reached the barbed wire that Castelani had strung, beat it down with their swords, and were through.

Of those who breached the wire, most died on the very lips of the Italian trenches, shot to bloody pieces by close-range volleys of rifle fire – but a few, a very few came on still. A group of three figures leaped the wire at a point where two dead Ethiopians had fallen and dragged it down, making a breach for those who followed.

They were led by a tall, skeletal figure in swirling white robes. He was bald, the pate of his head gleaming like a black cannon ball, and perfect white teeth shone in the sweat-coiled face. He carried only a sword, as long as the spread of a man's arms and as broad as the span of his hand,

and he swung the huge blade lightly about his head as he jinked and dodged with the agility of a goat.

The two warriors who followed him carried ancient Martini-Henry rifles which they fired from the hip as they ran, each shot blowing a long thick blue flag of black powder smoke, while the leader swung the sword above his head and loolooed a wild war cry. A machine gun picked up the group neatly and a single burst cut two of them down – but the tall leader came on at a dead run.

The Count, peering over the turret of the tank, was so astonished by the man's persistence that his own fear was momentarily forgotten. In the tank parked beside his, the machine gun fired, a ripping tearing burst, and this time the racing white clad figure staggered slightly and Aldo Belli saw the bullets strike, lifting tiny pale puffs of dust from the warrior's robes, and leaving bloody splotches across his chest – yet he came on running, still howling, and he leaped the first line of trenches, coming straight down towards the line of tanks, and it seemed as though he had recognized the Count as his particular adversary. His charge seemed to be directed at him alone, and he was suddenly very close. Standing fascinated in the turret, Aldo Belli could clearly see the staring eyes in the deeply lined face, and noticed the incongruity of the man's rows of perfect white teeth. His chest was sodden with dark red blood, but the swinging sword in his hands hissed through the air and the dawn light flickered on the blade like summer lightning.

The machine gun fired again, and this time the burst seemed to tear the man's body to pieces. The Count saw shreds of his clothing and flesh fly from him in a cloud, yet incredibly he kept coming onwards, staggering and dragging the sword beside him.

The last burst of fire struck him, and the sword dropped from his hand; he sank to his knees, but kept crawling –

now he had seen the Count and his eyes fastened on the white man's face. He tried to shout something, but the sound was drowned in a bright flooding gout of blood that filled his open mouth. The crawling, mutilated figure reached the hull of the stationary tank, and the Italian guns fell silent – almost as though in awe of the man's tenacity.

Laboriously, the dying warrior dragged his broken body up towards the Count, watching him with a terrible dying anger, and the Count fumbled nervously with the ivory butt of the Beretta, slipping a fresh clip of cartridges into the recessed butt.

'Stop him, you fools,' he cried. 'Kill him! Don't let him get in.' But the guns were silent.

With shaking hands, the Count slapped the magazine home and lifted the pistol. At a range of six feet he sighted briefly into the crawling Ethiopian.

He emptied the magazine of the Beretta in frantic haste, the shots crashing out in rapid succession in the sudden silence that hung over the field.

A bullet struck the warrior in the centre of his sweat-glazed forehead, leaving a perfectly round black hole in the gleaming brown skin, and the man slithered backwards and then rolled down the hull, coming to rest at last upon his back, and he stared up at the swiftly lightening sky with wide, unseeing eyes. Out between the slack lips dropped a set of artificial teeth, and the old mouth collapsed and fell inwards.

The Count was shaking still, but then quite unexpectedly a surging emotion swept away the terrors that had gripped him. He felt a vast proprietorial sense of emotional involvement with the man he had killed – he wanted to take some part of him, some trophy of his kill. He wanted to scalp him, or take his head and have it cured so that he might preserve this moment for ever, but before he could move, there was the shrilling of whistles, and a bugle began urgently to sound the advance.

On the slope ahead of them, only the dead lay in their piles and mounds, while the last of those who had survived that crazy suicidal charge were disappearing like wisps of smoke back among the rocks.

The road to Sardi was open, and like the hard professional he was, Luigi Castelani seized the chance. As the bugle sang its brassy command, the Italian infantry rose from the trenches, and the formation of tanks rumbled forward.

The corpse of the ancient Harari warrior lay directly in the track of the command tank, and the rumbling steel treads pressed it into the rocky ground as it passed over, squashing it like the carcass of a rabbit on a highway, as it bore Colonel Count Aldo Belli triumphantly up the gorge to Sardi and the Dessie road.

At the wall of rock built right across the throat of the gorge, the armoured column ground to a halt, blocked at the very lip of the valley, and when the Italian infantry, who had moved under cover of the black steel hulls, swarmed out to tear the wall down, they met another wave of Ethiopian defenders who rose from where they had been lying behind the wall, and immediately attackers and defenders had become so entwined in a single struggling mass that the artillery and machine guns could not fire for fear of gunning down their own.

Three times during the morning the infantry had been thrown back from the wall, and the heavy artillery barrage that they had directed against it made no impression on the granite boulders. When the tanks came clanking and squealing like great black beetles hunting for a breach, there was none, and the tracks had clawed sparks from the rock but been unable to lift the great weight of steel at the acute angle necessary to climb the wall.

Now there was a lull that had lasted almost half an hour, and Gareth and Jake sat shoulder to shoulder, leaning against one of the massive granite blocks. Both of them were staring upwards at the sky, and it was Jake who broke the silence.

'There is the blue.' They saw it through the last eddying banks of cloud that still clung like the white arms of a lover to the shoulder of the mountain, but were slowly smeared away by the fresh dry breeze off the desert.

A ray of brilliant sunlight burst into the valley, and threw a rainbow of vivid colour in a mighty arc from mountain to mountain.

'That's beautiful,' murmured Gareth softly, staring upwards.

Jake drew the watch from his pocket, and glanced at the dial.

'Seven minutes past eleven.' He read the hands. 'Just about right now they'll radio them that the clouds are open. They'll be sitting in the cockpits, eager as fighting cocks.' He patted the watch back into his pocket. 'In just thirty-five minutes they'll be here.'

Gareth straightened up and pushed the lank blond hair off his forehead.

'I know one gentleman who won't be here when they come.'

'Make that two,' Jake agreed.

'That's it, old son. We've done our bit. Old Lij Mikhael can't grouse about a couple of minutes. It will be as close to noon as pleasure is to sin.'

'What about these poor devils?' Jake indicated the few hundreds of Harari who crouched with them behind the wall of rock – all that remained of Ras Golam's army.

'As soon as we hear the bombers coming, they can beat it. Off into the mountains like a pack of long dogs—'

' – after a bitch,' Jake finished for him, and grinned.

'Precisely.'

'Someone will have to explain it to them.'

'I'll go and fetch young Sara to tell them,' and he crawled away, using the wall as cover from the Italian snipers who had taken up position in the cliffs above them.

Priscilla the Pig was parked five hundred yards back in a grassy wrinkle of ground, under a screen of cedar trees, beside the road.

Gareth saw immediately that Vicky had recovered from the state of collapse in which they had found her, although she was haggard and pale, and the torn rags of her clothing were filthy, stained with dried blood from the long flesh wound between her breasts. She was helping Sara with the boy who lay on the floorboards of the cabin, and she looked up with an expression which told of regained strength and determination.

'How is he doing?' Gareth asked, leaning forward through the open rear doors. The boy had been hit twice – and been carried back from the killing-ground of the gorge by two of his loyal tribesmen.

'He will be all right, I think,' said Vicky, and Gregorius opened his eyes and whispered, 'Yes, I'll be all right.'

'Well, that's more than you deserve,' grunted Gareth. 'I left you in charge – not leading the charge.'

'Major Swales.' Sara looked up fiercely, protective as a mother. 'It was the bravest—'

'Spare me from brave and honest men,' Gareth drawled. 'Cause of all the trouble in the world.' And before Sara

461

could flash at him again he went on, 'Come along with me, my dear. Need you to do a bit of translating.'

Reluctantly she left Gregorius and climbed down out of the car. Vicky followed her, and stood close to Gareth beside the side of the hull.

'Are you all right?' she asked.

'Never better,' he assured her, but now she noticed for the first time the flush of unnatural colour in his cheeks and the feverish glitter in his eyes.

Quickly she reached out and before he could prevent it she took the hand of his injured arm. It was swollen like a balloon, and it had turned a sickly greenish purple. She leaned forward to sniff the filthy stained rags that covered the arm, and she felt her gorge rise at the sweet stench of putrefaction.

Alarmed, she reached up and touched his cheek.

'Gareth, you are hot as a furnace.'

'Passion, old girl. The touch of your lily-white—'

'Let me look at your arm,' she demanded.

'Better not.' He smiled at her, but she caught the iron in his voice. 'Let sleeping dogs lie, what? Nothing we can do about it until we get back to civilization.'

'Gareth—'

'Then my dear, I will buy you a large bottle of Charlie, and send for the preacher man.'

'Gareth, be serious.'

'I am serious.' Gareth touched her cheek with the fingers of his good hand. 'That was a proposal of marriage,' he said, and she could feel the fiery heat of the fever in his finger-tips.

'Oh Gareth! Gareth!'

'By which I take it you mean – thanks, but no thanks.'

She nodded silently, unable to speak.

'Jake?' he asked, and she nodded again.

'Oh well, you could have done a lot better. Me, for

462

instance,' and he grinned, but the pain was there with the fever in his eyes, deep and poignant. 'On the other hand, you could have done a lot worse.' He turned away abruptly to Sara, taking her arm. 'Come along, my dear.' Then over his shoulder, 'We'll be back as soon as the bombers come. Get ready to run.'

'Where to?' she called after them.

'I don't know,' he grinned. 'But we'll try to think of a pleasant place.'

Jake heard them first, so far off that it was only the hive-sound of bees on a drowsy summer's day, and almost immediately it was gone again, blanketed by the mountains.

'Here they come,' he said, and almost immediately, as if in confirmation, a shell burst under the lee of the rock wall, fired from the Italian battery a mile down the gorge. The yellow smoke from the marker poured a thick column into the still sunlit air.

'Move!' shouted Gareth, and placed the silver command whistle between his lips and blew a series of sharp blasts.

But by the time they had hurried along the wall, making certain that all the Harari had understood and were running back down the valley into the cedar forests, the drone of approaching engines was growing louder.

'Let's go!' called Jake urgently, and caught Gareth's good arm.

They turned and ran, pelting back across the open ground to the lip of the valley, and Jake looked back over his shoulder as they reached it.

The first gigantic bomber came out of the mouth of the gorge, and the spread of its black wings seemed to darken the sky. Two bombs fell from under it; one burst short but the second struck the wall, and the blast knocked them both off their feet, slamming them savagely against the earth.

When Jake lifted his head again, he saw through the fumes and smoke the gaping breach it had blown in the rock wall.

'Well, now the party is definitely over,' he said, and hauled Gareth to his feet.

'Where are we going?' shouted Vicky from the cabin below them, and neither Jake in the driver's seat nor Gareth in the turret replied.

'Can't we just drive up the road to Dessie?' Sara demanded; she sat cross-legged on the floor of the cabin with Gregorius's head cushioned on her lap. 'We could fight our way through those cowardly Gallas.'

'We've got enough gas to take us about another five miles.'

'Our best bet is to drive to the foot of Amba Sacal.' Gareth pointed to the towering bulk of the mountain that rose sheer into the southern sky. 'Ditch the car there and try and make it on foot across the mountains.'

Vicky crawled up into the turret beside him, and thrust her head out of the hatch. Together they stared up at the sheer sides of the Amba.

'What about Gregorius?' she asked.

'We'll have to carry him.'

'We'll never make it. The mountains are crawling with Gallas.'

'Have you got a better idea?' Gareth asked, and she looked despairingly around her.

Priscilla the Pig was the only thing that moved in the

464

whole valley. The Harari had vanished into the rocky ground on the slopes of the mountains, and behind them the Italian tanks had not yet come in over the lip of the valley.

She lifted her eyes to the sky again, where only a few wreaths of cloud still clung to the peaks, and suddenly her whole mood changed. Her chin came up, and new colour flooded into her cheeks – her hand shook as she pointed up between the peaks.

'Yes,' she cried. 'Yes, I've got a better idea. Look! Oh, won't you look!'

The tiny blue aircraft caught the sun as it banked in steeply, turning in under the rearing granite cliffs, and it flashed like a dragonfly in flight.

'Italian?' Gareth stared up at it.

'No! No!' Vicky shook her head. 'It's Lij Mikhael's plane. I recognize it. It came to fetch him here before.' She was laughing almost hysterically, her eyes shining. 'He said he would send it, that's what he was trying to tell me before he was cut off.'

'Where will it land?' Gareth demanded, and Vicky scrambled down into the driver's compartment to direct him towards the polo field beyond the burned and still smoking town.

They watched anxiously, all of them except Gregorius, standing on the edge of the open field close beside the bulk of the car, all their heads craning to watch the little blue aircraft circle.

'What the hell is he doing?' Jake demanded angrily. 'The Eyeties will be here before he makes up his mind.'

'He's nervous,' Gareth guessed. 'He doesn't know what

465

the hell is going on down here. From where he is, he can see the town has been destroyed, and he can probably see the tanks and the trucks following us down from the gorge.'

Vicky turned from them and ran back to the car; she climbed up on to the turret and stood high, waving both arms above her head.

On the next circuit the little blue Puss Moth dropped lower, and they could see the pilot's face in the side window of the cockpit peering down at them. He banked steeply over the smoking remains of the town, with the lower wing pointing directly at the earth and then he came back at them, this time only ten feet above the field.

He was staring at Vicky, and with a lift of her heart she recognized the same young white pilot as had flown Lij Mikhael. He recognized her at the same instant, and she saw him grin and lift a hand in salute as he flashed past.

As he came out of his next turn, he was lined up on the field for his landing and he touched down and taxied tail-up to where they stood.

As the light aircraft rolled to a halt, they crowded up to the cabin door. The wash of the propeller buffeted them savagely and the pilot slid back the pane of his window and shouted above the noise of his engine.

'I can take three small ones – or two big ones.'

Jake and Gareth exchanged a single brief glance and then Jake jerked the cabin door and roughly they thrust the two girls into the tiny cramped cabin.

'Hold it,' Gareth shouted into the pilot's ear. 'We've got another small one for you.'

They carried Gregorius between them, trying to be as gentle as haste would allow. The pilot was already turning the machine into the wind and they staggered after it – lifting the boy's body into the open door as it was moving.

'Jake—' Vicky shouted, and her eyes were wild with grief.

'Don't worry,' Jake shouted back, as they tumbled Gregorius across the girls' laps. 'We'll get out – just remember I love you.'

'I love you, too,' Vicky called back, and her eyes swam with bright tears. 'Oh Jake—'

He was struggling to close the cabin door, running beside the fuselage as the aircraft gathered speed for the take-off, but one of Gregorius's feet was holding it open. Jake stopped to free the foot, and rifle-fire snapped past his head, and twanged into the canvas fabric of the fuselage.

He looked up in time to see the next shot star the side window of the cockpit and then go on to strike the young pilot in the temple, killing him instantly, and knocking his body sideways so that it hung drunkenly out of the seat, held only by the shoulder straps.

The aircraft slewed sideways at the loss of control, and Jake saw Vicky reach over the pilot's body and close the throttle, but he was turning away and running back towards Priscilla the Pig.

More rifle-fire kicked up spurts of dust around them as they ran.

'Where are they?' he shouted at Gareth.

'On the left.' Jake twisted his head and glimpsed the Italians in the scrub and grass two hundred yards away on the edge of the field. Beyond them was parked the transport that had carried them ahead of the lumbering tank formation.

Priscilla's engine was still running, and he headed her in a quick turn for the riflemen in the grass. Above him, Gareth fired the Vickers and the Italians jumped up and ran like rabbits.

One quick pass scattered them and a burst of Vickers fire exploded the transport in a dragon's breath of flame, and then Jake swung the car back to where the little blue aircraft stood forlornly on the edge of the field. He parked the tall steel hull close beside her to screen her from Italian snipers.

Sara and Vicky between them had dragged the pilot's body out of the cockpit. He was a big man, heavy in the shoulder and belly, and the blood oozed from the bullet hole in his temple into the thick mop of his hair as he lay on his back in the short grass under the wing.

Vicky turned away from him and scrambled up into the cockpit settling herself behind the controls.

'Jesus!' said Jake, relief shining on his face. 'She said she could fly.'

A rifle bullet spranged against Priscilla's hull and went wailing away over their heads.

Gareth glanced down at the pilot's body. 'He was a big 'un – poor beggar.'

'There's room for one more now,' Vicky shouted from the cockpit; 'with both of you we'd never make it over the mountains,' and they saw what torture the words caused her. Another bullet clanged against steel. 'We can take only one more.'

'Spin you for it.' Gareth had the silver Maria Theresa on his thumb and he grinned at Jake.

'Heads,' said Jake and it spun silver in the sunlight and Gareth caught it in the palm of his good hand and glanced at it.

'It had to come – your turn at last.' Gareth's grin lifted the corners of his mouth. 'Well done, old son. Off you go.'

But Jake caught the wrist, and twisted it. He glanced at the coin.

'Tails,' he snapped. 'I always knew you were a cheat, you bastard,' and he turned away towards Vicky. 'I'll cover the take-off, Vicky, I'll keep Priscilla between you and the Eyeties as long as I can.'

Behind him, Gareth stooped and picked up a stone the size of a gull's egg out of the grass.

'Sorry, old son,' he drawled. 'But I owe you two already,' and tenderly he tapped Jake above the right ear with the

468

stone held in the cup of his hand, and then dropped the stone and caught him under the armpits as his legs sagged and he began to collapse.

He put his knee under Jake's backside and with a heave boosted him headfirst and unconscious through the cabin door. Then he put his foot on Jake's protruding posterior and thrust him farther into the cramped cabin until he could slam and lock the door.

Rifle-fire pounded and crashed against the screening hull of Priscilla. Gareth reached into his inside pocket and pulled out the pigskin wallet. He dropped it through the side window into Vicky's lap as she sat at the controls.

'Tell Jake if I'm not there on the first to cash the Lij's cheque and buy you a bottle of Charlie from me – and when you drink it, remember I really did love you—' Before she could reply he had turned and darted back to the armoured car and scrambled up into the driver's hatch.

Like a team in harness, the car and the little blue aircraft ran side by side down the open field and the Italian fire drummed against the steel hull of the car.

Then slowly the heavily laden aircraft drew ahead of the speeding car, but by then they were beyond effective rifle range, and as Vicky felt the Puss Moth come alive and the wheels bumped clear of the rough turf, she glanced quickly backwards.

Gareth stood in the driver's hatch, and she saw his lips move as he shouted after her, and he lifted his bandaged arm in a gesture of farewell.

She did not hear the words, but she read them upon his lips. 'Noli illegitimi carborundum,' and saw the flash of that devilish buccaneer smile, before the aircraft lifted away from the earth and she must turn all her attention back to it.

Gareth halted Priscilla at the edge of the field and he stood in the hatch, shielding his eyes with his good hand, and watched the little blue aircraft climb laboriously into the thin mountain air. Again it caught the sun and flashed as it turned unsteadily towards the gap in the mountains where the pass led up into the highlands.

His whole attention was fixed on the dwindling speck of blue, so that he did not see the three CV.3 tanks crawl out of the main street of the village five hundred yards away.

He was still staring upwards as the tanks stopped, rocking gently on their suspensions, and the turrets with the long Spandaus traversed around towards him.

He did not hear the crash of cannon, for the shell struck long before the sound carried to him. There was only the earthstopping impact and the burst of shell that hurled him from the hatch.

He lay on the earth beside the shattered hull, and he felt downwards with his good hand, for there was something wrong with his stomach. He groped down, and there was nothing where his stomach should have been, just a gaping hole into which his hand sunk, as though into the soft warm flesh of a rotten fruit.

He tried to withdraw his hand, but it would not move. There was no longer muscular control, and it grew darker. He tried to open his eyes and then realized that they were wide open, staring up at the bright sky. The darkness was in his head, and the cold was in his whole body.

In the darkness and the icy cold, he heard a voice say in Italian, 'E morto – he is dead.'

And he thought with mild surprise, 'Yes, I am. This time, I am,' and he tried to grin, but his lips would not move and he went on staring up at the sky with pale blue eyes.

'He is dead,' repeated Gino.

'Are you certain?' Count Aldo Belli demanded from the turret of the tank.

'Sì, I am certain.' Warily the Count climbed down the hull.

'You are right,' he agreed, studying the man. 'He is truly dead.' Then he straightened up and puffed out his chest.

'Gino,' he commanded. 'Get a picture of me with the cadaver of the English bandit.' And Gino backed away, staring into the viewfinder of the big black camera.

'Chin up a little, my Colonel,' he instructed.

Vicky Camberwell brought the Puss Moth out over the final crest of the pass, with a mere two hundred feet to spare, for the small overladen aircraft was fast approaching its ceiling.

Ahead of her, the highlands stretched away to Addis Ababa in the south. Below her passed the thin raw muddy bisecting lines of the Dessie road. She saw the road was deserted. The army of Ethiopia had passed. The fish had slipped through the net – but the thought gave her no pleasure.

She turned in her seat and looked back, down the long gloomy corridor of the Sardi Gorge. From the cliffs on each side of the gorge, the rain waters still fell in silver white waterfalls and muddy cataracts – so that it seemed that even the mountains wept.

She straightened up in her seat, and lifting her hand to her face she found without surprise that her own cheek was wet and slick with tears.

user =

a/n a tural 1

confirm 2 ; V V 5 B L

password

Malthil 123